Suffer
the Children

Books by John Saul

SUFFER THE CHILDREN
PUNISH THE SINNERS
CRY FOR THE STRANGERS
COMES THE BLIND FURY
WHEN THE WIND BLOWS
THE GOD PROJECT
DARKNESS
SLEEPWALK
NATHANIEL
BRAINCHILD
HELLFIRE
THE UNWANTED
THE UNLOVED
CREATURE
SECOND CHILD
SHADOWS
GUARDIAN
THE HOMING
BLACK LIGHTNING
THE BLACKSTONE CHRONICLES
THE PRESENCE
THE RIGHT HAND OF EVIL

Suffer
the Children

John Saul

A DELL BOOK

Published by
Dell Publishing
a division of
Bantam Doubleday Dell Publishing Group, Inc.
1540 Broadway
New York, New York 10036

ISBN: 0-7394-0296-X

For Michael Sack, without whom this book would not have been written

PROLOGUE

One Hundred Years Ago

The surf was high that day, adding a backdrop of sound to the late summer afternoon. High above the sea, the same wind that built the waves seemed only to stroke the grass in which the child played.

She was a pretty thing, eleven years old, the cornflower blue of her dress matching her eyes, and the blond hair that only children possess cascading down her back and over her shoulders as she bent to examine one of the tiny creatures that shared her world. She poked at it with one small finger, then pulled the finger away almost before she heard the tiny snap that signaled the beetle's ascent into the air. She watched it fall back to earth, and before it could scuttle away into the grass she poked it again. Again it snapped, rose into the air, and fell back to earth. She smiled to herself, then picked up the beetle and put it in her pocket. Through the heavy material she could just feel the movement of the struggling insect; its snapping sounds were completely muffled.

She glanced toward the house a hundred yards away, then toward the road that wound down the hill and out of sight. She half expected to see a carriage coming up the hill, and her mother waiting expectantly on the porch. But it was too early, much too early. She wondered what her grandmother would bring. She hoped it would be a pet. The child liked pets.

Her attention changed as a gust of wind hit her, and she turned to face the stand of woods that separated the field from the high bank of the ocean beyond. For a long time she stared into the wood, almost as though she saw something there, something that was almost within her range of vision, yet hovered just beyond the edge of sight. She felt an urge to go to the woods, to step in among the trees and ferns and lose herself from the house behind her. She knew she shouldn't. She knew the woods were beyond the limits, that there was danger there. But still, it would be nice to wander in the trees . . .

Perhaps that was why she began to follow the rabbit.

Within the forest, hidden by the foliage and the shadows of the trees above, a man sat staring out into the field. His eyes never left the child, never glanced to the side or farther out to the house that loomed across the field. It was as if he were hypnotized, part of the scene, yet somehow separated from it.

He watched in silence as the child looked first toward the house, then to the road, and finally turned to look directly toward him. For a long moment, as she seemed to examine him, seemed to look into his soul, he was afraid she was going to turn and run. His muscles tensed, but he felt nothing as he stared out of the darkness. Then the moment was over. The girl turned away, and the man relaxed. His hand reached for the bottle propped against a rock next to him, and he took a long drink.

It was a small rabbit, and the child knew it couldn't have been more than a few months old. It peered at her from beneath a bush, as if it knew that it was visible but hoped that maybe no one would notice. For a long time it held very still as the child approached it, but when she was still ten feet away she saw it begin to twitch its nose. She knew that it was about to bolt.

Still, if she held herself completely motionless, maybe it would relax again, and then she could creep a little closer. She waited until the rabbit's nose stopped moving, then inched closer. Another foot. The nose began twitching again. She stopped. The rabbit sat up and cocked its ears. The child held still. Carefully, the rabbit eased back down to all fours, and it laid its ears back, as if to disappear entirely into the brush.

The child moved forward once again, and the rabbit bolted. Startled, the child jumped a little too, but her eyes never left the rabbit.

She saw that it was crippled.

One of its hind legs was much weaker than the other, so that when it leaped, it veered a bit to the left. And it seemed to be slow.

Maybe she could help it.

She began following, creeping as close to the rabbit as she could get, then watching in disappointment as it evaded her. The rabbit seemed to have no plan in mind, and for a long time it darted back and forth across the field, hiding first under one bush, then under another.

In the woods, the man watched the chase, his eyes never leaving the child. Occasionally he would see a grayish blur out of the corner of his eye, and he was half aware that it was a rabbit. But it didn't matter to him.

What mattered was the child.

He raised the bottle to his mouth again, and then it was empty.

Suddenly the rabbit seemed to develop a plan. It began making its way toward the woods, still not in a straight line, but with a series of leftward-veering hops that was drawing it directly toward the spot where the man waited.

The child, now conscious only of the rabbit, followed along, quickening her pace. She was beginning to be able to anticipate the rabbit, to correct for its error even before it made its jump. As it leaped into the woods, the girl was only a few feet behind.

The man rose out of the bushes, the bottle held aloft, the knuckles of his right hand white as they gripped its neck. He brought the bottle down hard, crushing the rabbit's skull just as it came to light at his feet. He straightened up in time to see the child step from the light of the field into the shadows of the forest. The wind seemed to pick up, and the roar of the surf grew louder.

She didn't see the rabbit die.

Rather, her mind held impressions:

The rabbit bouncing out of the field into the woods.

A shape looming before her that hadn't been there a second before.

A sound, not a crashing, but a sort of a dull crunching, and then the rabbit, the small animal that she had hoped to help, lying twitching at the feet of the man.

She looked up into his face.

The eyes were bloodshot, and a stubble of beard showed on his chin. His eyes, which might once have been the sparkling blue of an autumn sky, had gone dull, and the hair was a colorless tangle that made his features almost unrecognizable. A flicker of recognition crossed the child's face, but disappeared as the beginning of a cry built in her throat when the man dropped the bottle and reached for her.

One arm snaked around her small body, and the hand that had held the bottle moved to cover her mouth before the cry could be sounded. Her tongue touched his hand, and recoiled from the taste of whiskey.

He picked her up effortlessly and swung around to carry her deeper into the wood. As she struggled in his arms, his grip tightened, and he began to feel a heat in his groin not caused by the liquor in his blood.

He did it silently.

Silently he set her down in a small clearing, and silently he pulled at his belt.

When it was free, he used it to bind her wrists, and when she broke the silence with her cries, he slapped her, hard. Her cries died away to a moan, and she stared up at him with the fear of a trapped animal. The sun disappeared behind a cloud.

He dressed slowly, then removed the belt from the girl's wrists and replaced it around his waist. Then he rearranged the child's torn garments as best he could, and picked her up as gently as he knew how. He cradled her head against his shoulder as he carried her on through the woods, and then he was out of the woods once more, standing on the high bank, holding his child out to the sea, almost as an offering.

It began to rain.

For long moments he stood, as if waiting for a sign of some kind. Then, adjusting the child in his arms so that he would have one hand free, he began picking his way down the embankment, skirting the rocks with a sure step, his free hand steadying himself only when his weight tilted a loose stone.

When he was still fifty feet above the surf he began to make his way around a large boulder. Behind it, hidden from all but the most careful eye, the solid wall of the embankment was broken by a small opening. He pushed the limp form of the child into the opening; then he disappeared after it.

The sky seemed to open up as he emerged, alone, from the opening in the embankment, and the wind whipped rain and sea-spray into his face. The waters mixed, and a strange bittersweetness crossed his tongue. Without looking back at the cave entrance, he began making his way back up the embankment.

The rocks had grown slippery with the wetness of the storm, and the wind seemed to be trying to pluck him from his perch. Each time his foot slipped, his hands bled a little more, but he didn't feel it. He felt only the firmness of the earth below him, and the fury of the elements around him.

Then he had gained the top of the embankment, and he plunged back into the woods as if the sea would reach up to take him if he hesitated for even a second. When the forest closed behind him, he began to relax.

He walked purposefully through the woods now, past the trampled ground where he had so recently lain with the child, to the spot where the empty bottle still lay where he had dropped it.

And the rabbit.

He stopped then, and stared down at the rabbit, whose rain-soaked body lay pitifully still.

He picked it up, cradling it in his arms like a baby, and began to make his way across the field to the house beyond.

He didn't pause in the field, didn't take even a moment to look once more at the place where she had played. Instead he kept his eyes on the house, with the same hypnotic concentration with which he had earlier watched the child.

He left the field, crossed the lawn, and entered the house through the wide front door.

No one was there to watch him as he bore the body of the rabbit down the hall and into his study, nor were the gaslights yet casting the shadows he feared to see.

He closed the door to his study, then went to sit in a chair in front of the fireplace, the dead rabbit in his lap.

He sat there for a long time, huddled forward as if to draw warmth from the cold hearth in front of him, his hands stroking the rabbit's wet fur. Now and then he glanced up at the portrait of the beautiful child in the cornflower silk dress that hung above the mantel.

He didn't hear the carriage arrive, or the sound of the knocker as it fell against the front door.

He didn't hear the light tapping at his own door; didn't hear the slight click of the door opening, or the soft step of the maid who came into his study. She waited quietly by his chair until at last he noticed her.

"Yes?" The word was strange-sounding on his ear, as if someone else had uttered it.

"I'm sorry, Mr. John," the maid said softly. "I'm looking for Miss Beth. Her grandmother's asking for her."

"Miss Beth? Isn't she in the house? She was in the field."

"No, sir," the maid replied. "She doesn't seem to be in the house at all. I thought perhaps—"

He held up a hand wearily. "No," he said. "She isn't with me. Not any more."

The maid turned to go, then turned back.

"Mr. John?" He looked up at her. "What's that in your lap?"

The man looked down, and for the first time seemed to be conscious of the small creature on his lap.

"It's a rabbit," he said slowly.

"But what's wrong with it?" the maid asked.

"It's dead," he said. "It was so innocent, and now it's dead."

The maid left the room.

He sat there for a few more minutes, then he stood up. Carefully, he placed the rabbit on the chair, then glanced once more at the portrait above the mantel.

He left the study, closing the door after himself once more, and retraced his steps down the hallway.

He passed through the front door, then turned to follow a walkway around the corner of the house.

He followed the walkway until it ended, then followed the path that picked up from the end of the walk.

At the end of the path, a cliff fell away to the sea below.

He stood for a moment, staring at the sea that battered far below him, and his lips moved almost silently. And over the wind, lost in the noise of the surf, a word drifted soundlessly away.

"Beth," he whispered. Then he repeated the name, and as the sound fell away from him, he flung himself into the waiting sea.

For him, it was over.

BOOK I

Fifteen Years Ago

1

Port Arbello perched snugly on the bluffs above the ocean, its trees flourishing the last of their fall finery with a bravado that belied the nakedness soon to come. The breeze off the Atlantic signaled an end to Indian summer, and Ray Norton smelled the first signs of winter in the air as he turned the town's only police car onto Conger's Point Road.

Ray had grown up in Port Arbello, and now, in his mid-fifties, he was beginning to feel old. He had watched himself change and grow older as Port Arbello stayed the same. He tried to remember what changes had come to the town since he had been born, and realized that there just weren't enough to make much of a difference.

There was the new motel, doing its best to act as if it had been there since the beginning of time. It hadn't been, and as he passed it Ray wondered what would become of it when the losses finally became too great for even its management to tolerate. Maybe the town could buy it and turn it into a country club. Get rid of the neon sign. Put in a golf course.

Then he remembered that Port Arbello had already tried a country club, or at least a building near the old golf course. That had failed too, and the building now stood vacant and dying, serving only as a shelter for the few people who still used the golf course. There weren't more than forty or fifty of them, and it was all they could do to keep raising the funds to pay the greenskeeper each year.

All in all, other than the new motel (which was already fifteen years old), there wasn't much that was new in Port Arbello. A store occasionally changed hands, a house came on the market now and then, and once in a while a new family came to town. For the most part, though, the town kept to itself, passing its homes and its businesses from one generation to the next. Its small farms remained small farms, and its small fishing fleet continued to support a small group of fishermen.

But that was the way they liked it, Ray realized. They had grown up with it, and they were used to it. They had no intention of changing it. He remembered a few years back—how many he was no longer sure, but it must have been right after the War—when a real-estate developer had bought up a lot of acreage outside the town limits. He was going to turn Port Arbello into a summer town, filled with A-frames and summer natives.

The town had caught wind of the plan, and for the first time in its history, Port Arbello had moved quickly. In a single town meeting, with the support of everybody except the farmer who had sold his property, Port Arbello had passed zoning ordinances to prohibit such projects, then annexed the property that was to be developed. The developer fought it through the courts, but Port Arbello won. In the end, the developer had been unable to sell the property, and the farmer, a couple of hundred thousand dollars richer, had foreclosed on the mortgage, bought himself all the newest equipment he could find, and was still happily working his land at the age of eighty-six. Ray grinned to himself. That was the way of things in Port Arbello.

He tooted his horn as he passed the old farmer, but didn't wave. He didn't have to, for the farmer, intent on what he was doing, didn't look up from his field.

But Ray knew that the next time he saw him in town, the old man would touch the brim of his hat and say, "Nice to see you the other day, Ray." That, too, was the way things were done in Port Arbello.

A mile out of town the Conger's Point Road made the left turn that would take it partway out to the Point before it cut back inland on its way south. Ray supposed that this, too, was something new, though the road had been extended far beyond Conger's Point long before he was born. But in the old days, the really old days, it had probably ended at the Congers' front door, a direct pipeline from the heart of the town to the residence of its leading citizens.

The Conger family, though not the founders of Port Arbello, had been at the top of the social heap there for so long that it was now a tenet of faith with the people that not much could go on in Port Arbello without the approval of the Congers. It was also a tenet of faith that the Congers were rich. Not as rich, perhaps, as the Rockefellers and the Carnegies, but close enough so that, to Port Arbello, it didn't make any difference. They still remembered the days when the railroad had built a special spur into Port Arbello to accommodate the needs of the Admiral's private car. They still remembered the days when the staff at Conger's Point was twice the size of the Conger family (which, until recently, had never been small). They assumed that the Congers, being people of taste and sensitivity, had let the staff go not because they could no longer afford them, but because large staffs had come to be considered ostentatious.

Ray Norton, who lived on the Point Road himself, and had grown up with Jack Conger's father, knew better. Ray had been of an age that fell between Conger generations, and felt himself privileged to be on warm social terms with two generations of Congers, even though the older one was now dead. Ray had been seventeen years younger than Jack Conger's father, and was fifteen years older than Jack. That, plus the fact that he was a neighbor and the chief of police, had put him in a position of being close to power. He enjoyed that position. And he was careful not to undermine it by talking about what he knew of the Congers.

He pulled the car off the road and into the Congers' driveway. You could see the house even before you turned into the drive. Indeed, you could see it from the moment the road passed the end of the forest that flourished along the north bank of the Point, and began flanking the field that separated the house from the woods. But Ray was always careful not to look at the house until he had reached the end of the driveway. From there, he could absorb it, could enjoy the grandeur with which it sat at the end of its lane, its full veranda staring austerely through the double row of ancient oaks that lined the drive. It was a saltbox, nearly two hundred years old, but its simple square lines seemed to fit with the bleakness of the lonely point on which it stood. It had a pride to it, as if it were challenging the sea to reach up and sweep it away. So far, the sea had not met the challenge, and Ray Norton doubted that it ever would.

He parked the car and crossed the porch to the great oaken door. As always, he was tempted to raise the antique brass door knocker and let it crash against its plate to cause the resounding boom in the house that always brought visions of times past into his head. But, as always, he resisted the impulse and pressed the button that would sound the door chimes in the main hall within.

"Newfangled gimcrack," he muttered to himself, parodying his New England background.

Rose Conger opened the door herself, and her face broke into a pleased smile at the sight of Ray Norton.

"Ray! If you're looking for Jack, you're in the wrong place. He really does work these days, you know."

"I'll get to him later," Ray said. "Right now I need to talk to you. Have you got any coffee on?"

Rose stepped back to let him in.

"I don't, but I'm sure Mrs. Goodrich does. If anything ever happens to her, I don't know what we'll all do. Is this a social visit, or are we talking seriously? It makes a difference, you know. When this place was built, they had separate rooms for all kinds of conversations. Take your pick."

"How about the back study? I always liked that room. But only when a fire's lit."

Rose smiled. "It's laid, but it's not lit. Let's go fix that. Why don't you get the fire started while I find Mrs. Goodrich?" Without waiting for an answer, she started toward the back of the house, but turned toward the kitchen, leaving Ray to continue into the back study.

He lit the fire, then seated himself in the old leather wing chair just to the right of the fireplace. He glanced around the room, and realized how comfortable he was here. Often he wished the house were his.

When Rose Conger joined him, Ray was staring at the picture above the mantel.

"That's new, isn't it?" he said.

"Only for us," Rose replied. "I haven't any idea how old it is. We found it in the attic a year ago, but just got around to having it cleaned last month." She shuddered slightly. "Have you any idea how much it costs to have a portrait cleaned?"

"I don't have any ancestors worth cleaning. Who was she?"

"I haven't the vaguest idea. From the way she's dressed, I'd say the portrait must be just about ninety years old. We can't figure out who she was. There's no one in any of the family albums who looks like that, or who might have looked like that when she was young."

Ray looked at the picture carefully. "Well, it's obvious who she looks like. She looks like Elizabeth."

Rose nodded her head. "She does, doesn't she? She definitely has Elizabeth's eyes, and the hair seems to be the same color, too. But she looks like she's two or three years younger than Elizabeth."

They looked at the portrait together, and were still staring at it when Mrs. Goodrich appeared with their coffee.

"How children were expected to play dressed like that," she said, following their eyes to the painting, "absolutely beats me. No wonder there were so many servants around here. It'd take one girl all week just to wash that child's clothes. And with no machines." She shook her head. "All I can say is, I'm glad times have changed." She set the coffee down, nodded to Ray, and left the room.

"And if she had her way," Rose said as she poured the coffee, "she'd have Elizabeth and Sarah dressed that way all the time. And she'd keep the clothes clean, even if she had to beat them on a rock to do it. Times may change, but not Mrs. Goodrich."

Ray grinned. "I know. If I didn't know better, I'd swear she hasn't changed at all since I was a kid. I always wondered if there was ever a Mr. Goodrich."

"Who knows?" Rose shrugged. "One simply doesn't ask Mrs. Goodrich such questions." She settled down on the sofa opposite Ray and sipped the coffee. "So what brings you out here in the middle of the day? Run out of crooks in Port Arbello?"

"I wish we had. Have you heard about Anne Forager?"

"Anne? Has something happened to her?"

"We don't know. Her mother called us this morning, very early. Apparently Anne came in late last night, long after she should have been home, and she was a mess. Her dress was torn, she was covered with mud, and she had a few scratches."

Rose paled. "Good God, Ray, what happened to her?"

"So far, we aren't sure. She says she was on her way home from school and that something happened to her. But she won't say what. She keeps saying that she doesn't remember. That all she remembers is that she was walking home from school, and then she was walking toward town along the Point Road, covered with mud."

"What time was that?"

"She got home around eleven."

"My God, Ray, and you mean her parents didn't call you? I mean, Anne Forager can't be more than seven or eight years old—"

"She's nine."

"All right, so she's nine! You can bet that if Sarah or even Elizabeth were missing that late at night, you'd have already been out looking for her for two or three hours."

"That's you, Rose. But these people are different. Around here, nobody thinks anything bad can happen. Marty and Marge just assumed that Anne was with some friend, and that was that. Until she came home. Now we're trying to find out what happened."

"Has a doctor seen her?"

"She's there now. I should find out what he has to say later this afternoon. What I need to know from you is if you were home yesterday afternoon."

"Not until five or five thirty. Why?"

"I was hoping you might have seen something. Anne says she walked back to town from here, or very close to here. From the mud, it looks like she must have been near the embankment."

"Or the quarry."

Ray's eyebrows rose. "Of course. The quarry. I'd forgotten all about it."

"I wish I could," Rose said. "I wish I could fill it in.

Someone's going to get killed out there someday, and I don't care what Jack says, it's going to be our fault."

"Oh, come on, Rose. That old quarry has been there forever and nobody's ever come to grief there yet. Besides, the fishing is the best in town. Fill that old quarry in and half the kids in Port Arbello would be on your back."

"We could consider building them a swimming pool and letting them do their fishing in the stream," Rose said acidly. "I don't think anyone realizes how dangerous that place is."

"Well, be that as it may, we don't know where Anne was. She could have been at the quarry, she could have been on the embankment, or she could have been anywhere else. We won't know until she starts talking."

"If she starts talking . . ." Rose mused, wondering immediately if it had been wise to voice the thought. She glanced at Ray and saw compassion in his eyes. Well, they were old friends, and he had long been aware of the Congers' private torments.

"If?" Ray inquired gently.

Rose shrugged. "She may not, you know. If something happened to her, something she doesn't want to remember, she might simply block it out of her mind."

"Unless the doctor determines she's been raped," Ray said, "I can't imagine what it could be. And, frankly, I just don't think she's been raped. Not here. Not in Port Arbello."

Rose smiled thinly. "Things like that do happen a lot more often than anyone hears about."

Ray shook his head doubtfully. "If you want my opinion, I think Anne stayed out a lot later than she was supposed to, and has thought up a nice story to get herself out of the punishment she deserves. If she were my child . . ."

"Which she's not," Rose pointed out.

Ray chuckled. "No, she isn't, is she? But I am the

chief of police, and I have a job to do. Is that what you're saying?"

"That's what I'm saying." Rose smiled. "Let me call Elizabeth. Maybe she'll know something you don't."

She went to the door of the study and called her daughter. She was pouring them both a second cup of coffee when Elizabeth Conger came into the room.

She was about thirteen, but had none of the awkwardness of most children of that age. Ray noted that the resemblance to the old portrait was remarkable indeed. The same eyes, the same silky blond hair, and, if the hair had been combed differently to flow freely over her shoulders, the same features. Elizabeth wore a ponytail, with bangs in front, the blond hair almost blending into the pale skin that was set off by her incredible sky-blue eyes.

Behind Elizabeth another child, Sarah, hovered silently. Two years younger than Elizabeth, Sarah provided an odd contrast to the older girl. She was dark, and her eyes seemed to sink deeply inside her, as if she lived in another world. Her hair was cropped short, and was as dark as Elizabeth's was blond. And, while Elizabeth was dressed in a neatly pressed mini-skirt and ruffled blouse, Sarah wore blue jeans and a plaid flannel shirt.

Elizabeth came into the room and smiled at Ray.

"Hello, Mr. Norton. Did you finally catch up with Mother? She's been overparking again. If you want to take her now, I can have Mrs. Goodrich pack a bag for her." She sat down, enjoying the laughter of her mother and the police chief.

"Sorry, Elizabeth," Rose said. "He can't prove a thing." Then her voice took on a serious tone, and Elizabeth's smile faded as she was asked if she had seen Anne Forager near the house the previous afternoon. She thought carefully before she answered. When she finally spoke, there was a maturity in her voice that belied her age.

"I don't think so. The last I remember seeing Anne yesterday, she was walking toward Fulton Street, by herself. It looked like she was going home."

Ray nodded. "That's what Anne says, too. She was walking along Fulton Street, and then she doesn't remember a thing until she was out this way."

"This way?" Elizabeth asked.

"Anne says she doesn't know what happened. But she says she walked home along the Point Road about eleven."

"Then that lets me out," Elizabeth said. "I go to bed at nine every night."

"Well, then," Rose said, standing up. "I guess that's that. I'm sorry, Ray, but it doesn't look like we can help you. Your trip's been wasted."

Ray, too, rose, and all four of them walked together the length of the hall. Ray waited while Elizabeth led her sister up the stairs, then looked at Rose. There was concern in his eyes, and Rose was able to anticipate his question.

"I think she's getting better, Ray. I really do. She still doesn't talk, but she seems a little more animated than she did a year ago." Then some of the brightness left her voice. "Of course, I may be kidding myself. The school says that they don't think anything's changed, that she's the same as ever. But, on the other hand, Elizabeth seems to think she's better. And God knows, Sarah spends more time with Elizabeth than with any of the rest of us. I don't know what I'd do without her. I really don't."

They said their good-byes, and Rose stood on the porch and watched as Ray drove down to the Point Road. Then she turned and stared speculatively across the field to the woods that hid the embankment from her view. Finally she turned back to the house, and went upstairs to find her children.

* * *

They were in the playroom, and the door stood open. Rose stayed silently in the hall for a moment, watching as Elizabeth patiently built a tower, then rebuilt it after Sarah knocked it down. Rose once more was impressed with Elizabeth's patience with her strange younger sister.

Elizabeth looked up as her mother came into the room, and smiled.

"One of these days the tower is going to stand," she said. "And on that day I'm going to tell Sarah that it's time for a new toy. Until then, I build and she knocks over." Elizabeth immediately noticed the pain in her mother's face, and tried to reassure her. "I don't mind, Mother. I'd rather have her knock them over than not do anything at all."

Rose relaxed, but only a little. In her mind she blessed Elizabeth once more. Aloud she said, "Elizabeth, you don't go near the embankment or the woods, do you?"

"Of course not, Mother," Elizabeth said, not looking up from the new construction she was building for Sarah. "You've already told me how dangerous it is. Why would I want to go there?"

She put the last block in place, and watched as Sarah's arm came out to knock it over.

2

Jack Conger reached instinctively to adjust the mirror
as he turned off the Point Road into the long driveway.
He was a fraction of a second too late, and the glint
of the setting sun caught him in the eyes just before it
moved off his face to settle in a harmless rectangle in
his lap. He blinked reflexively, and once more cursed
his ancestor who had so conscientiously laid this road
out on its perfect east-west axis. New England neat-
ness, he thought. God, they were all so—he groped
for the right word, then made his choice as he looked
down the driveway at his home—severe. That was it,
all right. They were severe. An absolutely straight drive
leading to an absolutely plain house. He wondered just
which of his forebears had had the temerity to break
the line of the house with the wide porch. The porch,
he had always felt, didn't really fit the house, though
without it the house would have been totally lacking
in any kind of warmth. Jack parked the car in front
of the converted carriage house, now the garage, and
went around the corner of the house to go in the front
door. The Congers, he had been taught since birth,
always used the front door. The side door was for
children, and the rear for servants and merchants. Jack
knew it was silly, but habit was habit, and besides, it
was about the last of the old traditions that he could
still keep up. The squire to the end, he thought as he
closed the front door behind him.

No butler waited to take his coat, and no maid

scurried out of his study as he entered it. He supposed, wryly, that he could pull the old bell cord and ask Mrs. Goodrich to bring him a drink, but he knew he would only be told once more that "grown men can mix their own drinks. Things aren't the way they used to be, you know." Then dinner would be slightly burned, just to remind him that he'd overstepped his bounds. He mixed his drink himself.

He had settled himself in front of the fireplace, and was weighing the pros and cons of stoking up the fire when he heard his wife's footstep in the hall.

"Rose?" he called, almost as if he hoped it wasn't. "Is that you?"

Rose came into the room, crossed the floor to her husband, and gave him one of those kisses usually classified as a peck. She sniffed at his glass.

"Is there another one of those?"

Jack's eyebrows lifted slightly. "So early?"

"It's been one of those days. Will you do the honors, or do I have to fix it myself?"

Jack smiled, but it wasn't a comfortable smile. "Since you didn't make any cracks about 'practice makes perfect,' I'll do it for you. Aren't you home a little early?" he asked as he moved to the bar.

"I've been here since lunch," Rose replied, settling herself on the couch. "All my work this afternoon was on paper, and the office was just too busy. I close three deals tomorrow, making us fifteen thousand dollars richer. Shall we drink to that?" She took the glass from his hand and raised it toward him. "To the recouping of the Conger fortune."

Jack raised his own glass halfheartedly, and settled back into his wing chair.

"You don't seem too thrilled about it," Rose said carefully.

"The Conger fortune," Jack said, "should be recouped by a Conger, if it is to be recouped at all. Not a Conger wife."

"Well," Rose said shortly, "I guess we don't need to talk about that any more. I had a visitor this afternoon."

"Is that unusual?"

Rose stared at her husband for a moment, fighting the urge to rise to the bait. When she was sure she had herself under control, she spoke again. "Jack, let's not fight," she said. "Let's spend a quiet, comfortable evening at home, just like we used to."

Jack looked at her carefully, trying to see if he could spot a trap. After a moment, he relaxed, his shoulders dropping slightly and his breath, which he hadn't realized he'd been holding, coming deeply. Now, for the first time since she'd come into the room, his smile was warm.

"I'm sorry," he said. "I guess I'm just learning to be defensive all the time. Who came by? You made it sound important."

"I'm not sure if it was or not. It was Ray Norton, and he was here on business."

"That," Jack said speculatively, "would have to do with Anne Forager, right?"

"You already know?"

"You forget, my love, that I'm the editor of the only paper in town. Granted, it isn't much, but it is mine own. And in my illustrious position, there isn't much that goes on in this town that I don't hear about. The Port Arbello *Courier* may not be a major paper, but it is a fine gossip center. In short, yes, I've heard about Anne. Probably a lot more than you, since my sources, unlike Ray Norton's, are not sworn to stick to the facts, ma'am. What would you like to know?"

"What happened to her," Rose said.

"Ah, now that complicates things," he said, growing somber. "Anne Forager, at various times of the day, has been reported to be missing, to be dead, to have been raped and decapitated, to have been raped but not decapitated, and to have been decapitated but not

raped. Also, she has been reported as having been
severely beaten and now hovering between life and
death. Or she deserves to be spanked, depending on
who you listen to. In other words, you probably know
a lot more about it than I do, since you talked to Ray,
and everybody else talked to me." He drained his glass
and stood up. "Would you like me to fix that for you,
or are you going to nurse it along?"

"I'll nurse it," Rose said. She continued talking
while Jack fixed his second drink. She noted that it
was a double, but decided not to mention it. Instead,
she occupied herself with recounting Ray Norton's visit
that afternoon.

"—And that's about it," she finished. "Ray didn't
go down to see you this afternoon?" Jack shook his
head. "That's funny. I had the distinct impression he
was planning to go directly from here to your office."

"If I know Ray," Jack said drily, "he went from
here directly to the quarry, to have a look around.
Probably complete with a pipe and a magnifying glass.
Was he wearing his deerstalker hat?"

Rose grinned in spite of herself. "Jack, that isn't
fair. Ray isn't like that, and you know it."

"How do I know it?" Jack shrugged. "Ray hasn't
had a real case to work on since the day he went to
work for Port Arbello. I'll bet he was more happy
than concerned that something has finally happened
here, wasn't he?"

"No, he wasn't. He seemed to be very concerned.
And why are you being so hard on him? I thought you
were good friends."

"Ray and I? I suppose we are. But we also know
each other's limitations. I don't think he's Sherlock
Holmes, and he doesn't think I'm Horace Greeley. But
we like to act like we are. It makes us feel important."

"And you have to feel important?"

Jack's guard went up immediately. "What's that
supposed to mean?"

"Forget it," Rose said quickly. "It wasn't supposed to mean anything. What do you suppose really did happen to Anne Forager?"

"Anne? Probably nothing. I tend to go along with the idea that she stayed out too late and came up with a good story to avoid her punishment. Children are like that."

"Not ours," Rose said quietly.

"No," Jack said. "Not ours." He stared into his drink for a moment. "Where are they?"

"Upstairs. Elizabeth's playing with Sarah. Oh, God, Jack, what if the same thing happened to Anne that happened to Sarah?"

Jack recoiled as if he'd been slapped.

"It didn't, Rose. If something like that had happened, she wouldn't be talking about it at all. She wouldn't be talking. She'd be sitting—staring at the walls—just . . . sitting." He broke off for a moment, as if it was too painful to continue. Then he forced himself to speak again.

"She's going to get better. She'll be back in school next year . . ."

"She's in school," Rose said gently.

"I mean regular school, where she belongs. Not that other place." The bitterness in his voice hung in the air.

Rose bit her lip for a minute, trying to choose the right words.

"It's a good school, Jack. Really it is. And Sarah's doing well there. You know she isn't well enough to go to public school. Think what would happen to her. Why, the children alone . . ." She trailed off.

"We should keep her at home," Jack said. "She belongs at home, with people who love her."

Rose shook her head. "It isn't love she needs, right now. She needs to have people around her who understand her problem, who can help her. God knows, I don't have the time or the skills to devote to her."

"It isn't right," Jack insisted. "That school. That's

for crazy kids, and retarded kids. Not for Sarah. Not for my daughter. All she needs is to be around normal kids, kids like Elizabeth. Look how well she does with Elizabeth . . ."

Rose nodded. "Of course I know how well she does with Elizabeth. But do you think all children are like Elizabeth? How many other children would have her patience? Children can be cruel, Jack. What do you think would happen to Sarah if she were back in public school? Do you think they'd all play with her the way Elizabeth does? Because if you do, you're crazy. They'd tease her, and taunt her. They'd play with her, all right, but she wouldn't be a playmate; she'd be a toy. It would only make her worse, Jack."

He finished his drink and rose to fix a third. Rose watched him go to the bar, and a wave of pity swept over her. He suddenly seemed unsure of himself, his step wary, as if something were waiting to trip him. As he tilted the bottle to pour the liquor into his glass, she spoke again.

"Do you think you ought to?"

"Ought to?" Jack glanced back at her over his shoulder. "No, I don't think I ought to. But I'm going to. There's a difference, you know."

The scream came before Rose could reply. Jack froze where he stood, the liquor streaming out of the bottle, overflowing the glass as the terrified shriek filled the house. It seemed to root him to the spot, and it wasn't until it had finally died away that he was able to let go of the bottle. Rose was already in the hall by the time the bottle broke on the floor, and if she heard it, she didn't turn around. Jack glanced at the mess at his feet; then he too ran from the room.

The awful sound had come from the floor above. Rose and Mrs. Goodrich met at the bottom of the stairs, and Rose came close to toppling the housekeeper as she scrambled up the single flight. Mrs. Goodrich recovered, and made her way up the stairs as quickly as her age and arthritis would allow. Jack passed her halfway up.

"What was it?" he asked as he passed.

"Sarah," Mrs. Goodrich panted. "It was Miss Sarah's voice. God Almighty, hurry!"

Jack was at the top of the stairs when he saw his wife disappear into the children's playroom. By the time he got to the door, he realized that whatever had happened, it was over.

Rose stood just inside the door, a slightly dazed look on her face. In one corner, Sarah sat huddled against the wall, her knees drawn up under her chin, her arms wrapped around herself. She wore a flannel night-gown, whose folds spread around her and seemed to give her extra protection. Her eyes, unnaturally wide, stared vacantly outward, and she was whimpering to herself.

In the center of the room, Elizabeth sat cross-legged on the floor, her fingers on the indicator of a Ouija board, her eyes closed tight. She seemed oblivious of her sister's terror, as if she had not even heard the piercing scream of a moment before. As Jack came into the room, Elizabeth opened her eyes and smiled up at her parents.

"Is something wrong?" she asked.

"Wrong? Didn't you *hear* it?" Jack demanded.

Comprehension dawned on Elizabeth's face. "You mean the scream?" she asked.

Rose swallowed hard. "Elizabeth, what happened?"

"Nothing, really," Elizabeth replied. "We were just in here playing with the Ouija board."

"Where did you find—" Jack started to say, but Rose cut him off.

"Never mind that now. What happened?"

"Nothing happened, Mother. We were just playing with the Ouija board, and nothing much was happening. Then Cecil brushed up against Sarah, and she screamed."

"That's all?" Jack asked, disbelief sounding in his voice. "But look at her. She's terrified." Rose was moving toward Sarah now, and the little girl shrank farther into her corner.

"Well, of course she's terrified," Rose said. "If that cat had brushed up against me, I would have jumped too."

"But that scream," Jack said.

"I guess it was kind of awful," Elizabeth admitted. "But you have to get used to it."

"She's right," Rose said, stooping over Sarah. "Sarah doesn't react the way the rest of us do. Mrs. Montgomery tells me it isn't anything to worry about. It's just that Sarah doesn't react to very much, and when she does react, she tends to overreact. Mrs. Montgomery says the best thing to do is simply act as if nothing happened at all. For instance, if Cecil brushed up against me and I jumped, would you make a big fuss about it? Of course not. And that's what we should try to do with Sarah. If we stay calm, she'll be all right. If we make too much of a fuss, it will only scare her more."

"Can you do it?" Jack asked. "Can you get used to her being this way?"

"I'll never get used to screams like that," Rose muttered as she gathered Sarah into her arms. For a moment Sarah seemed to shrink away from her mother, but then, as if she suddenly realized where she was, her arms went around Rose's neck, and she buried her face in the warm breast. Rose, totally immersed in calming her child, carried Sarah from the room.

Jack, still standing at the door, moved aside to let his wife pass. He made a small gesture, as if to put a comforting hand on Sarah, but Rose was already through the door by the time he had made up his mind to complete it. His hand wavered uncertainly in the air for a moment, then disappeared into his pocket. He stared at the Ouija board.

"Where did you get that thing?" he asked.

Elizabeth glanced up. "It was in the storeroom. You know, the one where we found the old picture. How old do you think it is?"

"Not that old. Probably thirty, forty years. Those things were popular in the twenties. Everybody had one, and everybody was holding séances. I seem to remember my parents and their friends playing with one. Probably that one."

"Want to try it with me?" Elizabeth asked. "Maybe we could find out who the girl in the picture is."

Jack smiled at her. "We know who it is," he said. "It's obviously you. Same eyes, same hair. Only I don't understand why you never wear that dress any more."

"Oh, it's so old," Elizabeth said, her eyes twinkling as she joined the game. "I've had it for at least a hundred years. It's really just a rag now." She sighed. "I suppose I'll have to throw it out."

"Don't. I can't afford to buy you a new one. Maybe that Ouija board can tell me where the money goes."

"Maybe so," Elizabeth said, a note of eagerness in her voice. "Want to try it?"

For a moment Jack was tempted. Then he remembered Sarah, and shook his head. "I'd better get downstairs and see if I can help your mother with Sarah."

Elizabeth nodded. "Okay. I'll be down after a while." She watched her father leave the room, then glanced down at the Ouija board. Then she remembered the cat.

"Cecil," she called. "Cecil? Where are you?" She held still for a minute or two, listening, then called to the cat again.

"Cecil? I'll find you, you know, so you might as well come out now."

There was no telltale scuffling to tell her where the cat was hiding, so she began a search of the room. Eventually she discovered the cat, clinging to the inside of the draperies, halfway up from the floor. She pulled a chair over and stood on it while she disengaged the cat's claws from the thick material.

"Did Sarah frighten you?" she said. "Well, you frightened her first. If you don't want her to scream, you mustn't brush up against her like that. But it isn't your fault, is it? How would you know it would scare her? All you wanted was a little attention. So you let go of that curtain and come down here with me. Come on, let go. It's all right now."

She freed the last of the claws and, holding the cat close, stepped down from the chair. She carried the cat to the Ouija board and sank back to her cross-legged position, placing Cecil in her lap. She sat for a long time, stroking the cat, talking softly to him, waiting for him to calm down. When at last Cecil closed his eyes and began to purr, Elizabeth stopped stroking him and put her fingers back on the indicator of the Ouija board.

An hour later, still carrying the sleeping Cecil, Elizabeth came downstairs for dinner.

3

She watched the moon creep up from the horizon, watched the silvery road shoot across the sea toward the base of the cliff that supported the house high above the surf. She listened for a moment, as if expecting the pounding surf to lessen its dull roar in the new brightness of the full moon. But the noise did not abate. The end of the silver road appeared, just short of the horizon, and she felt depressed as the gap between the moon and its reflection widened. As the moon climbed out of the sea, it seemed to shrink.

"It always seems to get smaller as it gets higher," Rose said, more to herself than to Jack. He glanced up from the book he was reading, and adjusted his sprawling position as Rose came over to the bed.

"What does?"

"The moon. It always looks so huge when it starts to rise, then gets smaller."

"It's an illusion," Jack said. "Something to do with the proximity to the horizon."

She cuddled close to him, and tried to ignore the slight drawing away she felt in his body. "That's my Jack, literal to the core. Can't you try to imagine it as really shrinking? As though somebody was letting some of the air out?" She ran her fingers through the hair on his chest, feeling the ripple of muscles just below the skin. She reached across his stomach and snatched the book away from him. He rolled over and scowled at her.

"Hey," he said. "I was reading that book."

She grinned at him.

"Not any more. I'm tired of you keeping your nose in that book. I want to play." She sat up and slipped the book behind her.

"Oh? Okay, we'll play. Give me back the book before I count to ten." As he reached nine, Rose slipped the book into the bodice of her nightgown. Jack's eyebrows rose a notch. "So that's what you want to play?"

Rose lay back, striking a seductive pose. "If you want it, come and get it." Her eyes danced as she challenged him.

Jack made a grab at the book, and as he came close to her, Rose tossed the book aside and slid her arms around his neck. His hand, caught between them, was pressed against her breast.

"Touch me, darling," she whispered into his ear. "Please touch me." Jack hesitated for a moment, then began moving his hand over his wife's breast, feeling the nipple harden under his touch. Rose moved her face around and began kissing him, her tongue lightly probing between his lips, trying to find an entry. She pulled him down till he was lying on top of her, and her hands began to move over his back, caressing him, stroking him. For a moment—just a moment—she thought he was going to respond. As she felt his body go limp, felt the weight of him lying inertly above her, her fingers turned into claws, and she scratched at him violently. Reacting to the pain, Jack leaped from the bed.

"God damn you," Rose snarled. "God damn you to hell for the no-good man you are!" There was no laughter in her eyes now, only a blinding rage that frightened Jack.

"Rose—" he began. But she got up swiftly, her sudden movement cutting off his plea, and stood opposite him as though the bed had suddenly become a battlefield.

"Don't 'Rose' me, you bastard. Do you think that's what I need?"

"I'm sorry," Jack began again.

"You're always sorry. That's all I've heard for a year now. Did you know it's been a year? I've been keeping track!"

"You didn't have to do that."

"Didn't I? Why not? So you'd never have to know how long it's been since you made love to your wife? So you wouldn't have to know how long it's been since you acted like a man?"

"That's enough, Rose," Jack said.

"It's not enough," she shot back, her voice rising. "It won't be enough till you get through this thing, whatever it is. Look at me. Aren't I attractive any more?" She stripped the nightgown off and stood before him, naked, the moonlight streaming through the window to bathe her pale form in an almost metallic hue, the high breasts jutting out above the narrow waist, the full hips tapering into her long, lithe legs.

"Well," she demanded as Jack stared at her. "What about it? Have I turned into some sort of pig?" Jack shook his head, saying nothing. "Well then, what is it? What's happened to you? If it isn't me, it must be you. What's wrong with you, Jack?"

Again he shook his head. "I—I can't tell you, Rose. I'm not sure I know."

"Then shall I tell you?" There was a note of malevolence in her voice that frightened him. He moved back a step, then sank into a chair, waiting. Rose began pacing the room, her eyes wild. She seemed to be casting about, wondering where to start, and for a second Jack waited, trying to fathom the direction from which the attack would come.

"It's the money, isn't it?" she demanded. Safe, he

thought. "You just can't stand the idea that the fortune's gone, can you? That you, the last of the Congers, actually has to work, not for the fun of it, but for the money?" She stared at him as if waiting for a defense, then plunged on. "Well, when are you going to learn that it doesn't matter? There's enough left to pay the taxes on this place, though God knows why we even need it, and between us we certainly make enough to pay for whatever we need. It's not as if we were poor, for God's sake. And even if we were, so what? You don't have to be rich to be a man, damn it!"

He sat silently, knowing what was coming next. Rose didn't disappoint him.

"Or is it me? Do you feel like I've cut your balls off by making more money than you do? I happen to be good at my job, Jack, and you should be proud of that. But not you! Oh, no! You take it as some kind of personal threat to your manhood. Christ, I begin to understand what all those liberationists are talking about. You *do* resent a successful woman. Well, let me tell you something. Do you want to know why I went to work in the first place? I was bored, Jack, just plain bored."

"Rose, we've been all through this—"

"And we'll go through it again." Suddenly she sank onto the bed, her rage spent. "We'll go through it till we get to the bottom of it." The tears started, and Rose buried her face in her hands. "I don't know how much more I can stand, Jack. I really don't. I'm sorry I said I was bored. It wasn't that. I was really just frustrated." She looked up, as if imploring him to understand. "Jack, it's terrible to love a man who doesn't love you."

"That's not it, Rose," he said softly. "I love you very much. I always have."

She sighed. "Well, it's a strange way you show it. I don't know what to do. Sometimes I think it would help if I quit my job. But it's too late for that now." She smiled thinly. "Do you know what it's like to be successful? It's intoxicating. You want more, and more. And I'm going to have more, Jack. I don't get anything at home any more, so I have to have some fulfillment somewhere else."

"If it's that bad," Jack said dully, "why are you still here?"

She stared at him, and there was a hardness in her eyes that frightened him. "Someone," she said slowly, "has to protect the children. Since you don't qualify, that leaves me, doesn't it?"

His blow fell so fast that she had no time to move with it. His fist struck her hard on the cheek, and the force of the blow knocked her flat out on the bed, but she didn't cry out. Instead, she touched the bruise gently and stared up at him. "At least I'm fairly close to your size," she said softly.

He stared at her, then at his hand, and it seemed like an eternity before he realized what he had done. "My God," he breathed. He went to the bathroom and ran the water until it was cold. Then he soaked a washcloth and brought it to her, handing it to Rose to press against her cheek, knowing that she wouldn't let him touch her now.

"I didn't mean to do that."

"Didn't you?" Her voice was listless, as if nothing mattered. "I suppose you don't mean to do a lot of things you do."

"Rose, that isn't fair."

"Life isn't fair, Jack. Leave me alone."

He got up to leave the room. "Maybe it's the curse," he said, trying to keep his voice light. "Maybe the old family curse has finally caught up with me."

"Maybe it's caught up with both of us," Rose said miserably. She watched him leave the bedroom, and wanted to call him back, wanted to hold him and be held by him. But she couldn't. She turned off the light, rolled over, and tried to sleep.

* * *

Jack sank into his chair in the study and took a sip of the drink in his hand. He stared moodily out the window, watching the play of moonlight and shadows on the branches of the maple trees that broke the clean sweep of lawn from the house to the edge of the cliff beyond. The cliff looked inviting, but Jack knew that that was not one of the things that happened when he drank. Often he wished it were.

The memory was still not clear. Perhaps it never would be, sodden as it was in alcohol.

Rose was right; it was just about a year. It had been a Sunday, and it must have been a little over a year ago, for the leaves were still on the trees, glowing gold and red. Rose had gone off for a game of golf—who with? He couldn't remember. There was so much of that day he couldn't remember. He had been drinking, which wasn't unusual for a Sunday, and in the afternoon he had decided to go for a walk. With Sarah.

And then it was foggy. They had started off across the field, and Sarah had run ahead, calling to him to hurry. But he hadn't hurried, and she had waited for him. They had talked, there in the field, but he couldn't remember what they had talked about. And then Sarah had asked him to take her to the woods. There were so many things in the woods she wanted to see, and she never got to go there. And so they had gone to the woods.

He remembered carrying her out of the woods, but that was all.

He listened to the clock strike, and watched the shadows dance on the window. It was an ugly dance, and he didn't want to watch it. He looked at his drink, and tried to force himself not to refill it.

Sarah slept restlessly, and the dream swept over her again, as it did every night, over and over, never ending.

She was in a room, and the room was big. There

was nothing in the room except Sarah and her toys. But she didn't want to play with them. Then Daddy was there, and they were going out of the house together and into the field. She ran ahead of him and stopped to look at a flower. There was an ant on the flower, and she picked the flower to take back to her daddy. But she knew that if she tried to carry it, the ant would fall off. So she called him.

"Daddy! Hurry!"

But he hadn't hurried, and she had waited for him. When he was finally there, the ant was gone, and the flower too, blown out of her hand on a gust of wind. It had gone to the forest, and she wanted to find it.

"The flower's in the woods, Daddy. Take me to the woods."

And so they went to the woods, and her daddy was holding her hand. She felt safe.

They stepped out of the sunlight of the field into the deep shadow of the trees, and Sarah held her father's hand even tighter. She looked around for the flower, and saw a bush. The flower was in the bush. She was sure the flower was in the bush, and the ant would be there too.

She pulled her father toward the bush.

"Hurry, Daddy, hurry. We're almost there."

And then she was there, crawling under the bush, its branches catching at her hair, thorns reaching out to scratch at her. Then she felt something grab at her ankle. A vine. It must have been a vine. She tried to shake loose, but the thing held tighter to her ankle and began pulling her from the bush. She couldn't find the flower. Wait! There it was. If she could only grab it!

But she couldn't, and the thing was pulling her out of the bush. She cried out.

"Daddy! Help! Make it let go, Daddy!"

She twisted around, and the thing was Daddy. But it wasn't Daddy. It was someone else, and he looked like Daddy, but it couldn't be Daddy. Not this man with his wild look. This man who was going to hit her.

She felt the blow, and tried to cry out to her father to help her, but she had no voice. Her father would help her.

Her father hit her.

She wanted her father to pull the man off her.

She wanted her father to stop hitting her.

She wanted her father.

The hand moved up and down through the air, and then Sarah couldn't hear anything any more. She watched herself being beaten, but she felt no pain. She tried to get away, but she couldn't move. As Daddy hit her again and again, she watched herself fade away. And then there was only the gray, the gray that she lived in, and in a far corner of the gray a girl—a blond, blue-eyed girl who would take care of her.

Elizabeth. Elizabeth knew what had happened, and would take care of her. As the gray closed around her, she reached out to Elizabeth.

Sarah woke up, and the hands that were outstretched moved slowly back, and she held herself. When she slept, she dreamed the dream again.

Elizabeth lay in her bed, staring at the ceiling, watching the progress of the moonlight as it moved slowly toward the far wall. She listened to the silence.

She had tried not to hear it; tried to bury her head under her pillow as her parents fought. But the sounds came through the walls, under the door, into the bed, and she listened. Finally she heard her father as he went down the stairs. Now she waited, and watched the moonlight. She would wait until she heard him come back up the stairs, until she heard the click of her parents' door finally closing for the night. Then she would sleep.

Didn't her mother know what had happened in the woods that day? Elizabeth knew that she could tell her mother, but that she wouldn't. Elizabeth knew that she shouldn't know what had happened. And she also knew she couldn't forget it, either.

She had been watching them from the house, and had decided to go with them. She had called to them, but the wind had blown her words the wrong way and they hadn't heard. So she had followed them across the field. Then, just as she had been about to catch up with them, she had decided to play a game with them instead.

She had veered off to the left, toward the road, and cut into the woods about fifty feet from them. Then she had begun making her way back, moving from tree to tree, keeping herself hidden. At the last minute, when she was so close that they would have to see her, she would jump out at them.

She had heard a scuffling noise, and peeped around the tree to see Sarah crawling under a bush. She used the opportunity to dart closer and hide behind a fallen log, watching her sister through the tangle of rotting roots that thrust skyward. Sarah had pushed farther under the bush, and Elizabeth thought her father was about to crawl after her.

But instead he grasped her ankle and began pulling her back toward him.

She heard Sarah cry out, and watched as her father lifted his fist into the air. Suddenly, yanking Sarah free of the bush, he brought his fist down on her. Sarah screamed then, and turned to look up at her father.

Elizabeth stayed hidden behind the log, watching the scene before her with a strange detachment. Suddenly it had all seemed to be far away from her, not connected to her. She suddenly no longer saw her sister and her father, but two strangers, a little girl and a man, and the man was beating the child. And it seemed to have no effect on Elizabeth at all. She simply crouched there, watching it unfold before her.

When Sarah finally lay still, Elizabeth saw her

father straighten up, and she could barely recognize
him. There was a vacant look in his face, and his black
hair, usually so neatly brushed, hung in damp strings
around his face. He looked around wildly, then down
at the child at his feet. She heard a sob wrack his body,
then watched as he picked Sarah up and began carrying her across the field toward the house. She stayed
perfectly still until her father, still carrying her sister,
had disappeared through the front door. Then she
stood up and moved slowly to the spot where her sister
had lain. She looked once more toward the house, then
turned and began making her way through the woods
toward the embankment.

When she had returned to the house an hour later,
the doctors were there, and they had taken Sarah
away. Her father was nowhere to be seen, and her
mother was hysterical. Mrs. Goodrich had finally
noticed her, and asked her where she had been. She
said she had been for a walk. Down by the quarry. It
was the only thing she had ever said about that afternoon, and it was the only thing she would ever say
about it.

Elizabeth continued to stare at the ceiling, and when,
much later, she heard the click of her parents' door,
she slept.

Jack lay in bed, but he still didn't sleep. He remembered what he could remember.

He remembered the doctors coming, and he remembered them putting Sarah in the ambulance. He
remembered Rose coming home, and he remembered
that someone had given him a shot.

They had flown Sarah to a hospital, a hospital far
enough from Port Arbello that no one would ever
have known what had happened to Sarah. She had
been there for three months, and the doctors had been
able to repair her body. The ribs had healed and there
were no longer any scars on her face.

But they had not been able to repair her mind. When she had come home from the hospital, she had been changed. She was no longer the bright elfin child she had always been. She no longer laughed, or ran through the house. She no longer shouted, or played in the field.

She was quiet. She neither spoke nor laughed, and when she moved she moved slowly, as if something were holding her back.

Occasionally, she screamed.

She seemed to be frightened, but she learned to tolerate the presence of her mother. She was never left alone with her father.

She responded only to Elizabeth. She would follow Elizabeth whenever she could, and if Elizabeth could not be with her, she would sit quietly and wait. But that wasn't often.

Elizabeth was usually with her. Except when they were in school, Elizabeth spent most of her time with Sarah—reading to her, talking to her, not seeming to notice that Sarah never talked back. Elizabeth played with Sarah, never losing her patience when Sarah's interest wandered, always finding something new to distract Sarah from whatever was going on in her mind.

The doctors said that Sarah could recover someday, but they didn't know when it would be. Since they didn't know exactly what had happened to Sarah, and nobody seemed able to tell them, they weren't entirely sure how to treat her. But someday, they were sure, Sarah would be able to remember what had happened to her that day, and face it. When that day came, Sarah would be all right again. But until that day, Sarah might do anything. Schizophrenia, they said, was unpredictable.

4

Rose Conger stared across the breakfast table and wondered for the twentieth time how her husband could drink so much and never show the effects of it.

Had he been less engrossed in his morning paper, Jack would have noticed the look of annoyance on Rose's face as she studied his own. At forty, he looked ten years younger, and where the lines of character, or age, should have begun their march from his forehead to his jowls, only the smooth skin of youth was present, still unaffected by the years of drinking. It isn't right, Rose thought. Any other man would have veins standing on his nose, and the awful pallor would make him look skeletal. But not Jack.

"What time did you come to bed?" she asked.

He looked up, then went back to his paper. "One thirty. Two. I don't know."

"Would you like some more coffee?"

He put down the paper, and a twisted smile crossed his face.

"Do I look like I need it?"

"I wish you did," Rose said bitterly. "Maybe if it showed on your face you wouldn't drink so much."

"Oh, come on, Rose. Let's let it alone, shall we? The kids will be down in a minute." He glanced at his watch, as if the gesture would bring the girls into the room and rescue him from what he knew was coming.

"They'll be ten minutes yet," Rose replied. "Jack, what we were talking about last night . . ."

"Is it going to be the drinking this morning? Why is it, Rose, that it's always the money at night and the drinking in the morning? Why don't you, just for the sake of variety, talk about the drinking at night and the money in the morning? Then maybe we could both think of something new to say."

Rose glowered down at her plate and tried to keep her voice even. "I suppose I harbor the vain hope that maybe, if I don't talk about it at night, you won't do it. You'd think I'd learn, wouldn't you?"

"Yes," Jack said, "you would." He folded the paper noisily and tried to concentrate on the print. He read a paragraph, then reread it as he realized that he hadn't any idea of what it was about. He was on his third reading when Rose spoke again.

"How long can we go on like this?"

He put the paper aside and stared across at her. For a long time he was silent, and when he spoke his voice was hard.

"What do you mean, 'like this'? If you mean how long until I can get it up for you again, I don't know. If you mean how long before I'm going to stop drinking, I don't know. If you mean how long before you stop harping at me all the time, that's up to you. I have a strange feeling that I will stop drinking, and start screwing, when you decide to let the whole thing alone and give me some peace. There are reasons, you know, why I have problems, and your nagging doesn't help at all. So why don't you just leave it alone, Rose? Just leave it alone." He stood up and left the room, and Rose was amazed to hear the warmth with which he greeted his daughters before he left the house. His failure to slam the door as he left only increased her annoyance. She poured herself some coffee, and tried to match Jack's warmth as the girls came into the room.

"You have your choice this morning," she said. "Mrs. Goodrich says waffles and pancakes are equally easy, so you can have either one."

"We'll have waffles," Elizabeth said. She kissed her mother good morning and seated herself. Sarah pulled her father's recently vacated chair around and sat beside Elizabeth.

"Sarah? Don't you want to sit in your own chair?"

There was no response from the little girl. She sat quietly with her hands in her lap until Elizabeth poured her some orange juice. She picked it up, dutifully drained the glass, and set it down again. Her hand went back to her lap. Rose watched in silence, feeling helpless.

"Sarah," she repeated. "Are you sure you don't want to sit in your own chair?"

Sarah's head turned toward Rose, and she stared at her mother for a moment. Rose looked vainly into the tiny, dark face, trying to see if Sarah had understood her. It was like trying to fathom the feeling of a mask. After a few seconds, Sarah turned her face away again. A knot formed in Rose's stomach.

"Maybe she'd rather have pancakes," she said pensively. "But how can I know?"

Elizabeth smiled at her mother. "The waffles will do fine," she said. "She likes them. How come Daddy left so early?"

"I guess he had a lot to do at the office," Rose answered distractedly, her eyes still on her younger daughter. She felt that there was something she ought to do, something she ought to say to Sarah, but she didn't know what it was. She felt confused. Hurriedly, she put her napkin on the table and stood up.

"I have a lot to do myself," she said. "Can you manage by yourself, Elizabeth?"

"Sure," Elizabeth said. "If I have to leave before the van gets here, shall I leave Sarah with Mrs. Goodrich?"

"If you think it would be—" "All right" was what she was about to say, but it struck her that she was the mother, not Elizabeth, and that even if she did feel all at sea where Sarah was concerned, it was still her duty to be a mother. She should not defer to a thirteen-year-old child, even one as mature as Elizabeth.

"That will be fine," she corrected herself. "I'll be in my office. Come in before you leave."

She started to leave the room, then, on an impulse, leaned down to kiss Sarah. Sarah didn't respond at all, and, the knot in her stomach tightening, Rose left the room. As she made her way into the little parlor at the front of the house that she had converted into an office for herself, she heard Elizabeth chattering brightly to Sarah, never pausing to give Sarah a chance to say anything, never sounding annoyed at Sarah's—"Dumbness" was the word that came to mind, but Rose couldn't bring herself to use it. She avoided the issue completely by turning her mind to her work.

She pulled out the files she had been working on the previous afternoon and began checking her figures once more. She found two errors, and corrected them. She prided herself on her attention to detail, and had become even more careful as time went on. Since her first day in the real-estate business she had not turned in any paperwork that was less than perfect, and she knew that the men in her office resented it. It had become an unspoken game, good-natured on her part but played with a slight edge of envy by the others involved, to give Rose wrong figures and see how long it would take her to find them. She suspected there was a pot building that would eventually go to the person who succeeded in catching her in a mistake. She intended for that pot to keep on growing till they finally gave it up and either split it up among themselves or handed it all over to her. She finished the files just as Elizabeth came in.

"That time already?" she said.

"I told Kathy Burton I'd meet her before school. Sarah's in the kitchen with Mrs. G."

"Will you be home right after school?"

"Aren't I always?"

Rose smiled at her daughter appreciatively, and held out her arms. Elizabeth came to her mother and hugged her.

"You're a great help to me, you know," Rose whispered to her.

Elizabeth nodded her head briefly and freed herself. "See you tonight," she said. Rose watched as she pulled the door closed behind her, and turned to gaze out the window. In a moment she heard the front door open and close, then saw Elizabeth, pulling a coat on, skip down the steps and start the walk to the Point Road.

Rose went back to her work, thumbing through her listings and mentally pairing off houses with clients. She had discovered that she had a knack for picking the right house for the right person, and her reputation was spreading. She made it a practice to spend at least a couple of hours with each client, talking about everything but houses. Then, when she felt she knew something about her client, she would pull out her listings and give them a couple to look over. Finally she would pull out her own choice for them, and she was usually right. More and more, lately, people had begun to come to her, not so much to see what she had available as to ask her what she thought they ought to have. It was making her work much easier, and her volume much larger.

One more year, she thought, and I'll get my broker's license. Then, watch out, Port Arbello. Another Conger is on the rise.

She was only half aware that the little Ford van that served as a school bus had arrived to take Sarah to White Oaks School, and didn't look up from her work until she heard the tapping at her door.

"Come in," she called.

The door opened, and Mrs. Goodrich, looking resentful at having to intrude on Rose, stuck her head in.

"Sorry to bother you," she said, the deep Yankee voice rumbling from her immense bosom. "Mr. Diller wonders if he could have a word with you. I told him you were busy, but he wonders anyway." Her tone suggested that it was her strongly held opinion that if Mr. Diller had any sense of propriety whatsoever, he would have faded directly into the ground upon being told that Mrs. Conger was busy.

Rose suppressed a grin and did her best to impersonate the grande dame that Mrs. Goodrich obviously expected her to be. For a long time, when she had first come to live in the Conger house, Mrs. Goodrich had frightened her to death, and she had been painfully aware that she did not meet the standards that Mrs. Goodrich had set for the senior Mrs. Conger-in-residence. But she had eventually come to realize that, whatever she did, Mrs. Goodrich would see her as Mrs. Goodrich wanted to see her. In the last couple of years Rose had found a certain enjoyment in trying to play the role. So now, for the benefit of the old housekeeper, she stood up, drew herself as erect as she could, and tried to sound imperious.

"It's unusual that he should call without an appointment, isn't it?"

Mrs. Goodrich nodded a vigorous agreement.

"But I suppose it would be useless to try to send him away."

Again Mrs. Goodrich nodded vigorously.

"So I suppose you may show him in."

The door closed, and in a moment it reopened to allow George Diller to enter. Rose promptly relaxed and smiled at him. He was a little younger than she, and sported a full beard. He was one of the teachers at the White Oaks School, but since he seemed to have a special way with the children he taught, he also drove the van that picked them up and delivered them home every day. The school had tried other drivers, but things always seemed to go better when George Diller drove, as if the children, trusting him, tried to behave better for him.

"What was that all about?" he said, glancing back toward the door.

"You heard?" Rose replied, chuckling.

"You sounded just like my Aunt Agatha, down in Boston. She could order a servant to kill himself, and he wouldn't dare disobey. Fortunately for everyone, she never did."

"Mrs. Goodrich would have loved your Aunt Agatha. She's convinced that's the way a proper lady should talk, so I do my best for her. It's kind of fun, really."

/ "Well, it almost scared me off. But not quite."

"That's good. Would you like some coffee?"

"Not enough time. The kids won't wait long."

Rose glanced out the window and saw Sarah climbing into the front seat of the van. In the back, six or seven children stared out at her, and she could see that one or two of them were already getting restless.

"Then what can I do for you?" Rose asked.

"Nothing for me. It's about Sarah. It isn't anything serious, but the staff at the school would like you and Mr. Conger to come in for a talk."

"Oh?" Rose looked concerned, and George hurried on.

"Really, it's nothing. I think they're thinking of making some changes in Sarah's program, and they want to talk to you first."

Rose nodded. "Of course. Is there any time that's best for the school?" She moved to the desk and opened her calendar.

"Not really." George shrugged. "Afternoons are best, after the kids have gone home, but if you don't have time, we can always work around you."

Rose knew they could. White Oaks was a very expensive school, and had a policy of going out of their way both for their students and the families of their students. Consequently, they found that they very rarely had to go out of their way. Parents, realizing that the school would do what it could for them, tried to do

what they could for the school. So Rose searched for
a free afternoon, and picked up a pencil.

"How's Thursday? Of course, I'll have to check with
my husband, but I imagine he can get away."

"Fine," George said. "About four?"

"I'll mark it right now—" Rose broke off as she
heard a little cry from the front of the house. She
glanced up, and for a moment she didn't see anything
amiss. Then she saw it: The van was moving.

"George!" she yelled. "Quick! The van!"

Without asking any questions, George headed for
the door. It stuck, and he grappled with it for a moment. Rose was still staring out the window. The van
was moving slowly, but it was picking up speed on the
slight incline that led to the garage. She judged that if
it hit the garage, it would stop with little damage. But
if it missed the garage . . .

Her eyes moved across the wide lawn, and the unob-
structed path that led directly to the edge of the cliff.

"The door," George yelled. "It's stuck!"

"Push down," Rose snapped. "It jams at the top."
She glanced out the window again, and the van seemed
to be veering a little to the left. It would miss the
garage.

She heard George grunt, and spun to see him still
struggling with the door. Behind her she could hear
the terrified screams of the children as they realized
what was happening.

"Let me do it," she cried, pushing him aside and
grasping the knob. She lunged at the door and gave a
quick yank. It flew open, and George was through it
and running for the front door, a few feet away. In the
middle of the doorway, Mrs. Goodrich stood frozen,
her hand covering her mouth as if to stifle a scream.
George shoved her aside, and she would have fallen if
Rose hadn't moved quickly to catch her.

"It's all right," Mrs. Goodrich snapped. "Don't worry about me. Help Mr. Diller."

But it was obvious that there was nothing she could do. She watched as George raced after the coasting van. From where she stood it appeared that even if he caught up with it, he wouldn't have any way of stopping it before it shot off the edge of the cliff.

The driver's door was flapping wildly as George caught up with the van. He hurled himself into the driver's seat, and his left hand groped for the emergency brake as his right hand pulled the wheel around. He felt the rear wheels lock, and the van pulled around to the left and began to skid. There was nothing more he could do. He held his breath and waited. Behind him, the children screamed wildly, except for Sarah, who sat placidly in the front passenger's seat, staring out of the window.

It stopped only inches from the edge. If the door hadn't been open, George thought—but then he realized that there were too many ifs. He sat behind the wheel and waited for his nerves to calm down. By the time he was ready to begin guiding the children out of the van, Rose was there. One by one, they got the children out of the van, and Rose led them up to the house. Mrs. Goodrich, having seen that the van didn't go over the edge, had already disappeared into the kitchen. By the time all the children were safely in the house, she had produced a pitcher of hot cocoa. Rose left the children in her charge and went back to the van. George had climbed into the driver's seat again, and was preparing to jockey it away from the precipice.

"Be careful," Rose warned him.

With Rose waving him directions, he eased the van inward from the edge and, when it was far enough back, turned it around. He called to Rose to join him, and eased the vehicle back up to the driveway. When he parked it, he carefully left it in gear and checked the hand brake twice.

"What happened?" Rose asked him as they re-entered the house.

George shook his head. "I don't know. I must have forgotten to set the brake. But I was sure I had. It's almost a reflex with me." He thought a moment, then shook his head. "I can almost see myself setting it, but I must not have."

An hour later, with the children calm once more, George Diller herded them all back into the van. If Rose noticed that George made sure that Sarah was in the back seat this time, she didn't comment on it. She simply stood on the porch and watched the van make its way down the driveway. Then she returned to her office and tried to concentrate on her work. It wasn't easy.

George Diller drove even more carefully than usual on his way back to the school, and he kept one eye on the rear-view mirror. But it wasn't the road behind him that he was watching. It was the children. Particularly, he watched Sarah Conger.

She sat in the back seat, and as they drove along the Conger's Point Road she seemed to be looking for something. Then George remembered. Every morning the van passed Elizabeth Conger as she walked into town to school. And every morning Elizabeth waved to Sarah as the van passed.

But this morning they were too late. There was no one to wave to Sarah.

At the end of the day Mrs. Montgomery would note in her records that Sarah Conger had been much more difficult than usual. It was one more thing she would have to talk to Sarah's parents about.

5

Rose glanced at her watch as she left the house; she had just enough time to stop at Jack's office and still not be late for her appointment. As she walked to the garage, she glanced at the scars on the lawn, and shuddered once more at the memory of the van careening toward the cliff. She wondered if she should have kept Sarah home for the day, and felt a slight twinge of guilt at the relief she had felt when George Diller had insisted that it would be better for Sarah to continue the day as if nothing unusual had happened. She made a mental note to devote a little extra time to Sarah that evening.

A quarter of a mile toward town, Rose smiled to herself as she passed the old Barnes place. She had a feeling that today, as she drove home, she would be able to take down the FOR SALE sign that had been hanging on the fence for months. And it's a good thing, she thought. It's been on the market too long. Another couple of months and it would take on that awful deserted look and be impossible to sell at any price. But she had a feeling that she finally had the right customers for the house. Unconsciously, she pressed the accelerator, and as the car leaped forward some of the feeling of depression that had been hanging over her all morning dissipated.

She slipped the car into her space behind Port Arbello Realty Company, and dropped her purse on her desk as she walked through to the front door.

"You have an appointment in fifteen minutes," the receptionist reminded her. Rose smiled at the girl.

"Plenty of time. I'm just going to run across the square for a minute and say hello to Jack." She knew she could as easily have telephoned, but she liked to keep up the charade of devoted wife. In Port Arbello, solid marriages counted for a lot in the business community.

On her way across the square she glanced quickly at the old armory, standing forbiddingly on the corner just south of the courthouse. Another year, she thought, and I'll find a way to buy it. Then it would be a simple matter of a zoning variance, and she could go ahead with her plan to turn it into a shopping center—not one that would compete with the businesses already surrounding the square, nothing with a major department store. Rather, she envisioned a group of small shops—boutiques, really, though she hated the word—with a good restaurant and a bar. That way, she could increase the value of the property without taking any business from the rest of the merchants. In her mind's eye she saw the armory as she would remodel it: sandblasted, its century-old brick cleaned of the years of grime, with white trim, and a few changes in the façade to give it an inviting look instead of the grim air with which it had always looked down on the town around it.

She jaywalked across the street to the *Courier* office and went in.

"Hi, Sylvia." She smiled. "Is my husband in?"

Jack's secretary returned her smile. "He's in, but he's a bear today. What did you do to him this morning?"

"Just the usual," Rose said. "Tied him up and thrashed him. He squalls, but he loves it." Without knocking, Rose let herself into her husband's office, closing the door behind her, and crossed to his desk, leaned over, and kissed him warmly.

"Hello, darling," she said, her eye not missing the fact that the intercom was open. "I hear you're having a bad day." As Jack looked at her in puzzlement, she pointed to the intercom unit on his desk. He nodded and switched it off.

"You seem cheerful enough," he said sourly.

"I am, now. But we almost had a disaster this morning." She recounted what had happened with the van.

"George is sure he set the brake?" Jack said when she had finished.

Rose nodded. "But he must not have. If he did, then there's only one explanation for what happened. Sarah." Jack seemed to lose a little of his color.

"So the school wants to talk to us about her on Thursday afternoon?" He made a note on his calendar.

"Not about what happened this morning," Rose said quickly. "Although I should imagine that will come up too. My God, Jack, they all would have been killed. Not one of them would have had a chance."

"And you really think Sarah might have released the brake?"

"I don't know what to think," Rose said uncertainly. "I suppose I'm trying not to think at all until we talk to the school."

"I could take the rest of the day off," Jack offered. "We could play a round of golf."

Rose smiled, but shook her head. "If you want to, go ahead. But not me. I have an appointment that I'm almost late for, and I think it's going to be a good one. I'm going to try to sell the Barnes place. If I can pull that off, it will do a lot more for me than a game of golf." She stood up. "For some reason, work seems to relax me."

"I wish it did the same for me," Jack replied. He didn't get up, and Rose felt a surge of anger that he wouldn't play the game with her. "Send Sylvia in as you leave, will you?"

Rose started to make a reply, then changed her mind. Silently, she left the office, forcing her face into a cheerful expression for Sylvia Bannister's benefit.

"He is a bear," she said to Sylvia. "And he wants you in his den. Got to run." Without waiting for the secretary to speak, Rose left the building and hurried across the square. By the time she had reached her own office, she had put her personal life back into its compartment, and was ready to greet her clients.

"So that's about it," Rose said a couple of hours later. "As far as I can tell, these are the only three houses in Port Arbello that come anywhere close to what you're looking for. I could show you more, but I'd only be wasting your time. Why don't we start with these two, and save this one for last." She picked up the listing for the Barnes property, tucked it beneath the other two, and stood up.

"Can we all fit in your car, or shall we follow you?" Carl Stevens asked.

"Let's take mine. That way I can give you a running commentary on the town. If you want all the dirt, you'll have to talk to my husband. I've only been here twenty years, and the people don't really trust me yet."

Barbara Stevens grinned at her. "That's why I love towns like this. If you weren't born here, people leave you alone. And you can't paint if people won't leave you alone."

They left the office, and Rose followed through on her promise. It wasn't true that she didn't have the dirt; every time she sold a house, its owners gave her a complete history of the house in question and the immediate vicinity. Rose knew who had slept with whom, who had gone crazy, and who had done "odd things" in every part of Port Arbello for the past fifty years. But she never passed the information on to clients. Instead, she stuck to her business. Where other real-estate people pointed out the house where they'd found old Mr. Crockett hanging in the attic, Rose pointed out the fact that the school was only two blocks from the property she was showing. Consequently, she got the sales.

She ushered the Stevenses quickly through the first two houses on her list. They were noncommittal, and she didn't push the properties. Then she turned onto the Conger's Point Road.

"Any relation?" Carl Stevens asked as he read the sign.

"We are the last of the Congers," Rose said, doing her best not to sound pretentious, and succeeding. "Unless I manage to produce a son, there soon won't be any Congers at all on Conger's Point Road."

"I think it would be wonderful to live on a road that was named after you," Barbara said.

Rose nodded. "I have to say I sort of get a kick out of it. From what I can gather, this road used to be practically the family driveway. My husband's family used to own practically everything between the town and the Point. But that was a hundred years ago. It's been built up for years. We still live on the Point, but the road passes us now. Sort of symbolic: The road used to end at our doorstep, but now it passes us by."

"You're a philosopher," Carl said. "Which side of the Point is the property that we're going to?"

"This side, but barely. As a matter of fact, if I can sell it to you, we'll be neighbors. The Barnes place adjoins ours. But don't worry, the houses are a quarter of a mile apart, and there's a strip of woods, a field, and some water between them. The Barnes place is on the mainland; we're out at the end of the Point. Here we are," she finished. She braked the car and turned in to the long drive that led to the old house. She heard Barbara suck in her breath, and wondered how long an escrow they'd want.

"My Lord," Carl said. "How big is it?"

"Not as big as it looks," Rose said. "It's an odd

house, but I think you'll like it. Besides, if you don't, you can always change it. The first time I saw it, it struck me that an architect should have it. No one else could make it livable."

"What's wrong with it?" Barbara asked.

"Nothing, really," Rose said. She was parking the car in front of the building now, and she pointed to what appeared to be a pair of long, enclosed galleries, one above the other, that ran the length of the house. "See those?"

"Don't tell me," Carl said. "Let me guess. You go in the front door, and there's an entry hall that goes straight through the house. On each side of the entry hall there's a staircase, and the two staircases meet above the front door. From there, a hall extends the length of the house in both directions."

Rose nodded. "That's it exactly. With another hall on the bottom floor. It gives the place the feeling of an immense railroad parlor car. Every room has one door onto the hall. There's an incredible view of the ocean, but only from the far side of the house. And I don't have any idea at all of what to do about it. That's one of the reasons I brought you out here. Even if you don't buy it, I can get some ideas on what to do with it in case somebody else does."

They went into the house and explored it room by room, first the lower floor, then the upper. Rose, following her instincts, did little more than identify the use to which the Barneses had put each room. Finally they were back in the entry hall.

"Well?" Rose said. Carl and Barbara Stevens looked at each other.

"It does have some problems," Carl mused.

"And they'd be expensive problems, wouldn't they?" Barbara added.

"Not expensive," Rose said. "Very expensive. Count on putting in half again what you pay for it, and that doesn't include the plumbing. Also, it's going to need rewiring within five years, and a new roof in two."

"Honest, aren't you," Carl said with a grin.

Rose shrugged. "If I don't tell you now, you'll tell me later. And I wouldn't want the next-door neighbors mad at me."

"And they want how much for it?" Rose could see the wheels clicking in Carl's mind.

"Fifty-two five. If the floor plan weren't so weird they could get at least twice that."

"Okay," Carl said.

"Okay?" Rose repeated. "What does 'okay' mean?"

Barbara laughed. "It means 'Okay, we'll buy it.'"

"At the asking price?" Rose said vacantly.

"At the asking price."

Rose shook her head. "You're both crazy. You asked me how much they wanted for it, not how much I thought you could get it for. Don't you want to make them a lower offer?"

"Not particularly," Carl said.

"I see," Rose said numbly. "What am I saying? I don't see at all. If you don't mind my saying this, you're taking all the fun out of it for me. I get paid to write offers and counteroffers, and make everybody think he got a good deal. I've never heard of selling a house for the asking price. In fact, I know darn well you could get it for less."

Barbara nodded. "But it would take time. We don't want to wait. We don't want an escrow, and we don't want to finance it. We'll write you a check for it today. Can we move in this weekend?"

Rose nodded. "I suppose so," she said slowly. "There's no mortgage on it, so I guess there isn't anything to it but transferring the title. That doesn't take any time at all."

Carl began laughing. "You look like we've just spoiled your entire day. Let's go back to your office

and get this thing settled. Then we'll go home and pick
up Jeff and bring him out here. He'll love the place.
He loves the ocean, and he loves climbing. That bluff
should make him very happy."

Again Rose nodded. "Something's wrong," she said.
"Selling a house like this isn't supposed to be this
easy. Why are you in such a hurry to move in?"

"We're in a hurry," Barbara said, "because we've
been looking for a house for a year, we know exactly
what we want, we have the money to buy it and the
talent to fix it, and it's just what we're looking for.
Also, Jeff is fourteen years old, and we want to get
him started in school before it gets too far into the
year. In another month all the cliques for this year
will be formed, and Jeff will be out in the cold till
next fall. So if we can't move in next weekend, we
probably won't move in at all. Can you arrange it?"

"Sure," Rose said. "There isn't anything to arrange.
Like I said, you've taken all the fun out of it for me."

"Well," Carl said, "we'll do our best to make it up
to you."

On the way back to town, Rose decided she liked
the Stevenses.

Martin Forager stood in front of Jack Conger's
desk, his eyes blazing. He kept his hands stuffed deep
in the pockets of his plaid hunting jacket.

"I'm telling you, Conger," he was saying, "it's a
disgrace. It's been two days now, and nothing's been
done." He turned to stare out the window. "Nothing,"
he repeated.

"I'm sure Ray's doing his best," Jack began. Forager
whirled.

"His best ain't good enough. I don't know what
happened to my daughter, but I want to know."

Jack looked up helplessly. Martin Forager was a big
man. He had planted his fists on Jack's desk and was
leaning over him, glowering.

"I don't see what I can do," Jack said quietly.

"You can use your paper," Forager snapped. "That's what you can do. You can use it to light a fire under Ray Norton. Let him know that if he doesn't do something, and do it fast, the people of this town are going to get rid of him."

"I hardly think—" Jack started to say.

"I hardly think," Forager mimicked. "It didn't happen to your daughter, so why would you hardly think anything?"

Jack fought hard to control his temper. He began again.

"Just exactly what do you think happened to Anne?" he asked.

"Someone—" Martin Forager hesitated. "Did something to her," he finished lamely.

"Did what?" Jack asked.

Forager began to look uncomfortable. "Well—I don't know, really. But the doctor said . . ."

"The doctor said nothing much happened to her," Jack said firmly. "He told me so himself, at your request. He examined her thoroughly, and apart from a few bruises, which she could have gotten in any one of a number of ways, she isn't hurt. She certainly wasn't molested." He continued quickly, seeing the blood drain from Martin Forager's face. "I know, you never said she was, but that's what you've been thinking." He dropped his hands into his lap and slumped back in his chair. "Hell, Marty, that's what we've all been thinking. But apparently nothing happened. And you know how kids are. She came home late. Maybe nothing at all happened, and she made the whole thing up." He held up a hand as he saw Forager's temper begin to build again. "Don't start up again, Martin. If the doctor's report showed anything, anything at all I could get a handle on, I'd be raising as big a stink as you. But it doesn't. Unless Anne starts talking about what happened to her, there's nothing any of us can do."

Forager glared at him for a moment. "You mean like Sarah talks about what happened to her?" he snarled. He turned away, and was out of Jack's office before he could see the effect of his words. Jack remained in his chair, waiting for his heart to stop pounding. He was shaking.

When Sylvia Bannister came into the inner office a few minutes later, Jack hadn't moved. Sylvia started to put a file on the desk in front of him, but stopped when she saw his face.

"Jack?" she said. "Jack, are you all right?"

"I don't know, Syl," Jack said quietly. "Why don't you close the door and sit down." He looked up at her. "If you have time?"

"I always have time," Sylvia replied, closing the door. She sat down in the chair in front of the desk and lit a cigarette. The beginnings of a smile came over Jack's face.

"That's almost automatic, isn't it?" he said.

"What is?" she said, glancing around.

"The cigarette. Haven't you ever noticed that you never light a cigarette in here when you know it's business, but you always light one when you know it's just going to be us talking? It's as though you use the cigarette to change roles from secretary to friend."

"Does it bother you?" Sylvia asked anxiously, looking at the cigarette with an embarrassment that was not like her. Jack shook his head.

"Not at all. I kind of enjoy it. It reassures me that you can read me like a book."

Sylvia relaxed again. "Then I'll try not to remember it every time I do it. You shouldn't have mentioned it; now I'll be self-conscious about it."

"Not you." Jack grinned. "You're the least self-conscious person I've ever met."

"Well," Sylvia said shortly, beginning to feel that

Jack was avoiding whatever it was he wanted to talk about. "Instead of talking about my many, varied, and questionable virtues, why don't we talk about you? What happened?"

Jack shrugged. "I'm not sure anything did, really. Martin Forager just said something to me that shook me. Something about Sarah."

Sylvia drew on her cigarette and let the smoke out slowly, choosing her words. "Exactly what did he say?" she said softly. Jack recounted the conversation he had just had. When he was finished, Sylvia reflected quietly before she spoke.

"I think that's what's called a shot in the dark, Jack. He didn't even know what he was saying," she continued, as Jack looked unconvinced. "Jack, nobody in this town, including you, your wife, or me, knows what happened to Sarah. *Nobody* knows. But you have to face it. Sarah doesn't talk any more, and she goes to White Oaks, and everybody in town knows what kind of school it is. So there's bound to be speculation, and some of it's bound to focus on you."

Jack nodded. "I know. Just one more thing to worry about."

"One more? What else is there?"

"Well, there's the situation between Rose and me."

Sylvia wasn't at all sure she wanted to hear any more, but she knew she would. If only I wasn't so damned— fond—of him, she thought. She had almost used the word "love," but had shied away from it. Yet she knew there wasn't any use in shying away from it. She did love Jack Conger, and she knew it. Not that it made any difference. She had come to grips with being in love with her boss a long time ago, and it helped to know that he loved her too, in a certain way. Not a sexual way. That he had always reserved for Rose, and Sylvia was just as happy that he did. She wasn't sure she could handle an affair, and she was very sure that she didn't want to try. She liked things the way they were. In the office, she and Jack were close. They moved from a business relationship to a personal one and back again many times each day, and each was in tune with the moods and feelings of the other. It was, she supposed, like a marriage in some ways, except that it lasted only eight hours a day. Each afternoon Jack went home to his family, and she went home to her cat. For eight hours a day she had a job she loved and a man she loved. It was usually enough. But sometimes, like right now, she wished he wouldn't tell her everything, that he would hold back a little of himself from her. On the other hand, she knew that for the past year he really hadn't had anybody else. Not since the day he had carried Sarah out of the woods.

"Are things getting worse?" she said.

"I'm not sure if 'worse' is the word. What's your definition of 'worse'? Rose is starting to hate me, but why shouldn't she? My drinking seems to be getting a little worse, but not so you could notice. And then there's Sarah. Sylvia," he said, and the desperation in his voice was almost tangible. "Why can't I remember what happened that day?"

"You were drunk," Sylvia said. "People black out sometimes." She put it bluntly, but her tone held no condemnation, only understanding.

"But I've never blacked out before," he said. "Never. It makes me wonder exactly what I did to her in the woods. What did I do that I won't let myself remember?"

Sylvia lit another cigarette, and when she spoke her voice was gentle. "Jack, what's the use of killing yourself over it? If you'd done what you think you did, the doctors would have known immediately. There would have been some kind of damage to"—she groped for a word, then decided that he might as well hear it out loud—"her vagina. You didn't rape her, Jack."

The word hit him like a physical blow. "I never thought—"

"Yes you did," Sylvia interrupted him. "That's exactly what you thought, and it's exactly what you've always thought. And if you want the truth, that's probably what's at the root of your worries. Maybe Rose thinks it has to do with money and liquor. I don't know what she thinks, and frankly, I don't care. It's what you think that counts. And you think you raped Sarah. Well, you didn't, and you can't keep torturing yourself by thinking you did. It's over, Jack, and you've got to forget it. Maybe if you can forget it, you can stop drinking."

Jack avoided her eyes, staring instead at the blotter on his desk. He saw the note on the calendar, the note reminding him to go to White Oaks on Thursday afternoon.

"It's hard to forget it," he said, "when I have to face Sarah every day."

Sylvia nodded. "Of course it is. That's why the doctors suggested that she be institutionalized for a while. It wasn't just for her, you know. It was for you, too. It's hard to forget something when you're faced with reminders every day. Particularly reminders like Sarah."

"I can't put her away," Jack said miserably. "Not after what I did to her."

Sylvia came around behind him and put her hands on his shoulders. She felt the knots in the muscles, and began working to relax them.

"You're too hard on yourself, Jack," she said softly. "Much too hard. Let it go." But she knew he wouldn't.

6

Neither of them spoke until Rose turned the car into the gates of the White Oaks School. Before them, an expanse of well-tended lawn rolled gently up a rise dotted with maple trees. A gardener rode back and forth across the leaf-strewn grounds on a midget tractor, his progress marked by exposed strips of lawn. Here and there stood piles of leaves, some of them intact, others already scattered by the group of children moving from one pile to the next, systematically rescattering the leaves. The gardener seemed not to notice but drove patiently onward. Rose smiled at the scene, but it only depressed Jack.

"I love this place," Rose said. "It's so beautiful, no matter what season it is." When she heard no response from her husband, she continued. "I should think it would be good for the children, just being in a place like this."

"If they even know where they are," Jack said flatly. "You'd think the gardener would get upset with them, wouldn't you?"

"I suppose they hired him partly because he doesn't get upset," Rose replied. "I don't suppose it's an easy place to work. I admire the people who can do it."

"I certainly couldn't," Jack said. "I don't see how any of the people here can stand it. Look over there."

He pointed across the lawn to a spot where a small boy, not more than six or seven, sat under a tree. He had found a stick and was methodically tapping the trunk of the tree with it, with the regularity of a metronome. Rose stopped the car, and they watched him. He simply sat there, beating a steady rhythm on the tree trunk.

"The poor child," Rose whispered, after several silent minutes had passed. "What do you suppose he thinks about? What do you suppose makes him that way?"

"Who knows," Jack said uncomfortably. He watched the boy for a while, and finally his expression softened. "I'm sorry, Rose," he said. "I don't really hate this place. It's just that it makes me feel so—so helpless. I see all these children, and they all seem to be part of another world, a world I can't touch. And it tears me apart to think my own daughter is part of this world."

Rose reached across the front seat and squeezed his hand. She put the car in gear again, and they moved toward the main building. Behind them, the boy still sat beneath the tree, slowly tapping at its trunk.

Dr. Charles Belter stood up as they came into his office, and came out from behind his desk to greet them.

"Mr. Conger," he said warmly, his hand extended. "Mrs. Conger. I'm glad you could both be here. You'd be surprised how hard it sometimes is for us to get even one parent out here, let alone both. Of course, some of the parents have a difficult time being here, simply because of the nature of our work." He looked carefully from Rose to Jack, and noted the response to his comment that showed in Jack's face. And you, Mr. Conger, are one of those parents, he said to himself. Aloud he invited them to make themselves comfortable, and told them that Sarah's teacher would be joining them in a couple of minutes.

Charles Belter was in his late fifties, and had the look that psychiatrists are supposed to have. He sported an immense beard (no doubt the model for George

Diller's, Rose thought) and a walrus moustache, and still had a full head of bushy hair that was fast going gray. Behind his horn-rimmed glasses his blue eyes twinkled with a good humor that had always made it easy for him to relate to the children with whom he worked. Indeed, he had done his best for years to try to emulate Santa Claus, a role he was able to totally realize only once a year. The rest of the time, he felt, the red suit and bells would be a little too eccentric even for him. Consequently he contented himself with wearing a red blazer, which he did his best not to button. He didn't fool anybody.

White Oaks School had been his dream since the first day he had seen it, back in the days when it had been a tuberculosis sanitarium. Like so many similar facilities, the tuberculosis sanitarium had run out of clients. It was Dr. Charles Belter's dream that someday he, too, would run out of clients. But the prospects of that happening were dim, and he looked forward to spending the rest of his life at White Oaks. Which, he reflected, was not a bad prospect.

There was a tap at the door; then Marie Montgomery let herself into the office. Prim and thirtyish, she had a conservative look that suggested a spinsterish schoolmarm of fifty years earlier. People who had not seen her work always had reservations about Marie Montgomery; people who had taken the time to observe her in action were totally convinced of her abilities. Put her in a classroom full of disturbed children and her reserve disappeared. She seemed never to notice the children's peculiarities, and would work tirelessly with each of her ten students, seeing progress where others saw no change, inventing techniques where none had existed before. It was almost as if, by refusing to recognize her pupils' limitations, she overcame them. And, indeed, her pupils always seemed to make more progress than anyone else's. But now, as she perched herself in the vacant chair between Dr. Belter and Rose Conger, she wore a look of concern that went beyond her normal air of reservation.

"Marie," Dr. Belter said, "we've been waiting for you."

She smiled briefly. "I'm sorry. I was delayed for a minute. Oh, nothing serious," she went on as Dr. Belter's brow rose questioningly. "Just a matter of discipline. Two of the children seemed to want to discipline each other. They'll be all right."

"It must be difficult," Jack said.

"Not at all." Mrs. Montgomery was crisp but kind. "Don't forget, most of the children here don't really know there's anything the matter with them. They simply have a different standard of normality. And when you look at the state of the world, who's really to say they're wrong? Sometimes I watch Jerry tapping that tree trunk out there, and it occurs to me that that isn't really such a bad way to spend time. I sometimes wish I had his powers of concentration. Do you know, he's been working on that same tree for five months now? I'll be glad when he's finished."

"What's he doing to it?" Jack asked.

Mrs. Montgomery shrugged. "If you can find out, you're doing better than I am. But I'll know someday. Someday he'll tell me all about it. When he's ready. In the meantime, I have other things to keep me busy."

"Like Sarah?" Rose said.

The younger woman nodded. "Like Sarah. I hope you haven't been too worried. I asked George to make it absolutely clear that there isn't any emergency. I hope he did."

Rose smiled. "He did. But then we had an emergency of our own. I suppose he told you about it."

Dr. Belter's face clouded. "Yes," he said. "He did. Needless to say, that wasn't one of the things we wanted to talk about, since it hadn't happened when we decided to have this meeting, but I think—"

"Are you suggesting that Sarah had something to do with it?" Jack said coldly. "Because if you are—"

"I'm not suggesting any such thing," Dr. Belter said. "I doubt that we'll ever find out exactly what happened with the van. George Diller was sure he set the brake. He might be mistaken. Sarah, of course, can't tell us anything about it at all. But from my own observations of her, and from what Marie here tells me, I'm not going to suggest that Sarah released the brake. At least not deliberately. For one thing, saying Sarah released the brake implies several things. First, that she knew what would happen if she did. In other words, that she knew that if she released the brake the van would start to move, and that if the van started to move it would at best ram into the garage, hurting several of the children, and at worst plunge into the sea, killing everybody in it, including herself. Frankly, we're not at all sure that in her current state of mind Sarah is capable of putting all that together. It's possible that she is, of course, but her performance here doesn't indicate it. Further, we don't think she's suicidal, and releasing that brake would certainly have to be considered a self-destructive gesture."

"In other words," Rose said, "you don't think Sarah released the brake?"

Dr. Belter smiled wryly. "I wish it were that simple," he said. "It's entirely possible that she released the brake without the least idea of what she was doing. She may easily have been doing nothing more than displaying a fleeting interest in an object, with no concept of the possible ramifications of her actions. This, I'm afraid, is very much within the scope of her current behavior."

There was a long silence as Rose and Jack digested what the doctor was saying. Jack shifted uncomfortably while Rose played with a glove.

"What you're saying, Dr. Belter, if I read you right," Jack said tightly, "is that my daughter is dangerous."

Dr. Belter sighed and began again. "No, that's not exactly what I'm saying."

"Not exactly," Jack repeated, "but close?"

Dr. Belter nodded slightly. "I suppose you could say that if you wanted to. What Sarah is, right now, is irresponsible. From what we have been able to observe, she is often totally unaware of the effects her actions could have. In other words, she acts without thinking. That can be a dangerous thing for anybody. For her, with the emotional struggles she is going through, it can obviously be disastrous. The incident with the van, I'll admit, is an extreme example, but it is certainly illustrative of what could happen."

"If she actually released the brake," Jack said darkly.

"If she actually released the brake," Dr. Belter repeated. "And, of course, we have no way of proving it either way. Believe me, nothing would make me happier than to be able to show that it was carelessness on George Diller's part. It would be much more simply dealt with. But I can't."

"You said there's more," Rose said softly. "What else is there?"

"Marie?" Dr. Belter said, turning toward the teacher. "Why don't you run through it?"

Marie Montgomery picked a file up from the desk and opened it.

"It's all so minor," she said. "Really just little things, but when they're added up, I think we have to pay attention to it. First, Sarah seems to be retreating further into herself. It isn't anything major. It's just that a couple of months ago she would almost always respond to her name the first time it was spoken. Now she never hears until it's repeated, or if she does she seems to ignore it.

"Then there's the matter of her concentration. It seems to be getting shorter. As a matter of fact, I have some figures on that, but, again, they aren't anything major. What it boils down to is that she spends less time with any one thing than she used to. That in itself wouldn't bother me particularly—attention spans seem to expand and contract like rubber bands around here —but with Sarah it isn't as if she gets bored with what she's doing, exactly. It's more as though she finds herself more interesting than the real world. It's getting harder to keep her focused on the real world, and that bothers me. It's beginning to look like we're losing touch with her, instead of getting closer to her." Marie Montgomery saw the flash of pain in Jack's eyes and hurried on. "That's really the major reason for this meeting. To find out if the same things are happening at home."

Rose shook her head. "I don't think so," she said doubtfully, "but of course I can't really be sure. I find it awfully hard to look at her objectively. I'm afraid I try to see progress where there might not be any."

"There's progress," Jack said, but his voice indicated that his statement might be more wish than fact.

"Jack," Rose said, as gently as she could. "What progress has there been, really?" She turned back to Mrs. Montgomery. "I wish I could tell you whether or not there really has been any change in Sarah, but I can't."

"We're not expecting you to be able to tell us anything today," Dr. Belter put in. "As we've tried to make clear, nothing major has happened. This is simply to alert you to something that might be happening. We aren't sure, and we're asking for your help. It would be very helpful for us, and for Sarah, if you could simply be aware that something may be going on that we don't know about, and try to notice anything unusual or different in her behavior."

"Well," Jack said carefully, "there was that thing with the Ouija board the other night."

"Ouija board?" Dr. Belter said. "I haven't seen one of those things in years. Do they still make them?"

"Not this one," Rose said. "Elizabeth found it in a

storeroom or something. And the Ouija board really
had nothing to do with what happened."

She recounted the incident of a few nights earlier,
and Sarah's reaction to the cat brushing up against
her. As she talked, Dr. Belter took a few notes.

"It was really nothing," Rose finished.

"And they were playing with a Ouija board?" Dr.
Belter asked again. "Hmm." He made a final note and
looked up. "Does Sarah spend much time with her
sister?"

"That's putting it mildly," Jack said. "The worst
part of each day is when Elizabeth leaves for school
and Sarah has to wait for the van to bring her out
here. They're practically inseparable."

"And how does Elizabeth react to Sarah?" the doctor
asked.

"Considering her age," Rose said, "it's amazing.
You have to remember that Elizabeth is only thirteen
herself. But the way she takes care of Sarah, you'd
think she was five years older. She seems to understand Sarah, somehow. She plays with her by the hour,
and reads to her, and it never bothers her when Sarah
suddenly wrecks whatever they're playing, or grabs a
book out of her hands. And the other night, when
Sarah screamed, it was as if Elizabeth didn't hear it at
all. It upset Jack and me much more than it did either
of the girls."

"It's strange," Jack said, picking up the thread.
"Elizabeth talks to Sarah, and she never seems to notice
that Sarah doesn't talk back. It's as if Sarah doesn't
have to talk—Elizabeth seems to communicate with
her or something. Sometimes Elizabeth makes me feel
inadequate. I've tried to talk to Sarah so many times
I can't count them, but as soon as I pick her up she
starts wriggling around, and in a couple of minutes
she's out of my lap and off to find Elizabeth."

"Has she shown any signs of violence at home?"
Dr. Belter said quietly.

"Sarah? I don't think so," Rose said. "Why?"

"Again, it's nothing we can really put our finger on," Dr. Belter said. "The screaming when the cat brushed up against her reminded me of it. One day last week one of the children came up behind Sarah and touched her shoulder. She screamed, which isn't abnormal for her, but she also whirled around and hit the other child. She hadn't done that before, and we still don't know if it was an accident or if she struck at the child on purpose. Has she ever swung at either of you? Or at Elizabeth?"

Jack and Rose shook their heads.

"Certainly not at either of us," Rose said. "And if she'd ever done anything like that to Elizabeth, I'm sure we'd have heard about it." She paused a moment, as if reaching to remember something, then went on. "I'm afraid we don't really spend as much time with Elizabeth as we should. But Sarah takes up so much of our time. Well, Elizabeth doesn't seem to resent it."

"You're very lucky," Dr. Belter said. "Many parents find that they have more trouble with their so-called normal child than with their disturbed one. It's only to be expected, really. All children need attention, and when one is disturbed, the other often feels he needs to compete for his parents' attention. It sounds as if Elizabeth is a very exceptional child." He smiled and stood up. "Thank you for coming today. We'll be going over Sarah's case in our staff meeting tomorrow, and we may make some minor changes in her medication. Other than that, for the moment it's just a matter of keeping our eyes open and trying to spot a trend."

"Then that's it?" Jack said, getting to his feet.

"That's it," Dr. Belter said. "For the moment. I don't want you to feel alarmed. You should, however, be aware that if Sarah's condition deteriorates too far, we won't be able to keep her here. White Oaks is a school, not an institution." Seeing the anxiety in both their faces, Dr. Belter hurried to reassure them. "It's only an eventuality," he said. "For the moment, we aren't having any more problems with Sarah than with any of the others. And some of them are a lot worse than she is. For the foreseeable future, I look forward to having Sarah here."

"Can we take her home with us," Rose asked, "or has she already gone in the van?"

"She's waiting in my room," Mrs. Montgomery said. "One of the aides is with her. I'm sure she'll be glad to see you."

But Sarah wasn't waiting in Marie Montgomery's room.

In the house on Conger's Point, Elizabeth poured the last of a glass of milk into the cat's dish, and watched as Cecil lapped it up. Then she picked up the animal and listened to him purr.

"Come on," she said to the cat. "Let's go outside."

Scratching Cecil's ears, Elizabeth carried him from the house.

As she crossed the field, Elizabeth pulled the rubber band out of her ponytail and shook her head. The blond hair cascaded over her shoulders. Her step quickened.

No one saw her disappear into the woods.

7

The room was a shambles: desks and chairs were overturned; the items that were normally arranged across the top of Marie Montgomery's desk had been swept from it and now lay scattered and broken across the floor to the left of the desk.

"Jesus," Jack breathed. Before anyone could say more, they heard the sounds from the cloakroom—scuffling noises, as though whatever struggle had taken place in the classroom was now continuing in the small room behind the blackboard. The sounds were muted but somehow desperate. There were no cries, none of the shouts that should accompany the sort of battle that must have taken place. Led by Mrs. Montgomery, the three of them raced through the room.

In the back corner of the cloakroom the aide struggled with Sarah. The battle had come to a stalemate.

When she spoke, Mrs. Montgomery's voice was very low and completely controlled, but it held a note of authority that Rose Conger was sure had cut through worse confusion than confronted her now.

"Philip," she said, "what's happened here?"

Immediately the struggle stopped. The aide, who couldn't have been more than twenty, straightened and stepped away from Sarah.

The child was a mess. Her shirt was torn in several places, and she was covered with some sort of yellow substance. As soon as the aide let her go, Sarah's hand

moved to her mouth, and she began chewing. Rose
stared at her, and it was a few seconds before she
realized what her daughter was doing. The yellow
substance was chalk, and Sarah was chewing on a
piece of it. Philip watched her for a second before
turning to the small group that hovered in the doorway. Rose started to move toward her daughter, but
Marie Montgomery's hand held her back.

"It's all right," she said quietly. "A little chalk isn't
going to hurt her."

"It's not a little," Philip said. "She's been at it ever
since you left. She must have eaten almost a full box
by now."

"And you tried to stop her?" Marie asked.

The young man nodded. He looked miserable. "I
couldn't do it, though. I was afraid of hurting her."

"You probably scared her half to death," Marie
said. "If you'd let her alone, she might have stopped
of her own accord. A little chalk won't hurt her."

"But a whole box?" Jack said. He took a step toward
Sarah. The child shrank back farther into the corner
of the tiny room, and began to gnaw on another stick.
Her teeth made a strange grinding sound as she
crushed the chalk into powder. She swallowed some
of it, but most of it cascaded, mixed with saliva, into
her lap. Jack felt a queasy feeling developing in his
stomach.

Rose broke free from Mrs. Montgomery's grip, and
quickly moved past her husband to pick up her
daughter. Sarah let herself be lifted, but refused to
open her hand when Rose tried to remove the chalk
she clutched. Rose seemed to be about to struggle
with her when Mrs. Montgomery spoke again.

"Let her have it, Mrs. Conger. Really, it won't hurt
her. If she's had too much, she might throw it up.
Otherwise, it'll pass right through her. If it could hurt
her, we wouldn't use it here. Our kids do that all the

time." She looked accusingly at the aide, who seemed to wither.

"It just seemed like she was eating so much of it."

"So you scared her half to death, and wrecked the room?" the teacher inquired drily. "Don't you think the cure was a bit worse than the illness?"

"I guess I just . . ." Philip trailed off. "Didn't think," he finished lamely.

"I guess you didn't," Marie said, but the chill was gone from her voice, and she was smiling again. "Well, next time, keep in mind that chalk doesn't hurt children, and that desks cost money. And you can think about it while you clean up my room." She turned and led the Congers out of the room, walking with them to their car.

"Are you sure it won't hurt her?" Jack asked again as he turned the key in the ignition.

Mrs. Montgomery shook her head. "She might throw up, but that's all." She waved to them as they drove away, then turned back to the building. She'd changed her mind, and was about to help Philip clean up the mess.

Rose, holding a now passive Sarah on her lap, was still trying to get the scene out of her mind when the vomiting began. She wasn't sure it was going to happen at first; she felt a couple of involuntary flinches in her daughter, but then Sarah lay still again in her mother's arms. Then, without warning, it came.

The yellowish stream shot out of Sarah's mouth and ran down into her lap, where it overflowed. Rose could feel the heat of it as it soaked through her wool pants. She felt more than saw Jack glance over to see what had happened.

"Don't look," she said tightly. "Just keep your eyes on the road and get us home as quickly as you can. Mrs. Montgomery said this might happen." She was

trying to reach into her purse for the package of
Kleenex that was always there, when the second con-
vulsion hit. As she felt more of the vomit flow over
her legs, she realized the Kleenex would be futile. Instead, she used her free hand to roll the window down.

The cold air hit her face and cut through the sicken-
ing sweet-sour smell of the vomit, and Rose began to
fight down her own nausea. Then Jack had opened his
window, too, and she felt more fresh air. It wasn't until
Sarah began to throw up again that Rose realized their
mistake. There was a window open, and Sarah was
struggling to reach it.

"Dear God, this can't be happening," Rose said to
herself as the mixture of freezing air and vomit washed
over her face. She was sure she was going to lose her
own battle with nausea as she began to struggle to get
Sarah's face out of the wind.

The girl was crying now, and Rose began to panic
as she realized what could happen to Sarah if she
began to choke on her own vomit.

"Jack," she said. "I think you'd better try to stop
the car. Don't look. Just stop the car."

"There's a rest area just up ahead. Can you make it?"

"I'll have to," Rose said.

She felt the car surge forward, then swerve to the
right and brake sharply. She had the door open before
the car had quite stopped. She swung out of the car
and set Sarah on the asphalt of the parking lot. She
was just able to get off the lot and onto a patch of
bare earth when the first retching began. Mortified,
she stood with her forehead resting against the trunk
of a tree, her own vomit mixing with Sarah's as it
splashed against her legs. In a couple of minutes, it
was over.

She turned back to the car, and her teary eyes told
her that for her daughter it was not yet over.

Sarah sat miserably in the spot where Rose had left
her, and the convulsions were beginning again. Fran-

tically, Rose looked for her husband. For a second he seemed to have disappeared, but then she saw him coming from the men's room, a sodden paper towel in his hands. Ignoring her, he went directly to Sarah, knelt beside her, and began bathing her face with the dripping towel. Rose watched the scene in silence, then began making her way to the women's room.

For a long time she ran cold water, scooping it up and pouring it over her face, as if the water could wash away the experience that preceded it. Finally she returned to the car.

They saw Mrs. Goodrich standing on the porch when they turned into the driveway. The Congers glanced at each other, and their eyes held for a moment. There was a sudden warmth between them that neither of them had felt for a year. When Rose spoke, it was not to wonder why Mrs. Goodrich was on the porch.

"I'm sorry about all that," she said quietly.

"It's all right," Jack replied, his voice gentle. "It's nice to know that I'm still good at something, even if it's only looking after my sick womenfolk."

Rose saw the pain and tenderness flash in his eyes. She looked away, her gaze coming to rest on Sarah, who had fallen asleep in her arms.

"Do you think I ought to call the doctor?" She shifted Sarah's weight so that the child's head was cradled on her shoulder.

"If it'll make you feel better. But I suspect it's all over now. She's got all that crap out of her system. I think we can wait till she wakes up at least. Then we'll see." He stopped the car in front of the house, got out, and went around to open the door for his wife. Mrs. Goodrich had left the porch and was coming toward them, her ample figure moving as quickly as her age would allow. As Jack pulled open the passenger door, she stopped.

"Lord have mercy," she muttered, her eyes taking

in the mess that covered the inside of the car, Sarah, and Rose. Involuntarily she took a couple of steps backward.

"It's all right, Mrs. Goodrich," Rose said, disengaging herself carefully from the car so as not to disturb Sarah, in her arms. "We had a little trouble, but it's over with now."

Mrs. Goodrich surveyed the mess stoically. If she wondered what had happened, it didn't show in her face. "I'll have to take a hose to the inside of that car," she said, almost making it sound like a threat.

"I'll take care of it, Mrs. Goodrich," Jack began. "We can't really ask you—"

"I've cleaned up worse than that in my time," the housekeeper snapped. "Besides, you've got other things to do." There was an edge to her voice that captured Jack's attention. Rose had already disappeared with Sarah into the house.

"Other things? What other things?"

"It's Miss Elizabeth," the housekeeper said. "I think she's been playing where she's not supposed to." Jack waited for her to continue, and eventually had to prompt her.

"Well," Mrs. Goodrich said. "I saw her come out of the woods not too long ago. I don't know why, but I'm sure she was playing on the embankment. She denied it, of course." The last was said with the certainty of one convinced, by a lifetime of hard experience, that children will deny anything and everything, even when caught red-handed.

"Elizabeth's usually pretty honest," Jack said gently. He was reluctant to nettle the old woman; when he did, it usually showed up at dinner in the form of overcooked food. Mrs. Goodrich peered at him over her glasses and stood her ground.

"I'm well aware of that, young man," she said, and Jack prepared to give in. Ever since he had been a child, he had known that when Mrs. Goodrich called him "young man" she meant business.

"Nevertheless," she went on, "I think you'd better speak to her. She knows she's not to go into those woods, let alone anywhere near the embankment. And I know she was in the woods. I saw her come out."

"All right," Jack said. "I'll talk to her as soon as I clean up. Where is she?"

"In the field," Mrs. Goodrich said dourly, indicating that as far as she was concerned, the field was almost on par with the woods and the embankment. She pointed off to the distance, and, following her gesture with his eyes, Jack saw his older daughter. She was squatting down, and seemed to be looking at something.

He started to move toward the house but, seeing the glare Mrs. Goodrich was giving him, turned toward the field instead.

"No time like the present," he heard the housekeeper mutter behind him.

Elizabeth didn't see him until he was less than twenty feet from her. She suddenly looked up, as if she had heard something, but Jack was sure he had been silent. When she saw him a smile lit her face, and Jack could feel its glow brighten his spirits. He stopped, and the two of them studied each other for a moment. With her hair flowing free, Elizabeth looked more than ever like the girl in the portrait.

"How's my favorite daughter?" he said, breaking the silence.

"Am I?" she said, the smile growing even brighter.

"Well, if I am, you deserve this for telling me so."

She stooped, and when she stood up there was a single buttercup in her hand. She ran over to him and held the flower under his chin.

"Well?" he said. "Do I glow?"

"I'm not going to tell you." Elizabeth laughed. "Did

you bring Sarah home with you?" He nodded, and when Elizabeth turned and began to walk toward the house, he stopped her.

"Hold on. Can't you spend a little time with your favorite father?"

Elizabeth turned back to him. "I just thought—" she began.

"Never mind," Jack said. "Sarah had a little trouble on the way home, and your mother's cleaning her up. It's nothing serious," he added hastily as a look of concern twisted Elizabeth's face. "Just something she ate. She had a bit of an accident on the way home."

"Yuck!" Elizabeth said. "Does the car stink?"

"Mrs. G's cleaning it up. She wants me to talk to you."

"I thought she would," Elizabeth said. "She thinks I was out on the embankment today."

"Were you?" Jack tried to sound unconcerned.

"No," she said. "I wasn't. I don't know why she thinks I was."

"She said she saw you coming out of the woods."

"I know," Elizabeth said. "And I don't know why she thinks that either. I wasn't in the woods."

"Were you near them?"

Elizabeth nodded. "I thought I saw Cecil, and I was following him. But I don't think it was Cecil. It looked like him, but then, just as he was about to go into the woods, he jumped. 'Cecil' turned out to be a rabbit."

"How could you mistake a rabbit for Cecil?" Jack asked. "Of all the un-rabbitish cats I know, Cecil is the most un-rabbitish of them all."

"Search me," Elizabeth said. "But he sure looked like Cecil till he jumped."

"Well, I'm glad he did," her father said. "If he hadn't, you might have followed him into the woods."

"I'd have noticed," Elizabeth said. She was silent for a moment; then: "Daddy, why aren't I allowed to go into the woods or to the embankment?"

"It's dangerous, that's why," Jack said, his tone indicating that he would like to leave it at that. But Elizabeth was not to be put off.

"But, Daddy, I'm thirteen years old now, and I can take care of myself. I don't see how the embankment can be any more dangerous than the quarry, and you let me go there any time I want to."

"I'd just as soon you stayed away from there, too," Jack said.

"But why?" Elizabeth pressed. When there was no answer she said, "It's because of Anne Forager, isn't it?"

"Anne Forager?" Jack said guardedly.

"All the kids are talking about it. They say something awful happened to her, and that it happened out here. Is that true?"

"I don't know," Jack said truthfully. "I don't really think anything happened to her, and if it did, I doubt very much if it happened out here. At any rate, that doesn't have anything to do with you. It's just that the embankment is very dangerous."

"Not any more than the quarry."

Jack shook his head. "If you slipped at the quarry, you'd at least have a chance. You'd fall into deep water, and you can swim. With the embankment, you wouldn't hit water. You'd hit rocks and surf. That's a whole different story."

"I suppose you're right," she said. Then she looked up at him, and there was a glint of mischief in her eyes. "But in five years I'll be eighteen. Then I'll go see just what's at this embankment, and you won't be able to stop me."

"That's five years," Jack said. "In five years you could change your mind."

"I won't," Elizabeth assured him. Then she slipped her hand into his, and together they walked back to the house.

●　●　●

Dinner was a quiet affair for the Congers that night, at least at the beginning. Out of respect for the delicate stomachs of Rose and Sarah, Mrs. Goodrich had put together a light omelette, which she had restrained herself from burning. Conversation was dilatory, much of it in the form of encouraging remarks directed toward Sarah by her parents. Sarah seemed not to hear; instead she concentrated on her plate, calmly shoving each forkful of egg into her mouth, chewing stoically, and swallowing. To Elizabeth, Sarah seemed to be as she always was.

Mrs. Goodrich cleared away the plates and brought in the dessert.

"Here we go again," Elizabeth said.

"Hmm?" Rose inquired, turning her attention from Sarah to the older girl. Elizabeth grinned at her.

"I said, 'Here we go again.' We had the same pudding at school today. Except this is better."

"Oh?" Rose said. But she was not really interested; her attention was back on Sarah. "How was school?"

"Not bad. We got our history tests back. I think Mr. Friedman must have made a mistake. He gave me a perfect score."

Now both Rose and Jack turned to Elizabeth, and she could see the pleased expression in their eyes. But before they could speak, a sound rent the air.

Elizabeth turned, then ducked just in time to avoid the bowl of pudding that was flying toward her from her sister's place. The glass bowl shattered on the wall behind Elizabeth, but the sound of its crashing was inaudible over the shrieks and wails emanating from Sarah.

Her face contorted in rage, Sarah snatched all the silverware within her reach, and in a moment it was scattered across the room. One of the heavy silver knives shattered a pane in the French door and clattered to rest on the veranda outside. Her voice build-

ing, Sarah continued to howl as her arms moved wildly over the table, searching out other things to throw.

Rose sat as if frozen and stared at Sarah. Sarah had been so calm, and now— She began to rise as she saw Sarah's fists clutch at the tablecloth. She tried to prepare herself for the destruction that was imminent if her daughter followed through on what she apparently intended to do.

And then, over the din of Sarah's howling, she heard Jack's voice shouting.

"For God's sake!" he yelled. "Will you get her out of here?"

Rose's eyes widened, but the impact of his words seemed to free her from her chair. Wordlessly she swept Sarah into her arms, somehow freeing the clutching fingers from the tablecloth, and carried her from the room. As she passed Jack she sensed more than saw him slump weakly in his chair.

The dining room was suddenly silent, and the two of them sat there, Jack avoiding words, Elizabeth with nothing to say. Then, visibly, Jack began to pull him-self together.

"I'm sorry," he muttered, more to himself than to Elizabeth. "Every time she does something like that I get the most horrible feeling. I get the feeling that I made her nuts." He began sobbing, but silently.

"And I guess I did," he mumbled. Then he too left the room, and Elizabeth was suddenly alone.

She sat quite still for a time, as if she had neither heard what her father said nor noticed the chaos around her. When eventually she moved, it was to begin cleaning up the mess. She cleared off the table first, then began on the wall and floor. She moved slowly, carefully, as if her mind was far from what she was doing. When she finished, she surveyed the dining room.

"I was so sure that was Cecil," she said, for no ap-

parent reason. "But I guess it couldn't have been."
She was silent, then spoke once more to the empty
room. "I wish he'd come home."

Then Elizabeth, too, left the dining room.

8

To an observer they would have seemed no different from any other family at breakfast. Perhaps one child —the younger—was much quieter than the other, but such is the case in any family. Only a particularly careful observer would have noted a slight air of strain around them, as if they were avoiding something. As, indeed, they were.

Rose Conger was maintaining an almost grim good cheer, doing her best to prevent the silence that was normal for Sarah from becoming the norm for them all. But she knew no one was paying any attention to her. She could see Jack, his face mostly hidden, trying desperately to concentrate on his morning paper. And she knew that Elizabeth was devoting more energy to getting food into Sarah than she was to listening to her mother.

"And, of course," Rose chirped, "they have a son." She waited for a reaction, but there was none. She said, a little more loudly, "A fourteen-year-old son." She was gratified to note that she suddenly had her older daughter's attention.

"Who does?" Elizabeth said, putting down the knife she had been using to slice Sarah's sausages.

"You haven't been listening. The new neighbors. If you hadn't been so engrossed, you'd have heard me."

Elizabeth smiled sheepishly. "I'm sorry," she said, with a grin that let it be known that she was apologizing more for the sake of form than for anything else. "Don't tell me you actually sold the Barneses' old place." She made a face. "I hate that house. Who would want to live there?"

"It's a family," Rose said, smoothing the tablecloth unconsciously. "An architect and an artist. And their son. His name's Jeff."

"A boy," squealed Elizabeth. "A real live boy! What's he look like?"

"I'm sure he'll be terribly handsome," Rose replied. "Isn't the boy next door always supposed to be terribly handsome?"

Elizabeth blushed, and the sudden flushing disconcerted Rose. And then it hit her that she had somehow come to think of Elizabeth as being older than she was. She had to remind herself that Elizabeth was only thirteen, and that thirteen-year-old girls are very likely to blush when boys are mentioned.

"Actually, I don't know what he looks like. But we'll all know over the weekend. Carl and Barbara—they're the new neighbors," she added for the benefit of Jack, who had finally put his paper down. "Carl and Barbara Stevens will be coming down this morning, and I'm going to spend most of the day with them." Jack looked at her questioningly.

"Well," Rose went on, a little uncomfortably, "since the Barneses aren't around, somebody has to show them how the house works. Particularly a house like that." She saw a shadow of doubt cross Jack's face.

"All right," she said, putting down her napkin. "Also, I feel like being a busybody neighbor and seeing what I can find out about them. So far they seem to be a delight, and I think it would be nice to have neighbors who are also friends. It would be fun to have people we like close enough for dropping in, and I intend to promote it."

"Well," Jack said, the shadow of doubt now growing into a cloud. "I'm not so sure that's a good idea." Rose saw his eyes flick involuntarily toward Sarah. It was so fast that she was sure he wasn't aware that he had done it; she was equally sure she hadn't imagined it. She decided to face the issue directly. She began folding the napkin into smaller and smaller squares.

"I see no reason why we should behave like hermits," she said slowly. "If there is a reason, I'd like to know what it is."

The color drained from Jack's face, and he stared at his wife.

"I—I should think—" he began. Then he fell into an uncomfortable silence.

"I should think," Rose said definitely, "that we should keep in mind what century we are living in. Having a daughter in White Oaks School is not something we need to be ashamed of. If you think it is, then you have more of a problem than Sarah does." She paused as she saw Jack signaling with his eyes to where Elizabeth sat, listening to what her mother was saying. Making up her mind, Rose turned to Elizabeth.

"What do you think?" she asked.

"About what?" Elizabeth asked carefully, unsure of the direction things were taking.

"Well," Rose said, casting about in her mind for the proper words. "About Sarah, I suppose."

Elizabeth looked directly at her mother—almost accusingly, Rose thought. She seemed to be struggling with herself, and almost on the verge of tears. Then, she found her voice as her tears overflowed.

"I think," she said, fighting back a sob with a small, choking sound, "that we all should remember that Sarah isn't deaf. She doesn't talk, but she hears." She stared beseechingly at her mother for a few seconds, then turned back to her sister. "Come on, Sarah," she said. "Let's go get ready for school." She took Sarah's hand, and led her out of the dining room. Silently, Rose and Jack watched them go.

" 'From the mouths of babes . . .' " Jack said softly.

Then he saw the tears running down his wife's face. He moved from his chair and knelt beside her. She buried her face in his shoulder, and her body shook with her sobs.

"What are we going to do, Jack?" she said into his ear. "She makes me feel ashamed sometimes. Absolutely ashamed. And she's only thirteen."

Jack patted her gently. "I know, darling," he said. "I know. I guess sometimes children have an easier time of things. They seem to be able to accept things the way they are. And we have to fight it."

"It?" Rose looked up. Their eyes met, and there was closeness between them, a closeness Rose hadn't felt since the early years of their marriage.

"Life," Jack said. "Wouldn't it be nice if we could stop fighting life?"

Rose nodded. "But we can't, can we?" Jack didn't answer, nor did Rose expect him to.

A few minutes later Rose looked in on her daughters. Elizabeth, already dressed, was brushing Sarah's thick dark hair. Sarah sat quietly in front of the mirror, but Rose couldn't tell whether she was watching Elizabeth. She might have been, but she might also have been somewhere else, living a life that had nothing to do with this room, her sister, or anything else related to the house on the Point.

"Do you need anything before I go?" Rose said.

Elizabeth looked up and smiled. "An extra quarter for snack period?" she asked brightly. Rose shook her head. Elizabeth straightened up. "There," she said. "What do you think?" Rose noted that the barrettes Elizabeth had fastened in her sister's short, shiny hair did not match, and the part was not quite straight. She decided not to comment on it.

"What does Sarah think?" she countered.

"Oh, she loves it," Elizabeth said. "It keeps her hair out of her eyes."

"That counts for a lot," Rose said, smiling. "Could you do the same for me?"

"Sure," Elizabeth said eagerly. "Now?"

Rose laughed. "Later. I don't have time now, and neither do you. But maybe tomorrow," she added, seeing the light fade in Elizabeth's eyes. "Kiss me good-bye?"

Elizabeth approached her mother and tipped her head up to be kissed. Rose squeezed her quickly, then moved to the vanity, where Sarah sat, still apparently staring at her new hairdo. Rose knelt and wrapped Sarah in her arms.

"Have a good day, sweetheart," she whispered. She kissed the little girl several times, then hugged her once more. "See you this afternoon," she said.

Downstairs again, Rose stopped in the kitchen to speak to Mrs. Goodrich. The housekeeper looked up at her inquiringly.

"Has Cecil turned up yet?" Rose asked.

Mrs. Goodrich shook her head.

"Do me a favor and look around for him today, will you?"

"Cats can take care of themselves. He'll be back when he's a mind to," the old woman said.

"I'm sure he will," Rose said drily. "But would you mind having a look anyway? The children miss him. He might have gotten locked in somewhere."

"If he did, someone locked him," Mrs. Goodrich stated. Then she relented. "Sure. You go on now—I'll find him."

Rose smiled her thanks and went to find her husband. Jack had already left the house.

In the kitchen, Mrs. Goodrich continued loading the dishes into the dishwasher. She was convinced that no machine could get dishes nearly clean enough for someone to eat from, but she used the machine anyway. She simply washed them to her own satisfaction before loading them into the machine and left

out the soap. She supposed the machine was good
enough for rinsing, particularly since she rinsed them
herself, too. She closed the door and pressed the button to make the dishwasher start. All that racket, she
thought. It's a wonder they don't all smash. Then,
over the noise of the washer, she heard another sound,
from the front of the house. She moved to the kitchen
door, opened it slightly, and listened.

"No, Sarah," she heard Elizabeth saying. "You can't
come with me. You have to wait here for the van."

Mrs. Goodrich heard Sarah wail, and moved through
the door.

"Oh, Sarah," Elizabeth was saying, a little louder
now. "I wish you could come with me, really I do,
but you simply can't. It'll only be a few minutes."
There was another wail from Sarah. "Sarah, let go.
I'm going to be late if I don't leave now."

When Mrs. Goodrich appeared in the front hallway,
Elizabeth was valiantly trying to free herself from
Sarah's grasp. The smaller girl held on to Elizabeth's
wrist with both hands, and Elizabeth was making no
headway at all. Each time she pried one hand loose,
the other would grasp her anew. She saw Mrs. Goodrich, and signaled to her to hurry.

"Help," she said, keeping her voice as light as she
could. "Just hang on to her till I get out of sight, and
she'll be all right."

Mrs. Goodrich seized Sarah and held her firmly
while Elizabeth put on her coat. "You hurry along
now," the woman said. "The sooner you're gone, the
easier time I'll have. Not that I'm saying I don't like
having you around," she added.

"I know," Elizabeth grinned. "I'll see you this afternoon."

Elizabeth went to the front door, opened it, turned
to wave to Sarah, then closed the door behind her.
She tried not to listen as she heard Sarah's voice rise in
a howl of anguish. Instead, she concentrated on the trees

that lined the driveway. By the time she reached the Point Road, she'd almost convinced herself that Sarah had stopped her howling.

Behind her the battle that was raging was a strange one. Sarah's outraged screams filled the house, and she struggled, twisting and squirming in Mrs. Goodrich's arms. Her face set, the old woman drew every measure of strength she possessed to hang on as tightly as she dared, and hold the child without hurting her. Mrs. Goodrich saw no point in trying to talk to Sarah. She was sure the child would never hear her above her own din, and it would only be wasting her strength to try. Grimly, she held on.

Then Sarah bit her. The housekeeper felt the teeth sink into her hand, into the fleshy part at the base of the thumb. She steeled herself against the pain and lifted Sarah off the floor. She carried the child to a window and turned so that Sarah could see out. Sarah stopped howling.

Mrs. Goodrich set her down then, and examined the thumb. The skin was broken, but not badly.

"It's been a long time since a child did that to me," Mrs. Goodrich noted out loud. Sarah, her attention diverted from the window and the empty driveway beyond, stared up into the housekeeper's face. Looking down into the huge, empty brown eyes, a surge of pity swept over the old woman. She slowly knelt down and put her arms around the child. "But I don't suppose you meant anything by it, did you? And you're not rabid, so there's no real harm done." She continued to hold the child, soothing her until she heard the van coming up the driveway. Then she hauled herself to her feet and, taking Sarah by the hand, led her back to the front door. Sarah stood docilely while Mrs. Goodrich bundled her into her coat, and made no objection when George Diller led her to the van. Mrs. Goodrich stood by the door and watched the van till it was out of sight. She didn't wave; she was too tired from the struggle, and she didn't really think Sarah would see it anyway. When the driveway was empty once again, she closed the door slowly and retreated to her kitchen, where she bathed the injured hand, winced as she applied iodine, and bandaged it. Then she remembered the cat.

She was sure it was a waste of time, but she had agreed to make a search for Cecil, and she would. She decided to get the long climb to the attic out of the way first and work down from there. Getting to the second floor was no problem; she was used to that. She carried the key to the attic door in her pocket, but instinctively tried the door as she reached for the key. The key dropped back into her pocket as the door opened, revealing the steep staircase. "Supposed to be locked," she muttered to herself, pausing a moment to rest before tackling the stairs that led to the attic. As she climbed, she tried to remember the last time anybody had been up here. A month ago, when they had brought down the old portrait. She went into the attic and closed the door behind her.

"Cecil?" she called. "Here, kitty, kitty, kitty . . ."

Elizabeth was halfway into town when she saw Kathy Burton walking ahead of her.

"Kathy?" she yelled. The girl ahead of her stopped and turned around. "Wait up," Elizabeth called. She ran until she caught up with her friend.

"What are you doing out here?" she said when she was abreast of Kathy.

"I was baby-sitting last night," Kathy said. "At the Nortons'."

Elizabeth rolled her eyes. "They're weird," she said.

"What do you mean?"

"He's so much older than she is . . ." Elizabeth trailed off, mulling the peculiarities of her elders. Then another thought occurred to her.

"Your mother lets you baby-sit there?"

"Sure," Kathy said curiously. "Why wouldn't she?"

"I mean after what happened to Anne Forager . . ."

"Oh, that," Kathy shrugged. "My mother says nothing happened to her at all. She says she's a liar."

Elizabeth nodded. "That's what my dad thinks, too. But I'm not sure he believes it."

"Why?"

"I don't know," Elizabeth said. "He's just acting strange." She looked around, and pointed to a bird that swooped from a nearby tree. "Look," she said, "a jay."

Kathy followed her gesture, but missed the bird. "You sure are lucky, living out here," she said. "That's why I like to sit for the Nortons. I can stay over and walk back in the morning."

"I wish there was a bus," Elizabeth said. "It gets boring after a while."

"I wouldn't get tired of it if I lived out here," Kathy said confidently. "It must be fun to be able to go exploring any time you want to."

Elizabeth nodded, but her attention was no longer on Kathy.

A rabbit had flashed across the road ahead of the girls, and as Elizabeth watched it a strange expression crossed her face. She stopped, and seemed to be grasping at an elusive thought.

"There's a place," she whispered.

"What?" Kathy asked.

"A secret place," Elizabeth went on. She turned to Kathy and stared intensely into her eyes. "Would you like to go there sometime?"

Kathy's eyes widened. "What kind of place?"

"If I told you it wouldn't be secret any more, would it? If I take you there, you have to promise never to tell anybody about it."

"Oh, I wouldn't," Kathy said, the excitement of sharing a secret bringing a quiver to her voice. "It would be just ours."

Elizabeth seemed on the verge of saying something more when she heard the sound of a vehicle approaching from behind them. She pulled Kathy off the road, and the two of them waited while the White Oaks van passed them. George Diller waved and tooted the horn as he passed. From the back of the van the girls could see Sarah, her face pressed against the rear window of the vehicle, until the bus took a curve in the road, moving out of sight. When the van was gone, Elizabeth stopped waving, and she and Kathy once again began walking.

"What's wrong with her?" Kathy asked.

"Who?"

"Sarah," Kathy said.

"Who said something's the matter with her?" Elizabeth said defensively. It upset her to be asked questions about her sister.

"My mother," Kathy said matter-of-factly. "She said Sarah's crazy."

Elizabeth stared at the ground for a while before she spoke again.

"I don't think you should talk that way about Sarah."

"Well, is she crazy?" Kathy pressed.

"No," Elizabeth said.

"Then why does she go to White Oaks? That's a place for crazy kids. They come from all over the country to go there."

"And they live there, don't they?" Elizabeth pointed out. "If Sarah was crazy, wouldn't she have to live there too?"

Kathy thought it over. "Well, if she's not crazy, why does she go there at all?"

Elizabeth shrugged her shoulders. "I don't know. Something happened to her about a year ago. She was in the woods, and she fell or something. And now she can't talk. If she went to school in town, everybody would laugh at her. But she'll be all right, as soon as she starts talking again."

The two girls walked in silence for a while, and it wasn't until they were into town that either of them spoke again.

"Does Sarah know about the secret place?" Kathy said suddenly.

Elizabeth shook her head. "And you won't either, if you don't stop asking questions about it. It's a place you have to be. You can't talk about it."

"Will you show me?" Kathy asked defiantly.

"If you stop talking about it," Elizabeth countered. "It's a very special place, just for me. But I suppose I could take you there, since you're a friend of mine."

"When?"

But Elizabeth didn't answer. Instead, she gave her friend a mysterious look, then disappeared into the school.

Mrs. Goodrich spent nearly an hour in the attic, only part of it looking for Cecil. A quick inspection convinced her that the cat was not there, and she was about to go back downstairs when something caught her eye. She wasn't sure what it was—something out of place, or something missing, or something there that shouldn't have been there. She paused and looked around. For a long time she couldn't put her finger on what it was. It was more a feeling than anything tangible. As if someone had been here and moved things around, then returned them to their original places. Except that there was still an air in the attic. An air of having been disturbed.

The old woman began looking around more carefully, realizing as she did that the attic was as much the storehouse of her memories as it was the repository of the Conger family's castoffs. All the things that Congers had used and forgotten about were scattered around the attic—things that they had forgotten about but that Mrs. Goodrich had not. Her hand caressed the cradle that had been used for so many Conger babies—Sarah most recently, but Elizabeth before her, and their father before them. She wondered how many generations of Conger babies had slept in that cradle. And then she noticed that the intricate hand carving contained not a particle of dust. That was what had struck her about the attic: no dust. Everything that should have been covered with dust was clean.

She spent the next hour in the attic, looking for the dirt that should have been there. But it was not there, nor was Cecil.

Early in the afternoon she decided that, wherever the cat was, he was not in the house.

He'll come back, she thought. When he's a mind to.

9

"Are you sorry yet?"

Rose asked the question as she peered over the edge of her highball glass at Barbara Stevens. She had been right; she did like the Stevenses, and was looking forward to several years of happy neighborliness. Opposite her, sitting next to Carl, Barbara stared right back at her.

"Sorry?" she said. "Sorry we bought the house?"

"Well," Rose said, her eyes wandering through the ugly square living room, now filled with packed boxes and disarranged furniture, "I told you it was a mess. And it sure is."

Barbara laughed, and the sound seemed to make the room less ugly. "It isn't all that bad. There are lots of possibilities." Rose was sure she heard a touch of uncertainty in the words.

"Name one." It was a challenge.

"Carl has dozens," Barbara said, neatly avoiding the hook. "I'll take over after the remodeling is done."

"In other words," Carl put in, "never. Barbara is thoroughly convinced that 'remodeling' includes paint, paper, and, if she can persuade me, new furniture. Then, when it's all finished, she comes out of her studio, looks around, and says, 'My, we have done wonders with this place, haven't we?'"

"Now, it's not that bad at all," Barbara protested. "Besides, you know damned well that you think an architect should have full control of everything that goes into a building, from the day the ground is broken until the day the building is torn down." She turned her attention to Rose and winked. "He even has stipulations in his contracts to carry his instructions forth unto the fourth generation. The sins of the fathers may not be visited on the sons, but they're sure going to have to live with them."

"Enough," Carl said, standing up and brandishing a bottle that the three of them had half killed. "Any more, anybody, or shall we call it a day?"

Rose glanced at her watch, and it struck her that she had spent a lot more time here than she had intended. But it had been fun, and she'd found out a lot more about the old house than she had ever known. The three of them had spent most of the day exploring it from top to bottom, and the Stevenses were now well acquainted with the Barneses' lighting system, which had allowed some rooms to be lit only from other rooms. Some rooms, which Rose explained had been the children's, were without any switches at all, and the three of them had speculated that the Barneses had actually and literally kept some of their children in the dark on occasion. The day had gone fast, and it was close to four. Rose stood up.

"There's one more thing I should show you," she said pensively, "and I'd like to do it this afternoon."

Carl's brows rose curiously. "Sounds important."

"It may be, and it may not be. You'll know better than I, since I haven't met Jeff yet."

"Jeff?" Barbara echoed, now totally mystified. "What does he have to do with it?"

"Nothing, I hope," Rose said. "That's why I'd like to tell you about it now, before he gets here. Come on."

She led Carl and Barbara out of the house on the ocean side. There was a path leading along the cliff to the south, and it was along this path that Rose took the Stevenses.

"There should be primroses," Carl remarked. Barbara smiled at him appreciatively, but Rose appeared not to have heard the remark. She strode forward, and they walked for about a hundred feet before she stopped.

"There," she said, pointing.

Carl and Barbara stared out to sea, their eyes sweeping the horizon. The ocean was clear of boats and ships, an expanse of gray-green water broken only by the horizon and Conger's Point jutting out to sea another hundred yards south of them.

"It's beautiful," Barbara said. "But I don't know what I'm looking for."

"The Point," Rose said. "From here you have a good view of the north face of it. The woods at the top are really a pretty shallow stand. On the other side of the woods is our field, and, of course, on the other side of the field is our house. If it weren't for the woods, you'd have a straight shot at the house."

"So?" Carl said, still clearly baffled as to what Rose was getting at.

"It's the embankment," Rose said. "I think you ought to know about it. It's very steep, and it can be treacherous, particularly when the wind blows from the north. The sea can get wild out there, and the spray turns the face of the embankment into glass. There have been some accidents . . ." Her voice trailed off; then, catching the worried look in Barbara's eyes, she went on. "Oh, not for a long time," she said. "Not in this century, as far as we know. We've always been very careful about it, and the children are not allowed to go anywhere near it. In the Conger family, for generations children haven't been allowed to play either in the woods or on the embankment. Not only is it dangerous, but it's practically invisible. You can't see the face of the embankment from any point on our property, and only from a couple of spots over here. From your house it's totally out of sight. All you can see is the forest."

"Why haven't you cut the forest down?" Barbara said thoughtfully. "It wouldn't be as pretty, but at least you'd be able to see if any of the kids are playing along the top."

Rose smiled tightly. "I suggested it once. Part of it, of course, is the esthetics. Also, there's the wind. The woods protect the house pretty well when the wind is from the north. Which it is, during the winter. And, of course, the privacy thing. The Congers always liked the idea that none of their neighbors could see them."

"It's nice to be able to afford that sort of luxury," Carl murmured.

Rose nodded. "Very nice. If you can afford it, which we barely can. A couple of more tax hikes and we won't be able to afford it at all." She realized she was saying more than she probably ought, then realized that she didn't really care; in fact, it was nice to be able to admit to someone, anyone, that the Congers weren't what they used to be. Still, she decided it was time to get back to the subject at hand.

"So that's what I wanted to show you," she said. "Of course, you can do what you want, but I'd advise you to tell Jeff not to go anywhere near the place."

"Which would send him there directly, the minute our backs were turned," Barbara said. "I think we'll just have to trust to his good sense." She noted the expression on Rose's face, and her smile faded. "Is there something else?" she asked.

Rose hesitated a minute, then spoke again. "Yes," she said, glancing once more at her watch. "I don't have time to go into it all, but there's a legend about the embankment. There may be a cave there, and it's really quite dangerous." Rose smiled uncertainly. "I've got to be getting home. Both the girls will be there, and I don't like to leave them for long with nobody but Mrs. Goodrich."

"Mrs. Goodrich?"

"The housekeeper. She's getting older—she must be nearly seventy—and terribly set in her ways, but she's been with the family since long before Jack was born."

They chatted a little more on the way back to the Stevenses' new house, but Rose didn't go in again. She felt a sudden urge to get home.

Minutes later, she was striding along the Point Road, skirting the west end of the strip of woods. She saw a squirrel playing in one of the trees, something she normally would have taken a few minutes to enjoy, but she didn't give it a second glance. She passed the woods, and was walking along the edge of the field. Suddenly she stopped. Coming out of the woods, about one hundred and fifty yards from Rose, was Elizabeth. A couple of seconds later, Sarah, too, emerged from the woods. Rose felt her stomach tighten as she watched her children cross the field toward home. She didn't call out to them; indeed, she didn't even move until she saw them disappear into the house. Then, when they were no longer visible, she continued on her way. But her pace was slow, and her mind was filled with thoughts. None of them made any sense. All of them were foreboding.

When she got home, she didn't call out a greeting. Instead, she went directly to the small study at the rear of the house, poured herself a drink, and sat in the wing chair. As she waited for her husband to come home, she studied the old portrait above the mantel. It did look like Elizabeth.

So much like Elizabeth.

She sipped the drink, stared at the picture and waited.

She was still in the wing chair an hour later, when Jack came home. She heard his voice calling out as he opened the front door, heard the answer come from Elizabeth upstairs. Rose remained silent, and listened to his footsteps approach the study. She was watching the door when he came through. His eyes widened in surprise; then he grinned at her.

"Are we doing a role reversal? I'm the one who's supposed to sit brooding in the chair with a drink in my fist." His smile faded as he watched his wife's face. "Is something wrong?" he asked, and Rose was pleased to hear a concern that sounded genuine.

"Fix yourself a drink and sit down," she said. "And you might as well fix this one up. The ice has melted."

He took her glass, refilled it, and poured himself a neat Scotch. Setting Rose's drink on the table at her elbow, he seated himself opposite her.

"So what's up? Sarah?"

She shook her head. "I'm not sure, really." She recounted her day, skipping over most of it until she reached the end. She went over her final conversation with the Stevenses in detail, trying to remember exactly what she had told them. When she finished, he didn't seem particularly disturbed.

"Then what has you so upset?" he asked.

"On my way home, I saw the girls coming out of the woods. First Elizabeth, then Sarah."

"I see," Jack said quietly. "And you want me to talk to them?"

"Not both of them. Just Elizabeth. I don't care what you tell her, but convince her to stay away from there."

"Shall I tell her about the legend?"

"If you want."

"Well, Lord knows, if that won't do it nothing will. That legend has kept four generations of Congers away from that embankment."

"Four?" Rose said. "That many?"

"I think so," Jack said. He counted briefly on his fingers. "Nope. I'm the third. If it works, Elizabeth and Sarah will be the fourth. Well, no time like the present." He finished his drink and left the room.

Alone, Rose continued sipping from her glass and

staring at the portrait. For some reason, Carl Stevens's words echoed in her mind. "The sins of the fathers . . ."

Then she remembered the rest of the quotation, and she shuddered: ". . . even unto the third and fourth generations."

Jack climbed the stairs slowly, wondering what he would tell his daughter. At the top he paused and squared his shoulders. The truth, he guessed. Or at least what the Congers had thought was some sort of truth, among themselves, for more years than he knew.

He found them in the playroom. A frown creased his brow as he saw what they were doing. Between them was the Ouija board, and Elizabeth seemed to be concentrating on it. Sarah was concentrating on Elizabeth. Jack cleared his throat, and when nothing happened he spoke.

"Elizabeth," he said, and regretted the sharp sound that filled the room. His daughters jumped a little, and Elizabeth opened her eyes.

"Daddy! Did you come up to play with us?"

"I came up to talk to you. Alone." His eyes shifted to Sarah on the last word, and Elizabeth picked up on the message. She stood up, then leaned over to whisper into her sister's ear. Sarah, to Jack's eye, did not respond, but Elizabeth seemed to be satisfied that Sarah would be all right by herself. She followed him as he led her out of the playroom and into her own room. When she was inside he closed the door, and Elizabeth knew that she had done something wrong. She sat on the edge of her bed and regarded her father respectfully.

"It's the woods, isn't it?" she said.

Her father looked at her sternly. "Yes," he said, "it is. Unless I'm badly mistaken, it was only yesterday that we had a talk about that. Now I understand you were in the woods today. With Sarah."

Elizabeth looked straight into his eyes, and he tried

to find a clue in her own as to her mood. He wondered if she would be defiant, or angry, or stubborn. But he saw only curiosity.

"I know," she said. "I don't really know why I took Sarah to the woods today. We were in the field, playing, and then we were in the woods. I must have been thinking about something else, because I honestly don't remember going into the woods. The only thing I remember is suddenly realizing we were in the woods, and leading Sarah back out to the field."

Jack listened to his daughter silently, trying to decide if she was being truthful. He remembered his own youth, and all the times he had become so engrossed in something that he had lost track of his surroundings. He supposed it could have happened.

"Well," he said, "I expect you not to let it happen again. You're a big girl now, and you should be able to keep your mind on what you're doing. Or at least where you are, particularly when Sarah is with you."

"I take good care of her," Elizabeth said, and Jack thought he heard a defensive note in her voice.

"Of course you do," he said soothingly. "But please take good care of her only on this side of those woods." Now he definitely saw anger in Elizabeth's face. The beautiful features hardened slightly, and he realized he was going to have to amplify. While she posed the question, he tried to figure out where to begin his answer.

"I want to know why," she was saying. "I think it's getting absolutely silly. I'm old enough to go where I want to go, at least on our own property. When I was little, it was one thing. But I'm not little any more. You said so yourself," she finished.

"You're going to think we're all crazy," Jack said.

"Are we?" Elizabeth asked, but there was no twinkle in her eye.

"Who knows?" Jack replied, keeping his tone light.

"Okay, I'll tell you the story. There's an old family legend."

"I know," Elizabeth said.

"You know?" Now Jack couldn't keep the surprise out of his voice. "How?"

Elizabeth widened her eyes and tried to look spooky. "The Ouija board," she intoned. "It knows all and it tells all." Then she burst into laughter at the expression on her father's face. It was a mixture of awe, surprise, and fright. "I'm kidding, Dad," she said. "I don't know what it's all about." She thought carefully, then went on. "In fact, I don't really know what I know and what I don't know, or where I found out. But I know there's some kind of story and it goes back a long way. What is it?"

Jack felt a strange sense of relief that she did not know the legend, and he began to tell it to her.

"It does go back a long way," he said. "Your mother and I were just figuring it out, and it's four generations, counting you and Sarah. It has to do with your great-great-grandmother. It all happened somewhere in the neighborhood of a hundred years ago, and she was already an old, old lady then. I don't know how many of the details I can remember, since I don't think anybody ever wrote the story down, but here's what is supposed to have happened:

"The old woman—I think her name was Bernice or Bertha, something like that—was in the habit of taking a nap every day after dinner, which was what we'd call lunch nowadays. Apparently every day she'd go upstairs and sleep for an hour, then come back down, and that was that. Except that one day she didn't come back down."

"You mean she died?" Elizabeth asked.

"No," Jack said. "She didn't die. When she didn't come down from her nap, they went upstairs, I imagine expecting to find her dead, but she wasn't. She was still asleep.

"To make a long story short, the legend has it that she slept for two days and two nights, solid. They tried to wake her up, and couldn't. They called a doctor, but he couldn't find anything wrong with her at all. I suppose she might have had some kind of stroke and gone into a coma, but at the time they didn't know much about such things. Anyway, she eventually woke up, and she didn't seem to have anything wrong with her.

"I suppose the family would have forgotten about it, except that a couple of days later one of the old lady's sons, who would have been my great-uncle, I think, walked into the house carrying a dead rabbit. Then he proceeded to jump off the cliff behind the house."

"You're kidding," Elizabeth breathed.

Jack shook his head. "If I am, then your grandfather kidded me when he told me the story."

"But why did he do it?" Elizabeth asked.

"No one ever found out." Jack shrugged. "Or if they did, they never told anybody. Anyway, when the old lady heard about it, she wasn't surprised. Apparently she said she'd been expecting it. And from then on until she died, she told everybody who was going to die, and when. She said she had gotten all the information in a dream she had while she'd been sleeping those two days."

"And she was never wrong?" Elizabeth asked doubtfully.

"Who knows? You know the way stories grow. She could have been wrong most of the time, but the only thing anybody would remember and pass along would be the times she was right. She probably predicted everybody's death every day, so sooner or later she hit the nail on the head. It's like astrologers. They say so much that some of the things have to be right."

"Then what's the big deal?" Elizabeth said.

"Well, the last straw came just before she died. She claimed she'd had a vision."

"A vision? You mean like angels or ghosts?"

"Not quite. A vision, but not of angels. She claimed that in the vision she had been taken to a cave in the embankment. Inside the cave, she was shown a shaft that led straight down. Her 'angel,' or whatever it was supposed to be, told her that the shaft was the gates of hell. According to the old lady, all sorts of awful things were supposed to happen if anybody ever went through the gates of hell. Or, I suppose, down the shaft. Anyway, she told the family that she had seen visions of horrible things in the future, and that the only way to keep them from happening was to see to it that no one went near that cave. She made everyone in the family swear never to go near the embankment where the cave is supposed to be. Then she died."

Elizabeth stared at him silently for a minute before she spoke. He could hear incredulity in her voice.

"Is there really a cave there?"

"I don't have any idea."

"You mean they believed her?" Elizabeth said. "You mean nobody ever even went to look for it?"

Jack licked his lips uncomfortably. "Someone did," he said slowly. "My grandfather."

"Did he find it?" Elizabeth asked eagerly.

"No," Jack said. He hoped he could leave it at that, but Elizabeth wouldn't let him.

"Well, what happened?" she demanded.

"No one knows about that, either. He announced one day that he was going to find the cave, *if* there was a cave, and headed off by himself. When he didn't come back, a search party went to find him."

"Did they?" Elizabeth asked. "Find him, I mean?"

"They found him. They found him at the bottom of the embankment. His foot was wedged between two rocks, and he had apparently drowned when the tide came in."

An expression of horror came over Elizabeth's face. "What an awful way to die," she said softly.

"Yes," said Jack, "it is. The odd thing was that they

couldn't figure out exactly what happened. His foot was caught, but not tightly. He should have been able to get it loose without any trouble."

"Maybe he fell," Elizabeth suggested.

"Maybe, but they didn't find any bruises that would have indicated it. Well," he finished, "that's it. Whatever the truth of it, the whole family has always respected the old lady's dying wish. Except for my grandfather. If nothing else, it gives us a reason for staying away from a dangerous place. I hope you'll respect it as much as the rest of us have."

Elizabeth was very quiet, and when she spoke her voice was low. "Daddy," she said. "Do you believe it?"

Jack considered the question, and could find no answer. He had lived with the legend for so long that it never entered his mind to question the truth of it. Now, looking at it in the cold light of his daughter's ice-blue stare, he shook his head.

"No," he said, "I don't suppose I do, really. On the other hand, I don't believe it's bad luck to walk under a ladder, but I still don't walk under ladders. So maybe, deep down inside, I do believe the legend."

Elizabeth seemed to digest this for a minute, and Jack was about to lean over to kiss her when she asked another question.

"What about the little girl?" she said.

"What little girl?" Jack asked blankly.

"I'm not sure," Elizabeth said. "It seems to me that I've heard somewhere that there was a little girl in the legend."

Jack reviewed the story in his mind, then shook his head.

"No," he said. "Not that I know of."

"Well," Elizabeth said, "there should be. Let's make one up." Now Jack could see the glint of mischief in her eyes.

"You do that," he said. "And tell me about it over dinner. See you downstairs in thirty minutes."

He kissed her, then left the room. As he descended the stairs, he heard her calling after him.

"I'll ask the Ouija board about it," she said.

He heard her laugh as she went back to the playroom.

10

"What exactly did you tell her?"

Rose spoke in the dark, and her voice seemed to bounce off the walls and come back at her more loudly than she desired. Beside her, she felt Jack stir. She was sure he wasn't sleeping, but it was almost a minute before he answered her. In the silence, she began counting the ticking of the grandfather clock. She had reached forty when Jack finally spoke.

"The whole thing," he said. "The idea was to keep her away from the embankment, wasn't it?"

"I suppose so," Rose said unsurely. "How did she take it?"

She heard Jack chuckle in the darkness. "How would you take a story like that in this day and age? I'm not sure family legends and curses count for much any more."

"But a lot of it happened," Rose said.

"Some of it happened," Jack countered. "Granted that the old lady slept for a couple of days, that someone jumped off the cliff and someone else drowned. It still doesn't add up to much. And, of course, the old lady's vision at the end was probably nothing more than senility." He rolled over. "Still, it makes a good spooky story, and it's sure kept us all off the embankment for a lot of years."

"How did she take it?" Rose repeated. "Didn't she say anything?"

Jack smiled in the darkness. "She wanted to know about the little girl."

"Little girl?" Rose said. "What little girl? I never heard of a little girl before."

"Of course not. There isn't any. It just struck Elizabeth that there ought to have been a little girl involved in the legend. She said she thought she heard about one somewhere, but couldn't remember where. She said she'd consult the Ouija board."

Rose felt herself begin to shudder, but fought it off. "Ouija board," she said. "I'm not sure we should let her play with such a thing. Children are too suggestible."

She rolled over and nestled against her husband. She felt his body stiffen. Sighing, she moved away from him.

In her room, Elizabeth lay in her bed, listening to the murmur of her parent's voices. As the voices died away, the girl's eyes closed; then her breathing evened out and grew deeper. As the clock struck, her eyelids began to flicker. A sound struggled from her throat, then died away on her lips. She turned, and the covers fell to the floor. Her knees drew up, and she wrapped her arms around herself.

And then she rose from the bed.

She padded on her bare feet across the floor of her room and out into the hall. She moved, trancelike, to the attic door and stretched upward to take the key from the ledge above. Avoiding the loose third tread, Elizabeth glided up the steep stairs into the attic, unaware of the silent Sarah, who stood quietly watching the ascent.

After Elizabeth disappeared into the upper reaches of the house, Sarah returned to her bed, where she lay staring blankly at the ceiling.

Elizabeth stayed in the attic for an hour, but what

she did there, and what she saw, didn't register on her memory.

Lying awake, Rose felt as if she were suffocating. She tried to ignore the feeling, but it persisted. Finally, in frustration, she left her bed and went to sit by the window. Moodily, she sat and smoked and peered out into the night. There was a full moon, and shadows played across the field. It was peaceful, she thought, and she considered going for a walk. The cliff would be beautiful, with the light dancing on the sea, and the surf, turned silvery by the moon, crashing below her. And then, as suddenly as the feeling of suffocation had come over her, it left her. She crushed the cigarette out and went back to bed. In a moment she was asleep.

Had she stayed by the window, she might not have returned to her bed, for she might have seen the shape moving across the field.

Elizabeth crossed the porch at the moment that Rose went back to bed. She moved slowly, carefully toward the field, as if feeling her way with her feet. Then, suddenly, she turned and began walking quickly toward the old barn that stood a few yards from the garage. She let herself in by the side door and moved to the tack room. She picked up a bag and a strange coil of rope and wood. She slung the coil over her head, grasped the neck of the bag, and left the barn. Then, her step no longer cautious, she moved across the field toward the wood. Soon she was enveloped in its black shadows.

The dress Elizabeth wore was old—much older than any of the clothes she kept for playing in the field. Its ruffled hem caught on branches as she drew nearer the woods, but the ancient material gave way with so little resistance that she felt no pull. Her blond hair, flowing over her shoulders in an old-fashioned way,

caught the moonlight and, from a distance, seemed to
form a halo around her head.

She moved surely and gracefully, her eyes staring
directly ahead into the blackness before her. There
was no path or trail, but she advanced as easily as
though the way had been paved. Though the shadows
were deep, and the underbrush thick, her feet found
the places where no branches waited to trip her, or
stones to bruise her foot, or vines to ensnare her.

And then Elizabeth emerged from the woods, and
stood on the top of the embankment, staring out
across the sea. It was gentle that night, and the surf
murmured below, softly, invitingly.

Elizabeth began moving eastward along the edge
of the embankment, slowly, as if waiting for some sort
of signal to tell her she was at the right place. Then
she stopped again, and stared once more out to sea.
Finally she began moving down the steep face of the
embankment, her small feet finding holds that would
have been useless to a larger person. Occasionally her
free hand moved out as if to steady herself, but most
often it stopped short of touching anything. She moved
steadily downward, disappearing now and then from
the moonlight, then reemerging a few feet lower than
before. Finally she disappeared into the shadow of a
boulder, and crept into a hole that lay hidden in the
blackness. Fifty feet farther down, the surf pounded
against the Point.

Elizabeth crawled through the tunnel of the cave,
pulling the long skirt up every few minutes, then creeping farther forward until the dress grew taut as she
crawled across it. Then she would pause again, and
pull the material from under her knees, spreading it
once more before her. She felt her way forward, pushing
the bag carefully, as if it would disappear if she pushed
it too far. Then she stopped, crept as far over the bag
as she could, and felt the floor of the cave in front of
her. At the end of her reach she felt the lip of a shaft.

She moved a little closer to the edge and poked around in the depths of the bag. Her hand closed on a flashlight, and she drew it out. She tested it a couple of times, flashing the narrow beam on the walls that closed in around her. The tunnel widened into a room around the shaft, and the shaft itself appeared to be a well in the center of an oval room whose floor was littered with boulders.

Elizabeth removed the coiled object from around her neck, and, still clutching the flashlight, moved to the edge of the shaft. She pointed the light downward and stared into the depths. Far below, she wasn't sure how far, the light glinted on something that lay on the bottom of the shaft.

She laid the flashlight carefully in a cleft of stone, and jiggled it a little to be sure it was secure. Then she began uncoiling the object she had carried from the barn. It was a rope ladder that had once provided primitive access to the loft. For years it had lain in the tack room: the loft was no longer used, and the ladder had been deemed a danger to playing children. Elizabeth began wedging the ends of the rope into cracks in the boulders, chinking the rope tighter with bits of stone that lay scattered across the cavern floor. Finally she tested the ropes, pulling on them as hard as she could, bracing her legs against the boulders. The rope held.

She pushed the rest of the coil over the lip of the shaft. It clattered against the side of the shaft, then caught. She pulled it back to the surface and carefully untangled it. The second time, as she fed it carefully over the edge, it fell straight to the bottom. She felt a slight vibration as the bottom rung struck the floor below.

She picked up the bag and dropped it over the edge. She heard a soft *thunk* as it too hit the bottom. Then she worked the flashlight loose from its crevice, put it in a pocket of her dress, and began making her way down the ladder.

It was slow going, but Elizabeth didn't seem to notice the slime that rubbed off the walls of the shaft as she crept carefully from rung to rung, nor did the darkness frighten her. She felt the cool stone touch the sole of her foot as she found the bottom of the shaft. She reached into her pocket and pulled out the flashlight.

The yellowish beam flickered around the chamber at the bottom of the shaft. It was very much like the chamber above: smaller, and with a lower ceiling, but oval, and with a flat, rock-strewn floor. The shaft opened almost in the center of the small chamber.

Elizabeth played the light over the floor of the cavern, and the object which had glinted from above suddenly flashed once more. It was a gold bracelet, set with a small opal.

It was still on the wrist of its owner.

The skeleton lay directly below the opening of the shaft, sprawled in the position in which it had lain through the decades. Here and there small pieces of rotten cloth still clung to it, but they disintegrated into dust when Elizabeth touched them. The sack lay near it, where Elizabeth had dropped it, its impact having scattered some of the ribs across the floor. Elizabeth retrieved the bag and set it aside. Then she played the light over the skull. She picked up a rusted metal barrette that lay next to the skull and examined it carefully. She nodded to herself.

"I knew you were here," she whispered. "Everything will be all right now. You'll see."

She left the skeleton for a moment and found a new resting place for the flashlight. She left it on and trained it on the spot where the ancient bones gleamed palely in its light.

Elizabeth worked slowly, moving the bones carefully. She laid them out at one edge of the chamber, close to one of the walls. She found a small flat rock to cushion the skull, and when she was finished the remains lay on their back, the arms folded peacefully over the rib cage. Elizabeth smiled at the corpse, and there was a strange light in her eyes as she removed the bracelet from the fleshless wrist and slipped it onto her own.

She began moving some of the rocks around, wrestling a large one with a fairly flat surface into the center of the cavern. Then she moved four other, smaller rocks to form stools around the rough table. She placed the bag on the table and sat down on one of the stools.

From the bag she began removing a set of doll's clothing: a small blue dress, tiny stockings, and a pair of miniature patent-leather Mary Janes, together with a pair of white mittens and a small ruffled bonnet.

Then she opened the sack and Cecil lay on the rock slab, his body limp, his head at a strange angle from the broken neck that had killed him.

Elizabeth began dressing the dead cat in the doll's clothes, carefully working the dress over his head, front legs, and torso, forcing the forepaws through the sleeves, and meticulously buttoning the dress up along his spine.

Then she worked the tiny socks over his hindpaws, and forced the stockinged paws into the miniature shoes. She slipped the mittens onto the forepaws and, finally, put the bonnet on Cecil's head, tying the strings securely under his chin.

"Pretty baby," she murmured as she finished. "Aren't you my pretty baby?"

She set the grotesquely costumed animal on the rock opposite her and watched as it collapsed to the cavern floor. She tried to set it up twice more, but each time it fell. Finally she collected a number of small rocks and built a small pile of stones that would support the weight of the corpse. Eventually the dead Cecil sat propped across from her, its bonneted head lolling weirdly to one side. Elizabeth seemed not to notice the unnatural pose.

"And now we'll have a party," she said. "Would you like some tea?"

Her right hand picked up an imaginary teapot, and she skillfully poured from it into an equally invisible cup that she held steadily in her left hand. She set the imaginary cup in front of the dead cat.

"One lump or two?" she asked politely, offering her guest a bowl of sugar. Without waiting for an answer, she mimed placing two lumps of sugar in the cup that was not on the table.

"Well," she said, smiling brightly, "isn't this nice?"

Elizabeth waited, staring across at the tightly closed eyes of the cat.

"Are you sleeping?" she asked. She reached across the table and prodded the corpse with one finger. Then she left her seat and moved around to kneel beside Cecil. She carefully forced each eye open, peeling the lids far back until they did not snap shut again when she released them. She went back to her seat.

"There," she said. "Now we can have a nice conversation. Would you like a piece of cake?" Elizabeth picked up an imaginary cake plate and offered it to the vacantly staring cat. When there was no response, she pretended to scoop a slice of the cake onto a plate that was apparently already waiting in front of Cecil.

"Now," she said, pausing to take a bite of the cake that wasn't there and wash it down with a swallow of the imaginary tea. "What would you like to talk about?"

She waited for a response again and glared at the limp, unresponsive body that sat propped across from her. Empty eyes stared back at her.

"It's very rude not to talk when you're spoken to," she said softly. "Nice children answer questions."

There was still no response from the corpse, and Elizabeth's face flushed with anger.

"Answer me when I speak to you," she snapped. Still there was no response.

She peered balefully at the cat, and her eyes flashed in the strange yellow glow of the flashlight.

"Talk to me," she demanded, a hard edge of hatred coming into her voice. "You talk to me, you disgusting child!"

Elizabeth's anger mounted as the dead thing across from her failed to respond to her demands, and her voice rose and grew shrill.

"Don't you sit there like that, you bastard!" she yelled. "That's all you ever do. I spend my life with you, and what do I get from you? Nothing. *Nothing!* Well, now you'll talk to me, or I'll beat your ass bloody."

She suddenly leapt at the cat, grabbing the corpse and yanking it across the table. She flipped it over, held it on her knee, and began spanking it. The slapping of her hand against the cat's haunches echoed back at her, and she put all her strength into the beating she was administering. Then she set the cat back on the rock and smiled at it.

"There," she said. "Now that you've had what you deserve, we can get back to our tea party."

She went on chattering mindlessly for a few moments, miming the actions of refilling the cups and plates she imagined were before her. Then she asked the cat another question and waited for a response. When there was none, her anger flashed back, flooding over her like a red tide.

"Don't you do that to me, you fucking no-good monster!" she screamed. "I hate it when you do that to me. Hate it, hate it, *hate it!*"

As her voice rose, she grabbed the cat and began swinging it over her head, then brought it crashing down on the stone table. In her rage, she didn't hear the crushing of the skull.

"You'll answer me," she raved. "God damn you, you'll talk to me or I'll kill you!"

Suddenly she hurled the cat against the wall of the cave and grabbed the bag once more. She reached deep into it, and when she withdrew her hand she clutched a large butcher knife. Her anger cresting, she fell on the cat's limp body and began slashing at it with the knife, her voice rising as she cursed the unresponsive animal.

Suddenly she had the cat on the table again, and the knife flashed through the air once more. Cecil's severed head rolled away from the torso and fell to the floor. Elizabeth stared at it, not comprehending what had happened.

"Don't do that," she breathed. "Don't do that to me. I want you to talk to me. *Talk to me!*" she screamed once more, then stopped, her breath coming in gasps. She felt a pain throbbing through her head, and heard something that sounded like wind. Then the pain passed, and the sounds of the wind faded into a strange whimpering from above. She looked up into the darkness of the shaft.

Seeing nothing, she found the flashlight, and shined it upward. The beam illuminated Sarah's dark face, her huge brown eyes blinking in the glare of the light.

Elizabeth smiled up at her, and her face softened.

"Sarah," she almost whispered. "Did you see? Did you see that naughty baby? She isn't like you. She isn't like you at all. You're such a sweet girl, so sweet . . ." She turned back to look once more at the decapitated feline body, which lay, still clothed, on the rough rock. Then the light picked up the head, still encased in the old-fashioned bonnet, the eyes dully reflecting the glare from the flashlight.

"You should have talked to me," she hissed. "Really, you should have." She picked up the knife and placed it carefully on a ledge near the ceiling of the cavern.

Then she slipped the flashlight, still glowing, into

her pocket and began to make her way back up the rope ladder. Sarah crept back from the edge as Elizabeth emerged from the pit.

"It's late," Elizabeth whispered. "But not too late." Then she slipped the bracelet that was still on her wrist off her own arm and onto Sarah's.

"This is for you," she said. "It's from Beth. She wants you to have it. She says it should belong to you."

Ignoring Sarah now, Elizabeth crept through the tunnel and emerged once more into the night. Quickly, she made her way back up the face of the embankment and disappeared into the woods.

Elizabeth lay once more in her bed, staring at the ceiling. She wished she could fall asleep again, but she couldn't. She had awakened from a dream which had fled as she opened her eyes, and now sleep would not come to her. She thought she heard a noise outside, and went to the window. There, making her way slowly across the field, she saw her sister. Elizabeth went downstairs and met Sarah at the front door.

She was covered with mud and slime, and her hands were badly scratched. She stared helplessly up at Elizabeth.

Silently Elizabeth took Sarah upstairs and into the bathroom. She cleaned her sister up and threw the filthy clothes into the laundry chute. Then she tucked Sarah into bed.

Elizabeth wondered where Sarah had been. But soon she slept. It was a peaceful sleep, and there were no more dreams.

11

Mrs. Goodrich opened the trapdoor at the bottom of the laundry chute and watched the clothes tumble to the floor at her feet. She picked up a particularly dirty pair of blue jeans with a ragged tear at the knee and looked at them critically.

"Just look at that," she said to the empty room. "I've never in my life seen anything so filthy. Looks like she's been crawling around in some kinda slime."

She fished out an equally dirt-encrusted shirt and examined it carefully. The filth had dried overnight, and it flecked off into the old woman's hand as she held the shirt to the light.

She sniffed at it, and her face wrinkled even more deeply as she recoiled from the smell of rotting seaweed. Her face tightened, and she turned toward the laundry-room door with an air of determination.

She found Rose and Jack Conger sitting silently in the dining room, and would have noticed the strain in the air if she hadn't had other things on her mind. She stumped into the room without her usual pause, and Jack looked up curiously. Mrs. Goodrich ignored him.

"Miz Rose," she complained, her Yankee twang taking on a hint of outrage. "Just look at these. I don't know how I'm supposed to get things like this clean." She held the shirt up for Rose's inspection, primarily because the filth showed up better against the white of the shirt than the blue of the denim. Mrs. Goodrich was a great believer in the best effects delivering the best result. She shook the shirt slightly, for good measure, and was gratified to see some of the dried mud flutter to the carpet. The vacuum would take care of that.

"What is it?" Rose asked curiously. "It looks like mud."

"Mud? You call that mud? I call it slime." She held the shirt nearer, and Rose was able to get a good whiff.

"It smells like dead fish," Rose commented, wondering what was expected of her. "Whose is it?"

"Miss Sarah's," Mrs. Goodrich stated. "I don't know what that child's been up to, but it should be stopped. She didn't get this dirt from playing in the yard, or even the field. I don't know how I can get it out." She did know, of course, but saw no point in admitting it. Over the years she had discovered that life was much easier if she feigned incompetence, and this seemed like a good time to exercise that knowledge.

"Well, do your best," Rose said, still not sure how she was supposed to deal with the situation. "I don't really see how we can find out where she picked up that dirt, under the circumstances."

Mrs. Goodrich, her feelings aired, stumped back out of the room, leaving the air filled with grumblings. Rose thought she heard a reference to things like this not happening in the old days, and wondered if it could have been true. Then she saw Jack staring at her, and suddenly felt uncomfortable. Briefly she wondered what had happened to the peace they had had so recently.

"Well, what was I supposed to say?" she said, feeling a little guilty but not sure why.

"Nothing," Jack said. "Don't worry about the dirt—Mrs. Goodrich can handle that with a good hard look. But where *did* Sarah pick it up?"

"I'm sure I don't know," Rose snapped. "Why don't you ask her?"

"That's cruel, Rose," Jack said quietly. "And not just to me. It's cruel to Sarah, too."

Rose took a deep breath, then exhaled slowly, willing the tension from her body. She chewed her lower lip for a moment, then tried to smile at her husband.

"I'm sorry," she said. "Of course you're right. But, God, Jack, what am I supposed to do about it? If she went somewhere by herself, there's absolutely no way in the world that we're going to find out where it was."

"It probably has something to do with the scratches," Jack said.

Rose nodded. "And she could have gotten those anywhere."

Then they looked at each other and they both remembered. Early this morning, Rose had looked in on Sarah. The child had thrown her blanket off in the night, and as Rose bent to cover her she saw that Sarah's hands were badly scratched, and one knee was scraped. But she had been clean. The wounds had been clean too. They'd assumed that something had happened during the night, that the wounds had been somehow self-inflicted. But now, with the filthy clothing, they had to reassess the whole thing. They each avoided the subject in a different way: Rose by stirring her coffee moodily, Jack by mopping up the last of his egg with a piece of danish.

"It did smell like the sea," Rose said at last.

"Around here everything smells like the sea," Jack countered.

"I suppose she could have decided to go down to the beach."

"In the middle of the night?" Jack said. "Besides, that trail's not slimy, and it's an easy trail. Even if it was pitch-black, all you have to do is keep one hand on the guardrail and walk. And the beach is sand."

"There are rocks," Rose offered, and it was true. There were rocks on the beach, but they weren't of the rough variety. They were, for the most part, beach pebbles worn smooth by years of tumbling in the light surf of the south side of the Point. The rough rocks, both of them knew, were on the north side, jutting out of the face of the embankment. Neither of them was willing to confront that possibility yet.

"What about the quarry?" Jack asked suddenly. "She could have walked over to the quarry for some reason. It's always muddy there, and God knows those old slag heaps are hard on the hands."

Rose stared speculatively into space and tried to believe in the idea of the quarry. It would be easy, except for the smell. Her nose wrinkled as she remembered the awful rotting kelp odor that had permeated the shirt. She decided to put it out of her mind.

"Well, I don't see that there's a thing we can do about it now," she said. "It's too late. Besides, we've got other things to worry about," she added pointedly.

Jack felt the familiar sick feeling begin to form in his stomach, the feeling he was not getting used to— and was experiencing more and more.

"Don't you think things are bad enough?" he asked, his voice carrying a quaver that he hoped Rose wouldn't hear. "Let's not make them any worse."

"How could it get any worse," Rose said bitterly. She kept her voice low, ready to break off the conversation if she heard the children coming downstairs. But she was not about to let it go. She remembered the previous night—his rejection, her long, thoughtful vigil at the window—and wondered how many more of them there would be, how many more of them she would be able to stand without blowing apart from the rage, the frustration, and the humiliation.

Last night she had taken herself in hand and squeezed her anger back, forcing herself to sleep through it. But this morning it was still there, waiting to be served up to Jack along with his coffee and orange juice. He had not been surprised.

"Don't you think it's time you got back into therapy?" she asked softly, trying another tack.

"I don't want to go into it," Jack said sourly.

"The subject or the therapy?"

"Take your pick," he said. "Is there a difference?"

"That depends," Rose said, deliberately keeping the poison out of her voice. "I know you don't get off on therapy—"

"I don't get off at all," Jack finished for her. "You're getting predictable."

"And you aren't?" Rose snapped, no longer bothering to hide the hostility she was feeling. "Listen to me," she hissed as he began turning away, as if his back might shield him from her words.

"It's no good, Jack, it's just no good. I'm a normal woman, with normal desires, and I deserve some kind of normal satisfaction. Although God knows why I should expect that in a home that's anything but normal. Maybe there's nothing we can do for Sarah, but I should think that you, at least, would want to do what you can before you get just like her."

"It's not that easy—" Jack began, but she didn't give him time to defend himself.

"What is easy? Is it easy to live with a man like you? Easy to live with a child like Sarah? Easy to keep on acting as if nothing is the matter? Business as usual? How long do you think I can keep it up? God knows, every woman that's ever married into this family has had her hands full just being the latest Mrs. Conger for this godforsaken village. But that's not enough, not any more. Not only do I have to be Mrs. Conger, but I have to be a loving mother to a traumatized child, a loving wife to an impotent husband, and push real estate on the side."

"You don't have to do that," Jack put in, grabbing at the only available straw.

"Don't I?" Rose demanded. "Don't I? Well, let me

tell you one more thing. Pushing real estate is the easy part. It's the only fun I get out of life any more, and besides, it gives us enough money to keep Sarah at White Oaks. So don't talk to me about what's easy. For Christ's sake, all I'm asking you to do is go and *talk* to somebody!"

Talk to somebody. Talk to somebody. The words echoed in his mind, bouncing back and forth off the inside of his skull. It sounded so easy.

Just go talk to somebody.

But about what? About what he'd done to Sarah? About why he'd done it? He wasn't even sure what he'd done, and if he wasn't sure what he'd done, how could he begin to be sure why he'd done it? And it wasn't as if he hadn't tried. He'd spent months with Dr. Belter. The psychiatrist had spent hours with him, hours with Sarah, hours with the two of them together, watching them interact, trying to discover from some clue in the way they related to each other what had happened. He'd beaten her—Jack knew that now. But he couldn't remember starting to beat her; he couldn't remember administering the blows. All he could remember was being in the woods, then carrying Sarah out of the woods. And her face. For some reason he could remember her face, the tiny, dark, great-eyed face, peering desperately up at him, the frightened eyes not understanding what was happening, pleading with him to help her.

If he could remember, he could deal with it. But it was as if it had all happened to somebody else and he had been a witness to it. A witness who didn't want to see.

They had even tried hypnosis. But that too had failed. Dr. Belter had warned him that some people simply cannot be hypnotized, and he had proved to be one of them. Deep inside he harbored the distinct feeling that he could have been hypnotized, but simply didn't want to be; that whatever was inside him was too fearsome to bring out, that he was protecting himself from a weakness too ugly to face. And it had formed a vicious circle, the guilt feeding on the doubt, the doubt growing as the guilt increased. Finally, when he could no longer face those awful silent hours with the doctor, sipping coffee and wishing desperately that he could bring himself to talk, if not about the incident with Sarah then at least about the impotence that had resulted, he had given up. He had come to terms with himself, and they were not easy terms. He would live with the guilt, and he would live with the impotence, and he would live with the questions about what had really happened. But he would not have to know. And he had come to believe that to know what had happened would be the worst thing of all.

He stared silently across the table at Rose, wondering if there was any way to convey all of this to her, trying to think of what he could possibly say, when he was rescued from having to say anything at all. Mrs. Goodrich's voice was pouring forth from the kitchen.

"Miss Sarah, you stop that, do you hear me?"

There was a crash, the sound of pots and pans falling to the floor, followed by the sound of Sarah's voice rising into the wordless wail that for a year had been her only means of communicating her pain to the world.

"Dear God," Rose breathed, letting her head sink into her hands. "How much more?" Then she pulled herself together and started toward the kitchen, wondering what it would be this time. She didn't see Elizabeth enter the dining room from the other door.

Elizabeth paused as her mother left the room and waited a moment, listening to the chaos from the kitchen. As it subsided, she relaxed and moved to the table. Still in his chair, Jack stared vacantly at the door leading through the butler's pantry to the kitchen, his face pale. Elizabeth reached out a hand to touch him.

"It's all right, Daddy," she said softly. "It's over now."

At the touch, Jack started. His mind registered the fact that he hadn't been aware of Elizabeth's presence, and he felt the fear sweep over him again. He tried to cover it with a smile.

"Hello, Princess," he said, fighting to control the shakiness in his voice. "I didn't hear you come in."

"I wonder what she was doing," Elizabeth said, standing close to her father. "I hope she didn't hurt herself."

"I'm sure she didn't," Jack said, though he was far from sure. "Have a seat, and I'll pour you some juice."

Elizabeth grinned at him crookedly. "How about if I sit on your lap?" she said.

"My lap? Aren't you getting a little big for that?"

"Sometimes I like to feel small again," Elizabeth replied. "Do you ever feel like that?"

"Everyone feels like that," Jack said, opening his arms. "Climb on up and be small for a while."

The girl sat on his knee, and Jack put an affectionate arm around her waist. And then the door opened once more, and Rose stood staring stonily at him.

"I beg your pardon," she said, her voice icy and her eyes accusing him. "I didn't mean to interrupt anything."

"You're not—" Elizabeth started to say, but she wasn't allowed to finish.

"Take your chair, Elizabeth," her mother snapped. Obediently Elizabeth left her father's lap and sat down in her chair. She reached for the orange juice and poured herself a glass.

Jack started to rebuke his wife, then changed his mind. "Is everything all right out there?" he said instead.

"Mrs. Goodrich has it under control, and Sarah seems to have settled down, but the kitchen's a mess.

Mrs. Goodrich thinks she was trying to get at the knife case for some reason."

"The knife case?" Jack repeated. Elizabeth began buttering a piece of danish.

"Well, of course, she's not sure," Rose continued. "I can't imagine what she'd want to do with a knife."

"No," Jack said briefly, "I can't either." Then he searched his mind for another subject, something that would take all their minds off what had just happened. Suddenly he brightened and turned to Elizabeth.

"Did you ever find Cecil?" he said.

Elizabeth shook her head. "I don't know what happened to him. He must've run off somewhere. He'll be back. Cats are like that, I guess. I'd rather have a dog, anyway. They pay more attention to you."

"I asked Mrs. Goodrich to look for him the other day," Rose said, her foot moving to the button on the floor that would summon the housekeeper. "But I forgot all about it till this minute." Rose, too, was glad for the distraction from the unpleasantness that had clouded an otherwise beautiful morning. Outside the sun was shining brightly. The door to the butler's pantry opened, and Mrs. Goodrich's stocky frame appeared.

"Yes?"

"I'm sorry to bother you, Mrs. Goodrich, I know it hasn't been the best morning. But I was just wondering, did you ever find Cecil the other day?"

"I got better things to do than search for an independent cat," the housekeeper said shortly. Then she relented. "No, I didn't. And I searched this place from top to bottom." She seemed to think a moment, then spoke again. "Which reminds me. Somebody around here not satisfied with my work?"

"Not satisfied?" Rose said blankly. "What do you mean?"

"Well," Mrs. Goodrich said, shifting her weight from

one leg to the other, "someone's been up in the attic, cleaning. If you'd wanted the attic cleaned, you might have told me. I'm getting along, but I can still keep this house."

Rose glanced at her husband and her daughter; they both shrugged their innocence. "I'm sure I don't know who cleaned it," Rose said, trying her best to suggest that it probably hadn't been cleaned at all. "And you didn't see any traces of Cecil?"

"Cats don't leave traces," Mrs. Goodrich said bluntly. She turned, then stepped aside. " 'Scuse me," she said, and edged around the small form of Sarah, who had been standing, hidden behind the housekeeper's bulky form, through the whole conversation about the cat. Her eyes were filled with tears, and she was shaking.

Elizabeth moved quickly to her sister and put her arms around her, stilling Sarah's sobs with her embrace.

"It's all right, Sarah," she said softly. "If Cecil doesn't show up, we can get another cat. Or maybe even a dog," she added wistfully. Sarah's trembling increased, and she seemed about to scream. Then she relaxed under Elizabeth's loving smile.

Rose watched Elizabeth dry Sarah's eyes and lead her to the table, and wished once more that she had the compassion for Sarah that her older daughter clearly had. She banished the twinge of guilt she felt pass through her and poured more coffee, first for herself, then for Jack. It was in the way of calling a truce, at least for a while.

12

Port Arbello basked in the unusual warmth of the fall afternoon, and the sun warmed not only the air but also the atmosphere within the house at the end of the Point. By noon, a feeling of peace had overtaken the house, a peace all the Congers felt. The strain of the morning dissipated, and the undeclared truce between Jack and Rose seemed to be blossoming into an armistice. Within themselves, they wondered how long it would last, but each of them was determined to enjoy it while it was there.

"I love Indian summer," Rose commented over lunch. "Let's do something this afternoon."

"Can't," Jack said apologetically. "I already promised Ray Norton a round of golf."

Rose felt a caustic phrase concerning neglect of family rise to her throat. She fought it down before it had the chance to ruin their lunch.

"I've got some work to do anyway," she said, and there was nothing in her voice to suggest disappointment, hostility, or anything else that might destroy the good mood she could feel in the room. Jack, who had been expecting some sort of dart, looked up in surprise.

"I could cancel it," he offered, and Rose knew it was a genuine offer.

"No, you go ahead," she said, the intention being sufficient for the fact. They finished lunch in the comfortable silence that often occurs between people who love each other, but which had been absent from their lives for so long. They greeted it with appreciation, and did nothing to disturb it.

Jack left for his golf game, and the children disappeared upstairs. Rose wandered to her office in the small room at the front of the house and shuffled some papers around. She found she couldn't concentrate. She left the office and rambled down the hall to the study at the rear. She entered the study, and something caught her eye. It was so fast, she wasn't sure it had happened—one of those instants when one is sure one saw something, but has no idea what. She glanced around the room, but nothing was amiss. She closed the door behind her and sat down. It was a pleasant room, and the sun streamed through the window. It flashed off an ancient brass spittoon that had been converted to a standing ashtray, and it occurred to Rose that that must have been what caught her eye as she entered. Then she glanced up at the old portrait above the mantel.

It had to be an ancestor, she knew. The resemblance to Elizabeth was too remarkable for the girl in the picture not to be a Conger. But which one?

They had found the picture up in the attic more than a year ago. But then the trouble with Sarah—as Rose liked to phrase it—had started, and it had not been until a month ago that she had remembered the portrait and brought it downstairs. It was odd, she reflected, not for the first time, how the painting had been tucked away in a corner. The Congers, who had apparently been much given to ancestor worship, had a large rack in the attic upon which those ancestors not currently on display in the lower portion of the house could be neatly stored. At the moment, the group in storage included nearly everybody; only Jack's mother still enjoyed the light of day over the fireplace in the living room. Even with all the ancestors in residence, there had still been plenty of room in the rack for the picture of the young girl. But she hadn't been there. Instead, she had been hidden away in a corner.

The other odd thing was that the girl was not identified. The frames of all the other portraits bore neat brass plates giving the name, date of birth, and date of death of their subjects. Except this one. This one had once borne such a plate, as evidenced by the two tiny nail holes in the bottom rail of the frame, but it had been removed.

Rose stared at the portrait and wondered what had banished the little girl from the family gallery. Her imagination ran wild, and she entertained herself for some time creating scenarios to account for the girl's fall from grace.

And then it hit her. It had not been the sunlight on the spittoon that had caught her eye. It had been something in the portrait. She studied it carefully, trying to force her mind to make the connection again, to tell her what it was that she had recognized. Then it came to her.

It was the bracelet. The bracelet on the girl's wrist. She had seen it before, very recently. But where? It was a gold bracelet, and it seemed to be set with some sort of stone. It looked like opal, but in the old oil she couldn't be sure. It could have been something else.

She concentrated on remembering where she had seen the bracelet, why it was suddenly familiar. She drew a blank, and the longer she stared at the picture, the surer she became that it was not a real memory, but a simple *déjà vu*. The illusion of memory. She reached up to adjust the picture, which seemed to be tilted just slightly off center, and decided that she wasn't going to spend any more time worrying about a bracelet in a picture. She really did have work to do.

She returned to her study, determined to avoid looking out the window until she was well into the rhythm of her work. The day was just too pretty, and she knew that if she looked out too soon she would find an excuse to close her files and go out into the sun. But the sun could wait. She burrowed into the stack of papers on the desk.

She didn't really hear the door open an hour later, but was aware that she was no longer alone. She looked around and discovered that Sarah was with her, standing just inside the door, her huge brown eyes fixed on her mother. Rose put down her pen.

"Sarah," she said, and held out her arms. Slowly, almost warily, Sarah approached her. The little girl stopped when she was just beyond Rose's reach.

"She wants you to play with her," Elizabeth said from the door. Rose glanced up.

"I didn't see you," she said. "Come in."

"Not now," Elizabeth said. "I'm going outside for a while. Sarah wants you to play with her."

"What does she want me to play?"

"Whatever," Elizabeth said. "I'll see you later." She disappeared, and a moment later Rose heard the front door open and close. She turned her attention back to Sarah.

"What would you like to play?" she asked the silent child.

Sarah merely stood there; then, after a few seconds, she backed a few paces away from Rose and sat heavily on the floor. Rose frowned slightly, then left her chair and joined her daughter on the floor.

"Pease porridge hot," Rose tried, clapping her hands first on her thighs, then together, then silently outward. There was no response from Sarah, who simply sat on the floor, her face in repose, staring steadily at her mother. Rose decided to try it again, this time guiding her daughter's hands through the routine.

"Pease porridge cold," she said. "Now let's try it together."

She went through the routine again, and on the first

"Pease" Sarah's hands clapped against her thighs. But as Rose resumed the chant, the child's hands continued to slap her thighs, never progressing to the other variations. Rose found herself playing with empty air. Determinedly, she continued the game. Sarah's hands clapped a steady rhythm against her thighs. Finally, when Rose stopped the game, Sarah's hands continued to move, clapping hollowly into the silence.

Rose watched the mindless clapping for a minute or two, then could stand it no more. She picked the child up and sat in a large chair, Sarah in her lap. The girl did not resist, but Rose had the distinct feeling that if she did not continue to support her daughter, the child would slip to the floor. She picked up a magazine from a table next to the chair, and began to leaf through it. Every now and then Sarah's hand would reach out to stop the pages from turning. The third time it happened, Rose realized that Sarah was stopping the pages wherever there was a picture of a cat.

"I know, darling," she whispered. "If Cecil doesn't come back in another day or two, we'll get you another cat."

And suddenly Sarah was gone. Before Rose could do anything, the girl had wriggled from her lap and dashed out of the room. Rose could hear her retreating footsteps pounding up the stairs, and started to follow. Then she stopped, realizing that there was little she could do, since she had no way of finding out from Sarah what had gone wrong. She stood in her office door for a minute, listening carefully, but heard no sounds from above. It wasn't until she was sure of the silence that she allowed herself to realize that she had not been expecting silence. She had been expecting pandemonium, an encore of this morning's tantrum. When it failed to materialize, she felt relief. She left the office door open and returned to her desk.

She had no idea how much later it was when she

once more got the feeling that she was not alone. She
glanced over her shoulder, and there, standing once
more just inside the door, was Sarah. She seemed to
start slightly when Rose glanced at her, and Rose
turned quickly back to her work. But she was careful
to listen for her daughter's slightest movement.

Sarah came into the room and began moving around,
touching objects, picking things up to examine them,
then putting them back where she had found them.
Rose heard the small feet shuffling around the room,
heard the tiny clicks as Sarah replaced the things she
picked up. Then there was a silence, but Rose restrained herself from looking around to see what the
girl was up to. Then she felt something touch her leg,
and realized that Sarah had crept under the desk. Rose
smiled to herself as she remembered how much fun
she had had as a child pretending a desk was a cave.
If her daughter was anything like she had been, she
would be happy there the rest of the afternoon. Rose
turned all her attention back to her work.

As the afternoon wore on, Rose was occasionally
aware of movement under the desk, but it wasn't until
she felt something being fastened around her ankle that
she finally put her work aside. She sat very still, wondering what it was that Sarah was attaching to her.
She waited, expecting something to touch her other
leg, and she wasn't disappointed.

The girl was tying her feet together. Rose began
planning the show she would put on for her daughter
when Sarah had finished. She had tried the same trick
as a child, tying her father's shoestrings together as he
sat at his desk, and had been gratified when he stood
up, stumbled violently, then crashed around the room
for almost a full minute before collapsing to the floor
in a hopeless tangle. At the time it had never occurred
to her that her father had not actually been out of control of the situation, and, indeed, it wasn't until this
very minute that she realized that he had put on the

same carnival for her that she was about to stage for Sarah. Then she felt Sarah finish.

"Well," she said loudly. "That's that. I guess I'll stretch my legs." She could picture the child grinning and quivering with suppressed laughter beneath her.

Rose pushed away from the desk and moved her feet carefully to test the length of the string she was sure was hobbling her ankles. It seemed to very long indeed, and she wondered how she was going to be able to fake the thing convincingly.

It wasn't until she was fully away from the desk that she realized that there was no string at all, that it was something entirely different that was around her ankles.

She reached down and felt something hard. When she looked, she felt her heart skip a beat, and had that feeling in her stomach that she often got when an elevator dropped away beneath her feet. It was the bracelet.

She pulled it from her ankle, forgetting about Sarah for the time being, and examined it carefully. Yes, it was the bracelet from the picture: gold set with a small opal. Tiny flecks of dirt clung to it, as if it had been lying outdoors for a long time. She stood up, intending to take it into the rear study for a careful comparison, and felt something else, something flopping against her other ankle.

She looked down once more, and didn't immediately recognize the other object. It was a pale, whitish color, but badly stained, and seemed to have a buckle of some kind on it. Then she realized what it was.

A collar.

A cat's plastic flea collar.

"Where in the world—" she muttered as she unfastened the collar from her ankle. She straightened up and examined the collar. It was dirty too, but it was not the same kind of dirt that was on the bracelet. The collar bore specks of a reddish-brown substance.

It took a while for Rose to realize that the substance looked like dried blood. When she did realize what it was, she stepped to the office door.

"Mrs. Goodrich," she called. "Come here, please. Quickly."

When she turned back to the study she realized that Sarah was still under the desk, tightly crouched, her small face peering out of the darkness like a rabbit trapped in a hole. Rose stared back at the child, not having any idea what to say. When Mrs. Goodrich appeared at the door, Rose hadn't moved.

"I sure hope my pies don't get ruined," the old woman said, wiping her hands on her apron. Then, when Rose didn't turn around to face her, she stopped wiping her hands and spoke again.

"Is something wrong, Miz Rose?" she asked.

"I—I don't know," Rose said unsteadily. "Look at this."

She held out the flea collar, and Mrs. Goodrich reached to take it from her.

"Looks like a flea collar," the housekeeper said. "Same kind we put on Cecil." Her eyes caught sight of the stain. "Here, what's this?"

"I'm not sure," Rose said, hoping Mrs. Goodrich would offer an alternative.

"Why, it's blood," the woman said. "Well, if that don't beat all. Where'd this come from?"

"Sarah," Rose said vaguely. "Sarah put it on my ankle."

"Well, that's a peculiar thing to do," the old woman said. "Where do you suppose she got it from?"

"I'm not sure," Rose said. "I don't have any idea at all, really."

"Well, if she got it off that cat, I wish she'd tell us where the cat is." She sniffed the air. "I smell my pies." She bustled away, and Rose listened to her footsteps fade down the hall.

"Sarah?" Rose said. The child crept a little way out

from under the desk. "Sarah, darling, it's all right," Rose said, not knowing if it was all right or not. "Come out from under there."

She reached down and gently pulled her daughter the rest of the way out, then picked her up and carried her upstairs. She set Sarah on the bed and covered her with a comforter. "Take a little nap," she said, and bent down to kiss her gently on the forehead. She was behaving with a calm that she did not feel.

She heard Jack's car coming up the drive as she went back down the stairs, and waited for him at the front door.

"Hi," he said, but the smile faded from his face when he saw how pale she was. "What's wrong?" he asked. "Has something happened?"

"I don't know," Rose said quietly. "Let's go into the study. I'll be with you in a minute."

She stepped into her office and picked up the bracelet and the collar. Then she followed Jack down the hall.

"Why don't you pour us both a drink," she said, closing the door behind her. Jack looked at her curiously.

"You sound upset," he said. "What's been going on around here?"

She told him what had happened and showed him the two objects. He examined the collar briefly, then turned his attention to the bracelet.

"This looks familiar," he said slowly. "I'd swear I've seen it before, but I can't remember where."

"The picture," Rose said.

"Picture?" Then he looked to where she was pointing, and his eyes found the bracelet on the little girl's wrist. "Good Lord," he breathed. "Are you sure it's the same one?"

"I haven't compared them yet, but yes, I'm sure," Rose said. "And the strangest thing is that earlier, before Sarah put it on my ankle, I was looking at the bracelet in the picture. I was almost sure I'd seen it somewhere before, other than in the picture."

"Has Sarah been wearing it?" Jack asked.

"I don't know. If she has, I hadn't noticed it consciously. But I suppose she must have been."

Jack moved to the picture and held the bracelet up next to its representation in the portrait. It was the same bracelet.

"It's the collar that worries me more," Rose said, taking a long swallow from her drink.

"The collar?"

"Well, where do you suppose she got that? And how do you suppose the blood got on it?"

"You mean Cecil?" There was clear disbelief in his voice.

"What else could it be?"

"Oh, now, come on, Rose. Sarah loves that cat."

"I know," Rose said miserably. "But put it all together. The cat's gone, Sarah was apparently trying to get at the knives just this morning, then she got upset at pictures of cats this afternoon. And now that." She pointed to the bloody collar.

"You think she's killed Cecil."

The words hit Rose, and she recoiled almost visibly. She realized that that was exactly what she thought; she had merely refused to put words to it. She nodded dumbly.

"I don't believe it," Jack said. "I just don't believe it."

"Then where did she get that collar? And the bracelet, too, for that matter."

"I don't know," Jack said. "But I don't believe she killed Cecil. She wouldn't do a thing like that."

"How do we know she wouldn't, Jack? How do we know what she would do or wouldn't do?" She was on the verge of tears, and Jack reached out to comfort her, but she turned away.

"What do you think we ought to do?" Jack said.

"Call the school, I suppose," Rose said. "Talk to Dr. Belter. He wanted to know if anything unusual happened. And God knows this is unusual."

"What are we going to tell him?" Jack said uneasily. "That Sarah found a couple of things and we think she killed the cat?"

"I don't know," Rose replied. "I'll just tell him exactly what happened and see what he thinks about it."

"When are you going to call him?" A note of belligerence had crept into his voice.

"Right now," Rose replied, moving to the phone. She dialed the telephone, and was connected to the doctor a couple of minutes later. He listened to her story, and when she finished he asked some questions.

"How is she now?" he wanted to know.

"Sarah? I guess she's all right. She doesn't seem to be upset, if that's what you mean. She's upstairs, sleeping."

Dr. Belter considered, then spoke again.

"Why don't you both come to the school on Monday? You and your husband? Then we can talk about it. Can it wait until then?"

"Well, I suppose so," Rose said, but she wasn't sure it could. Dr. Belter heard the uneasiness in her voice.

"I'll tell you what. If anything else happens, you call me, and I'll be right out there. Otherwise, I'll see you on Monday."

"All right," Rose agreed. "I suppose that'll be fine. Thank you, Doctor." She hung up the phone, and was about to tell Jack what had been arranged when she saw his eyes move from her own to a spot behind her and the blood drain from his face. She whirled around, not knowing what to expect.

It was Elizabeth, and she was a mess. The dress that had been so clean when she left the house was now filthy, covered with mud, and the muck was streaked over her face as well.

"My God," Rose said. "What happened?"

"I'm sorry," Elizabeth said, and it was the voice of a small girl. "I was out by the quarry. I slipped in the mud."

"What were you doing out there?" Jack demanded. "You could have killed yourself."

Elizabeth seemed on the verge of tears. "I said I was sorry," she repeated. "I'm all right. It's—it's only mud."

"That dress," Rose snapped. "You've ruined that dress. Get it off immediately and give it to Mrs. Goodrich. Maybe she can save it."

Elizabeth burst into tears and fled from the room. Rose watched her go, and doubted that Mrs. Goodrich would be able to save the dress. It looked to be as ruined as the afternoon. Rose, too, felt like crying.

"Oh, shit," she said miserably.

"It's only a dress," Jack said soothingly.

"No it's not," Rose said. "It's everything." She felt the hopelessness sweep over her.

13

"And that's where we are as of now," Dr. Charles Belter concluded, closing the file in front of him. He glanced around the room, noting that Marie Montgomery looked unhappy and Josephine Wells looked annoyed. The three of them were waiting for Jack and Rose Conger, and Josephine Wells had suggested that it would be a good idea to review the entire file before their arrival. The mind of a bureaucrat, Dr. Belter had thought, but he had complied. Now he looked at Josephine Wells. "Any questions?"

"It strikes me," Josie Wells said, and Dr. Belter noted to himself that things invariably "struck" Josie Wells, "that there must be a lot more going on here than we know about."

Dr. Belter tried to keep his face straight, and did his best to nod gravely. "Go on," he said, knowing that she would anyway.

"It strikes me," Miss Wells said again, and this time Charles Belter had to fight down an impulse to do exactly that, "that we should be looking beyond Sarah as an individual, and trying, rather, to fathom the greater socio-psychological factors involved within the structure of the prime unit."

"If you mean we should talk to her family," Dr. Belter remarked drily, "that's exactly what we're about to do. If they ever get here." He glanced at his watch and noted that it was still five minutes until the time

the Congers were due. He braced himself to tolerate
further pontificating from the social worker.

"What I'm trying to say," Miss Wells said, tapping
her front teeth with the end of the Pentel she always
carried, apparently for no other purpose, since she
rarely took notes, "is that what we seem to have here
is a clear case of regression." Miss Wells, who felt that
her Master of Social Welfare degree qualified her as a
psychologist, a sociologist, and a sage, leaned back and
looked pleased with herself.

"And?" Dr. Belter prompted.

"And therefore it strikes me that we should be
trying to find out toward what she is regressing."

Dr. Belter shot a glance to Mrs. Montgomery, but
the teacher's face was a bland mask of innocence.
Marie Montgomery had discovered long ago that with
Josie Wells it was best to sit quietly and listen. Any
response was all too likely to carry Miss Wells further
into the mazes of gobbledygook that she mistook for
erudition. Marie caught Dr. Belter's glance, and wondered how he was planning to deal with the social
worker's impossible idea.

"I think you're absolutely right," Dr. Belter said
gravely. "I suggest that you have copies made of the
entire file immediately, and begin comparing common
factors between the prenatal experience of Sarah and
the postpartum depression futeriundus of her mother."
The doctor was pleased to see Josie Wells's Pentel
scribble a word. He wondered how many books she
would search before she finally decided there was no
such word as "futeriundus." Then it struck him that
it was more likely she would simply attach a meaning
to the word, and proceed to carry out his instructions.
He sighed to himself and cursed the necessity of having
a social worker in his midst. When he saw the Congers
driving up to the building, his sigh became audible. He
braced himself and put on a broad smile as they were

ushered into his office, so that neither of them was aware that he was, while greeting them, examining them minutely.

He noted the obvious strain in Rose's face, the strain that had been growing there for a year. It didn't seem any worse than the last time he had seen her, but there were other signs now, signs that her composure was wearing thin. Her hair, usually perfectly set, was beginning to show the first signs of disarray. Not that it was messy—not by any means; it simply wasn't as perfect as usual. And there was a tiny spot on the jacket of her pants suit, a spot that most people would never notice but nevertheless a spot that Dr. Belter knew Rose Conger would not normally tolerate.

Jack, on the other hand, seemed totally unchanged. It should be showing, Dr. Belter thought. Unless he's some sort of monster. But Charles Belter did not believe people were monsters, so he looked more closely. He found what he was looking for in Jack's fingernails: He was beginning to chew on them. Not enough so they looked chewed, but just slightly uneven, as if he would chew one, then smooth it out with a file, leaving it shorter than the others.

"Sit down," Dr. Belter said warmly. "We've just been discussing Sarah. Since you didn't call again, I gather yesterday was quiet?"

"Well," Rose said, "I'm not sure what quiet is any more. If you mean nothing happened, nothing out of the ordinary, I suppose you could say nothing happened. But I'm afraid I have to say that I think she's getting worse."

"Rose!" Jack said. "I don't think that's fair."

"No," Rose said tiredly. "I know you don't think it's fair. And it may not be. I will grant you that I'm not a psychologist, and I will grant you that I have no training in the sort of disorders Sarah has. But I'm a mother, and I know how I feel. And I feel worn out, and I feel sick, and I feel my daughter isn't getting any better—"

"That's a lot different from getting worse," Jack interjected.

"All right, maybe I'm wrong. You tell us," she appealed to the doctor. Then she recounted the events of Saturday, leaving out none of the details. Dr. Belter listened carefully, as did the teacher and the social worker. When Rose was finished, he leaned back in his chair, closed his eyes, and seemed to be considering something. No one in the room spoke, and it passed through Jack's mind that the doctor looked just like Santa Claus. Had he known of the thought, Dr. Belter would have been pleased.

Eventually he opened his eyes again, and turned to Marie Montgomery. "Any ideas?"

She shook her head. "Not at the moment. Frankly, it doesn't sound to me like Sarah's getting worse."

Jack's eyes lit up. "No?" he said eagerly.

"Well," Marie Montgomery said carefully, "it seems to me that the fact that she was able to concentrate on something as long as she did in order to get that collar onto your ankle indicates that she may be getting a little better. Granted, it was a macabre thing for her to do— at least, it seems so to us, but it may not have been macabre to her at all. It may have been something else entirely." She reviewed the incident with the magazine and Sarah's reaction to the pictures of cats. "She may have been trying to tell you something."

"Such as?" Rose asked.

The teacher shrugged. "That's the hard part. You have to remember that Sarah's mind isn't working the same way as yours and mine. There's really no way for us to know what she was trying to communicate. But whatever it was, it must have been important. She doesn't normally spend that much time doing anything, let alone anything that takes the dexterity of fastening one of those plastic collars. They're tricky."

Dr. Belter nodded his head in agreement, and seemed

to come to a decision in his own mind. He spoke to his colleagues. "I think I'd better talk to the Congers alone, if you don't mind."

Josephine Wells started to protest, but Mrs. Montgomery was already on her feet. "Of course," she said, over the social worker's voice. "If you need us, page us." Before Josie could say anything, Marie Montgomery was pulling her out of the office. Dr. Belter waited until the door was closed before he spoke.

"You two are having a rough time of it, aren't you?" he said at last. Rose and Jack stared at him, each waiting for the other to speak. The silence lengthened, until Rose broke it.

"Yes," she said, barely audibly. "We are. And it isn't all Sarah."

Dr. Belter's head bobbed. "Not directly, anyway. Do you want to tell me what's going on at your house?"

Rose waited for Jack to speak, but when he didn't she began talking about their problems. As she talked she became aware of a strange detachment, as though she were talking about two other people, not herself and her husband. She recounted the fights and the cruelties they had inflicted on each other, and was surprised to discover that she was being fair; she was presenting Jack's side of things as well as her own. When she was finished, Dr. Belter turned to Jack.

"You want to add anything?"

"No," Jack said. He smiled at his wife. "I have to hand it to you—I couldn't have been that fair."

"Mrs. Conger," Dr. Belter said, "has it occurred to you that maybe you should be in therapy too?"

"What do you mean?" Rose said defensively.

Dr. Belter smiled easily. "Well, let's face it. Generally speaking, I consider emotional problems to be a communicable disease. If one person in a family is having problems, others usually are too, if for no other reason than that it is difficult to live with someone who is mentally ill. It is quite easy for someone with no particularly severe problems to develop some severe problems simply because of the extra pressure involved in living with a person as disturbed as Sarah."

"And you think I'm developing some severe problems?"

"Are you?" Dr. Belter tossed the question back to her.

Her initial impulse was to deny it, but Rose realized that she couldn't, not if she was honest. She remembered the moments of panic she was having, the tight feelings in her stomach, the sudden flashes of anger she felt, the way she had begun to overreact. An image came to her mind of Elizabeth fleeing from the study in tears, simply because Rose had yelled at her about getting her clothes dirty.

"You're suggesting that I could use some therapy too?" she asked noncommittally.

"I'm suggesting that both of you could use some therapy. You don't seem to be handling your problems very well, either of you, which is understandable, considering the circumstances. All I'm suggesting is that you both could use some help."

"Maybe we should throw in Elizabeth, too, and qualify for a family discount," Jack said. When the chuckle died away, Dr. Belter's face took on a serious cast.

"What about Elizabeth?" he said.

"She's incredible," Rose said. "Other than when I yelled at her on Saturday for getting her dress dirty, she's been an angel. She's patient with Sarah, takes care of herself. Sometimes I wonder what I'd do without her."

"She must be an amazing child," Dr. Belter mused. "Generally, a child her age, with a sibling like Sarah, would show at least intermittent hostility toward the sick brother or sister. It's because of the extra attention the sick one gets, of course, and it's perfectly natural."

"Well," Rose said, "we've had none of that sort of thing."

Jack grinned. "I guess Elizabeth is the only one of us who's immune to the family curse." He laughed, but his laughter faded when he noticed that the doctor had not joined him.

"Ah, yes," Dr. Belter said, leaning back once more and closing his eyes. "The Conger family curse."

"You've heard about it?" Jack said.

"Around Port Arbello, who hasn't? As a matter of fact, I probably know more about your family curse than you do."

"Oh?" Jack said guardedly. "How so?"

Dr. Belter smiled at him. "I make it a practice to find out everything I can about all my patients, and their families. So when I first met you people, I started snooping."

"And what did you find?" Rose asked.

"A certain Reverend Caspar Winecliff," Dr. Belter said, savoring the name.

"You mean the old Methodist minister?" Jack said, his brows arching. "We hardly know the man."

"Ah, but he knows you," the doctor intoned, enjoying the baffled looks on the Congers' faces. Then he dropped the air of mystery.

"Actually, Caspar Winecliff simply has a passion for local legend and folklore, particularly with reference to New England curses and that sort of thing. My personal opinion is that he enjoys the subject because he thinks it's wicked and flies in the face of his good Methodist background. If you ask me, he believes every word of every legend he's ever heard, though of course he denies it. And the Conger legend happens to be his favorite."

"You're kidding," Jack said. "I knew the legend wasn't any great secret, but I didn't know anybody was that interested in it."

"I didn't either, until I was down at the library one day asking some questions. I was hoping to find some old papers or something that would have the legend written up. They didn't, but the librarian put me onto Caspar Winecliff. How much do you know about your legend?"

Jack recounted as much of it as he knew, and when he was finished the doctor nodded his head.

"That's it, all right, except for the story about the little girl."

Jack and Rose glanced at each other, and Dr. Belter thought he saw alarm in their eyes.

"What little girl?" Jack said apprehensively. For some reason, an image of the portrait in the study came to his mind.

"It has to do with the relative who went off the cliff," the doctor began, looking inquiringly at Jack.

"I know about him," Jack said. "I'm not sure what his name was."

"It was John Conger, actually," Dr. Belter said seriously. "The same as yours."

Jack felt a chill in his spine. "What about him?"

"Well," Dr. Belter said, "the story is that the reason he jumped off the cliff was that he had just molested and killed a little girl. His daughter."

The blood drained from Jack's face, and he stared coldly at the doctor.

"Just what are you trying to say?"

The doctor smiled reassuringly. "I'm not trying to say anything. I'm just telling you the story. And, of course, it could be entirely apocryphal. Caspar Winecliff tells me they never found a body, and, for that matter, there don't seem to be any records of John Conger's ever having had a daughter."

Rose saw the portrait in her mind's eye, with the nameplate removed from the bottom of the frame.

"Did Reverend Winecliff have any idea of how old

the girl was, or what she looked like?" She was almost afraid to hear the answer.

Dr. Belter shook his head. "Nothing about what she looked like, but she was supposed to have been about ten or eleven years old."

"About the same age as Sarah?" Jack said, a distinct edge in his voice.

"Yes," Dr. Belter said, meeting his troubled gaze, "about the same age as Sarah."

"Dr. Belter," Rose said, "just what are you getting at? It sounds as though you believe in the whole silly legend."

Dr. Belter thought carefully before he answered, and when he spoke he chose his words precisely.

"Whether or not I believe in the legend isn't what's at issue here. What's at issue is whether or not your husband believes in it. Do you, Mr. Conger?"

Jack started to speak, but the doctor stopped him.

"Don't answer quickly, please. Think about it. And try to think about it on two levels. I'm sure your conscious mind doesn't believe that there could be any kind of curse on your family. In this day and age we tend to think of such things as silly. But there is also your subconscious mind. Often we find that the things our conscious minds refuse to take seriously our subconscious minds deal with in a very serious manner. Essentially, that is what dreams are all about, and, sometimes, neuroses and psychoses. One might say that mental illness results when our conscious minds and our unconscious minds try to do each other's jobs. So think about it before you answer my question."

Jack did, and found that he was amazed by the answer he came up with. He smiled sheepishly at the doctor.

"Okay," he said. "I guess I have to admit that I do believe in the legend, including the curse. I suppose with us Congers it's like religion. We were brought up with it, and while we know it's nonsense, it's still lurking there, just below the surface."

Dr. Belter nodded. "But you say you never heard of the little girl before?"

Jack shook his head. "No. I'm sure. I'd have remembered. Why?"

"Isn't it obvious? If the story of the little girl is true, there are some pretty strong parallels between what happened to her and her father, and what happened to you and Sarah. Except that with you and Sarah no molestation took place, and nobody died. But otherwise, it's the same thing."

"History repeating itself?" It was Rose's voice, and the two men turned to her. "I don't believe it."

"That's not exactly what I meant," Dr. Belter said. "Although the effect would be the same. Do either of you know anything about voodoo?"

"That it's a lot of hoodoo," Jack said, too quickly.

"Not quite," Dr. Belter replied. "It's based on the power of suggestion. Essentially, what it boils down to is this: If someone believes strongly enough that something will happen, it will, in all likelihood, happen. For instance, voodoo tradition has it that you can cause pain in a person by sticking pins in an effigy of that person. The catch is that the person has to *know* that pins are being stuck in the doll. Once he knows the pins are being placed, his own mind will create the pain. Do you see?"

Jack mulled it over. "In other words, you think I might be a victim of the legend, simply because I believe in it?"

"That's it," Dr. Belter said. "Simplified, but that's essentially it."

Rose smiled wryly. "Except that we didn't know anything about the relevant part of the legend. The little girl. You said yourself that there's no evidence she exists."

"But she does, Rose," Jack said quietly. "Don't you want to tell Dr. Belter what she looked like?"

Dr. Belter turned questioningly to Jack.

"We found a picture in the attic," Jack explained, and went on to tell the doctor about the portrait.

"But how can you be sure it's the same little girl? How can you even be sure it's a Conger child?"

"Because," Jack said, his voice a whisper now, "the girl in the picture looks exactly like Elizabeth."

"I see," Dr. Belter said after a long silence. "Mr. Conger, are you sure you never saw that picture before, or heard anything about it?"

"Not until a year ago," Jack said definitely. "Not that I can remember."

"Not that you can remember," the doctor repeated thoughtfully. "But we don't always remember everything we want to remember, do we? I think maybe it would be a good idea to try to find out exactly what you do remember."

Jack appeared to be about to object, but at the look on Rose's face, a look that told him he'd better agree, he sagged in defeat.

"Very well," he said. "When shall we begin?"

Dr. Belter examined his calendar. "How about two weeks from tomorrow, at one P.M.? Both of you."

Before Jack could protest Rose said, "We'll be there."

The session with Dr. Belter ended.

Neither of the Congers felt better about anything.

They were more frightened than ever.

14

Fifteen miles from White Oaks School, while Jack and Rose Conger sat chatting with Dr. Charles Belter, the final bell rang through the halls of Port Arbello Memorial School, and the children poured out of the classrooms. Elizabeth Conger picked Kathy Burton's face out of the crowd and hurried toward her.

An eager smile lit Kathy's face. "Is today the day?" she asked.

"What day?" Elizabeth's face was blank.

"Is this the day you're going to take me to the secret place?"

Elizabeth looked at her oddly, and Kathy's eyes widened as she felt a thrill of excitement run through her. Then she sagged with disappointment.

"I can't," Kathy said. "I'm supposed to go right out to the Nortons' to baby-sit."

"That's all right," Elizabeth said, her eyes suddenly seeming to bore into Kathy's. "The secret place is only a little farther out than their house, and it won't take very long."

"I don't know," Kathy said doubtfully, "I told Mrs. Norton I'd be there right after school."

The two girls left the school building and began walking toward the Conger's Point Road. As they left the town behind, Elizabeth began talking quietly about the secret place and the wonderful times she had there. As she talked, Kathy Burton began to wish she hadn't promised Mrs. Norton her baby-sitting services for the afternoon.

"Why don't we go tomorrow?" she asked.

Elizabeth shook her head. "No. It has to be today."

"Well, I don't see why it can't wait," Kathy sulked.

"It just can't, that's all," Elizabeth stated. "But if you don't want to go . . ." She let her voice trail off.

"But I do want to go," Kathy insisted. "It's just that I promised Mrs. Norton." She waited for a response from her friend, but when none came she looked at her watch.

"Maybe if we hurry," she said. "I could be a little late."

Elizabeth smiled at her and quickened her pace. "It'll be all right," she said. "You'll see. You'll love the secret place."

As they passed the Nortons' driveway, Kathy felt a twinge of guilt and wondered if Mrs. Norton was watching for her. When she didn't see anybody, or hear anyone calling her, she relaxed. When they were out of sight of the Nortons' house, she spoke.

"How much farther is it?"

"Not far. Just past the old Barnes place. Have you seen the people who bought it?"

"He's cute," Kathy said. "What's his name?"

"Jeff Stevens. He's fourteen. His mother's an artist."

"Does he know about the secret place?" Kathy asked.

Elizabeth shook her head. "I don't think I'll tell him," she said. "We'll keep it just for us."

They passed the old Barnes house, and looked curiously at it. They'd both heard that it was being remodeled, but from the outside it looked the same as ever.

"It sure is ugly," Kathy said.

"The Barneses were crazy," Elizabeth commented. "It's even weirder on the inside."

"You've been in it?" Kathy asked.

"Not for a long time," They were coming to the

woods now, and Elizabeth took Kathy by the arm. "We go through here," she said. Kathy looked at the woods nervously.

"I don't know," she said. "I'm not supposed to go in there. They think that's where something happened to Anne Forager."

"Nothing happened to Anne Forager," Elizabeth scoffed. "You know what a liar she is."

Kathy mulled it over. It was true, Anne Forager *was* a little liar, and she did want to see the secret place, but still . . . She made up her mind.

"All right," she said. "But you lead. I don't know the way out here."

They left the road and plunged into the woods. Their route took them through the center of the woods, and every now and then they caught a glimpse of the sea through the trees on one side or the field on the other. There was no trail, but Elizabeth seemed to have no trouble making her way through the underbrush. Kathy stumbled now and then, and had to call to Elizabeth to wait. She was determined not to fall behind. Then Elizabeth made a left turn, and in a couple of minutes they stood on the embankment, high above the surf.

"Isn't it beautiful?" Elizabeth whispered.

"Is this the place?" Kathy asked, looking around. Somehow it was not what she had expected.

"No," Elizabeth answered. "It's over that way." She led Kathy along the embankment, and at a certain spot, a spot that looked to Kathy to be no different from any other spot, Elizabeth started down the face of the embankment. Behind her, Kathy stopped.

"It looks awfully dangerous," she said. Elizabeth turned and looked up at her, and Kathy thought she saw something in Elizabeth's eyes, something that made her uneasy. "I'm not sure I ought to," she said nervously. "I really should be at the Nortons' by now."

"Are you chicken?" Elizabeth said scornfully. "Look, it's easy." She leaped from one rock to another, and

Kathy had to admit to herself that it did look easy. Besides, she wasn't chicken, and she wasn't going to let Elizabeth think she was. She began picking her way down the embankment, trying to follow the path Elizabeth had taken. It was not so easy.

Kathy told herself that she was having a harder time of it just because she hadn't done it before. Next time, she assured herself, she'd know the way and be able to go as fast as Elizabeth. She glanced up and saw Elizabeth disappearing behind an immense boulder. That must be it, she said to herself.

When she got to the boulder Elizabeth was waiting for her. Kathy crouched down in the deep shadow that cast the crevice between the boulder and the face of the embankment in almost total darkness.

"Is this it?" she whispered, and wondered why she was suddenly whispering.

"Almost," Elizabeth whispered back. "Look." She pointed to a spot deep within the blackness, and Kathy suddenly realized that it was not a darker shadow, but a small hole in the embankment.

"We aren't going in there, are we?" she whispered.

"Sure," Elizabeth whispered back. "Are you scared?"

"No," Kathy lied, and wondered how much face she would lose if she turned back now. "It's awfully dark, though, isn't it?"

"I have a light," Elizabeth said. She reached into the hole and pulled out the flashlight from its niche behind a rock just inside the mouth of the cave. She clicked it on and shined it into the opening.

"It's a tunnel," Kathy whispered. "Where does it go?"

"To the secret place," Elizabeth said. "Come on." She crept into the tunnel, and Kathy saw that there was enough room for Elizabeth to crawl along without hitting the roof of the cavern. Swallowing her fear, she followed Elizabeth.

In half a minute they were in the cavern surrounding the shaft. Elizabeth waited for Kathy to emerge from the tunnel, and heard Kathy say, "This is neat."

"We're not there yet," Elizabeth said. "The secret place is down there." She shined the light into the shaft, and heard Kathy suck in her breath.

"Where does it go?" she breathed.

"Down to the secret place. I have a ladder, see?" Elizabeth directed the beam of the flashlight to the rope ladder, which still hung in the shaft, securely anchored to the rocks on the cavern floor.

"I've never climbed one of those before," Kathy said, wondering if her lack of experience would get her off the hook.

"It's easy," Elizabeth said. "Look. I'll go first, and when I get to the bottom I'll hold the light for you. It isn't very far, and you won't fall. Besides, even if you do, you won't fall far enough to hurt yourself. I've done it lots of times, and there wasn't anybody to hold the light for me."

"How did you find this place?" Kathy asked, wanting to delay the moment when she knew she would have to conquer her fear.

"I don't know. I guess I've known about it for a long time. My friend told me."

"Your friend?"

"Never mind," Elizabeth said mysteriously. "Come on." Holding the light, she began climbing down the rope ladder, and in a few seconds she was on the floor of the pit. She shone the light up and saw Kathy's frightened face peering down at her.

"I can't see you," Kathy hissed.

"That's because I'm behind the light," Elizabeth hissed back. "Come down."

Kathy pondered the situation. She was afraid of the shaft, and of going down the ladder, but she didn't want Elizabeth to know how frightened she was. She glanced back toward the entrance to the tunnel, and the blackness there made up her mind for her. She wasn't about to try to make her way through the tunnel in the total darkness behind her. She eased herself over the lip of the shaft, and her feet found the ladder. The descent was much easier than she had thought it would be.

"I have some candles," Elizabeth whispered, keeping the flashlight trained on Kathy's face. In the glare, Kathy barely saw the flare of the match as Elizabeth struck it. Elizabeth put the match to two candles, then snapped the flashlight off. For a moment Kathy couldn't see anything in the gloom except the twin points of light, and Elizabeth's face looming in the glow.

"This is spooky," she said uncertainly. "I'm not sure we should be down here."

Her eyes began to adjust to the gloom, and she looked around the cavern. There didn't seem to be much to it—just a large, uneven room with some boulders strewn around. In the middle, some of the boulders had been arranged in a circle, like a table and chairs. Then Kathy saw something behind Elizabeth.

"What's that?" she asked. Elizabeth stepped aside, and Kathy's eyes slowly took in the skeleton that was neatly laid out along the wall.

Her scream was cut off by a sharp slap.

"You have to be quiet down here," Elizabeth said, in a whisper that seemed to Kathy to echo through the cavern more loudly than her scream. She wanted to scream again, but the sting of the slap kept her silent.

"We're going to have a party," Elizabeth whispered. "Just you and me and my baby."

"Baby?" Kathy repeated hollowly. "What baby?" She wasn't sure what Elizabeth was talking about, and her mind, clogged with confusion, couldn't seem to get a hold on anything. Then she knew that Elizabeth must be referring to a doll.

"Sit down," Elizabeth ordered her. "I'll bring the baby."

Slowly, Kathy sank onto one of the rocks that served

as a stool and watched in fascination as Elizabeth produced a sack and placed it on the tablelike boulder.

"It's broken," Kathy said as Elizabeth pulled a bundle of doll's clothes from the bag. "There's no head."

"Yes there is," Elizabeth muttered. "Here." She pulled the bonnet out of the bag and set it on the table. It rolled over, and the cavern echoed with another scream as Kathy saw the distorted features of the cat's face, the eyes open but sunken in now, the stump of flesh at the severed neck beginning to putrefy.

Kathy fought to control herself. She thought she was going to throw up.

"I don't want to stay here," she said, her voice quavering with the beginnings of hysteria. "Let's go home."

"But we have to have a party," Elizabeth said, her voice carrying a silky sweetness that somehow frightened Kathy even more. "That's why we came here." She began propping the body of the cat up on one of the rocks, and Kathy watched in horror as Elizabeth tried to balance the head on the decapitated torso.

"Stop that!" she cried. "Don't do that!" She felt the sting of another slap, and this time she struck back. Her hand flashed out, but before it could make contact with Elizabeth, the other girl had leaped on her.

Kathy felt Elizabeth's weight coming down on her and tried to brace herself, but there was nothing to brace herself against. She rolled off the rock to the floor of the cavern, and felt Elizabeth's fingernails digging into her face. She screamed again.

"Don't do that down here," Elizabeth said, the silkiness gone from her voice and her breath coming in quick, shallow gasps. "Down here you have to be quiet. My friend doesn't like noise."

Beneath her, Kathy whimpered, and tried to regain control of herself. She had to, she knew, or the beating would continue. She forced her body to go limp.

"Let me up," she whispered desperately. "Please,

Elizabeth, let me up." The beating ceased then, and Kathy felt the pressure ease as Elizabeth let go of her. She lay quietly, her eyes closed tightly, waiting for whatever would come.

"Sit there," she heard Elizabeth hiss. "Sit over there, and I'll pour us some tea."

Kathy opened her eyes slowly, and looked around. Elizabeth was sitting on the rock nearest the end of the dangling rope ladder, and Kathy felt her hopes fading. She had thought she might be able to climb out of the shaft before Elizabeth could stop her. Now, she could see, that would never happen. She got shakily to her feet, and sat carefully on the rock opposite Elizabeth. Between them, the macabre corpse of the cat sat propped on a third rock, its lips stretched back in a deathly grin. Kathy tried not to look at it.

"Now," Elizabeth said. "Isn't this nice?"

Kathy nodded dumbly.

"Answer me," Elizabeth snapped.

"Yes," Kathy whispered, afraid to raise her voice.

"What?" Elizabeth demanded, and Kathy was afraid for a moment that Elizabeth was going to hit her again.

"Yes," she said, louder this time.

"Yes what?" Elizabeth said relentlessly.

"Yes," Kathy said, wrenching every word out, "this is very nice." Elizabeth seemed to relax, and smiled at her.

"Tea?" Elizabeth asked.

Kathy stared at her.

"Answer me!" Elizabeth demanded. "Do you want some tea?"

"Y-yes," Kathy stammered. "Some tea . . ."

Elizabeth began to mime pouring tea and passing a cup to Kathy. Kathy hesitated for a split second, but quickly pretended to accept the invisible cup Elizabeth was holding out to her. There was an odd, wild look in Elizabeth's eyes, and Kathy felt panic beginning to grow in her. She wanted to bolt for the ladder, but knew there was no way she could get to it before Elizabeth got to her.

"I think we should go now," Kathy said slowly. "I really think we should. Mrs. Norton will be looking for me."

"Fuck Mrs. Norton," Elizabeth said quietly. Kathy's eyes widened at the word, and her fear grew.

"Please, Elizabeth," she said fearfully. "Can't we go now? I don't like it here."

"You don't like it?" Elizabeth said, glancing around at the dimly lit cavern. The flames flickered, and shadows danced evilly on the walls. "It's my secret place," Elizabeth went on. "And now it's yours, too. Only we know about this place."

Until I get home, Kathy thought. She fought to stay calm, and watched Elizabeth carefully.

Elizabeth was engrossed in the tea party, and was busy pouring for the wreckage that had been her pet, and pretending to pass cakes around. Her eyes fell once more on Kathy.

"Talk to me," she said.

"Talk to you?" Kathy repeated. "About what?"

"They don't talk to me, you know. None of them do. They only talk to Sarah, and she can't answer. So I come here, and my friends talk to me." She was staring into Kathy's eyes again, and there was a cold light in her own eyes. "All my friends talk to me here," she said again. Kathy licked her lips.

"I—I like your secret place," Kathy said carefully, hoping she was choosing the right words. "I'm glad you brought me here. But, please, I'm going to be awfully late for my job. If I get in trouble, I won't be able to come here with you again."

"You will," Elizabeth said with a smile, but the smile only made Kathy more uncomfortable. "You'll learn to love this place. You'll learn to love it as much as I do."

"Y-yes," Kathy said. "I suppose I will. But I have to go now. I really do," she pleaded.

Elizabeth seemed to consider it, then nodded.

"All right," she said at last. "Help me clear off the table."

She stood up and began to go through the motions of stacking up all the imaginary dishes. Kathy watched her in silence, but when Elizabeth glared at her she stood up and tried to convince Elizabeth that she was helping. She also tried to move near the shaft, but Elizabeth managed to keep herself between Kathy and the ladder.

"Blow out the lights," Elizabeth commanded. She stood at the bottom of the ladder, the flashlight in her hand.

"Turn on the flashlight," Kathy countered. Elizabeth snapped it on.

"Will you hold it while I climb up the ladder?"

Elizabeth nodded. Kathy moved toward the ladder.

"The candles," Elizabeth said softly. "I told you to blow them out."

Obediently Kathy turned back to the stone slab. She blew out one of the candles, then stooped over the other one. Just before she blew on its tiny flame, she stared over the flickering light and saw Elizabeth smiling at her. She blew out the candle.

As the flame died, Elizabeth snapped off the flashlight and darted up the rope ladder. Below her she could hear the first scream of terror burst from Kathy's throat.

"*Eliiiiiiizabeth!*" Kathy wailed. "*Noooooooo! Oh, God, Elizabeth, don't leave me here!*"

The screams built in intensity, and Elizabeth heard the other child stumbling around in the blackness of the pit, knowing that Kathy was trying to find the end of the rope ladder that should have dangled somewhere in the suffocating darkness. But she had already pulled the rope ladder out of the pit. Kathy's screams echoed around her, resounding off the walls of the upper chamber, pounding against her eardrums. She coiled the ladder, then moved once more to the top of the shaft.

She threw the beam of light downward and watched
Kathy swarmed into it like a moth around a lightbu

Kathy's face tipped up, drained of blood and shin
palely in the uncertain light of the electric torch. I
mouth was contorted into the shape of the screams t
tore upward from some spot deep in her guts, and
arms were upraised, pleading.

"Noooooo!" she screamed. *"Pleeeeeaaaase noooo*

Elizabeth held the flashlight steady and stared do
at her friend.

"You have to be quiet in the secret place," she s
softly. Then she snapped the light off and moved to
entrance of the tunnel by memory, surely, swiftly. §
began crawling toward the surface.

By the time she emerged on the embankment,
roaring of the surf drowned out whatever remnants
the screams might have found their way through
tunnel, and Elizabeth was pleased that she no lon
heard sounds from the secret place.

She began making her way deftly up the embar
ment and disappeared into the woods.

15

Marilyn Burton didn't begin worrying until eight o'clock that night. If she had been home earlier in the day she would have begun worrying then, but, having closed her shop at six as usual, she had decided to treat herself to a dinner out. She didn't mind eating alone; in fact, she rather enjoyed it. She talked to people all day in the store, and it was a relief to spend a few hours by herself, alone with her thoughts. She heard the phone ringing as she put her key in the door, just before eight, and a feeling came over her that something had gone wrong, that she was about to be alone with some thoughts she wouldn't enjoy.

"Marilyn?"

She recognized Norma Norton's voice immediately, and the feeling of unease intensified.

"Yes?" she said. "Something's happened, hasn't it?"

There was a short pause before Norma spoke again. "Well, I don't know," she said uncertainly. "That's why I'm calling you. I've been calling you all afternoon."

"Why didn't you call me at the store?"

"I did, but the line's out of order."

Marilyn frowned, then realized that she hadn't had any calls all afternoon. Nor had she had any reason to call out. The sound of her daughter's name brought her mind back to Norma Norton.

"I'm sorry," she said, "I was drifting. What about Kathy?"

"That's what I want to know," Norma said, her exasperation coming clearly over the line. "What about Kathy? She never showed up after school."

"She didn't?" Mrs. Burton said blankly. "That's strange."

"It's damned inconsiderate is what it is," Norma fumed. "I thought she might have gotten sick, but she could at least have called."

"Just a minute," Marilyn said. "I'll check here. I just got in." She set the phone down, but even as she walked toward Kathy's room she knew it would be empty. She was doing the same thing she had done when they'd called her to tell her that Bob was dead. Postponing the inevitable. Even knowing what she was doing, she still walked through the entire house before she returned to the telephone.

"She's not here," she said. She stood dumbly, waiting for the woman at the other end to pick up the conversation. There was a long, awkward silence as the memory of Anne Forager's strange story went through both their minds. Neither of them wanted to mention it.

"Maybe she went over to see a friend," Norma Norton said gently. "Maybe she forgot all about baby-sitting for me today."

"Yes," said Marilyn numbly. "I'll tell you what. Let me make a couple of calls, and I'll call you back when I find her. She certainly owes you an apology."

"Do you want me to call Ray?"

"Of course not," Marilyn replied, too quickly. "I'm sure everything is fine." But she knew it wasn't. She dropped the receiver back in its cradle and sat silently for a few minutes. Postponing the inevitable. Then she picked up the phone and dialed.

"Mrs. Conger?" she said. "This is Marilyn Burton."

"Hello," Rose said warmly. "Don't tell me you've finally decided to sell that store of yours?"

"No," Marilyn said. "That's not why I'm calling. I was just wondering if Kathy's out there."

"Kathy?" Rose said blankly. "No. Isn't she home?" She reproved herself for asking a dumb question. "I'm sorry," she said immediately. "Of course she isn't home, is she?"

"No," Marilyn said reluctantly. "I wish she were. Is Elizabeth there?"

"Yes, of course," Rose said. "Just a minute, I'll call her."

Jack looked at her curiously as she went to the door of the study. "Kathy Burton hasn't gotten home from school yet," she said. "Mrs. Burton is wondering if Elizabeth knows where she might have gone." She stepped into the hall and called Elizabeth's name, then waited until her daughter came down the stairs.

"It's Kathy's mother," she explained. "She's wondering if you know what Kathy was doing this afternoon."

Elizabeth walked to the phone, and picked it up.

"Mrs. Burton? This is Elizabeth."

"Hello, dear, how are you?" Marilyn Burton plunged ahead without waiting for an answer. "Did you see Kathy this afternoon?"

"Sure," Elizabeth said. "She walked most of the way home with me. She was baby-sitting for the Nortons today."

"And she walked with you all the way to the Nortons'?"

"Farther," Elizabeth said. "We were talking about something, and she walked with me all the way past the Stevenses' house."

"Stevenses?" Marilyn Burton said blankly. "Who are they?"

"Oh, they're the people who bought the Barnes place," Elizabeth said. "They just moved in."

"I see," Marilyn said. "And Kathy was going to go right back to the Nortons'?"

"That's what she said," Elizabeth replied. "I tried

to talk her into coming here for a little while, but she said she didn't have time."

"I see," Marilyn Burton repeated, though she had barely heard what Elizabeth had told her. "Well, I'm sure she's perfectly all right."

"Didn't she get to the Nortons'?" Elizabeth asked.

"No," said Marilyn Burton. "She didn't. But don't worry. I'm sure she's somewhere." She dropped the receiver back in its cradle, then called Norma Norton back.

"Norma?" she said. "It's Marilyn. I think you'd better call Ray."

Rose saw the apprehension in her daughter's face as Elizabeth hung up the phone.

"What is it?" she asked. "Has something happened to Kathy?"

Elizabeth shrugged and shook her head slowly. "I don't know. She never got to the Nortons'."

"Where did she leave you?" Jack asked.

"At the edge of the woods," Elizabeth replied. "We were talking about the Stevenses, and Kathy was hoping if we walked by, maybe she'd get a glimpse of Jeff."

"And did you?" Rose asked archly.

Elizabeth shook her head. "I don't think anybody was home," she said. "At least, we didn't see anybody. So when we got to the woods Kathy said she had to be getting back to the Nortons'."

There was an uncomfortable silence, and Rose was sure that all three of them were thinking about Anne Forager. "Well," she said finally, breaking the silence. "You'd better get back upstairs before Sarah misses you."

"Yeah," Elizabeth said blankly. "I hope nothing's happened to Kathy." She searched her parents' faces, as if looking for reassurance that her friend was all right. Rose did her best to smile brightly.

"I'm sure it's nothing serious," she said, with a con-

fidence she didn't feel. Then she decided to voice what
they were all thinking. "After all, nothing happened to
Anne Forager, did it?"

"No," Elizabeth agreed. "But she's a little liar anyway. Kathy isn't like that." She left the room, and Jack
and Rose listened to her steps echoing up the stairs.

"We ought to get a carpet for that staircase," Jack
said absently.

"That's a stupid thing to say," Rose snapped. She
stopped, surprised at what she'd said. Jack stared at
her.

"What did you expect me to say?" he said coldly.
"Are we supposed to sit here speculating on what
might have happened to Kathy Burton?" He saw the
anger flare in his wife's eyes, and wished he'd kept his
mouth shut. He picked up his glass and headed for
the bar in the corner of the study.

"I wish you wouldn't do that," Rose said.

"Do you? Well, I'm sorry," Jack said irritably, and
poured twice as much liquor into the glass as he had
intended to. He was preparing for the battle he could
see brewing when the phone rang again. This time it
was Ray Norton.

"That you, Jack?" he said when Jack picked up
the receiver.

"Hello, Ray," Jack replied. "Shall I guess what
you're calling about?"

"I was wondering if it would be all right with you
if I dropped over for a couple of minutes."

"Here?" Jack said. "Why here?"

"Well," Ray answered. "It seems like Elizabeth was
the last person to see Kathy—"

"You're talking like she's dead," Jack interrupted.

"I didn't mean to." Ray Norton was apologetic but
firm. "But she does seem to be missing, and I'd like
to hear Elizabeth's story straight from her."

"What do you mean?" Jack said defensively.

Ray Norton heard the tone of his voice, and hurried to dispel Jack's thoughts.

"Stop jumping to conclusions," Ray said. "I just don't like getting information secondhand, even from a mother. In fact, especially from a mother. I'd rather get it directly from the source, and from what I know of Elizabeth, she's a pretty reliable source. Can I drop over for a few minutes?"

"Officially or unofficially?" Jack asked.

"Oh, come on, Jack," Ray replied. "If you're wondering if you need a lawyer—"

"No," Jack interrupted, "I was wondering if I should have a drink waiting for you. See you when you get here." He dropped the phone back on the hook, cutting off Ray Norton's relieved laughter, and turned to his wife.

"We're having company," he said.

"So I gathered," Rose said drily. "I take it he wants to talk to Elizabeth?"

"That's it." Jack nodded. "I guess Marilyn Burton's pretty upset, and gave him a garbled version of what Elizabeth told her."

"Well, she has a right to be," Rose said. "Upset, I mean." She looked at the drink in Jack's hand and was suddenly sorry she'd criticized him.

"If I apologize for snapping at you, would you mix me one of those?" She smiled.

Jack mixed the drink, and they sat in front of the fireplace, waiting for Ray Norton's arrival. "I wonder what really happened," Jack said finally.

Rose glanced up at her husband, and saw that he wasn't looking at her but at the portrait of the little girl. She, too, stared up at it for a moment.

"What do you mean?" she countered. "You mean to her? Who knows? Who even knows if there really was a girl such as Dr. Belter was talking about. And even if there was, there's no way of knowing if that's the girl."

"If there *was* a girl, that's the girl," Jack said positively.

Rose looked quietly at him, trying to fathom what was going on in his mind. "You sound so sure," she said at last.

Jack's lips pursed, and he frowned a little. "Yes," he said slowly. "I do, don't I. And you know what? I am sure. I can't tell you why, but I'm sure there was a girl and that that picture *is* the girl. And it terrifies me." Then they heard the sound of a car coming up the drive, and Jack stood up to go to the front door. While he was out of the room Rose examined the portrait once more, and thought about the legend.

What nonsense, she thought. What utter nonsense.

Ray Norton closed his notebook and smiled at Elizabeth. "I wish all witnesses were like you," he said. Once more he ran through Elizabeth's recounting of what had happened that afternoon.

"And you're sure you didn't hear my wife calling to you?" he said.

"I'm sorry," Elizabeth said. "But we didn't. In fact, we were both listening for her. Kathy said she'd have to go in if Mrs. Norton called her, even though we were early. I'm sorry we didn't hear her."

Ray Norton nodded noncommittally. Norma hadn't called to the girls as they passed the house, hadn't even seen them. Ray liked to throw a curve now and then, just to see if a witness would change his story. But Elizabeth hadn't. They'd been alone, and they hadn't seen anybody or anything unusual, but of course, as Elizabeth explained, they hadn't been looking for anybody, either. Except while they were passing the Nortons', they had been engrossed in talking about Jeff Stevens.

"And you didn't turn around and wave?" Ray said once more.

"I cut across the field," Elizabeth said. "So I couldn't

have seen Kathy anyway. The woods would have been in the way."

"Okay." Ray sighed. He looked at Jack. "I'll have that drink now, if it's still around. I probably shouldn't, since I'll have to go into town, but I hate things like this." He caught Rose's frown and remembered that Elizabeth was still in the room. "Not that anything has happened," he added hastily. He took the drink that Jack was offering, gratefully. "Thanks."

"Can I ride into town with you?" Jack asked. "As a newspaperman, not as a friend. I'd like to be on top of this one, after what I took from Martin Forager. Besides, I still have all of this afternoon's work to catch up on."

"Fine with me," Ray said, draining the drink. "But I can't guarantee what time you'll get back."

"I'll find a way," Jack said. He went to find a coat, and while he was gone Ray looked up at the portrait. "It looks just like you," he said to Elizabeth.

"I know," Elizabeth said. "But it isn't. It's somebody else. She's not at all like me."

Rose and Ray Norton stared after her as she left the room.

"Now what did that mean?" Ray said, puzzled.

"Don't ask me," Rose said. "She and Sarah found an old Ouija board up in the attic. Maybe she's been talking to ghosts."

"Right," Ray said with mock seriousness. "I'm sure that's what it is." Jack returned, his coat buttoned up to his chin.

"See you when I see you," he said, and kissed Rose perfunctorily. The two men left the house, and seconds later Rose heard Ray Norton's car grinding away down the driveway. Not knowing why, she fixed herself another drink.

Ray Norton pulled the car up in front of the Port Arbello *Courier*, but didn't turn off the engine.

"Looks like you got burglars," he commented, pointing to a shadow moving across the drawn curtain of Jack Conger's office. Jack smiled.

"Looks like Sylvia is trying to catch up on my work, is what it looks like."

Ray Norton shook his head ruefully. "Sure wish I could get a secretary like that. At the station they don't even want to do their own work, let alone mine."

"Yes," Jack said easily, "it is a problem, isn't it. On the other hand, Sylvia can do my work better than I can, and your girls can't do your work at all. Any idea how long you'll be?"

"None whatever. Call me when you're through, or I'll call you. If you wander over later, and ask me nicely, I'll fill you in on what's happening with Kathy Burton."

"What do you think's happening?" Jack asked.

The police chief looked grim. "If we're lucky, it'll be the same story as Anne Forager. But we won't be lucky."

"You sound awfully sure," Jack said.

"Call it a hunch. And knowing kids. Don't quote me, but I tend to agree with the people who say nothing happened to Anne. She's always been that kind of kid. Kathy Burton's different, though."

"Oh?"

"Norma and Marilyn Burton have been friends for years, ever since they were kids. So I know Kathy. She's a good kid. Responsible, not the kind that would have let Norma down the way she did today, unless something happened. Been that way ever since her father died." Norton shook his head sadly. "That was a tough break, for Kathy and her mother both. I really hand it to them."

"It was a hunting accident, wasn't it?"

"Yup. Just about three years ago. Really dumb one. He wasn't wearing the colors, and someone mistook him for a buck. I tell them the same thing every year:

Wear the colors. There's always one or two who don't
listen. But Burton's the only one who ever caught a
shot for his trouble." The chief glanced at his watch.
"Well, enough jawboning. Got work to do." He shifted
the car into gear as Jack got out. "See you later."

Jack watched him pull away and head around the
square to the police station. It was one of the things
he liked about Port Arbello—being able to watch the
whole town from his front door.

He had been right: Sylvia Bannister *was* in his office,
and she *was* trying to do his work. She smiled at him
as he came in.

"You just wrote one of the best editorials that's ever
come out of this office," she told him.

"Oh? What's it about?"

"Read it yourself," she said, handing him a sheaf of
papers. "Pure dynamite. You are fearless, courageous,
and willing to put your reputation on the line. But
modest and humble."

"Sounds great," Jack said. "But what am I being all
this about?"

"Rose's plan for the armory."

"How'd you hear about that?" Jack asked, puzzled.
"That's supposed to be a secret."

"Not in this town," Sylvia said. "Anyway, you're
against the plan."

"I am?" Jack said blankly. "That'll be great for me
at home."

"It won't hurt. You couldn't very well be for it—
everyone would accuse you of corruption. This way,
you get credit for being honest and courageous and
Rose gets her plan talked about."

"Have you talked this over with Rose?" Jack said
doubtfully.

"Of course," the secretary said. "Who do you think
thought of the idea? Didn't she tell you about it?"

"She doesn't tell me about much," Jack said, and

a sudden wave of despondency flowed over him. He saw Sylvia's face cloud over.

"I'm sorry," she said. "I thought maybe things were getting better."

Jack smiled, but it was a wry smile. "I thought they were. But you can never tell. One day things seem to be going well, and the next all hell breaks loose."

"And today all hell broke loose?"

Jack shrugged and slumped into a chair. He folded his hands over his stomach and stretched his legs. He was comfortable, and he hadn't been comfortable for a long time.

"Not really, but it might yet. The night isn't over."

Sylvia looked at him curiously, and he filled her in on the disappearance of Kathy Burton. When he was finished she seemed puzzled.

"Well, I'm sorry to hear about Kathy, of course, but I don't see how it could have any bearing on you and Rose."

"Rose has problems with reference to me and young girls," he said quietly. He saw the outrage flash into Sylvia's eyes, and it pleased him.

"But that's ridiculous," Sylvia declared. "For God's sake, she's been with you all day. What does she think, you spend all your time, even when you're with her, making trouble for children?"

Jack held his hands out helplessly. "I know. But it makes her nervous. And I suppose I can't blame her, all things considered."

"Well, I think it's awful," Sylvia said, and Jack could hear indignation boiling in her. "Is she going to hold one incident against you the rest of your life? I don't think you should stand for it. Really, I don't!"

"My God, Sylvia," Jack said. "You sound really angry."

"Well, I guess I am," the secretary flared. "I guess I just don't think it's right. We know you didn't really do anything to Sarah, and we know you weren't responsible for what happened. Not really. You were drunk . . ." She trailed off.

"But I am responsible," Jack said quietly. "I wasn't that drunk, and I guess I did beat her. So I do deserve some punishment." His voice grew quieter. "But it gets hard sometimes," he said softly. "You have no idea."

"Oh, I might have some idea," Sylvia said gently. She came to stand behind him, her hand resting gently on his shoulders. As she continued to talk, her fingers began massaging the tight muscles of his neck, and he relaxed under her touch. "I'm not inhuman, you know. I hurt. I carry some pain and guilt with me, too. And I do the same thing you do. Try to hold it in, and try to deal with it. Sometimes I wish I could do what you do and get drunk a few times." She smiled wanly. "But I don't. I'm not allowed."

"What stops you?" Jack said quietly.

"Me, I suppose. Me, and my puritan background, and my high ideals, and all the other stuff that got bred into me and keeps me from liking myself."

Jack reached up, and his hand closed over hers. He felt her stiffen, but she did not pull her hand away. Slowly he drew her around until she stood in front of him and he was looking up into her eyes. They were blue, a deep blue, and Jack had the feeling he had never seen them before. He stood up.

"I'm sorry," he whispered, and put his arms around her.

"Sorry?" she said. "For what?" She tried to keep her eyes on his, but she couldn't. After a moment she broke their gaze and leaned her forehead against his chest.

"I'm not sure," Jack said above her head. "For everything, I guess. For all the trouble you've had, and for all the things I haven't been able to give you." He tilted her head up and kissed her.

It was a soft kiss, a tender kiss, and it surprised Jack. He had not planned to kiss her, nor had he realized he wanted to. But as he kissed her it became very clear that he did want to kiss her and did not want to stop with a kiss. He felt a heat flood through him that he had not felt in a long time. And then he felt Sylvia pull away, and he was ashamed.

"I'm sorry," he repeated, and this time he was sure she knew what he meant. And then he had the distinct feeling that she was no longer in a serious mood, that, indeed, she was laughing at him. He looked at her, and there was a mischievous delight playing in her eyes and at the corners of her mouth.

"I thought you weren't supposed to be able to do that," she said, suppressing a giggle. Jack felt his face flush as he realized what she was saying.

"I haven't, for the last year," he said nervously. "I certainly didn't expect—" He began floundering. "What I mean is, I hadn't intended—"

"Don't apologize." Sylvia laughed. "Be happy. At least you know the problem isn't all yours. Apparently it's your wife you don't turn on to, not everybody."

Jack stared at her, and he felt a weight lifting off his whole being. Maybe, he thought, things aren't so bad after all.

"Now what do we do?" he said.

She shrugged and walked from the room. "Nothing," she tossed back over her shoulder. "Not for a while, anyway." He heard her close the front door of the office behind her, and realized she was right. He would need time to think. So, he hoped, would she.

16

Port Arbello sat up late that night.

At ten o'clock, when she was usually in bed, Marilyn Burton found herself getting into her car and driving out the Conger's Point Road to spend however long it took with Norma Norton. The two women sat drinking coffee and talking quietly about anything except their children, each of them mentioning several times that the coffee would surely keep them awake all night. They carefully avoided mentioning that they expected to be awake all night anyway. Instead, they simply went ahead and drank the coffee.

Shortly after eleven, Martin Forager appeared at the police station, his breath reeking of whiskey and his manner truculent.

"Well," he demanded. "Now what have you got to say for yourself?"

Ray Norton glanced up at Forager, and his finger stopped dialing the telephone on his desk. He was in the last stages of organizing a search party, and Marty Forager's interruption was annoying. But he put his annoyance aside and spoke mildly.

"About what, Marty?"

Forager sat heavily in the chair opposite the police chief, a surly expression darkening his face. "She hasn't showed up yet, has she?"

"No," Norton agreed, "she hasn't. But I still don't see what you're getting at."

"I know what this town thinks," Forager challenged.

"I hear the rumors too. They think my Annie lied. That nothing happened to her."

"By now Anne was home, wasn't she?" Norton replied quietly. He glanced at his watch. "Unless I'm wrong, Anne came in at eleven. It's nearly eleven thirty now."

Forager glared at him. "You wait," he said. "You just wait, and you'll see. She'll turn up, and she'll turn up with the same story."

"I don't care what story she has," Norton said. "I just hope she turns up."

"She will," Marty Forager repeated. "You just wait."

"I will, Marty," Ray Norton said as the man opposite him got to his feet. "Where you heading?"

"Saw Conger's lights on," Martin Forager said thickly. "I thought I'd go over there and see what he's up to."

Ray Norton put on his best policeman manner. "I think I'd go on home if I were you," he said, his voice turning it from a suggestion into an order. Forager swung slowly around to stare at the police chief.

"You telling me what to do?"

"Not really," Norton said affably. "But it's a busy night around here, and I think it's a busy night at the *Courier*, too. And it doesn't concern you, Marty. Go on home, and talk to Jack Conger in the morning if you still think you want to."

"You and he are pretty buddy-buddy, aren't you?" Forager said suspiciously. "And you both live out on the Point Road, where all the trouble seems to be, don't you?" He leered drunkenly at the policeman, who considered the advantages of putting him in the one cell Port Arbello possessed to sleep it off. He decided against it. Instead, he smiled agreeably.

"That's right, Marty. I thought you knew. Ever since I got to be chief of police and Jack Conger took over as editor of the *Courier*, we've been entertaining ourselves by kidnapping little girls. The woods are full of the bodies, but nothing will ever be done about it, because everybody knows that Jack and I are buddies and covering up for each other. In fact, and don't spread this around, we're queer for each other, and the real reason we're out messing with little girls is so that no one will suspect that it's really each other we turn on to." He stood up. "Now, why don't you go out and spread that one around, even though I asked you not to? It's at least as plausible as the story your daughter told."

He immediately regretted his last statement, but then he realized that Forager was too drunk to put together everything he'd said.

"That's all right," Forager muttered under his breath. "You'll see. Somethin's going on in this town, and it started with my daughter. You'll see." He shambled out the door, and Ray Norton stepped out from behind his desk to see where Forager was headed. He watched until he was sure the drunken man wasn't headed toward the offices of the *Courier*, then went back to his desk. On an impulse, he picked up the phone and dialed quickly.

"Jack?" he said when he heard his friend's voice answer. "If I were you I'd lock my front door."

"What are you talking about?" Jack Conger said, and Ray Norton thought he heard a sharpness that didn't fit with the light tone in which he'd couched his suggestion.

"Sorry," he said. "I didn't mean to scare you. Marty Forager's wandering around tonight, and he's pretty drunk. He was just here, and he said he was going to see you next."

"Is he headed this way?" Jack asked.

"Nah. He looked like he was heading for the tavern, but after a couple of more belts, he just might forget what I told him. Or worse, he might remember."

"What'd you tell him?" Jack asked curiously.

Ray Norton recounted the ludicrous story he had

made up for the benefit of the drunk, and was surprised when Jack Conger didn't seem to think it was funny.

"That's great," Jack said, annoyance twisting his voice.

"Well, I wouldn't worry about it," Norton said uneasily. "I imagine he'll forget all about it by morning."

"I hope so," Jack Conger replied. Then he changed the subject. "What about Kathy Burton?"

"Nothing," Ray Norton replied, shifting to his business tone. "She hasn't turned up, and no one's seen her. I don't know what to think. Marilyn Burton's out at my house now, and Norma's staying up with her. I have a feeling they'll be up a long time."

"Along with the rest of the town," Jack observed. He had swung his chair around, and was staring pensively out the window. There was a lot of traffic; cars cruising slowly around the square, and knots of people standing talking under the street lamps. He knew what they were talking about, and it made him uncomfortable. "This town talks too much," he said.

"Only when they have something to talk about," the police chief responded, "and that's not often enough. How much longer are you going to be over there?"

"I've about got it wrapped up. What about you?"

"Same here. I was just finishing the calls for the search party when Marty came in. The boys should all be here in another half-hour, and I want you, too."

"Why me? Not that I'm objecting."

Norton chuckled. "You'd better not. We're starting the search at your place, and I need you to help me lead it. Since we know the area best, and we're both more or less responsible citizens, I thought we'd split into two groups. I'll take my bunch to the quarry and you can comb the woods."

Jack felt a sudden chill, and beads of sweat formed on his forehead. He hadn't been in the woods for a year. He tried to keep his discomfort out of his voice when he spoke again.

"All right. I'll close up here and head over your way. See you when I get there."

He didn't bother to wait for the chief to say good-bye before dropping the phone back in its cradle. He cleared his desk off and locked it, then his office. He left the lights on in the main office of the paper, and made sure he locked the door behind him when he stepped out onto the sidewalk. What with the traffic, and the questions of the curious, it was a half-hour before he made it to the police station. That worked out to just about ten feet a minute.

Rose Conger had tried to work after her husband had left the house, but hadn't been able to concentrate. She had given it up, and turned her attention to a book, but again had found herself unable to concentrate. Finally she had given it up, and simply sat, listening to the old clock strike away the quarter-hours, the half-hours, the hours. The night was beginning to seem endless. Then she had decided to call Norma Norton, to see if she had heard anything about Kathy. Norma, a bit uncertainly, had invited her to come over and join the watch. Though their husbands were close, the women had never hit it off particularly well—partly, Rose suspected, because Norma Norton regarded her not as a human being but as *the* Mrs. Conger. She welcomed the opportunity to try to dispel the image.

"I'd love to," she said. "I've just been sitting here getting more nervous by the minute. Let me find out if Mrs. Goodrich is still up. If she's not planning to go to bed for a while, I'll have her keep an eye on the girls. I'll be there in ten minutes, or call you back."

She found Mrs. Goodrich watching television in her room off the kitchen, and the old woman assured her that she'd be up most of the night. "Seems like the

older you get, the less sleep you need," she said grump-
ily. "Or maybe it's just arthritis. But you go ahead.
Nothing's happened in this house for fifty years that I
haven't been able to handle."

Rose thanked her and went upstairs to check on the
girls. They were sleeping peacefully, and she kissed
Sarah lightly on the forehead. She didn't want to disturb Elizabeth. Two minutes before the end of the
allotted ten, she had parked her car in the road in
front of the Nortons', and a minute later she was gratefully accepting a cup of coffee from Norma.

"I'm so sorry about what's happened," she told
Marilyn Burton. "But I'm sure Kathy's all right. It'll be
just like Anne Forager." The trouble was, none of
them knew what had happened to Anne Forager. They
sat together, an uneasy group, and tried to numb their
fears with caffeine.

Elizabeth's eyes snapped open when she heard the
click of her bedroom door closing. She didn't know
why she had pretended to be asleep when her mother
opened the door. Usually she would have spoken, if
only to say good night. But she had kept her eyes
closed, and maintained the slow, steady, rhythmic breath
of sleep. And now, with the door closed again, and her
eyes open, she still maintained that slow, steady rhythm.
She lay quietly, listening to the night sounds, and heard
the purring of her mother's car as it moved quickly
down the driveway.

When the sound of the engine faded from her hearing, she rose and went to the window. She stared off
across the field, and almost felt that she could see into
the woods that stood darkly in the night. For a long
time she remained at the window, and a strange feeling
came over her, a feeling of oneness with the forest and
the trees and a desire to be closer to the sea beyond
the woods. She turned away from the window and, her
eyelids fluttering strangely, began to dress.

A few moments later she left her room and moved to the top of the stairway. She paused there, seeming to listen to the silence, then began to descend, as silently as the night. She passed the grandfather clock without even noticing its loud ticking. At the bottom of the stairs she turned and began making her way toward the kitchen.

She didn't hear the droning of the television set in the little room next to the kitchen; if she had, she might have tapped at the door, then opened it to see Mrs. Goodrich dozing fitfully in her chair.

Elizabeth opened the refrigerator and stared blankly into its depths for a moment. Then her hand moved out and her fingers closed on a small package wrapped in white paper. She closed the refrigerator door and left the kitchen. In the little room next door Mrs. Goodrich's sleep was not disturbed by the soft clicking of the front door, or by the heavy chiming of the clock as it struck midnight.

Elizabeth moved across the field quickly and faded into the woods. Once she was there, hidden by the trees, her pace increased.

The lights of the searchers bobbed in the darkness around her, but if she was aware of them she gave no sign. Twice Elizabeth disappeared into the shadow of a tree only seconds before one of the searchers would have discovered her, and just before she emerged from the woods onto the embankment she passed within ten feet of her father. She neither noticed him nor made any sound that could have penetrated Jack's concentration. He was too intent on overcoming his fear of the forest to have heard. He forged on, stolid in his grim search for Kathy Burton.

Soon Elizabeth was once again on the embankment over the sea. She listened to the surf, and it seemed to her to be a sound she was used to, a sound she had lived with for much longer than she could remember. She began making her way down the embankment, until she disappeared into the black shadow behind the boulder.

The sounds of the surf, or something else, prevented her from hearing the snapping of twigs and the breaking of branches behind her as others fought a path through the woods above.

Kathy Burton wasn't at all sure she was hearing anything, she had been hearing so much in the past hours. First there had been the sound of her own screams, echoing back at her like some vile, dying creature, hammering into her ears. She had screamed until her voice gave out, then had lain on the floor of the pit for a long time, crying to herself, her body heaving with exhaustion and fear. Then the panic had passed, and she had begun listening to the muffled sound of the surf, which made a soft backdrop of noise, preventing silence from multiplying the terror of the unrelieved blackness. And then she had begun hearing the small sounds, the tiny scurrying sounds to which she had at first been able to attach no meanings. Her mind began producing images in the darkness, images of rats chasing each other around the cavern, circling just beyond her reach. As the images in her imagination grew stronger, she began to feel the rats, if rats they were, moving closer to her, sniffing the air toward her, and her fear grew. She retreated to the top of the rock that only a few hours earlier had served as the table for Elizabeth's manic party.

She had stayed there, huddled against the darkness, and had felt herself growing smaller. She imagined herself disappearing, and it was the least frightening of her imaginings, for if she disappeared she would at least be away. And she wanted to be away, desperately.

As the hours had worn on, her joints had become stiff from the inactivity, and from the dank chill that pervaded the cavern. Finally she had been forced to move, but she had not dared to leave the flat surface of the rock, afraid of what she might encounter in the darkness that surrounded her.

And now she heard a different noise, a scuffling noise from above. She felt a scream forming in her aching throat, but she held it back. The scuffling continued.

Kathy craned her neck, trying to find, somewhere in the darkness above, the shaft that led out of her prison. She thought she knew where it was, for there was the slightest draft, nothing more than a general disturbance of the air, and she was sure that the shaft lay directly above that tiny current of air that was the only real movement in the pit. Earlier she had stood up and tried to reach the low ceiling of the cave, but it was just out of reach, and the inability to even locate the limitations of her confinement had only served to increase her fear. She lay on her back now, her face tipped upward into the draft of air she was sure came from the shaft.

And then she was blinded. She felt her face contract as the light struck her eyes, dazzlingly brilliant. Like a doe trapped in the beam of an automobile's headlight, she was frozen to the stone slab.

Above her, Elizabeth held the flashlight and peered down into Kathy's terrified face. There was a wild look in Kathy's eyes that somehow comforted Elizabeth, and she smiled to herself. Then she heard Kathy speak.

"Who is it?" Kathy managed, her voice sounding strange to her ears. "Please, who is it?"

"Be quiet," Elizabeth hissed down at her. "You must be quiet here."

"Elizabeth?" Kathy asked uncertainly. Then, when she heard no answer, she repeated the word.

"Elizabeth," her voice rasped. "Please, Elizabeth, is that you?"

Above her Elizabeth continued to hold the flashlight steady with one hand, while the other hand pulled at the white paper that wrapped the bundle she had brought from the kitchen. When the paper was free, she spoke.

"Here," she said, her voice almost as harsh as Kathy's strained rasp. "Here's your dinner."

She flung something downward, and watched as the piece of raw and bloody meat slapped wetly into Kathy's face.

Kathy didn't see it coming, and when the slab of meat hit her she recoiled reflexively, and her voice found itself once more. A howling of fear mixed with revulsion at the unknown wet coldness that had hit her face roared out of her throat and filled the cavern with sound. The dull roar of the surf disappeared, and all the small noises were drowned in the sound of Kathy's terror. And then Elizabeth's voice, harsh and ugly, cut through the scream.

"God damn you!" Elizabeth shouted. "Shut your fucking mouth! Shut up!" she kept screaming, as Kathy's voice slowly died away. *"Shut up!"* And then the silence closed over the cave again, until the murmur of the surf found its way in once more.

"Eat it," Elizabeth commanded. "Eat your dinner."

Below her, Kathy's eyes began to adjust to the rent in the darkness. She looked down and saw the raw steak gleaming redly in the circle of light from the flashlight above. She stared at it and tried not to listen to Elizabeth's voice commanding her from above.

"Pick it up," Elizabeth was saying. "Pick it up, you little bitch, and eat it! Come on, pick it up and eat it. Pick it up. Pick it up. Pick it up."

The voice from above took on a hypnotic quality, and suddenly Kathy found herself holding the limp and bloody object in her hands. And then the order from above changed.

"Eat it," Elizabeth commanded. "Eat it. Eat it. *Eat it!"* Helplessly, Kathy moved the raw meat to her lips. The light clicked off.

Kathy sat for a long time, crouched on the slab of rock, the piece of meat clutched in her hands, listening to the scuffling sounds dying away above her. And then, finally, it was silent; still she sat in the blackness, like some wary animal, waiting for an unseen enemy to leap forth from the night.

She became aware of the fact that she was hungry. Slowly her mind began to focus once more on reality, and she wondered how long she had been trapped in the hole, how long it had been since she had eaten. She thought about the bloody object in her hand. Somewhere in her mind she found some little note, some scrap of information, that told her that some people ate raw meat. She felt her stomach jerk, and for a moment she thought she was going to throw up. Then the nausea passed, and once more she felt the pangs of hunger. She made up her mind.

Kathy forced the raw meat into her mouth and began chewing. She was glad now for the dark. She knew she wouldn't have been able to eat it if she had been able to see it.

The scuffling began again when she was halfway through the steak. She stopped gnawing at the meat and listened. It grew louder; then, when it sounded as though it was directly above her, it stopped.

Kathy started to say something, then thought better of it. Acting more on instinct than on reason, she suddenly leaped from the rock, something in her subconscious telling her that the danger from the pit was less than the danger from above. She huddled against the wall of the cavern and waited for the beam of light to come once more through the shaft, heralding a fear that would be bigger than the fear of the darkness and the silence. But there was no beam of light, no rasping, ugly voice obscenely commanding her from above. Instead, there was a sharp crash, as though some object— some hard object—had been dropped from above. There was another silence, and then the scuffling began again, fading slowly away until it melded fully into the background of the surf. Kathy stayed huddled against the wall.

When her legs told her that she would have to move, she began groping her way once more toward the center of the cavern. Her hands found the large slab of stone, and she began cautiously going over its surface, not wanting to find the object that had been dropped, but afraid not to find it.

And then her fingers brushed against something. She drew away as though the object were hot, then moved back. She began examining the object with her fingertips. It was hard, and round, and sort of flat. It seemed to be covered with some sort of cloth—and then she knew what it was. She picked up the canteen and shook it. It sloshed.

Carefully she unscrewed the top and sniffed at the contents. There was no odor.

Finally she worked up her courage and tasted it. It was water.

Thirstily, Kathy drank. The water was soothing to her painful throat.

As she awoke the next morning, Elizabeth's eyes widened in surprise at the pile of dirty clothes sitting in the center of her bedroom. She stared at it curiously, wondering where the clothes could have come from. She decided that Sarah must have left them there during the night, and gathered them up. Depositing them in the laundry chute, she went downstairs for breakfast.

A few minutes later Sarah woke up, and she too found a heap of filthy clothes on the floor of the room. She got out of bed and put them on. Then Sarah, too, went downstairs and silently took her place at the breakfast table. Her parents looked at her in horror. Elizabeth stood up, came around beside her, and took her hand.

"Come on, Sarah," she said gently. "You don't want to wear those to school."

Elizabeth led her sister back upstairs as Rose and Jack Conger looked at each other. Neither of them could think of anything to say. They were too frightened.

17

Time crept slowly through Port Arbello that week. Marilyn Burton, still valiantly postponing the inevitable, opened her shop each day, and each day she smiled at her customers and assured them that, no, she was sure nothing too bad had happened to Kathy and she would turn up. Deep inside, though, she knew that Kathy would not turn up.

Ray Norton expanded the search parties, and the men of Port Arbello began a systematic search of the entire area, each day sweeping a wider arc around the town. Norton did not expect them to find anything, but it kept them busy, and kept them from listening too closely to Martin Forager's charges, repeated drunkenly in the tavern each evening, that the police weren't doing anything. Norton hoped he could keep the searchers working for at least ten days, at the end of which time he hoped to have something more solid to go on than a simple vanishing.

The women of Port Arbello found they were drinking much more coffee than usual, and burning much more gas than usual, as they all took to transporting their children to and from school. All except the people along Conger's Point Road, where Anne Forager had allegedly been attacked, and where Kathy Burton had apparently disappeared. The families on Conger's Point Road did not discuss what was happening, nor did they consult each other on the best way of handling the situation. It was as though, individually, they had each decided that nothing would happen if they did not admit that anything was wrong. So the children of Conger's Point Road continued to walk to and from school each day. If anyone noticed that there was an unusual amount of automobile traffic on the Point Road as each of the mothers found an errand or two to do in town during the hours the children would be walking, no one commented on it. Silently they preserved the appearance of normalcy, and the sight of the constant search parties reassured them.

Thursday morning Elizabeth found herself almost running from the house to the Conger's Point Road. She would have cut across the field, coming to the Road at the base of the woods, but she felt slightly embarrassed. When she got to the Road she glanced quickly to the right, then deliberately slowed her pace and tried to assume an air of nonchalance. For the third morning in a row, Jeff Stevens was waiting for her.

Tuesday morning she had assumed it was a coincidence. She hadn't questioned him about how he happened to leave his house just as she passed the woods. Instead, she had simply fallen in beside him, and surrendered her books when he had taken them from her.

Wednesday morning he had been waiting for her by the Stevenses' mailbox, and she wondered if he had been told to escort her to school. As if he had read her thoughts, he reached for her books and smiled.

"Tomorrow morning you can carry mine," he'd said. "I'm glad you live out here. It isn't any fun, walking by myself."

So on Thursday morning Elizabeth approached Jeff and held out her hands.

"My turn," she said, grinning at him. When he failed to respond, she spoke again. "You said I could carry your books today."

Jeff handed his books over silently and told himself not to forget to get them all back before they were in sight of the school. The teasing had been bad enough when he'd carried Elizabeth's; if she were seen carrying his, he'd never live it down.

He tried to think of something to say, but nothing came to his mind. Which was all right with him, since he seemed to find himself stammering a lot when he tried to talk to Elizabeth. He wondered if he was developing a crush on her, and decided he probably was.

"You're awfully quiet this morning," Elizabeth said, making Jeff blush a deep red.

"I was . . . uh . . . I was just thinking about Kathy Burton," Jeff managed to say, and the blush deepened. What was wrong with him? He'd known what he was going to say. Why couldn't he just say it?

"I wonder what happened to her," Elizabeth said, frowning a little. "Maybe Anne Forager wasn't lying after all."

"Except she's still around, and Kathy isn't." This time Jeff pronounced each word carefully and managed not to stammer.

"I hope they find her," Elizabeth said. "She's a good friend of mine. She baby-sits for the Nortons a lot, and we used to walk together."

Jeff suddenly found himself hoping maybe they wouldn't find Kathy Burton. He wasn't sure he wanted to walk with Elizabeth and someone else too. He decided being fourteen was lousy.

He forgot to retrieve his books from Elizabeth until they were inside the building. Thursday morning Jeff Stevens took a terrific ribbing at school.

By Thursday afternoon Port Arbello had begun to accept the reality of the situation. Marilyn Burton found that her cash receipts were dropping back to a normal level; fewer people were stopping by "just to have a little chat" and staying to buy an article or two out of guilt more than need.

Ray Norton was beginning to cite the cars that were

habitually overparked on the square; he had decided on
Thursday morning that an investigation of a missing
child should not be used as an excuse for overlooking
less serious matters.

Things were getting back to normal.

Mrs. Goodrich was once more in the laundry room,
and when she saw the extra sets of filthy clothes she
shook her head ruefully. She thought about separating
them from the rest of the laundry and bringing them up
again to Miz Rose, then remembered what had happened the last time she had taken such action. She decided it would be wasted effort. So she put the soiled
clothing in a tub and added extra soap and bleach to
them as they soaked. Two hours later, when they came
out of the dryer, they were as clean as new. As clean
as Mrs. Goodrich's demanding standards called for.

Outside the Port Arbello school, Elizabeth Conger
stood uncertainly, searching the faces of the children as
they emerged from the building. For a moment she
thought she might have missed the one she was watching for. Then she suddenly smiled and waved. When
there was no response from the object of her efforts, she
called. "Jimmy," she yelled. A small boy looked up.
"Over here," she called, waving once again.

Jimmy Tyler was small for his age, but not by so
much that it was a strong disadvantage to him. It was
only an inch, and his father had told him that by the
time he reached his next birthday he would surely be
as big as the other eight-year-olds. But when you are
seven, eight seems like a long way off, so Jimmy made
up for his slight disadvantage in size by being more
agile than anybody else. Particularly in climbing. Jimmy
Tyler would climb anything, and one of his favorite
sports was climbing higher and faster than any of his
friends. Then he could look down on them, and that
made him feel good.

He looked up when he heard his name, and saw Elizabeth Conger waving at him. He waved back, then saw that she was waiting for him. He hurried his step.

"Want to walk home with me?" Elizabeth asked him. The Tylers lived even farther out the Point Road than the Congers, and this week, much to Jimmy's surprise and pleasure, Elizabeth had been waiting for him each afternoon, and walking home with him. He liked Elizabeth, even though she was a girl. He supposed that, since she was almost twice as old as he, that didn't count. Anyway, none of his friends had teased him about walking with a girl yet.

"Okay," he said brightly.

They walked silently for most of the way, and it wasn't until they were in front of the Stevenses' house that Jimmy spoke.

"This is where it happened, isn't it?" he said curiously.

"Where what happened?" Elizabeth asked.

"This is where Kathy Burton disappeared," Jimmy said, his young voice expressing no particular reaction to Kathy's disappearance.

"I don't know," Elizabeth said. "I guess it must be."

"Do you suppose they got her?" Jimmy asked, pointing to the ugly old house above the sea.

"No, I don't," Elizabeth said flatly. "Those people aren't like the Barneses were."

"Well," Jimmy said doubtfully. "I still don't like that house."

"I used to think it was haunted," Elizabeth said, teasing him, "when I was your age."

"I don't believe in ghosts," Jimmy said, wondering whether he did or not.

"You don't?" Elizabeth said, but there was a new sound in her voice, as if she was suddenly talking more to herself than to Jimmy. "I didn't used to, but now I'm not so sure."

"Why?" Jimmy said.

Elizabeth seemed to jump back into the here and now. "What?" she asked.

"I said, why?" Jimmy asked again. "Why do you believe in them now if you didn't used to?"

"Oh," Elizabeth said. "I don't know." She suddenly felt uncomfortable, and quickened her pace. Jimmy Tyler almost had to trot to keep up with her.

"Slow down," he said finally. "I can't keep up."

They were near the woods now, and Elizabeth paused, staring into the trees.

"If anything's haunted around here, it's in there," she said.

"In the woods?" Jimmy asked. "Why would anybody want to haunt a woods?"

"Because of something that happened there. Something bad, a long time ago."

"What happened?" Jimmy demanded.

"I don't know," Elizabeth said. "I almost know, but I don't know yet."

"Will you tell me when you find out?" Jimmy's voice rose a notch. "Please, Elizabeth? Will you?"

Elizabeth smiled down at the child beside her and reached down to take his hand.

"I'll tell you what," she said softly. "I'll try to find out what happened this afternoon. Can you come over to my house at four thirty?"

"I don't know," Jimmy said doubtfully. "Why don't you call me? My mother doesn't usually let me go outside that late. It's starting to get dark by then now, and she doesn't like me to be outside in the dark."

"If you want to know what happened in the woods," Elizabeth said enticingly, "come over at four thirty. It won't be dark till after five. Besides, Sarah wants to play with you."

"How do you know?" Jimmy said truculently. "Sarah can't talk."

"I just know," Elizabeth said. "You be here by four

thirty, and I'll tell you about why the woods are haunted."

"All right," Jimmy agreed finally. "But it better be good. I don't believe in ghosts." He started to walk away.

"By the mailbox," Elizabeth called after him. "Meet us by the mailbox." Jimmy Tyler nodded and waved, and Elizabeth watched him continue down the road. She wondered what she'd tell him that afternoon, and why she'd told him the woods were haunted at all. It occurred to her that it was a silly thing to say. Jimmy was right, of course. There was no such thing as ghosts. Well, she'd make up some kind of story, and at least Sarah would have someone besides herself to play with. That would be nice.

At four thirty Elizabeth and Sarah were waiting by the mailbox that stood across the road from the end of the Congers' long driveway. Elizabeth saw the small form of Jimmy Tyler trudging toward them and waved. He returned the wave.

"See?" Elizabeth said to Sarah. "Here he comes, just like I told you."

Sarah stared at Elizabeth, and there was nothing in the huge brown eyes that told Elizabeth that her younger sister had even heard her. But she knew she had. She smiled at Sarah, but Sarah still did not respond. She simply stood, patiently waiting, as Jimmy Tyler approached.

"I can't stay very long," Jimmy said when he caught up with the girls. "My mother told me I have to be in before it gets dark." He glanced at the sun, which was falling steadily toward the horizon behind them.

"Let's go out in the field," Elizabeth suggested. "Let's play tag."

"Does Sarah know how?" Jimmy said, neither knowing nor caring whether the subject of his question could hear or understand him. Elizabeth looked at him reproachfully.

"Of course she does," Elizabeth said. "And you'd better hope you're never It, because she can run a lot faster than you. She can even run faster than me."

"Who is going to be It?" Jimmy wanted to know.

"I will be," Elizabeth said. "I'll give you both till I count to five to get away. One—two—three—" Jimmy Tyler was already bounding across the field. Sarah simply stood there, looking at her sister. Elizabeth stopped counting and put her hands gently on Sarah's shoulders, bending her knees a little so she was on the same level as the smaller girl.

"We're going to play tag," she said softly. "And I'm It. You have to get away from me." Sarah seemed not to hear for a moment; then she bolted suddenly, as if the idea had at last penetrated her mind, taking off across the field in the direction that Jimmy Tyler had taken. "Four—*five!*" Elizabeth called out the last number and set off after the two other children.

She knew she could catch either of them whenever she wanted to, but she didn't try too hard. They seemed to be enjoying dodging away from her, and a couple of times she deliberately let her foot slip when she was only inches from one of them, and listened to Jimmy laugh as she tumbled to the ground. Then, when she sensed Jimmy's interest in the game lagging, she suddenly caught up with him. "You're It," she cried, dashing away from him. He stopped suddenly, as if stunned at the turn the game had taken. Then he grinned happily and set off after Sarah.

Sarah played the game with a determination not to be found in other children. When Jimmy ran toward her, she turned and fled from him at a dead run, her head bent forward, her small legs pumping beneath her steadily. It was quickly obvious that Jimmy didn't stand a chance of catching up with her. Elizabeth worked her way around and headed Sarah off. When she got close to her sister, she called to her, and the sound of her name caused Sarah to look up. She broke her stride and paused for a minute. Elizabeth dashed toward Jimmy as Sarah watched.

"I told you you'd never catch her," she crowed to the boy.

"But I bet I can catch you," Jimmy shouted back, and he shifted his concentration from Sarah to Elizabeth. Chasing Elizabeth was more fun, anyway; she dodged around, and didn't try to keep a straight course. He began trying to outguess her, and didn't notice that as Elizabeth darted to and fro she was working her way closer and closer to the woods. He didn't realize it until she suddenly collapsed in a heap and let him catch her.

"I give up," she laughed, trying to catch her breath. "I can't outrun you."

He fell on the grass beside her, then sat up.

"Look," he said. "We're almost into the woods."

"Yes," Elizabeth said. "I didn't think we were this close. Maybe we'd better go back."

"No," Jimmy said firmly. "I want to hear about the woods. Did you find anything out?"

"There isn't anything," Elizabeth said. "Nothing at all."

"I'll bet there is." Jimmy pouted. "You just don't want to tell me."

"Well," Elizabeth said slowly, gazing off into the trees, "there is a secret place. Only Sarah and I know about it."

Jimmy's eyes widened with interest. "A secret place?" he echoed. "What kind of a secret place?"

Elizabeth shook her head. "I don't think you'd like it," she said. "It's kind of scary."

"I'm not afraid," Jimmy declared. "I'm not afraid of anything. Where is it?"

Elizabeth smiled at him. "It isn't really in the woods," she said. "It's on the other side."

A frown knit Jimmy's brow. "There isn't anything on the other side. Only the ocean."

"That's where the secret place is," Elizabeth insisted.

"I want to go," Jimmy demanded, his voice rising a little.

"Shhh," Elizabeth cautioned him. "Don't frighten Sarah."

"Does she frighten easily?" he wanted to know.

"Sometimes. Not always, but sometimes."

Sarah sat quietly with them, and it would have been impossible for an observer to tell whether she was following the conversation. She would look first at one, then at the other, but not always at the child who was speaking. She seemed to be hearing a conversation of her own, a conversation completely separate from the one Elizabeth and Jimmy were having. Jimmy looked at Sarah speculatively.

"Is she afraid of the secret place?" he asked.

"I don't think so," Elizabeth said uncertainly.

"Are you?" Jimmy asked, hearing the hesitation in her voice.

"I don't know," Elizabeth said after a long pause. "I think maybe I should be, but I'm not."

"I want to see it." It was no longer a request, but a demand. Jimmy Tyler set his face in an expression of stubbornness and looked steadily at Elizabeth. "I want to see it," he repeated.

"It's getting late," Elizabeth said carefully.

"I don't care," Jimmy said firmly. "I want to see the secret place, and I want to see it now."

"All right." Elizabeth gave in. "Come on."

They got to their feet, and Elizabeth led them into the woods. She did not move through the woods as swiftly today, or as sure-footedly. Instead, she moved carefully, and several times had to stop and look around, as if she was looking for markings on a trail. At last they came out of the woods and stood on the embankment.

"Where is it?" Jimmy asked. "Is this it?" There was disappointment in his voice. Elizabeth looked around and wasn't sure which way she should go. She felt uncomfortable today, and something inside her was telling her not to go any farther, to turn back before it was too late. But she didn't know what it would be too late for. All she knew was that she seemed to have lost her bearings somehow, and was unsure of which direction to take. She heard a strange buzzing sound in her ears, a buzzing that didn't drown out the sound of the surf, but seemed to make it hazy. She struggled with herself, and was almost on the verge of turning back into the woods when she heard Jimmy's voice.

"Look," he was saying. "Sarah knows the way. Let's follow her."

Elizabeth looked frantically around, and there was Sarah, picking her way slowly down the face of the embankment, moving back and forth from one toehold to the next. Jimmy followed behind her, his agile little body having no difficulty in keeping up. Elizabeth hung back for a moment, then reluctantly followed.

As she moved down the embankment, the confusion lifted from her, and she knew where she was going. Her step grew sure, and she began moving with the suppleness and agility that had always before taken her so swiftly to the large boulder that hid the entrance to the cavern tunnel.

And then they were there. The three of them huddled together in the shadow of the immense rock, and Jimmy looked at Elizabeth quizzically.

"Is this it?" he said, his voice implying that it was less than he had expected.

"This is the entrance," Elizabeth whispered. "Come on."

And suddenly she was gone. Jimmy stared at the spot where she had crouched an instant before, and then he realized that there must be a tunnel. Eagerly, he followed Elizabeth into the hole in the face of the embankment.

In the pit, Kathy Burton was not immediately aware of the scuffling sounds from above. She lay on the floor of the cave, the water container clutched in her hand. She had lost it once in the darkness, and had had to spend what seemed like an eternity searching for it, ranging back and forth across the cold damp floor of the cavern, not knowing whether she was searching all the area or only circling over a small portion of it. At one point in her gropings in the dark her hand had closed on a strange object, and it had been a few moments before she realized that it was a bone, a part of the skeleton that still lay neatly along one wall.

Another time her hand had brushed against the furry surface of the corpse of the cat, and she had retched for a few moments before being able to continue her search.

The smell in the cave was getting foul, for the flesh of the cat was beginning to rot, and Kathy had had to relieve herself several times. Mixed in was the sour smell of her retching.

She had found the water bottle at last, and had developed the habit of clutching it whenever she was awake. When exhaustion overcame her and she fell into a fitful sleep for a few moments, the bottle stayed beside her, and it was the first thing she groped for when she woke up.

She had stopped hearing the sound of the surf long ago, she wasn't sure when, and the only sounds that still registered on her mind were the scrapings of what she thought had been rats. It had turned out that they weren't rats, but tiny crabs, scuttling among the rocks, finding refuge and food among the small pools of sea water that collected here and there from seepage. She had not yet tried to eat one of them, but she was afraid she was getting close to the point where she would have to. She was pondering the wisdom of this when she suddenly became aware of the sounds from above.

She froze where she was and waited quietly. She wanted to cry out, but was afraid to; she didn't know what was above her. And then the beam of the flashlight hit her, for the first time in three days. By now her eyes were so used to the total blackness that the light was physically painful. She heard a voice above her, but could not make out the words.

"Look," Jimmy Tyler was saying, his voice kept low by sudden fear. "There's somebody down there."

"Shh," Elizabeth said. "They'll hear you."

"I'm afraid," Jimmy said, his fear of the cave overcoming his fear of being thought a coward.

"It's all right," Elizabeth soothed him. "They can't get up here."

And then Kathy Burton opened her eyes, and moved her head into the beam again, looking upward. She tried to speak, and found to her dismay that she couldn't. All that came out was a low gurgling sound.

"It's Kathy," Jimmy said. "We've found Kathy Burton."

"Yes," Elizabeth said slowly. "We have, haven't we." Jimmy Tyler did not notice the strange tone that had crept into her voice, the odd rasping sound.

"What's wrong with her?" he whispered. "Is she all right?" He raised his voice. "Kathy," he called. "It's me. It's Jimmy."

Below, Kathy Burton felt a surge of relief come over her. She was safe. Jimmy Tyler would bring help, and she would get out of here.

"Go get someone," she whispered hoarsely.

"I can't hear you."

She heard his voice echo down. "Help!" she croaked, a little louder.

Jimmy turned to Elizabeth. "We've got to get her out of here," he said. "I'd better go get someone."

"No," Elizabeth whispered. "Let's get her out now. There's a ladder here. Look." She showed him the ladder. "It won't hold me, but I'll bet it would hold you. You can climb down and find out if she's all right. If she is, she can climb back up with you."

Jimmy considered it for a moment. He had never climbed a rope ladder before, but, on the other hand, he was the best climber he knew. And he thought of how neat it would be if he got the credit for saving Kathy Burton after the whole town hadn't been able to find her.

"It's all right," he called down the shaft. "I'm coming down."

And suddenly, in the pit, Kathy realized with terrible clarity what was about to happen. She tried to call out to him, but her voice wouldn't carry through her fear. She watched in horror as the rope ladder appeared in the shaft. She tried to get up, to move to the ladder and grasp the end, but she was too weak. She watched in silence as Jimmy Tyler started climbing slowly down the ladder.

It happened when he was a little more than halfway down: Above him, Elizabeth gathered all her strength, and clutched at the rope ladder with both hands. And then she yanked.

If he'd been expecting it, Jimmy would have been all right. But he wasn't expecting it, and he felt first one hand and then the other come loose from the slippery ropes. He was falling. He tried to break the fall, but it was too late. He landed on his head beside Kathy Burton, and lay still.

The shock of it forced a scream from Kathy's ragged throat, and she found enough strength to make a single lunge at the rope ladder. Helplessly she watched it disappear up the shaft once again. And then she heard the ugly, rasping voice that she had come to associate with Elizabeth.

"Take care of him," Elizabeth said. "Take care of your little brother. He needs you."

The light clicked off, and Kathy listened as the scuffling sounds faded away once more. She began groping in the dark for Jimmy Tyler.

It was almost dusk as Elizabeth and Sarah made their way through the woods, and as they crossed the field night fell darkly over Port Arbello.

18

The next day there was no school in Port Arbello. The school had opened as usual, but by nine o'clock it had become obvious that the teachers would be sitting in all but empty classrooms. The few children who showed up were dismissed. But they refused to go. All had explicit instructions from their parents not to leave the school. They would be picked up, even the ones who lived only a block or two away.

The panic had built all through the night, from the moment Jimmy Tyler's mother had called Ray Norton to advise him that her son had not come home that afternoon. Well, actually, he had come home, she admitted under questioning, but he had gone right out again to play. And then he had not come home.

No, she did not know where he had gone.

Yes, she supposed she should have found out, but she had assumed that he was going to stay near their house; after all, there weren't any children his own age to play with. In fact, the only children close enough to be convenient were the Conger children.

Ray Norton's forehead creased into a frown when Lenore Tyler mentioned the Conger children. That made three cases in the area, though he was still inclined to doubt Anne Forager's strange story. He wondered what time Marty Forager would show up to begin abusing him about his handling of things in general and the case of his daughter in particular.

When he finished talking to Lenore Tyler, Norton started to call Jack Conger, then thought better of it. He decided to wait awhile and see what developed. He turned his attention instead to another problem, a problem that he thought could be potentially worse than the one of the missing children. The children's disappearance was a fact. There was nothing he could do about it for the moment, except try to find out where they had gone.

The reaction of Port Arbello to the disappearances was something else again. This, Ray Norton thought, was predictable, and he didn't like what he saw coming.

Port Arbello was not used to dealing with crime. Port Arbellans, in fact, were part of that great mass of Americans who knows that crime exists but never feels it personally. They lived in an atmosphere of trust; they had no reason not to. For most of his career, Ray Norton's time had been taken up with citing speeders (most of them tourists) and keeping the peace at the tavern. There had been an occasional suicide in Port Arbello, but that was not unusual for New England, particularly during the winter. The crimes that plagued the country, the urban crimes that make urban people barricade their doors, were essentially unknown in Port Arbello. There had never been so much as a mugging, let alone a murder, at least not in the last hundred years. The town was so innocent, indeed, that it was only in the last few days that the people had begun installing new locks on their doors. Until now they had felt perfectly comfortable with the old locks, locks that could be opened with almost any key that came to hand.

But now they were frightened, and Ray Norton found it worrisome. Particularly with a man like Marty Forager doing his best to fan the fires. Ordinarily nobody paid much attention to Marty Forager, but now he had something to use as leverage, and Ray Norton was convinced that he would use it to his best advantage. Ray was very much aware that Martin Forager resented

"Jack," he said when the editor was on the phone. "I'm afraid we've got trouble."

"Not another child," Jack said. "I don't think the town could stand it."

"No," Norton replied. "It's not that. It's the town I'm worried about now. Martin Forager was just here again." Quickly he filled Jack in on what Forager had told him, and made sure that the editor understood Forager's manner as well as his words.

"In other words," Jack said after he'd heard Ray Norton out, "you see a lynch mob developing."

"I wouldn't say that," Ray said slowly.

"Not for publication, anyway," Jack gibed at him. "But that *is* what you're saying, isn't it?"

"Well, I don't think it's gone that far yet," the police chief began.

"—But that's the direction it's taking," Jack Conger finished for him. "Any ideas about who Forager wants to string up?"

"I think I'm at the top of the list," Ray replied, trying to put some banter into his voice. Then he became more serious once again. "Frankly, it's you I'm worried about."

"Me?" Jack said, his voice reflecting a disbelief he did not feel. "Why me?"

"Well, we might as well face the facts," Norton said. "All the things that have been happening have been happening near your place."

"That's not quite true," Jack corrected him. "Anne Forager says she was near our place, but no one knows for sure. Kathy Burton was last seen near our place, but it would be more exact to say she was in front of the Stevenses' house. After all, Elizabeth said they parted at the woods, and that's right at the property line. And as for Jimmy Tyler, we don't know anything about him at all. The Tylers live a good quarter of a mile farther out than we do. So why do you think they'll focus on me?"

the position he held in Port Arbello. Not that he
blame him; who, after all, would want to be kno
"poor Marty Forager"—a phrase always accomp
by a sorrowful shake of the head and words of pi
his wife and daughter.

He was pondering the situation, trying to figu
the best way to defuse it, when his main worry app
in his office.

Marty Forager loomed over him, and Ray N
could see immediately that he had already been
ing.

"I came to tell you," Forager said, his voice
"There's going to be a meeting tonight. A town
ing. Since you don't seem to be able to do an
about what's going on in this town, we're going
if we can come up with some ideas of our own
stared down at the chief of police as if waiting
challenged. Ray Norton looked up at him.

"Am I invited?" he asked mildly. The questic
parently took Forager by surprise, as he stepped
pace.

"No way we can keep you from coming," h
reluctantly. "But you ain't running it," he added.

"I would assume that Billy Meyers will be r
it," Ray said quietly. "He's still president of the c
isn't he?"

"This's a citizens' meeting," Forager sneered. '
council meeting. Nobody's gonna run it."

"I see," Norton said, standing up. He was plea
note that Forager moved back another pace. "I
case, you can count on me showing up. I always v
to see a meeting nobody was running. It ought
fascinating."

Marty Forager glowered at him, and Ray thou
was going to say something more. Instead, F
simply wheeled and stalked silently out of the
station. Norton watched him go and decided it wa
to call Jack Conger.

"It's natural," the policeman said smoothly. "Everything's happening on Conger's Point Road. So who comes to mind when you think of Conger's Point Road? Conger, of course."

"I see," Jack said slowly. "What do you think I should do?"

"I think you should come to that meeting tonight, and I think you should come to it with me."

"After what you told Marty Forager about us?" Jack said, still managing to cling to a shred of humor, however black. Ray Norton chuckled.

"Well, if we have the name, as the man says, we might as well have the game. Seriously, though," he went on. "I think you'd better plan to be at that meeting tonight, if for no other reason than not to be conspicuous by your absence."

"Well," Jack said doubtfully, "I'm not sure I go along with your reasoning, but I'll be there, if not as a private citizen then as the editor of the *Courier*. If they all know they're going to be quoted, it might help to keep the lid on things."

"Maybe with some of them, but not with Marty Forager. I think he's beginning to think of this whole mess as a one-man crusade."

"Yes," Jack mused. "He is that sort of person, isn't he? Do you want to ride in to the meeting with me?"

"Fine," Ray agreed. "Pick me up a little before seven. I'll find out where it's going to be, and either get back to you or tell you when I see you." The conversation ended.

"Is there anything I ought to do?" Rose asked.

They were in the small study. Rose had listened in silence as Jack told her of the meeting he would have to attend, and the direction that Ray Norton was afraid it was going to take.

"Maybe I ought to go with you," Rose continued.

"No," Jack said. "I don't see any reason for that. I think you ought to stay here with the girls."

Rose looked at him, trying to fathom his mood. He seemed worried about something, but she wasn't sure what it was.

"Surely you don't think anything's going to happen to them, do you?" she asked.

Jack shrugged. "I don't see how. Not as long as you're here and they stay in the house," he said. "But I'd feel more comfortable if I knew what was going on."

"Jimmy Tyler," Rose said slowly. "That's odd."

"What's odd?"

"That he should disappear. I mean, suppose Anne Forager's story is true, and frankly I'm beginning to think it is. Well, then, at least it makes some kind of sense for Kathy Burton to have disappeared. But Jimmy Tyler?"

"I don't see what you're getting at," Jack said, although he was afraid he did.

"Well, let's face it," Rose said. "There haven't been any kidnap notes or ransom demands, have there? So what does that leave? A nut. Some crazy person who gets turned on to children. Little girls. Except that now Jimmy Tyler is missing, too, and he doesn't fit the pattern."

"If there is a pattern," Jack said reluctantly.

"Isn't there?" Rose was looking into his eyes. "Don't you see a pattern?"

"Yes," Jack said finally, "I suppose I do." He hoped that what was hanging between them, unsaid, would remain unsaid. "And it doesn't help matters that it's all happening out here, does it?"

"No," Rose said quietly. "It doesn't." She was about to say more when Elizabeth appeared at the door. Rose wondered how long she had been standing there.

"Mother?" Elizabeth said uncertainly.

"Come in, darling," Rose said, glad of the interruption.

"Is it true that Jimmy Tyler's gone too?"

Rose glanced at Jack, unsure of how to handle the question, and saw that she was on her own. She could see no point in denying it.

"Yes, he's been missing since yesterday afternoon."

"What time?" Elizabeth wanted to know.

"Why, I don't know," Rose responded, puzzled. "I don't think anybody knows, really. But no one's seen him since after school."

"I walked home with him yesterday," Elizabeth said slowly, as if trying to remember something.

"You did?" Rose said. "You didn't tell me that."

"I guess it didn't seem important," Elizabeth said, and Rose got the definite impression that her daughter was thinking about something else.

"Is something bothering you, dear?" she asked the girl.

"I—I don't know," Elizabeth said hesitantly. "It's just that I'm not sure—" She broke off, and Rose prompted her again.

"Sure of what, Elizabeth?"

Elizabeth shifted her weight from one foot to the other, uncomfortable. Finally she sat down and looked at her mother, a worried expression on her face.

"I don't know, really," Elizabeth said. "But I thought I saw Jimmy yesterday afternoon."

"You mean after you walked home with him?" Jack asked.

Elizabeth nodded. "But I'm not sure it was him," she said, as if it was somehow important that whoever she had seen might *not* be Jimmy Tyler.

"Where did you think you saw him?" Jack pressed.

"In the field," Elizabeth blurted. "Playing with Sarah."

"But you couldn't see them clearly?" Rose asked, knowing what was coming.

"They were too far away," Elizabeth said miserably. "They were almost to the woods."

"I see." Rose sighed. She avoided looking at Jack, afraid to see if he was feeling the same thing she was feeling. Instead, she spoke again to her daughter.

"They were by themselves?" she asked, and hoped that Elizabeth wouldn't hear the implied criticism. After all, Rose reflected, she *isn't* Sarah's nurse. She wished she could have retracted the question, but didn't see how she could.

"Yes," Elizabeth said apologetically. "I was in my room. I wouldn't have seen them at all if I hadn't looked out the window. I thought Sarah was in her room. I—I'm sorry."

"It's all right," Rose heard Jack say. "You aren't responsible for Sarah." Rose wished she'd said it. "Why don't you go upstairs, honey, so your mother and I can talk."

Elizabeth left the room. Rose had the impression that she left only because she had been told to, that she wanted to stay. But there was nothing more to be said. She looked at her husband, but he was avoiding her gaze. The silence stretched until Rose could bear it no more.

"I don't know what to think," she said at last. "I'm not sure I want to think at all."

"Maybe we'd better call Dr. Belter," Jack said.

"No," Rose said, too sharply. "I mean, call him about what?"

Now it was Jack's turn to sigh tiredly. "Don't you think it's time for us to face up to it?" he said.

"I don't know what you're talking about."

Jack smiled ruefully. "What do you suppose would happen to us if we both decided to bury our heads in the sand at the same time?"

"All right," Rose said after a short silence, her voice stronger. "You're right, of course. I suppose we're going to have to accept the possibility that Sarah is getting dangerous. Is that it?"

"That's it," Jack said. "Of course, it may easily not

be true, but I don't think we can sit here and do nothing. Not considering what's been happening."

"Let's talk to her," Rose said desperately. "Let's at least try to talk to her before we do anything."

"What good'll it do?"

"I don't know," Rose said. "But we can at least try, can't we?" Her eyes were beseeching him, and finally Jack stood up.

"All right," he said. "Shall I go get her?"

"No!" Rose said immediately. "I'll get her. You wait here."

While she was gone, Jack mixed himself a drink. The hell with the meeting, he thought.

A few minutes later Rose was back, leading Sarah by the hand. She followed along docilely, almost as if she were unaware of what was happening. She wasn't resisting, but she didn't seem to be actively involved, either.

Rose sat the child down, then knelt beside her. Sarah sat quietly on the sofa, staring vacantly into the air in front of her face. After a minute or two her right hand went up and her thumb disappeared into her mouth.

"Sarah," Rose said quietly.

Sarah continued to sit, sucking her thumb, apparently not hearing her mother's voice.

"Sarah," Rose repeated, a little louder. "Do you hear me?"

Sarah's head turned, and she peered blankly at her mother. Rose made a distinct effort not to turn away.

"Sarah!" Jack said sharply. The child's head swung around, and her gaze fell on her father. Jack met her eyes for a moment, but he was not as strong as Rose. He broke the eye contact, and sipped his drink.

"Sarah," Rose said again. "Were you playing with Jimmy Tyler yesterday?"

No response.

"We need to know," Rose said. "Can't you at least nod your head? Were you playing with Jimmy Tyler yesterday? Jimmy Tyler!" she repeated, more loudly, as if her child were hard of hearing. Her frustration rose as her daughter continued to stare vacantly into her eyes. Her hand moved to her forehead and brushed back a nonexistent stray hair.

"Sarah," she began again. "We know you were playing with Jimmy Tyler in the field yesterday. It's all right. All we need to know is if you went into the woods. Did you go into the woods?"

No response.

"For God's sake, Sarah," Rose pleaded. "It's terribly important. Please, please, try to understand. He went home, didn't he? Jimmy Tyler went home?"

Sarah continued to stare at her mother. The silence hung heavy in the room. And then, very slowly, Sarah shook her head.

The meeting in town was chaotic, and Jack was sorry he had agreed to take Carl Stevens with him. Jack was embarrassed for the town, and he knew he had not been good company. All he could see, first on the way to Ray Norton's house and then as they drove into Port Arbello, was a vision of Sarah staring darkly into the distance and slowly shaking her head. Over and over again Jack tried to tell himself that it was a good sign, that Sarah finally had responded to something. But over and over he would remember what she had responded to, the question Rose had asked, and despair would close in on him again. Jimmy Tyler had not gone home. Sarah knew that Jimmy Tyler had not gone home. The time was getting very near when all of them—he and his wife and Elizabeth and Mrs. Goodrich—were going to have to accept the fact that Sarah would no longer be with them. But not yet.

The faces of the people of Port Arbello loomed around him, and Jack found himself unable to meet some of the eyes that he imagined were staring at him accusingly. Marilyn Burton greeted him warmly, but he was sure he heard a false note in her voice. Lenore Tyler smiled and waved, and Jack wondered why she hadn't spoken. Had she guessed?

Although Marty Forager had claimed that there was to be no chairman at the meeting, he did his best to run it his way.

"There's something going on in this town," he shouted, "and it's going on out at Conger's Point."

Suddenly all the eyes in the packed auditorium were turned on Jack, and he realized he would have to say something.

He stood up and faced the town. Suddenly they were no longer his old friends; suddenly he was no longer Mr. Conger of Conger's Point Road. Suddenly Conger's Point was something to be afraid of, not respected. And he was the man who lived there.

"I don't know what's going on," he began, and a murmur ran through the crowd, a murmur that Jack was afraid could turn the crowd into a mob. He'd have to do better than that. He listened to his own words and wondered where they came from.

"My daughter saw Jimmy Tyler yesterday afternoon."

"How did she tell you that? Sign language?" a mocking voice shouted from the rear. Jack flinched and fought to contain his sudden rage.

"Elizabeth saw Jimmy Tyler," he heard himself say. "Down by the old quarry. She talked to him. She told him to go home. She told him it was a dangerous place to play, but he didn't pay any attention to her. She told me that when she came home, just before dark, he was still there. That's all."

Jack sat down, and felt the eyes of the town staring curiously at him. He wondered if they knew he was lying, and tried to convince himself that he had lied only because of the way the meeting was going, because of the feeling he had gotten of a mob on the verge of rampage. But he knew that that wasn't true either. He had lied to protect his daughter. His baby daughter.

Then they formed a posse. They called it a search party, but Jack knew it was a posse. Ray Norton tried to stop them, but there was nothing he could do. Perhaps if Marilyn Burton hadn't been there, or Lenore and Bill Tyler had stayed away, Norton could have controlled the situation. But the fact was that they were there, and their very presence, combined with the rantings of Martin Forager, aroused in them the desire to *do* something. Anything.

And so they went out to the old quarry. Ray Norton made sure that he was in the lead, and found a spot to park his car that effectively blocked the road. If there was anything there, Ray Norton wanted to make sure it stayed there. He didn't want any evidence obliterated by fifteen cars driving over the soft ground. Norton organized them as best he could, and the men of Port Arbello spread out to search the area. It was ironic that the only person to find anything was Martin Forager.

What he found was tire tracks. They were fresh, and they were of an odd sort. As the men gathered to examine them, Jack Conger smiled to himself. The tracks would strengthen his story.

They were preparing to leave the quarry when Ray Norton drew him aside.

"Well," Jack said when they were sitting alone in Norton's car, "at least you have something to work on."

"Yeah," Norton said, but he didn't look too hopeful. "I just wonder what those tracks will lead to. If you ask me, we'll never even find the car that left them. But that's not what I wanted to talk to you about."

Jack looked at the police chief questioningly. Norton looked uncomfortable, as if he weren't quite sure how to begin. He decided that the best way was the most direct way.

"Look, Jack," he said. "I know what I'm about to say sounds silly, but I have to say it anyway. Or, rather, ask. How much do you know about the old legend about your family?"

Jack tried to smile, but underneath the smile he felt chilled.

"I know there is one," he said carefully. "What's it got to do with all of this?"

"Nothing, probably," Norton said. "If I remember right, there was supposed to be a cave involved, wasn't there?"

Jack nodded. "Yup. The old lady claimed it was somewhere in the embankment. But of course she never claimed to have seen it, except in her so-called vision."

"Well, what about it?"

Jack looked at the policeman blankly. "What about it?"

"Does it exist?"

"The cave?" Jack said incredulously. "Are you serious? My God, Ray, the cave was never anything but the figment of an old lady's imagination. If someone told the same story today they'd say she was senile. And they'd be right."

"But didn't anyone ever look for it?" the police chief persisted.

"Sure," Jack said. "My grandfather did. And it cost him his life. That embankment is a dangerous place. It's steep and slippery and treacherous. Fortunately, we've had the legend to keep all the kids away from the place."

"And none of them ever went to find out if there was anything there?" Norton said curiously. "You know, when I was a kid the one thing I always wanted to do was go look for that cave. But I couldn't."

"Why not?" Jack asked. "The embankment was there."

"Ah, but it was on the Congers' property. Don't forget, when I was a kid your family was almost royalty around here. We may have wandered all over everybody else's land, but not the Congers'."

Jack chuckled, remembering. It had almost been like that when he had been a boy. "Well, let me set your mind at rest," he said. "Of course I went to look for the cave. And I imagine my father did too. But I didn't find it, probably because it simply isn't there. If it was, I'd have found it."

"Okay," Norton said. "I was almost hoping you'd never looked, and that we could turn the damned thing up. I can't turn the whole town out searching for it, not when all I have to go on is an old tale of a senile woman's visions. We'd probably lose three men in the looking. So I guess it's back to the quarry. I hope you won't have any objections to my sending out a crew to drag it?"

"Of course not," Jack said. "Any time you want. But, God, I hope they don't find anything."

"So do I," Norton agreed. "So do I."

An hour later Jack Conger was home. He went upstairs to say good night to his daughters, and it seemed to Rose that he was staying much too long with Elizabeth. She was on the verge of going up to see what was keeping him when he came down. When he entered the study he looked tired but he was smiling.

"Well," he said, fixing himself a nightcap. "If nothing else, at least I've bought us some time."

19

Neither Rose nor Jack slept that night, but they were quiet, each of them with their own thoughts, each of them wanting to postpone the time when they would have to make decisions.

They tried to avoid their thoughts as they lay in bed, side by side, separated by their fears. Jack kept repeating the story he had told to the town meeting, over and over, until even he began to believe it. Before the blackness of night began fading into a gray dawn, he had almost convinced himself that Sarah had not been playing in the field with Jimmy Tyler; that instead Elizabeth had seen Jimmy at the quarry and instructed him to go home. But with the dawn the truth came back at him, and reality reentered his life along with the sun.

As if by mutual consent, they began talking about it at breakfast. They had risen early, since neither of them had slept, and they sat in the silent house, sipping coffee and trying to figure out what they should do.

"I suppose we should call Dr. Belter," Rose said.

"No. Not yet." Jack knew she was right, but somehow calling Dr. Belter symbolized defeat for him, and he wasn't ready for that yet. "I mean, what could we tell him?" he went on, and he knew he was rationalizing as much for himself as for his wife. "Because Elizabeth saw Sarah and Jimmy playing together is no reason for us to jump to conclusions."

"No," Rose agreed. "It isn't. But it seems to me we have a duty that goes beyond our own family. If Sarah has anything to do with this, even if she only has something to do with Jimmy Tyler, I think we have to tell *somebody*. And Dr. Belter seems the logical person to tell. And, of course, there's Sarah to be considered."

"Sarah?"

Rose wore a pained expression, and Jack knew it was difficult for her to say the things she was saying. He wondered if it was as difficult for her to speak as it was for him to listen.

"What about her?" Rose said. "If she is doing something, and I'm not saying she is, she isn't responsible. She needs help. How can she get the help she needs if we aren't even willing to talk about what she's doing?" She stopped talking for a moment and stirred her coffee fitfully. "Maybe we ought to search the woods," she said. "If something did happen, it must have happened there. Unless they got as far as the embankment." She smiled, but there was no warmth in it. "At least we know there's no cave, so we don't have to look for that."

"I don't know whether there's a cave or not," Jack said quietly. Rose looked at him sharply.

"What do you mean? Didn't you tell Ray Norton last night that you'd spent most of your boyhood looking for it and it doesn't exist?"

"Yes," Jack said uncomfortably. "That's what I told him. But it wasn't any truer than anything else I told anybody last night."

Rose set her cup down and stared at him. "You mean you lied about the cave, too?" she said incredulously.

He nodded miserably, and it struck Rose that he looked very much like a small child caught with his hand in the cookie jar. For some reason it made her want to laugh, though she felt anything but mirthful.

"Why on earth did you lie about that?" she asked him when her laughter died. Her voice was mocking, and it made Jack flush.

"Because I didn't want them poking around the

woods and the embankment, that's why," he said vehemently.

"But they'll poke around the woods anyway," Rose said, taking on the voice of a teacher with a recalcitrant pupil. "Besides, they've already searched the woods. They did that when they were looking for Kathy Burton."

Then a thought came to her, and she searched Jack's face carefully, looking for the answer to the question that had come into her mind. It was there, in his hangdog expression, in the defensive light that glimmered in his eye.

"You believe it, don't you?" she said. "You believe in the legend. Is there a cave there?"

"I don't know," Jack said softly. "I never looked."

"Why not?" Rose demanded. "Are you going to sit there and tell me that, with a wonderful legend like that, you never once, you and your friends, never once went looking for that cave?" Her eyes widened in astonishment as he shook his head. "Well, for heaven's sake. That legend actually worked." Now her laughter came in gales, partly at the idea of her husband putting enough faith in the legend never to investigate it, but mostly as a simple release. A release of the stress she had been carrying. It was not pleasant laughter, and it did not make the house ring. Instead it echoed dully through the room, and then came back to hang heavily between them.

"I think," Rose said finally, "that it's time we had a look at that embankment. If there is a cave there, I think we should know about it. I think the whole town should know about it."

"You look if you want," Jack said softly. "Frankly, I'd rather not know."

Jack Conger arrived in his office early that morning, before any of the staff had gotten in. When they arrived, at eight thirty, they found his office door closed and the red light above it lit. All of the staff except Sylvia Bannister respected the warning light.

Sylvia ignored it.

She walked into the inner office without knocking. Jack looked up but did not speak.

"Bad night?" Sylvia said sympathetically.

Jack put down his pencil and leaned back, rubbing his eyes. "It depends on what you call a bad night. If you call lying to the whole town, lying to the chief of police, asking your oldest daughter to lie too, getting no sleep, and then topping the whole thing off with making yourself look like a fool to your wife—if you call that a bad night, then I suppose I had a bad night. Otherwise it was fine."

Sylvia sat down. "Do you want to tell me about it?"

"No," Jack said irritably, "I don't. I want to be left alone, to try to get my head straightened out. If that's all right with you."

He was already staring again at the piece of paper on the desk in front of him, and chewing on the end of the pencil, so he couldn't see the look of hurt that came into Sylvia's face. She stood up and smoothed her skirt.

"Of course," she said coolly. "I'm sorry I bothered you." She left the room, and when Jack heard the door close he looked up again, looked helplessly at the door through which the woman had just passed. He wanted to call her back. He didn't.

He worked for an hour, writing and rewriting, and when he was finished he read what he had written. Then he crumpled the pages and threw them into the wastebasket.

It had been an editorial, and when he had finished writing it and reread it he realized that it could as easily have been written by Martin Forager as himself. He had attacked the police chief, even suggested that perhaps it was time Ray Norton was replaced. He had demanded some answers about what had really happened to Anne Forager. And he had suggested, but in terms that denied their own content, that it was time for the citizens of Port Arbello to form a lynch mob. He had not, of course, used that term. He had called instead for a "protective association," but it amounted to the same thing. In short, he had written a hypocritical, self-serving editorial, designed to undermine the police chief and at the same time entrench Jack Conger as a concerned citizen. Jack Conger realized that he was trying to throw Ray Norton off a trail that Ray Norton didn't even know he was on. A trail that could lead only to Sarah, who couldn't possibly be considered responsible for anything she might have done. He retrieved the editorial from the wastebasket and read it once more. He decided, objectively, that the editorial had served its purpose very well.

He burned it in the wastebasket and picked up the telephone. It was time to talk to Charles Belter.

Dr. Charles Belter listened carefully to everything Jack Conger told him. It took more than three hours for Jack to put it all together for the doctor, and several times he had to backtrack, going over a point several times, filling in background or amplifying. Dr. Belter listened patiently, interrupting as little as possible; he felt it was important to listen not only to what was being said but also to how it was being said, and in what order. The mind tended to attach priorities to things, Dr. Belter knew, and often much could be learned not from the points being made, but from the order of the points and their relative importance to the person making them. When Jack finished Dr. Belter leaned back, his hands folded comfortably over his ample stomach.

"So you don't know whether or not there really is, or was, a cave?' he said.

"Was?" Jack repeated. "What do you mean, was?"

"Only that there might have once been a cave, but that it got filled in, or collapsed. It isn't important. Just a mind that deals with details functioning in its usual picky way. Forget I said it. The important thing is that you don't know whether or not the cave is real."

"No, I don't. And I don't see how it matters."

Dr. Belter lit a cigarette and shook the match out before he spoke again. "I don't know," he said at length. "Does it matter?"

"What are you getting at?" Jack asked suspiciously.

Dr. Belter smiled at him. "Well, it just seems to me that you've attached a lot of importance to that cave. After all, you did go so far as to tell the chief of police that it definitely doesn't exist. That tells me a couple of things."

"Such as?" Now there was definite hostility in Jack's voice.

"First, that you think there is a cave. If you were really sure that there was no cave, and that the legend was only a legend, why would you want to try to talk Norton out of searching for it? After all, if you're sure it doesn't exist, then you don't have to worry about it being found, do you?"

"What's the second thing?" Jack asked, without conceding the first.

"Why, that's easy," Dr. Belter said with a grin, leaning forward over his desk. "You're not only sure there's a cave, but you're afraid of what might be found in it."

"That's the stupidest thing I've heard of in a long time," Jack said angrily.

"Is it?"

Jack knew he was reacting more out of fear than out of anger, and he wondered why. What was he afraid of? Then he decided he wasn't afraid *of;* he was afraid *for.* He was afraid for Sarah.

"It's Sarah I'm worried about," he said nervously.

"Are you?" the doctor asked, and Jack thought he heard a mocking tone in his voice. "Let's talk about that for a minute then. Exactly what are you worried about? Are you worried that Sarah has been terrorizing

little children, then shoving them into a cave? That's
what I would call one of the stupidest things *I've* ever
heard of. For one thing, take a look at Sarah's size.
She's not big, is she? In fact, she's small for her age,
and a bit underdeveloped." He noticed the look of anger
that was coloring Jack's face and held up a hand. "Oh,
come on. I didn't say she was abnormally small or underdeveloped. Physically she's well within the normal
range. But on the small side of the average, rather than
the large side. Now tell me, do you really think a girl
the size of Sarah could do much to a girl the size of
Kathy Burton? Kathy Burton, from what I've found out,
was big for her age, and somewhat athletic. So, considering that she's also a year older than Sarah, I don't
see much chance that Sarah could have done anything
to her. Anne Forager and Jimmy Tyler I don't know
about. They're both younger than Sarah, and a bit
smaller. But Kathy Burton wouldn't have taken any guff
off of Sarah."

"I understand that children with . . . mental problems
. . . sometimes show remarkable strength," Jack said.

"You've been watching too many movies. Oh, sure,
it can happen, but it's rare, and it only happens for
short periods of time, under what we call hysterical
conditions. The same things happen with so-called
normal people. The mother who lifts the car off her
crushed child? Those things can happen. Under severe
stress, the body simply shoots itself up with adrenalin,
and you have a surge of strength. But it's rare, and it's
for very brief periods of time. Seconds, not the time it
would take to do what you're suggesting."

"I'm not suggesting a thing," Jack said coldly.

"Aren't you? I think you are. I listen carefully, you
know. It's my profession. And here's what I heard you
saying. Not directly, mind you, but by implication. And
all because Elizabeth said she saw Sarah playing with
someone who looked like Jimmy Tyler.

"You see Sarah dragging children into the woods,

beating them, and then taking them and dumping them in a cave somewhere. Am I right?"

Jack shifted in his chair with discomfort. The doctor had stated his thoughts too closely. "Go on," he said, not at all sure he wanted to hear any more, but feeling that he must.

"Well, if you don't mind my saying so, that theory is ridiculous. Not only would Sarah be totally unable to sustain the kind of abnormal strength that would be necessary for such a feat, but even if she could, can you imagine the difficulties in hauling someone your own size down the face of that embankment? You've said yourself that it's tricky for an adult by himself. It sounds like it would be impossible for a child carrying another child of almost the same size."

Jack thought it over and felt an odd sense of relief. The doctor was right; it didn't make sense. He and Rose had been overreacting. And why not? The last days had not been easy for anyone in Port Arbello, and Rose and Jack Conger were no exception. He felt a grin come over his face, and it felt good.

"Well, that's done with, anyway," he said. "Have you got any other ideas?"

Dr. Belter leaned forward, and his expression took on a seriousness that made the grin fade from Jack's face.

"Yes, I have. Mr. Conger, have you ever suffered from blackouts? Recently?"

It took nearly a full minute for the implications of what the doctor had just said to sink into Jack's mind. When it finally did and he grasped what Dr. Belter was suggesting, he had to fight to control himself. Trembling, he got to his feet.

"Only once, Doctor," he said coldly. "And we both know what happened that time. Since then, never." He left the doctor's office without another word, and without waiting for Charles Belter to respond.

"How can you be sure?" the doctor said to the closed

door and the empty room. "How can you be sure you never have blackouts?"

It was noon when Jack returned to the paper. He closed the door behind him, and a moment later the red light above his door flashed on. The staff of the *Courier* looked at one another curiously, but none of them was willing to speculate on what was going on. Instead, they all glanced at the clock and began drifting away to lunch. When the office was all but empty, Sylvia Bannister looked at the closed door. She hesitated a minute, then punched the button on the intercom on her desk.

"I'm going to lunch now," she said. She waited for an answer, and when none came began putting on her coat. She was ready to leave the office when the intercom suddenly came alive.

"Can you spare me a minute?" Jack's voice crackled through the wire.

Sylvia took off her coat and rehung it on the hook. Then she smoothed her skirt and entered the inner office.

She had been prepared to be cool to her employer, but the expression on his face changed her mind.

"You're not all right, are you," she said, making it more a statement than a question. Jack looked up at her, and she was sure she saw tears trying to make their way out of his eyes.

"I just got back from talking to Dr. Belter."

"I wondered where you went," Sylvia said, lowering herself into the chair opposite him. "Why did you go see him?"

"I'm not sure, really. I thought I was going to talk about Sarah. About what to do about her. But he didn't want to talk about Sarah."

"Oh?"

"He wanted to talk about me."

Sylvia smiled at him reassuringly. "Is that such a bad idea? We can all stand to talk about ourselves now and then. And you haven't been having it too easy lately, have you?"

"That wasn't what he wanted to talk about. He seems to think that I might be the one who's after the kids."

Sylvia stared at him in complete disbelief. "You? You must have misunderstood him."

"No. I didn't misunderstand him. He wanted to know if I've been having any blackouts lately."

"That is the most disgusting thing I've heard in a long time," Sylvia said, her voice reflecting the sickness she felt in her stomach. "That happened a year ago. Not last week, not last month. A year ago. Thirteen months, actually. Does he seriously think it would happen again now? Three times? Besides, we know where you were when the children disappeared."

"On the day Kathy Burton disappeared I was in his office, as a matter of fact," Jack said, smiling thinly.

"Then what's he trying to do?" Sylvia demanded.

"I don't know," Jack said. "But, God, it scares me. If that's what he thinks, what will the rest of the town think?"

"I haven't any idea, but I know what I think. I think it's insane, and I think Dr. Belter needs to have his own head examined."

She stood up. "And I think you and I should go have some lunch. At my place."

Jack looked at her with no comprehension.

"Jack," Sylvia said softly, "don't you think you've absorbed enough? Take some time off for yourself. Even if it's only a few hours with me. You need it. Really, you do. And so do I."

They drove in silence to Sylvia's house, and talked quietly while she fixed their lunch. They avoided the sensitive subjects, but it wasn't the studied avoidance that created a distance between Jack and Rose when they were consciously staying away from something. Instead, it was an easy avoidance, a mutual agreement to talk about things that made them comfortable, and they grew closer.

They didn't go back to the *Courier* that afternoon. They started to, but they changed their minds. Instead, they spent the afternoon in Sylvia Bannister's bed, and it was good. It was good for both of them. For the first time in a year, Jack Conger lay comfortably in a woman's arms. Sylvia Bannister was content. And, for the moment, so was he.

The two children in the cave clung together, as they had for almost thirty-six hours. Jimmy Tyler had been unconscious for the first hour he was in the cave, and for a long time Kathy had been sure he would die. But he hadn't died, and eventually he had awakened, terrified in the darkness. Kathy had tried to soothe him and explain to him what had happened. Her voice had been weak, and she had had several periods of incoherence, but the very sound of a human voice in the blackness had seemed to soothe Jimmy, and eventually he had calmed down. And then they had waited.

They stayed close together, never moving far enough apart so that they couldn't touch each other, and when they slept, they slept in each other's arms.

Jimmy was terrified by the strange scrabbling sounds, but when Kathy told him what they were he tried to catch one of the tiny crabs. Eventually he succeeded, and popped one into his mouth. It was bitter, and he promptly spat it out, retching. Kathy gave him a mouthful of the water to wash the taste away.

They talked now and then, Jimmy mostly, since Kathy's voice was weak and her throat hurt her badly now, but for the most part they simply sat silently, holding hands, wondering how long they had been trapped in the cavern and how long they would be kept there.

It was during one of the times that Jimmy was talking that Kathy suddenly squeezed his hand.

"Shhh!" she hissed. He felt her hand grasp his even more tightly, and stopped talking. Above him Jimmy heard an odd scuffling sound. As the scuffling grew louder, Kathy's hand continued to tighten on his, until it began to hurt. He sensed that the sounds from above were frightening Kathy, and the fear was contagious. He forgot the pain in his hand as he strained to hear what was happening overhead.

"Put your hand over your eyes," Kathy whispered to him. He didn't know why he should, but he followed her instructions. A moment later he saw a dim red glow through the flesh of his fingers. He opened his fingers slightly and saw a beam of light shining down from the shaft above. Squinting, he removed his hand from his eyes, then opened his eyes completely as they grew used to the light. Kathy still sat huddled next to him, one hand clutching his, the other clasped tightly over her eyes.

"It's all right," he whispered. "If you squint the light doesn't hurt your eyes."

Tentatively, Kathy took her hand from her face, and began letting her eyes adjust to the unaccustomed light. The light held steady, and there was silence from above. Curiously, the two children looked at each other. While they were searching each other's faces, they heard a plopping sound. Jimmy started to speak, but Kathy clapped a hand over his mouth. Both of them saw the small package, wrapped in white paper, that lay in the middle of the pool of light. Jimmy struggled free from Kathy's grip and scurried into the light to snatch it, like a rat snatching a piece of cheese from the middle of a floor, then darting back to its hole.

He unwrapped the package. "Look," he said. "Sandwiches."

Kathy looked at the food, and her hunger overcame her fear. She grabbed at one of the sandwiches and

shoved it into her mouth. Jimmy was gobbling at the food with the hunger of a small child not used to going without.

The nausea hit both of them simultaneously, and suddenly both of them were lying on the floor of the cave, retching furiously. The sandwiches, the wonderful gift from above, were stuffed with sand. Sand, and seaweed.

From above they heard the awful, maniacal laughter, and they knew that it was Elizabeth up there, holding the light steady, watching them puke. Instinctively Kathy and Jimmy squirmed away into the protective darkness, like subterranean animals creeping away from the sun. When they were completely out of the pool of light, the beam of whiteness suddenly disappeared, and they heard the sounds of Elizabeth creeping away toward the surface. Kathy and Jimmy cried quietly, clutching each other's hands.

20

The following Sunday was one of those leaden, gray days when fall seems to take a perverse pleasure in giving a preview of the winter to come. In Port Arbello the weather only accented the depression that hung over the town, and the tavern did a brisker business than usual. On an ordinary Sunday morning, only Marty Forager could be counted on to step over the threshold, announcing that he was there for "services." He would then stay through the day, and shuffle out only after he had finished "vespers." But on the Sunday following Jimmy Tyler's disappearance, the churches of Port Arbello found their pews packed for the early service, and the tavern found its stools packed for Marty Forager's services.

The Congers did not go to church that Sunday morning, nor did they show up at the tavern. They wouldn't have gone to the tavern anyway, and they had omitted church by mutual consent, neither stating why they chose to stay home, neither wanting to hear the reasons voiced. It was as if they sensed something coming, and hoped they might be able to avoid it by staying in their house. They were observing their morning coffee ritual, silently, when the telephone rang.

"I'll get it," they heard Elizabeth call from upstairs. A moment later they heard her call down again. "It's for you, Mother. Mrs. Stevens."

"Barbara," Rose said, trying to sound more cheerful than she felt. She had, indeed, been growing as depressed

as anybody else in Port Arbello, but was able to hide it
by using her "professional" voice. "I was beginning to
think you people had—" She'd been about to say
"died" when she thought better of it. She didn't bother
to try to find a better word. "That was a hell of a thing
to say, wasn't it. Well, I guess that's what's on all our
minds these days."

"That's why I'm calling," Barbara Stevens replied.
"I'm tired of the only topic of conversation in Port Arbello, and I should imagine you are too. And the
weather's too lousy to work on the house, so Carl
thought a game of bridge on a wet afternoon might be
in order. Do you play?"

"I'd love to," Rose said. "What time and where?"

"Here, about one-ish. And bring the girls."

"Let me check with Jack. I'll call you right back."

She hung up the phone and returned to the dining
room.

"That was Barbara Stevens. She and Carl want us to
come to their place for a game of bridge this afternoon.
With the girls," she added as Jack looked doubtful.

"I don't know. You know how Sarah can be in a
strange place."

"Then we'll leave them home with Mrs. Goodrich,"
Rose said promptly. Jack saw that there was going to be
a bridge game and decided to go along with it gracefully, even though he hated the game.

"Why don't we play here instead?" he suggested.
"Unless there's some reason why the Stevenses want
us at their place?"

"Fine," Rose said, smiling. "Barbara said one. Is
that all right with you?"

Jack glanced at his watch automatically. "I can't see
any reason why not," he said.

Rose grinned at him. "Except that you hate the
game, right?" Without giving him time to answer, she
continued. "Well, at least it will give us something new

to think about. After this week, you might even find you enjoy it."

The same thought had occurred to him, and he smiled at Rose, then watched her leave the room. He listened to her talking to Barbara Stevens, but didn't really hear what she was saying. He was, instead, trying to decide why it was that ever since the afternoon with Sylvia, which had been wonderful, he had been feeling better about his marriage. He supposed that it was simply that he was feeling better about himself. He found that he was actually looking forward to the bridge game. It was nice to be looking forward to something.

"One club."

"Pass."

"One spade."

"Pass."

"One no-trump."

The bid was passed out, and Barbara Stevens looked at her partner.

"Does your husband make you play one bids?" she asked.

"Only if he thinks he can set me," Rose replied. Barbara looked first at Jack, then at Carl.

"Well, boys, what about it? Do I have to play this one?"

Jack examined his hand carefully, then closed it and threw it in. "Not when fourth best is a four from a seven," he said. "You underbid. Score yourself forty, and we'll count ourselves lucky."

Carl Stevens dealt the next hand, and as he began sorting it he glanced up at the ceiling.

"Mighty quiet up there," he observed. "I didn't know three children could be that quiet. Knock on wood." He finished sorting his cards, and tried to keep his glee from showing.

"Two no-trump," he announced, and was pleased to hear a groan from the women.

Upstairs, the three children sat on the floor of the playroom, finishing a game of Monopoly that Sarah had won, primarily because both Jeff and Elizabeth, taking turns playing on her behalf, had made good deals for her. For her part, Sarah was sitting quietly, staring at the Monopoly board and occasionally picking up one of the pieces to examine it carefully before putting it down on the exact spot from which she had picked it up.

"She's just lucky, that's all," Jeff commented as he shoved the last of his money over to Sarah. Sarah, as if sensing somehow that the game was over, suddenly swept the board clean. Elizabeth began picking up the scattered money and sorting it out again. She smiled at Jeff.

"She does this all the time," Elizabeth said. "Whenever I play a game with her, she always wins. Then she dumps it." Elizabeth did not add that the only active part Sarah ever took in any of the games was in the dumping. She was sure Jeff understood that without being told. "Have you ever seen a Ouija board?" she asked him.

"You mean one of those things that's supposed to tell your fortune?"

"They don't really tell your fortune. You're supposed to be able to talk to spirits with them."

"I don't believe in spirits," Jeff said. Then: "Do you have one?"

Elizabeth nodded. "I found it up in the attic. Sarah and I play with it all the time. Want to try it?"

"Sure," Jeff said. "Why not?"

Elizabeth finished packing the Monopoly set in its box, then pulled out the Ouija board. She set it on the floor between Jeff and herself, then called to Sarah, who drifted back from the window she had been looking vacantly out of. Silently Sarah sat down on the floor and rested her fingers on the indicator.

"What do we do?" Jeff asked.

"It's easy," Elizabeth said. "Just put your fingers on that thing, the same way as Sarah, and then ask a question. Pretty soon it starts moving."

"All by itself?" Jeff said skeptically.

"Sure. Come on. Let's try it."

She put her fingers on the indicator, and after a moment, and feeling a bit silly, Jeff did likewise.

"Is anybody there?" Elizabeth intoned. For nearly a minute, nothing happened. Jeff was about to give it up as stupid when he thought he felt a vibration under his fingers. Then the indicator moved. It slid across the board and stopped at the "B."

"Did you do that?" he said to Elizabeth.

She shook her head. "Shh. You shouldn't talk."

Jeff's lips tightened, and he felt the indicator try to move again. He pressed down, trying to immobilize it. He could feel it straining under his fingertips and glanced surreptitiously at Elizabeth to see if she was trying to move it. She looked relaxed. Under his fingertips, which were growing white from the pressure he was applying, the indicator started to move.

"You can't stop it," Elizabeth whispered. "I tried that too. I thought Sarah was moving it. But I couldn't make it stop."

Jeff watched, fascinated, as the indicator moved across the board to stop at the "E." He tried once more to hold it immobile, but it moved relentlessly onward, coming to rest at the "T."

"Bet," Jeff said. "What's that supposed to mean?"

"It hasn't stopped yet," Elizabeth said. "But I know where it's going." The indicator swung slowly over the other way now, and stopped at "H." A sensation came over Jeff, and he knew that the indicator wouldn't move again.

"Beth," he said. "That's your name. Short for Elizabeth."

"I know," Elizabeth said. "But it isn't me. It's a spirit, and the spirit's name is Beth. She must want to tell me something."

"Why not me?" Jeff said, grinning. "I'm here too, you know."

Elizabeth shook her head seriously. "No, it's me she wants to talk to. I've talked to her before."

"Sure you have," Jeff mocked. "I suppose she was your great-great-grandmother, or something like that?"

Now Elizabeth looked at him nervously, and seemed to be less sure of herself. "Why did you say that?" she asked uncertainly.

"What?" Jeff countered.

"What do you mean, my great-great-grandmother?"

Jeff seemed to be baffled. "I didn't mean anything. Isn't it always a great-great-grandmother that people talk to?"

"Have you heard anything about my great-great-grandmother?"

"Why should I have?" Jeff challenged.

"I don't know," Elizabeth said. "I just thought you might have heard about the legend."

"What legend? Don't tell me Beth *was* your great-great-grandmother. Because if you do, you're crazier than your sister."

"Don't talk that way about Sarah," Elizabeth snapped. "It's not nice." She turned to Sarah. "Don't listen to him, Sarah. He doesn't know anything."

Jeff looked embarrassed and tried to mumble an apology. Then he asked Elizabeth to tell him about the legend.

"There's supposed to be a cave on the Point somewhere," she began. "My great-great-grandmother, or maybe it's three greats, had a dream about it. It was an awful dream, and the cave is supposed to be an awful place. My father told me that my great-great-grandmother said it was the gates of hell. Anyway, she had a dream about it, and then terrible things started happening."

"What sort of terrible things?" Jeff asked eagerly. "Did people get killed?"

"I guess so," Elizabeth said. "I think Beth was one of them."

"Who was she?"

"I'm not certain," Elizabeth said. Her voice had softened to a whisper, and a strange blank look had come into her eyes. "She was only a little girl when she died. A little younger than Sarah. I keep asking her what happened to her, but she won't tell me. But it had something to do with the woods, and the cave. That's why we're not supposed to go there."

"Is that all?" Jeff seemed disappointed, as if he had been expecting much more than what Elizabeth had told him.

"Well, there was my great-great-uncle. He killed himself."

"How do you know?"

"I just know. He came home one day, and he was carrying something. I think it was a dead cat, or something like that. Maybe it was a rabbit. Anyway, you know that study in the back of the house?"

"The one with the picture of you in it?"

Elizabeth nodded. "But it isn't a picture of me. Anyway, they say my great-great-uncle took the cat or the rabbit or whatever it was into the study. Then he went out to the back of the house and jumped off the cliff."

Jeff's eyes widened. "Really? Into the ocean?"

"Of course into the ocean," Elizabeth said. "There isn't anything else down there, except for the rocks."

"Gosh," Jeff breathed. "Did anything else happen?"

"There was one other person, my great-grandfather. They don't really know what happened to him, but he went to look for the cave one day, and he never came back."

"Did they ever find him?"

"Yes. But he was dead. He got his foot caught in the rocks, and when the tide came in he drowned."

"I don't believe any of it," Jeff said, hoping there was more.

"I don't care if you believe it or not," Elizabeth said. "It happened."

"Who told you?"

"My father. And his father told him. Or his mother. Anyway, it's true."

"Have you ever seen the cave?" Jeff demanded.

"No," Elizabeth said uncertainly. "But nobody else has ever seen it either."

"Then how do you know it's real?"

"I just know."

"How?"

"I just do."

"Well, if you can't tell me how you know, then you don't know," Jeff said tauntingly.

"I *do* know," Elizabeth insisted. "Beth told me," she blurted out.

Jeff rolled his eyes. "Sure she did. Except that you don't even know who she is."

"I do too," Elizabeth said shakily. "She—she's the girl in the picture downstairs. The one who looks like me."

Jeff looked at her with scorn. "Sure she is," he sneered.

"She is," Elizabeth insisted. "She talks to me through the Ouija board, and she told me so."

Jeff lounged back, propping himself up on one elbow, and grinned at Elizabeth. Neither of them noticed that Sarah had moved out of the circle and was back at the window, staring out and shifting her weight nervously from one foot to the other.

"I'll tell you what," Jeff said. "If you can tell me where that cave is, then I'll believe the rest of it."

Elizabeth looked at him petulantly and tried to figure out how to convince him.

"Well," she said nervously. "There's a place . . ."

Sarah turned from the window and stared vacantly across the room at Elizabeth. Neither Elizabeth nor Jeff seemed aware that she was there.

"What kind of place?" Jeff said, disbelief filling his voice.

"A—a secret place," Elizabeth said.

Sarah began screaming. The first high-pitched wail tore out of her throat as she charged across the room. Her face contorted, she grabbed the Ouija board and flung it at the window. It shattered the glass, then clattered down onto the roof of the porch.

Jeff leaped to his feet and stared at Sarah, who was running wildly around the room, as if she was looking for something. Suddenly she bolted for the door, flung it open, and disappeared into the hall. Jeff, his face pale, looked helplessly at Elizabeth, but Elizabeth was unruffled. She went to the window, opened it, and picked the Ouija board from among the splinters of glass in which it lay, brushing her finger against one of the fragments accidentally as she did. Carefully she sucked at the wound after making sure it didn't have any glass in it. When she was finished she turned back to Jeff and smiled. "It's all right," she said. "It happens all the time. Don't worry, she'll be all right."

As Sarah's first scream resounded through the house, Barbara Stevens dropped her cards, and her hands flew to her mouth.

"My God," she said. "Something's happened to the children." She was halfway out of her chair before Rose could stop her.

"It's Sarah," Rose said. "It's all right. It happens every now and then, and I know it's awful, but please, just sit still."

Barbara sank uncertainly back into her chair, her

face pale, and Carl Stevens sat as if rooted to his seat as the screams built in intensity. And then they heard the pounding of feet coming down the stairs.

The door of the living room flew open, and the room was immediately vibrating with the agonized screams of the hysterical child. Sarah looked around wildly, her eyes seeming to be searching for something but seeing nothing, and then she was across the room, charging toward the French doors, her arms outstretched.

She hit the doors full force, and her hands struck the wood frames of the panes rather than the glass itself. The doors buckled under the strain and flew open, banging back against the walls, shattering the panes. Sarah was already across the porch.

"Jack," Rose cried out. "Stop her! Hurry!"

Jack was already on his feet, and as the Stevenses looked on in horror, he bolted across the room and through the doors. They heard Sarah's screams begin to fade as she raced into the field, and watched in fascination as Jack chased her. In her hysteria Sarah moved unnaturally fast, and the three people in the living room saw that she was almost outrunning her father. She was heading toward the woods.

In the sudden silence of the house, Rose moved to the French doors to watch the pursuit. Upstairs, directly above her, Elizabeth and Jeff also watched the activity in the field, which, in the grayness of the day and the slight drizzle, seemed to be some manic form of tag. No one spoke, and time almost seemed to stop as Jack Conger tried to catch up with his fleeing daughter.

Jack felt the rain in his face as he leaped the five steps from the porch and dashed into the field. He could see Sarah ahead of him, her small legs pumping as she charged headlong for the forest. He had thought he would have no trouble catching her, but as she maintained the distance between them Dr. Belter's words came back to him and he realized that her body was working on adrenalin, not strength. He wondered how long she could hold her pace.

She began slowing perceptibly when she was a little more than halfway across the field. She ran straight as an arrow, as if she had a spot picked out and was heading for it. As he chased her Jack felt his feet slip on the wet grass, and twice he stumbled. Sarah did not, and each time Jack lost his footing she widened the gap again.

And then, finally, she began to falter, and Jack could feel that the race was almost over. He would catch up to her at the forest's edge, or slightly inside it.

Inside it. The thought chilled him for some reason, and then he felt an odd sensation. His system had now taken over for him, and he felt the tingling of adrenalin as it coursed suddenly through his body. He saw the woods loom up in front of him as he lunged after Sarah.

His arms closed around her legs, and he felt her fall more than he saw it. And then she was wriggling in his arms, trying to get free of him, and her screaming mounted. The two of them struggled there in the mud, and Sarah's thrashing became stronger, as if for some reason her fears had multiplied. He almost lost his grip on her, and then, as suddenly as it had begun, it ended.

Her screams stopped, and she lay in the mud, her small chest heaving with the exertion, her throat choking on tight little sobs. Jack picked her up gently and turned toward the house.

He started across the field, his mind a blank. Then it began to come back to him. This was like another day, a day a year ago when he had carried Sarah across this field, and it had been raining, and she had been crying. That day her dress had been torn, and she had been bleeding. Reluctantly he looked down at the limp child in his arms.

Her face had gotten scratched in the struggle, and there was a thin line of blood on her left cheek. Her denim overalls were muddy, and the bib had been ripped open and flapped beneath her. Jack felt panic building in him.

He looked toward the house, and through his blurred eyes he saw them waiting for him, waiting for him to bring his child home, waiting for him to tell them what he had done. What had he done? He didn't know what he'd done. He was bringing his child home. But they were waiting for him. Why were they waiting for him?

He no longer felt the rain on his face, or the spongy softness of the wet field under his feet. It was as if he was walking through a tunnel, and he didn't know what lay at the other end, nor did he know what lay at the end he was coming from. He felt himself getting dizzy, and he forced his eyes from the group that waited for him at the French doors. He forced himself to look up.

He saw Elizabeth. She stood at a window on the second floor, and she was watching him. She was smiling at him. It was a gentle smile, and it comforted him.

Jack felt the panic begin to recede, and he concentrated on watching Elizabeth—on watching Elizabeth as she watched him, beckoned him onward, somehow comforting him as he carried Sarah through the rain.

Elizabeth disappeared from his view as he stepped onto the porch. The panic came upon him once more.

He carried Sarah into the living room and laid her gently on the sofa. Then he gave in to the panic and the hysteria and began to sob. He backed away from Sarah, as if he never should have carried her into the house at all, and watched, strangely detached, as Rose and the Stevenses gathered around her, clucking over her and fussing. No one saw him leave the room. They were busy with Sarah. He found his way up the stairs and into the bedroom he shared with Rose. He lay down on the bed and began to cry. He was remembering. He hated it.

* * *

Downstairs, the three adults in the living room stared helplessly at the sobbing child on the sofa. All they could do, they knew, was wait till it passed. But the sobs were heart-rending, and it almost sounded as though Sarah was trying to say something.

They strained their ears and tried to make words out of the strange sounds that were being wrenched out of Sarah, as if by some unseen force.

"Secret," she seemed to be saying. "Secret . . . secret . . ."

But they couldn't be sure.

21

Barbara Stevens felt totally helpless as she watched Rose try to comfort Sarah. The child lay trembling on the couch, and her vacant eyes darted wildly around the room, as if searching for a way out. If there were any coherent thoughts going through her mind, it was impossible to interpret what they might be.

"It's all right, baby," Rose crooned over and over. "It's all going to be all right now. It's over, and Mother's here." She was trying to cradle the child's head in her arms, but Sarah kept jerking spasmodically. It was all Rose could do to keep her on the sofa.

The Stevenses' eyes met over the crouching Rose, and a look of pity passed between them. Then they heard a noise at the living-room door and saw Elizabeth and Jeff standing there. Carl started to wave them back upstairs, but Rose had seen them too.

"It's all right," she said. "She's quieting." She turned her attention to the two children, who were now inside the living room, standing quietly, though Jeff was fidgeting.

"What happened up there?" Rose said quietly. She glanced at both children, but her gaze settled on Elizabeth. "What set her off?"

"I don't know," Elizabeth said. "We were playing with the Ouija board, and then I started telling Jeff about the old family legend."

"Was Sarah listening?"

"I don't know," Elizabeth said again. "I wasn't really

paying much attention to her. Jeff and I were arguing."

"Arguing?" Barbara Stevens asked. "What about?"

"She was telling me a story," Jeff said. "It was really crazy, and she got mad when I told her I didn't believe it."

"But it's true," Elizabeth insisted.

"About the cave?" Barbara asked. Her son looked at her in surprise.

"You mean you've heard about it too?"

"Yes, I have. But whether it's true or not, you shouldn't have argued with Elizabeth about it."

"But—" Jeff began, but his father cut him off.

"No buts," he said. "You know better than to argue about something you don't know anything about. Apologize to Elizabeth."

For a moment it looked as if Jeff was about to argue some more, but then he turned to Elizabeth. "I'm sorry I argued with you," he said, then couldn't resist adding, "but I still don't think there's a cave."

Elizabeth opened her mouth, but Rose spoke first.

"It doesn't matter right now whether there's a cave or not. What matters is what got Sarah so upset. What happened?"

Elizabeth picked up the story. "I was telling Jeff about the legend, and I got to the part about the cave. And we started arguing about whether or not it was real, and then all of a sudden Sarah started screaming. There's a broken window in the playroom."

"A broken window?"

"She threw the Ouija board through it," Jeff explained."

"What in the world were you doing with the Ouija board?" Carl Stevens wanted to know.

Jeff started to speak, but this time it was Elizabeth who got there first.

"We were just playing with it. It spelled out 'Beth.' "

"That's your name," Barbara Stevens said with a smile.

"Yes," Elizabeth said, shrugging. She flashed a quick glance at Jeff, and he caught her meaning immediately. *Don't let the grown-ups know too much about it. It's our secret.* He smiled at her.

"But what set Sarah off?" Rose said doggedly, casting about desperately for a rational reason for her daughter's outburst. Please, she begged, directing a prayer heavenward. Let me understand. Just once.

Jeff and Elizabeth looked at each other and shrugged. Rose was about to begin cross-examining them, but changed her mind when she saw her husband making his way slowly down the stairs. He didn't come into the living room, though. Instead, he started across the hall toward the back study. The back study and the bar, Rose thought.

"Well," she said, "I guess that more or less takes care of our bridge game, doesn't it. I don't think I could concentrate on the cards any more." She produced one of those bright and cheery smiles that tell the recipient it's time to leave. The Stevenses got the message.

Carl glanced at his watch nervously. "It's time for us to be getting home anyway," he said. "I'm sorry this had to happen. If there's anything we can do . . ." He trailed off helplessly, knowing there wasn't.

"We'll do it again," Barbara said quickly, coming to his rescue. "Soon. Call us, okay?"

Rose smiled at them, and Elizabeth escorted them to the door, holding the door open while they got into their coats. Outside the rain still fell quietly from the gray skies.

"Not too pleasant," Carl said.

"No," Elizabeth agreed. "But we get used to it." As they left, neither Carl nor Barbara was sure whether Elizabeth had been referring to the weather or to her sister's outburst.

Neither of them spoke until they had turned onto the Point Road.

"It must be hard," Barbara said finally.

"What?"

"Having a daughter like Sarah. I feel so sorry for them both."

Carl nodded his agreement. "I'm not sure I could cope with it at all, let alone as well as they do. Elizabeth is remarkable too," he added. "They're lucky to have her. In a way, I suppose, it balances things out."

"She's crazy," Jeff commented from the back seat. Carl reproved his son for talking that way. It never occurred to him that Jeff might be talking about Elizabeth, not Sarah. And it didn't occur to Jeff that his parents had misunderstood him.

Elizabeth watched the Stevenses drive away through the rain, then quietly closed the door and went back to the living room. She watched her mother try to comfort Sarah for a moment, then walked over and knelt beside her.

"I'll do it," she said. "I can calm her down."

Rose stood up in relief. She never knew what to do in these situations, and she always wound up feeling helpless and frustrated—feelings which she was sure were somehow transmitted to Sarah. Gratefully she let Elizabeth take over, and when she saw that Sarah was indeed getting through her seizure, or whatever it was, she started grimly for the study in the rear of the house. There, at least, she would be dealing with the familiar, and her husband, at least, would understand what she said. Until he got too drunk. An image of Martin Forager flashed into her mind, and then Forager's features suddenly faded and were replaced by Jack's. She shook off the image and went into the study without knocking. Jack was sitting in the wing chair, a stiff drink in his hands, his eyes fixed on the portrait of the young girl hanging above the cold fireplace.

"I could have Mrs. Goodrich build a fire," Rose volunteered cautiously.

"It wouldn't make any difference," Jack said dully.

"I'd still be cold." His eyes didn't move from the portrait.

"Are you all right?" Rose asked.

"I suppose so. I'm sorry I fell apart like that. I had a bad time out there."

"I noticed," Rose said, a trace of acid edging her voice.

Jack held up a hand. "Don't start, Rose, not now. I'm still on the edge, and I don't want to talk about it yet."

"You're going to have to, sooner or later."

"I know. But let's make it later, shall we?"

Rose sat down in the other chair by the fireplace, then felt the chill of the room. She decided to ask for a fire anyway, and went to find Mrs. Goodrich. When she returned Jack hadn't moved, but his drink was fuller than it had been when she left. She knew he'd finished the first and refilled his glass, but he didn't seem to have changed his position at all. His eyes were still fixed glassily on the portrait, as if it held some sort of magnetic force over him. Rose, too, gazed at it, and tried to see whatever it was that Jack was seeing.

A few minutes later Mrs. Goodrich came in to build the fire. She said nothing, nor was she spoken to. When she left the room her employers still sat silently, gazing at the picture. Only now, a fire blazed cheerfully at their feet. Mrs. Goodrich, returning to her small room by the kitchen, felt vaguely worried. She picked up her *TV Guide* and settled herself into her chair.

Elizabeth slipped out the front door and made her way through the drizzle to the barn. When she was inside she walked quickly to the old tack room and pulled the door shut behind her. She took off her raincoat and hung it on a peg. Then she began to unbutton her dress. When all the buttons were open, she slipped it off and folded it neatly. She set it on an empty shelf and covered it with an ancient horse blanket. Then she rummaged

around in the pile of old hay in one corner of the
tack room and pulled out a small bundle of wadded
material. She shook it out. It was the old dress she
had found in the attic, torn and stained now, but still
in one piece. She put it on carefully, then began
loosening her ponytail. When the blond hair was flowing freely over her shoulders, she glanced around the
tack room, then opened the door once more. In a moment she was out of the barn and walking slowly
across the field toward the wood. The rain began to
fall harder now, and by the time she was twenty yards
from the house her dress was sodden, her hair streaming. She didn't feel it. She moved slowly but deliberately through the storm.

She reached the edge of the woods, and didn't pause
to enjoy the protection the trees gave her from the
downpour. Her hair was plastered shroudlike over her
shoulders now, its wet sleekness accenting the features
of her face. Her pace quickened, and she moved
through the woods with a sure-footedness that would
have seemed impossible to an observer, had there been
one.

Lightning was beginning to play across the horizon
when she emerged from the woods, and a roll of thun-
der greeted her as she stepped out onto the crest of the
embankment. It was dark, very dark, though the sun
had not yet set. The storm seemed to blot it out almost completely, and the sea, barely visible through
the rain, had the menacing look of an animal in the
night. Elizabeth, slowed by neither the rain nor the
darkness, began gliding down the face of the embankment. As the storm intensified she disappeared behind
the boulder that guarded the entrance to the tunnel.

She found the flashlight in its niche next to the tunnel
entrance, but didn't turn it on until she had reached
the upper chamber. By now the stench from the dead
cat, mixed with the sour smells from the children's

vomiting, had fouled the air throughout the cavern, but Elizabeth didn't seem to notice it.

She crept to the top of the shaft, clicked the light on, and peered down. She could see nothing except the large flat table-rock, but she could hear soft moaning drifting upward. She knew Kathy and Jimmy were still down there, cowering somewhere in the darkness. She smiled to herself and began to lower the rope ladder into the pit.

She tested it briefly, then began to climb down, the still-lit flashlight casting eerie shadows as it glowed in the pocket of her peculiar, old-fashioned dress. She felt her foot hit the floor of the cave and stepped away from the ladder. She drew the flashlight from her pocket and shined it around the cavern.

Kathy Burton and Jimmy Tyler sat huddled together against the wall of the cavern opposite the place where the skeleton lay. Kathy's eyes were tightly shut against the sudden brightness of the light, but Jimmy Tyler held one hand out, shielding himself from the worst of the glare. He was squinting, trying to see past the source of the light. Kathy was whimpering softly to herself, and except for the hand clasped over her face was apparently unaware of what was going on. Jimmy didn't try to get up, but his eyes moved alertly in the light. Elizabeth shifted the beam to the old skeleton, and a sound crept from her lips as she saw that it was in disarray, the bones scattered a couple of feet in every direction.

Elizabeth reached into her pocket and brought out some candles she had found in the tack room and a small cigarette lighter she had taken from the house. She wedged the candles into cracks in the walls and lit them, placing the lighter carefully into a crevice just below the candles. Then she snapped the flashlight off, and it disappeared back into the large pocket of her dress. The flames of the candles flickered, then grew steady, and a warm light suddenly bathed the interior of the cavern.

Ignoring the two children huddled together, Elizabeth began tending to the old bones opposite them. Tenderly she moved each bone back into its proper position, and in a few minutes the skeleton was complete again, its arms folded once more over its empty rib cage. Only then did Elizabeth turn her attention back to Kathy Burton and Jimmy Tyler.

"It's time to have another party," she whispered. Kathy didn't seem to hear her, but Jimmy shrank closer to the girl next to him, his mind filling with fear. He knew this was Elizabeth, but she was not the Elizabeth he had known all his life. It was another Elizabeth, a terrifying Elizabeth.

She was covered with mud, and her hair, muddy now, as well as wet, clung to her face and shoulders. The torn dress, soaking wet and slimy with the muck of the cavern, clung to her body in lumpy folds, and there was an emptiness in her face that reminded Jimmy of his grandmother, when he had seen her at her funeral two months ago. She looks dead, Jimmy thought. Elizabeth looks dead. He tried to burrow in closer to Kathy Burton.

As he watched in horrified fascination, Elizabeth found the remains of the dead cat, its doll's clothes now covered with the cave slime, and propped it up carefully on one of the rocks that sat like stools around the table-rock. She discovered the head of the cat, now eyeless, but still wearing its grotesque bonnet, and tried to balance it on top of the torso. When she couldn't make it stay, she grasped the head firmly and ground it into the torso like an orange onto a juicer. The rotting flesh of the torso gave way, and the end of the spine protruded upward into the foramen magnum. The head held, squatting deeply between the cat's shoulders.

"Come to the table," Elizabeth said softly, beckoning Jimmy Tyler to leave the security of the cavern wall and join the cat at the strange table. He shook his head.

"Come to the table," Elizabeth repeated, her voice becoming menacing. Jimmy Tyler pulled his knees up to his chest, and tightened his grip on Kathy Burton's hand.

Elizabeth moved toward him, and her hand drew back to strike him. Just before the blow was delivered, Jimmy scuttled away from Kathy and crouched, shivering, on one of the small rocks.

Elizabeth turned to Kathy.

"You too," she ordered. Kathy didn't move, but her eyes flickered open a little, and her mouth worked as if she was trying to speak.

"Now," Elizabeth demanded. This time the blow fell, and Jimmy Tyler cringed at the sound of the sharp slap against Kathy's face. Still Kathy didn't move. Instead, a small gurgling sound escaped her lips.

Elizabeth glared down at the inert child for a moment, then began dragging her toward the center of the cavern by her feet. Weakly Kathy Burton tried to kick loose, but Elizabeth's grasp was firm. In seconds Elizabeth was setting Kathy on the third stool. When she stepped away Kathy slumped back to the floor, and Elizabeth kicked her.

"Sit up when you're at the table," she snapped. Kathy seemed to become slightly conscious of what was going on, and managed to pull herself upright. "That's nice," Elizabeth said. She stepped back and looked over the strange tableau.

"Now," she said. "Kathy, you're the mother. And Jimmy's the father. And Cecil is your baby. Your crazy baby. Feed your baby, Mother."

Kathy sat quietly, barely able to keep herself upright.

"I said to feed your baby!" Elizabeth demanded. When Kathy still made no move toward the cat, Elizabeth raised her fist and brought it down hard on

Kathy's back, driving her face first into the center of the table. "You do what I tell you," Elizabeth snarled through her teeth.

"If Mother can't feed the baby, you do it," Elizabeth said to Jimmy. He looked at her, puzzled, trying to figure out what he was supposed to do. He saw her fist closing again, and decided the best thing to do was to pretend. He quickly mimed putting a bottle in the baby's mouth.

"She's too old for a bottle," Elizabeth hissed. "She eats real food."

Jimmy quickly pretended to pick up a spoon and shovel some food toward the cat.

"Talk to her," Elizabeth commanded. "Talk to your baby."

Jimmy froze for a moment, then found his tongue.

"Nice baby," he said. "Here's some nice food for the nice baby."

"Her name's Sarah!" Elizabeth screamed. "Don't you even know your baby's name? What kind of a father are you?"

"Sarah," Jimmy repeated quickly. "Here's some food for nice little Sarah."

He continued pretending to shove food into the dead cat's mouth, and kept babbling at it, not knowing what he was saying but being careful to call the cat Sarah every few seconds.

"She doesn't answer, does she?" Elizabeth said softly. Jimmy shook his head.

"Do you know why she doesn't answer?" Elizabeth asked smoothly.

Jimmy shook his head again.

"Because she's crazy!" Elizabeth screamed. "But children are supposed to answer when they're spoken to, aren't they?"

Jimmy nodded dumbly.

"Then she's a bad child," Elizabeth said. "She's crazy

and she's bad. Punish her." Jimmy didn't move. *"Punish her!"*

His eyes fixed on Elizabeth, and on the hand that was flexing rhythmically into a fist. Jimmy slowly picked up the dead cat. The head tumbled from the body and rolled into the shadows. Shuddering, he put the corpse over his knee and began spanking it.

Elizabeth smiled.

Kathy still huddled over the table, cradling her head in her arms, and she must have moved slightly, for Elizabeth's attention was suddenly drawn to her.

"Don't sleep at the table," she said menacingly. Jimmy, afraid that Kathy was about to receive another of Elizabeth's terrible blows, reached out to shake her.

"Don't touch her," Elizabeth commanded. "You don't like to touch Mother, do you? She wants you to touch her, but you don't like to. We know what you like, don't we?" She leered at the little boy, who stared at her in bewilderment.

"You like the baby, don't you? We know you like the baby better than you like Mother, don't we?" And suddenly her voice rose, and the cavern was filled to overflowing with the sound of her words.

"Well, if that's what you want, that's what you can have!"

Elizabeth leaped on Jimmy, and began pulling at his clothes. He struggled, but he was too weak from hunger and fear to fight very hard. Soon, before he had a chance to realize what was happening, Elizabeth had stripped his clothes from him and flung them in a corner. Naked, he huddled on the floor of the cavern.

Elizabeth picked up the torso of the dead cat.

"This is what you want, isn't it?" she hissed. "You want your baby, don't you?"

And she fell on Jimmy Tyler, forcing the rotting flesh of the dead cat against his crotch, mumbling incoherently that if he wanted it so badly, here it was.

Jimmy Tyler's helpless sobbing mixed with Elizabeth's ramblings, filled the cave. He didn't understand what was happening to him.

Kathy Burton, the strange sounds penetrating her fogged mind, looked up and watched the vile scene that was transpiring in front of her. She couldn't grasp it at first, couldn't sort it all out into anything that made sense. Then her mind cleared a little more and she realized what was happening. She looked on in horror as Elizabeth continued in her efforts to force Jimmy Tyler to copulate with the corpse.

Kathy Burton screamed, and with the last of her reserves of strength she pulled herself to her feet and moved toward the spot where Elizabeth struggled with Jimmy Tyler.

"Don't," she croaked. "Please, Elizabeth, don't."

Elizabeth wheeled, and Kathy wished she hadn't tried to interfere. She began backing away, the light in Elizabeth's eyes driving her backward until she reached the wall of the cavern. Her terror grew as she saw Elizabeth pick up a rock from the floor of the cavern. She felt the strength suddenly ebbing from her body when Elizabeth raised the stone over her head, and she began collapsing to the cavern floor as Elizabeth brought the rock downward.

For Kathy Burton, the horror was over.

An hour later Rose Conger found her older daughter emerging from the shower.

"I was just going to tell you that if you wanted a shower before dinner, you should get started. I see I'm too late."

Elizabeth nodded and smiled at her mother. Rose smiled back, and silently thanked God for sending her Elizabeth. Without Elizabeth, she didn't know how she would manage.

"Will you bring Sarah down with you?" she said.

"Sure," Elizabeth replied. "As soon as I get dressed."

* * *

In the cave, Jimmy Tyler lay where Elizabeth had left him, too weak and too confused even to try to find his clothes. He lay shivering, naked in the darkness.

22

Rose lay stiffly in bed later that night, listening to the rain pound on the roof, her thoughts as turbulent as the weather outside. She could hear nothing from Jack's inert form beside her, but she sensed that he wasn't asleep.

"There's something about that portrait, isn't there?" she said finally. Jack snapped on the lamp by his side of the bed and raised himself up on one elbow.

"Do you feel it too?" he asked.

"No," Rose said flatly. "I don't. But all evening long you sat and stared at it. What is it about it? It's as if you're trying to see something in it."

Jack lay back down again and stared at the ceiling.

"I'm not sure," he said. "It just seems like—like the portrait should look more like Sarah than like Elizabeth."

"Sarah? Why Sarah?"

"Nothing I can put my finger on. Just a feeling. I keep thinking about what Dr. Belter told us. About the little girl who was supposed to have been killed. I keep getting the feeling that the picture must be of that girl."

"What does that have to do with Sarah?" Rose's voice was sharper now, as if she was guarding herself against what was to come.

"I remembered today. I remembered it all. Rose, that day a year ago. I almost killed Sarah."

"But you didn't."

"No, I didn't," Jack said miserably. "I wanted something else."

"Something else?"

"I wanted to rape her," Jack said quietly. He waited for a response from Rose, and when there was none he went on. "I don't have the vaguest idea of what it was all about, but today, when I was bringing Sarah back in from the rain, I looked up and saw Elizabeth watching me. And then, suddenly, I remembered it all. I remembered being in the woods, and watching Sarah crawl under a bush. And suddenly I wanted her. Sexually. Don't ask me to explain why—I don't know. It was the most awful thing I've ever felt in my life. I felt like I was someone else, but I was still myself. It was like I was being made to do something, or want to do something, that I didn't want to do. And then an awful feeling came over me that . . . that Sarah was seducing me."

Rose sat up. "Seducing you?" she demanded. "Seducing you? My God, Jack, she was only ten years old!"

"I didn't say she *was* seducing me. I said I *felt* like she was. And so I started beating her. I really wanted to kill her. Oh, Jesus, Rose, it was awful." The pain of memory swept over him once more, and he began crying softly. Rose, failing to understand what had happened to him, her own feelings in turmoil, searched for something to say.

"What's all this got to do with the portrait downstairs?" she asked finally.

"I'm not sure," Jack muttered. "When I look at that portrait I get the strange feeling that what happened to Sarah a year ago, happened to that girl a long time ago."

"And that, I suppose, takes you off the hook, doesn't it?" Rose said icily. "Suddenly, instead of being the aggressor you're the victim? My God, Jack."

Jack cringed at her words, but Rose plunged on.

"And what about today? Were you a victim again

today? Did some strange force come over you again today? Were you not yourself again today?"

"What are you talking about?"

"I saw it today, Jack. I saw it all. And I was ashamed that Carl and Barbara Stevens saw it too."

Jack sat up and stared at his wife. "I don't know what you're talking about," he said.

"I'm talking about you out there in the field with Sarah. I'm not sure which was worse, watching her charging across the field, screaming, or watching you rescue her. You were vicious, Jack. It wasn't like you were helping her. It looked like you were attacking her! It was like it was all happening all over again."

Jack sat up, his eyes blazing. "Are you out of your mind? Today was nothing like a year ago. Nothing at all. For one thing, I was stone sober today."

Rose frowned. "Maybe you don't have to be drunk," she said. "Maybe something more serious is wrong with you."

Something snapped inside Jack, and he grabbed Rose by the shoulders and pinned her down to the bed.

"We'll see who I can rape," he snarled, and as Rose lay back limply, as if he weren't worth fighting against, his rage grew. He grabbed at her nightdress and tore it from her body. Still she lay there, taunting him with her passiveness. He hurled himself on her and tried desperately to mount her.

And he couldn't.

Now she began squirming under him, and for a moment he wasn't sure whether she was trying to free herself or help him.

"You can't do it, can you?" her mocking voice came from beneath him, slightly muffled by his chest. "Only little girls? Well, I'm not a little girl, Jack. I'm a woman, a real woman. Now get off me." She pushed up against him, and once more he tried to thrust himself inside her. Again he failed.

Then the struggle began in earnest, and Rose suddenly became frightened by what might happen to her. She redoubled her efforts, and finally succeeded in freeing herself. She scrambled from the bed and turned to face him. His eyes blazing, his anger still growing, he stared at her, and Rose was frightened. She felt she knew what Sarah must have experienced in the woods that day so long ago. She reached out to pick up an ashtray from the table by the bed.

"Don't come near me," she screamed. "I swear, Jack, if you so much as lay a finger on me, I'll—"

"You'll what?" Jack thundered. "You'll kill me? Do you really think I care?" He was standing now, and the bed separated them. Both of them were shouting, neither hearing the other. And then, when they both paused for a breath, they heard it. Someone was tapping at their door. They stared at each other, stricken. The children.

But it was Mrs. Goodrich's voice out in the hall. "Are you all right?" she was saying. "Land sakes, you're waking up the whole house."

There was a silence; then Rose spoke. "It's all right, Mrs. Goodrich," she called softly. "I'm sorry we disturbed you. We were just—just talking about something."

"Some people like to sleep at night," Mrs. Goodrich said. They heard her retreating back toward the staircase, her footsteps heavy as she plodded down.

"I suppose the children heard it all, too," Rose complained.

"Don't try to blame it on me," Jack said. "You might try listening to me once in a while, instead of accusing me."

"You're never responsible, are you?" Rose said, making an effort to keep her voice down. "You'll never take the responsibility for anything, will you?"

"Yes," Jack said. "I will. But not for everything, Rose. Not for everything." He began dressing.

"Where are you going?" Rose demanded.

"You don't need to know," Jack said. Then he smiled cruelly. "I'll take the responsibility for where I'm going. And I'll take the responsibility for what I'm going to do."

He left her standing next to the bed in her torn nightgown, and she hadn't moved when she heard his car roar off down the driveway two minutes later. Only when the noise of the car had faded did she sink back down to the bed. Shakily she reached for a cigarette and lit it. The smoke, sucked deeply into her lungs, seemed to calm her.

She finished her cigarette and lay down on the bed, turning off the light. She lay still for a long time, keeping her breathing even and forcing her tense muscles to relax. She tried to sort out her thoughts, and when that failed decided to drift with them and see where they led.

Thirty minutes later, she was still trying to relax her muscles, and her mind was as chaotic as it had been when she lay down. She decided to get something to eat.

She padded into the kitchen and turned the light on. She listened for a minute and heard the rhythmic snoring of Mrs. Goodrich in the next room. She crept to the refrigerator and opened it.

She thought she heard the click of a door opening as she poked among the leftovers neatly packaged on the shelves of the refrigerator, but it wasn't until she felt a draft on her legs that she turned around. The back door stood open.

A stab of fear ran through her, and she instinctively moved toward the drawer where the knives were kept. Then she saw who had opened the back door.

Sarah, her flannel nightgown soaking wet and covered with mud, her dark hair glistening with the rain, stood by the knife drawer, as if trying to decide whether to open it or not.

"Sarah?" Rose breathed, her heart pounding and a terrible fear rising in her. "Sarah," she said again.

She approached the child and knelt down. She reached out to touch Sarah, very gently, for fear that her daughter was sleepwalking and not wanting to wake her if she was. But at the touch Sarah turned around and stared at her mother. She blinked a couple of times, and Rose was sure she was awake.

"Sarah," she said quietly. "What is it? What were you doing outside?"

Sarah peered blankly at her mother, and Rose didn't know whether she had been heard or not. Then a large tear formed in one of Sarah's eyes and slowly ran down her face, streaking the mud in its path. It collected on her chin, then, when it was too heavy to hang on any longer, fell to the floor. Rose gathered the girl into her arms. Sarah did not resist.

"Come on," Rose said. "I'll take you upstairs and put you to bed."

She picked the little girl up and closed both the back door of the house and the refrigerator door. Snapping off the kitchen light and crooning to the child who shivered in her arms, she made her way upstairs to the bathroom. She set Sarah down and began running a tub of hot water. Then she went to get towels.

When she returned, Sarah still sat where Rose had left her, unmoving, as though she were thinking about something. But her eyes, the huge, beautiful brown eyes, still seemed vacant, staring at the tub of water. Rose undressed her and placed her in the tub.

When she finished bathing Sarah, Rose put her to bed. She tucked the child in carefully, then sat with her till she was sure Sarah was asleep. Finally she left Sarah's room, leaving the light on, and went downstairs. She knew she would not sleep if she went back to bed; knew she would not sleep until her husband came home. She wished he were home now, or at least had told her where he was going. She sat in the study and waited. Above her the little girl who looked so much like Elizabeth smiled down at her. The picture comforted Rose, and made her waiting easier.

Jack drove fast through the storm, the pounding of his heart echoed by the beating of the windshield wipers as they fought vainly to keep the glass clear in front of his eyes. He didn't need to see, really; he was so familiar with the Point Road that he felt he could have driven it blindfolded, navigating by the bumps and chuckholes.

He drove automatically, his mind racing, his thoughts chaotic. Then he saw the lights of Port Arbello glowing dimly ahead in the rain, and he knew where he was going.

He pulled the car into Sylvia Bannister's driveway, and left it there for anybody who wished to see. The house was dark, but he didn't consider going elsewhere. Instead, he walked up to the front door and knocked loudly. When there was no response, he knocked again, louder. Finally he saw a light flash on and heard feet coming toward the door.

"Who is it?" Sylvia's sleepy voice called.

"It's me. Jack."

He listened as she unfastened the chain and threw the bolt. Then the door opened, and she squinted out at him.

"Excuse me," she said, and flipped the switch for the porch light. "I didn't mean to leave you in the dark."

"It's all right," Jack said, grinning crookedly. Seeing her made him feel better. "I seem to be in the dark a lot these days anyway."

She pulled the door open and let him step inside before she closed it again, and fixed the chain and deadbolt. "I suppose it's silly," she said. "But they make me feel safer." Then she looked at him closely, and con-

cern came into her face. "Are you all right?" she said.
"Let me get you a drink. You look like you need one."

"I do," Jack said. "I suppose I shouldn't but I could
really use one."

"She's got you convinced, hasn't she?" Sylvia said
as she led him to the kitchen.

"Convinced?"

"That you're an alcoholic," Sylvia said, pouring them
each a drink.

"I suppose I am." Jack accepted the glass she handed
him.

"No," Sylvia said definitely. "You're not. Martin
Forager is an alcoholic. You're not. At least not yet. But
I suppose if you wanted to you could become one. Do
you?"

"I'm not sure sometimes. But yes, sometimes I do
want to become one. Sometimes I'd like to stay drunk all
the time. I would, except I suffer from terrible hang-
overs. They don't show, but God, do they hurt."

"Well, I suppose as long as you're suffering you're
safe. At least, that's what my mother taught me. Do you
want to sit here, or shall I build a fire?"

"This'll be fine," Jack said, settling into one of the
chairs at the kitchen table. "It makes it different from
home. Mrs. Goodrich does not tolerate any Conger
sitting in the kitchen. I think she thinks it's beneath
our dignity. Not that we have any dignity left, after
tonight." He told Sylvia what had happened at home.

"It must have been awful," she said when he had
finished.

He swirled his drink and smiled wryly. "Well, it
wasn't pleasant. So I took off, and here I am."

"I meant the remembering. It must have been terrible."

Jack nodded. "It was. In a way, I wish I hadn't remembered. Not knowing what I'd done was bad enough.
I think knowing what I was trying to do is even worse."

"Nonsense," Sylvia said. "You seem to be forgetting something. You didn't rape her, and you didn't kill her."

"But I wanted to," Jack said miserably.

"Wanting to do something and doing it are two entirely different things. If I had to feel badly about all the things I've wanted to do, I'd be a mess. And this town wouldn't be in very good shape, either. I can think of at least three people right off the bat that I've wanted to kill. I mean really kill. Complete with fantasies of doing it, and getting away with it. So stop feeling bad." She glanced at his drink, then held her own glass up. "And fix us both another. I'm not your secretary now, you know. I'm a woman, and I want to be waited on."

"You can kick me out if you want to go back to sleep," Jack said. "But I hope you don't."

"Kick you out? Not much chance of that. You might fire me in the morning, when you're my boss again. Besides, I happen to like you."

"Do you, Sylvia?" Jack said seriously. "Do you really? I guess I haven't been feeling particularly likable lately."

"And it hasn't occurred to you that that might have something to do with the way Rose has been treating you? It's hard to feel good about yourself when someone you love is making you feel bad about yourself."

"I'm not sure I love her," Jack said slowly.

Sylvia glanced at him, and the corners of her mouth flickered upward. "I suppose I could read a lot into that, if I wanted to, but I won't. You love her, Jack, even if you don't believe you do. You're used to her, and a lot of love is nothing more than habit."

"I thought love had something to do with passion," Jack said, trying to keep his voice light.

"Passion? I'm not sure passion has anything to do with it at all. Look at me, for instance. I've loved you for a long time." She smiled at his expression of surprise. "You didn't know? Well, why should you? It wasn't the kind of love that demands attention. It was the kind of love that's comforting. I knew it was there, and it helped me. If you didn't know it was there, or nobody knew it was there, it didn't matter. It was my love, and I liked it. And it had nothing to do with passion."

"And what about the other afternoon?"

"That was passion," Sylvia said softly. "And I liked it. But it scares me."

"Scares you?"

"Yes. I keep wondering—after the passion dies, will I still have my love? Or will that fade too? I don't want it to, Jack. I want to be able to go on loving you."

Their eyes met, and Jack reached out to touch her hand.

"And I want you to go on loving me, Sylvia. I want you to very much."

Together they walked to Sylvia's bedroom and closed the door. Their drinks sat forgotten on the kitchen table, and the ice in the glasses slowly melted.

Rose heard the car grinding up the driveway and glanced at the clock. He'd been gone almost three hours. She wondered if he'd notice the light under the study door when he came in, or whether he was too drunk. She heard the front door open, and her husband's footsteps in the hall. They stopped, then started again, and she heard him coming toward the study. He'd seen the light.

She waited till the study door opened before she spoke.

"I hope no children disappear tonight," she said coldly. "I won't be able to vouch for your whereabouts." She looked at him icily, but he didn't flinch. She realized he was sober.

"If it becomes necessary, Sylvia Bannister can tell

anyone who's interested where I've been tonight. And what I've been doing."

"I see," Rose said quietly, absorbing what he was telling her. "I suppose I should have known. She's been in love with you for years. I didn't know it was mutual."

"I didn't either, until recently," Jack said. "Are we going to have a fight about it?"

"Do you want one?" Rose countered.

Jack smiled and sat down. "No, I don't. I've had enough of fighting, Rose, with you, with everything. If you really want to know, I didn't want to come home tonight. Sylvia sent me."

"Sent you?" Rose asked, her brows arching. "Was she afraid the neighbors would talk?"

"No. She was worried about you. She likes you, you know."

"And I like her. But not so much that I'll let her take my place."

Jack chuckled. "It wasn't very long ago that you were thinking about leaving me."

"A woman has pride. If I left you it wouldn't be so that you could marry Sylvia Bannister. You'd be so broke that you wouldn't be able to marry anyone."

"I see," Jack said, standing up. "Somehow this conversation seems to have gotten out of hand. I have no intention of asking you for a divorce, at least not right now. So I think I'll go to bed."

"Not yet," Rose said. She realized that it sounded like a command, and that Jack wouldn't respond to a command. Not tonight. She softened her voice. "Please," she said. "Something happened tonight, and I don't know what it means or what we should do about it."

Jack sank back into the chair he had been occupying. "You mean after I left?"

Rose nodded. "I couldn't sleep, and after a while I decided to get something to eat. I went down to the kitchen, and while I was there Sarah came in."

"So?"

"I'm sorry. She came in from outside. She was dripping wet and covered with mud. Needless to say, I haven't the slightest idea where she'd been, or why."

"What did you do?"

"What could I do? I took her upstairs, bathed her, and put her to bed. I waited till she fell asleep, then came down here. I've been here ever since, trying to figure out what she could have been doing."

"Did she do anything in the kitchen?"

"If you mean, did she make one of her scenes, no. But I had the strangest feeling. I was burrowing around in the fridge when she came in, and I didn't hear her. I didn't realize there was anyone there till I felt the draft from the open door. When I realized there was someone in the room, my first thought was to grab a knife. And that's when I saw Sarah. She was standing by the knife drawer, and it seemed like she was trying to make up her mind about something."

"About what?"

"I don't know," Rose said uncomfortably. Then: "Oh, yes, I do know. It seemed to me that she was trying to choose one of the knives. I'm probably wrong, but that's the way it seemed."

Jack considered it, turning everything over in his mind, but he could come up with no answers.

"Is she still in her room?" he asked.

"Yes. I'd have heard her if she'd come down."

"Well, I don't see what we can do tonight. Let's go to bed, and look in on her. Then I'll call Dr. Belter in the morning. I doubt if it's anything serious, though. She was probably sleepwalking."

"No," Rose said definitely. "She wasn't sleepwalking, I'm sure she was awake, and I'm sure she knew what she was doing. And I'm very much afraid of what it might have been."

She was thinking of Kathy Burton and Jimmy Tyler, and Jack knew it. But he saw no reason to try to talk to her about it. It would be better to let Dr. Belter handle it in the morning.

"Come on," he said gently, "let's go to bed."

As he led her upstairs, he realized that Sylvia was right. He did love his wife. He loved her very much. He hoped it wasn't too late for them.

23

The next day, Columbus Day, dawned bright and cold, with a north wind rattling the house at the end of Conger's Point. By nine o'clock the brightness was gone, and the gray skies blended into an almost invisible horizon with the leaden sea. There was a heavy swell running, and the surf pounded at the Point with a winter strength.

"I know it's a holiday," Rose heard Jack saying into the telephone as she came down the stairs. "But I think it's pretty important. She seems to have been sleepwalking."

Fifteen miles away, in his cramped apartment at White Oaks, Charles Belter was stifling a yawn. He came awake at the word and his brows knit into a frown. Sleepwalking? It didn't fit the pattern. "Just what do you mean by sleepwalking?" he inquired. He yawned again, covering the mouthpiece of the telephone, and reached for his coffee. He was glad Jack Conger was at least aware it was a holiday, even if he didn't intend to respect the fact.

"Well," Jack was saying, "I'm not really sure she was sleepwalking. It just seems to be the most logical explanation. She was wandering around in the rain last night."

Belter set his coffee down and straightened up. "In the rain?" he said. "You mean outside?"

"That's right."

"What time was this?"

"I'd say about eleven thirty. Maybe midnight."

"How long was she outside?"

"I don't have any idea. We didn't know she'd gone anywhere. My wife came down to get something to eat, and while she was in the kitchen Sarah came in. Soaking wet and muddy."

"I see," Dr. Belter said. "Did she seem to be all right otherwise?"

"I—I don't really know," Jack faltered. "I wasn't home."

When there was no reply, Jack felt he ought to explain a little more. "I had to go out for a while," he said.

"What time did you get back?" Dr. Belter inquired, hearing something in Jack's voice that made him want to pry a little.

"I'm not sure," Jack hedged. "Late. I guess around three."

"I see," Dr. Belter said again. "May I assume you want to talk to me today?"

"If it wouldn't be too inconvenient for you. We think we're going to have to make up our minds about what to do with Sarah, and we'd like to talk it over with you. And after last night it suddenly seems urgent."

It seems urgent to you, anyway, Dr. Belter thought. Aloud he said, "Suppose you and your wife come out here about one?"

"Shall we bring Sarah with us?"

Dr. Belter thought about it. "I don't think so," he said. "There really isn't any need for it, and most of the staff is off today, so there isn't anyone around to look after her while we talk."

"All right," Jack said. "We'll see you at one, then." He hung up the phone and smiled at Rose. She did not return his smile.

"One o'clock," he said. "But he doesn't want us to bring Sarah."

Rose looked doubtful. "I don't know," she said. "I hate to leave her alone."

"She won't be alone. Elizabeth will be here, and Mrs. Goodrich."

"It just seems to me, with everything that's been happening, it's not a good idea to leave the children alone."

"I don't call being left with Mrs. Goodrich being left alone. When I was a boy she used to watch me like a hawk when my folks were away. I think she had visions of the Lindberghs in her mind."

"That was a long time ago," Rose commented. "She's getting a bit old to be watching children."

"Not that old," Jack said.

"Oh, I don't know," Rose said. "I suppose I wouldn't worry, but with Sarah . . ." Her voice trailed off, and she poured some coffee into her cup. Jack pushed his toward her, but she ignored it.

"It'll be all right," Jack insisted, and reached for the coffeepot.

"What will?" Elizabeth asked. Jack looked up and smiled at his daughter. He looked for Sarah behind her, but she wasn't there.

"Where's your sister?" he asked.

"Still asleep," Elizabeth replied. "She didn't want to wake up this morning, so I left her in bed. If you want, I'll go up and get her." She paused, then repeated her question. "What'll be all right?"

"We have to go see Dr. Belter this afternoon," Jack said. "Your mother's a little worried about leaving you and Sarah alone while we're gone."

"Won't Mrs. Goodrich be here?"

"Of course she will."

"Then why should you worry?" Elizabeth asked her mother. "I'm old enough to stay by myself, and I can take care of Sarah."

"I'm sure you can," Rose said reassuringly. "Ordinarily I wouldn't worry at all, but with the things that have been happening lately, I just want to be extra careful. That's all."

Elizabeth smiled at her mother. "Well, stop worrying. Nothing's going to happen."

It began drizzling at noon, and Rose wished she didn't have to go out. She looked longingly at the fireplace in the study and thought about how nice it would be to simply curl up on the sofa and spend the afternoon reading. But she couldn't. There were things that had to be done, and decisions that had to be made. But not right now. She sank down into the wing chair and stared moodily into the fire. She felt melancholy coming over her, and tried to force it away. She glanced up at the portrait, and found that her first thought was that it actually was a picture of Elizabeth. She reminded herself that it was not, and wondered once more who the girl in the portrait was. Could she really be the little girl that Dr. Belter had heard about? No, she told herself. The whole thing is silly. She stood up and straightened the picture. In the flickering light of the fire the child's expression seemed to change a little; something in the eyes. She looked again and decided that her own eyes were playing tricks on her. Whatever she'd thought she had seen was gone.

"Well," Jack said from the door, "we might as well get going."

"Already?" Rose said. "We have plenty of time." She wanted to put it off, and she knew it. She had a feeling about today, a feeling that today was going to be some kind of turning point. She wanted to put the interview with the doctor off as long as possible.

"I know," Jack said gently. "I'm not looking forward to it either. But it's something that has to be done."

"Yes," Rose sighed. "I suppose so. All right. Let me put on my coat. Are the girls downstairs?"

"I think they're in the playroom."

"Call them down, will you? I want to kiss them good-bye."

Jack looked at her curiously. "Rose, we're only going to talk today. You're acting like it's the end of the world or something."

She smiled tightly. "I suppose I am. But call them down anyway, will you?"

She began putting on her coat and heard Jack's voice calling from the foot of the stairs. When she got to the front door the children were waiting for her.

She kissed Elizabeth perfunctorily, then knelt by Sarah and put her arms around the child. She nuzzled Sarah's cheek, and felt the little girl withdraw slightly.

"You be good now," she whispered. "Mommy and Daddy have to go out for a while." She stood up again and smiled at Elizabeth. "We should be back by four thirty or five," she said. "Please stay in the house."

"Who wants to go out in that?" Elizabeth said.

"I know," Rose agreed. "It's awful, isn't it?"

"I wish it would snow," Elizabeth said. "At least it's pretty. This is depressing."

Rose smiled at her daughter's use of the word. She was definitely growing up, if she was starting to find the weather "depressing."

She left the house with her husband and got into the car. She turned to wave to the children as they drove away, then began preparing herself for the interview with Dr. Belter.

Elizabeth watched the car until it reached the Point Road, then closed the door. She was about to go upstairs when the phone rang.

"I'll get it," she called to Mrs. Goodrich. "Hello?" she said into the receiver.

"Who's this?" a voice asked.

"It's Elizabeth. Who's this?"

"Jeff Stevens. What are you doing?"

"Nothing. My parents had to go some place, and I'm taking care of Sarah."

"Oh." Jeff sounded disappointed. "I thought we might go look for the cave," he said.

"The cave? I thought you didn't believe there was a cave."

"I don't. And if we can't find it you'll have to admit I'm right, won't you?"

"I don't know," Elizabeth said noncommittally. "I don't see how our not finding it would prove it isn't there. That doesn't make sense. All it would prove is that we didn't find it."

"If it's there, we can find it. You want to try?"

Elizabeth thought about it. "Why don't you come over here?" she said. "Will your parents let you?"

"They're out playing golf," Jeff said.

"In the rain?"

"It doesn't bother them. They always play until it snows. Sometimes they even play in the snow."

"Weird," Elizabeth commented.

"Yeah," Jeff said. "I'll see you in a little while."

Elizabeth hung up the phone and went to find Mrs. Goodrich, to tell her Jeff Stevens was coming over. In the kitchen she could hear the sound of the old housekeeper's television droning from the next room. Elizabeth tapped lightly on the door. When there was no response, she tried the door, and finding it unlocked opened it and looked into the room. Mrs. Goodrich was sitting in her chair, facing the television. She was sound asleep. Elizabeth smiled to herself and closed the door again.

Twenty minutes later Jeff Stevens arrived, and Elizabeth led him to the back study. Sarah followed silently along behind, her wide brown eyes seeming to take in everything and see nothing.

"This is where my great-great-uncle left the rabbit," Elizabeth said, pointing to the wing chair.

"And that's the little girl who was supposed to have

been killed?" Jeff asked, pointing to the portrait above the fireplace.

"That's Beth," Elizabeth said, nodding her head.

"She looks just like you," Jeff said.

"I know. But she isn't me. I don't like her."

Jeff grinned at her. "You sound like you know her."

"I do," Elizabeth said. "I've talked to her."

"That's dumb," Jeff said. "You can't talk to dead people."

"Yes you can," Elizabeth insisted. "With the Ouija board."

"It didn't say anything the other day," Jeff said sarcastically. "All it did was spell out a name. And I'll bet you did that."

"It was her," Elizabeth said defiantly.

"Well, if it's all true, let's go find the cave. If there is one, I'll bet that's where your friend Beth is."

"I don't know," Elizabeth said. "The cave is supposed to be on the embankment, and I'm not supposed to go there."

"I'm not either," Jeff said. "But I'm not going to let that stop me. Are you chicken?"

"No, but I just don't think we should."

"You're afraid we won't find it and you'll have to admit you're wrong."

"All right, then," Elizabeth said suddenly. "Let's go." She turned to leave the room, and Jeff smiled. It had worked.

Elizabeth found her coat and put it on. "We'll have to take Sarah with us," she said. "I can't leave her here by herself."

"What about the housekeeper? Can't she watch her?"

"She's asleep. Besides, she wouldn't know what to do if Sarah gets upset."

Jeff decided it was better to take Sarah with them than not to go at all.

"All right," he agreed. "Let's go."

Elizabeth put Sarah into her coat and buttoned it up. Then the three children left the house.

The rain seemed to have let up slightly as they crossed the field, and when they were in the woods the trees protected them from it almost completely. As they entered the woods, Jeff looked around.

"Which way?" he asked.

"There's a path," Elizabeth said. "You can hardly see it, but it's there. Come on." Her voice seemed suddenly different to Jeff, and he thought her eyes looked odd.

Silently and quickly she led the way through the woods, and Jeff was amazed at her sure-footedness. Elizabeth seemed to know exactly where she was going, and where to put each foot in the tangle of roots and rocks that carpeted the path. Nor did she look back to see if the others were keeping up. Twice Jeff had to call to her to wait, and he stopped two more times to help Sarah, who was picking her way with great difficulty. And then they emerged from the woods and stood on the embankment. The rain had begun coming down harder now, and the wind whipped it into their faces. Below them the sea looked angry. Jeff felt himself shiver a little, and wondered if he should have talked them into this. The embankment looked as dangerous as his parents had told him it was.

"Where do you suppose it is?" he said, hoping that Elizabeth would suggest that they give it up.

"I'm not sure," Elizabeth said. "Let's try this way." She led them along the embankment, and Jeff was about to suggest that it was too dangerous when Elizabeth suddenly started making her way down the face, following a path that Jeff couldn't see at all. He watched her move surely from rock to rock and decided that if she could do it, so could he.

But he found it more difficult than he had imagined. The rocks were slippery, and he couldn't seem to find the same toeholds that had served Elizabeth so well. He made his way slowly, trying to keep one eye on Elizabeth to try to see where she was putting her feet. Now and then he glanced back to see how Sarah was faring, but she seemed to be able to keep up with him, and in a couple of minutes he stopped worrying about her. The rain was making the rocks more slippery every minute, and he was afraid he was about to lose sight of Elizabeth as she made her way nimbly downward. He called to her, but she didn't hear him over the roar of the wind and the surf. And then she disappeared behind a large boulder.

He crept cautiously along, picking his way from one rock to another, and concentrated on keeping the large boulder behind which Elizabeth had disappeared in sight. Behind him Sarah was matching his slow pace.

"Here."

Jeff jumped at the sound of the word, and peered into the shadow of the huge stone. There was Elizabeth, crouching low to protect herself from the rain and wind.

"What?" he said.

"It's here," Elizabeth told him. "I found the cave."

Jeff frowned and searched the darkness. "There's nothing there," he said.

"Yes, there is," Elizabeth insisted. "Come down here."

He climbed down till he was beside her. "Where?"

"Right there," Elizabeth said, pointing. Then he saw it. There, in the rock's deep shadow, almost invisible in the darkness, was a hole in the embankment. He moved closer and peered in. He was aware of Sarah behind him, pulling at him and making small, sobbing noises. He shook her off, and when she reached out for him again Elizabeth took her hands and stared into her eyes. A moment later, Sarah was calm.

"What do you suppose is inside?" Jeff asked.

"I don't know," Elizabeth replied. "Shall we look?"

Jeff looked doubtfully at the hole. It seemed just

large enough to crawl into, and he wasn't sure it led anywhere. Still, he didn't want to look like a coward.

"I'll go first," he said, trying to sound much more confident than he felt.

He made his way into the tunnel, and found that there was enough room to crawl comfortably. He eased forward, feeling his way in the darkness.

Behind him Elizabeth took the flashlight from its hiding place, but she didn't turn it on. She followed along behind Jeff. Sarah followed Elizabeth.

Jeff wasn't sure how far they had gone in the tunnel, but in the blackness it seemed like a long way. He was beginning to get frightened, and was on the verge of telling Elizabeth that he thought they had gone far enough when he felt a change around him. Though he could see nothing in the blackness, it felt as though there was more space around him than there had been. He reached out and realized that he was right. He could no longer feel the close walls of the tunnel. He wondered how large the cavern they were now in was, and crept cautiously onward. His hand felt the lip of the shaft, and he stopped. He felt around in the darkness, trying to determine how deep the drop was. He felt Elizabeth bump into him. He drew himself up and crouched in a squatting position next to the shaft.

"There's something here," he said. "It drops off. I can't tell how deep it is, or how wide."

And then he felt the push from behind him, and he grabbed wildly in the dark. But there was nothing for him to grab on to, and he felt himself falling through the darkness. He hit the bottom before he could scream, and the blackness deepened. Jeff Stevens lay still on the floor of the pit.

In the upper cavern, Elizabeth turned on the flashlight and moved to the edge of the shaft. She shined the light downward. It illuminated Jeff's inert form sprawled by the large flattish rock that she had used as a table for her tea parties. She could see nothing else in the pool of light, and after a moment she set the flashlight down and began uncoiling the rope ladder. Behind her, Sarah emerged from the tunnel and sat cross-legged, trembling, watching her sister. Elizabeth lowered the ladder into the shaft, and a moment later, the flashlight glowing dimly in her coat pocket, she disappeared down into the blackness below. Sarah crept forward and peered into the depths.

The candles still stood wedged into the cracks where she had left them, and the cigarette lighter still lay in its crevice beneath one of the candles. When she had lit the candles, Elizabeth turned off the flashlight and looked around.

Kathy Burton lay where she had fallen, her forehead badly discolored from the blow of the rock. Her eyes were open, and her face was beginning to bloat. Elizabeth poked at her curiously, and when there was no movement Elizabeth tried to close the eyes. They wouldn't close.

Jimmy Tyler lay naked, huddled against the wall of the cave. His eyes, too, were open, but they held the expression of a small and terrified creature. He was whimpering and shivering. When Elizabeth approached him he seemed not to see her, and there was no reaction when she touched him. He was clutching the torso of the dead cat to his chest, as if it were a teddy bear. The smell of death filled every corner of the cavern, and Elizabeth breathed deeply of it. She smiled at the skeleton that lay against the wall.

"It's good, isn't it?" she whispered. "Look, they're all here now. Mommy and Daddy and their baby. And your father, Beth. I brought your father to visit you today. Do you want to talk to your father?"

She dragged Jeff Stevens's unconscious body over to the skeleton and laid it out next to the fleshless bones. She moved the arms of the skeleton so that Jeff lay in its cold embrace.

Slowly Elizabeth began setting up another tea party,

the last tea party. She dragged the body of Kathy Burton from the spot where it lay and wrenched it into a sitting position on one of the small stones that surrounded the table. It pitched forward and lay face down on the larger slab of rock. Then Elizabeth began working the torso of the cat loose from Jimmy Tyler's grasp. He fought with her mindlessly, unaware of what was going on but not wanting to be disturbed in whatever place his mind had taken him to. He fought passively, his small arms trying to hold on to the body of the cat, but he did not try to kick out at Elizabeth. He fought silently, against a force that no longer made any sense to him. The cat slipped loose from his grip, and his arms closed on the empty space.

She propped the cat up once more, but was not able to make the head balance on the rotting shoulders. She watched it roll off, and let it lie where it came to rest, a no-longer-recognizable object in a soiled blue bonnet.

Then she began moving Jimmy Tyler. He didn't resist; he didn't realize that anything was happening to him. With nothing left to hold on to, he seemed to give up, and Elizabeth was able to prop him up, his vacant eyes staring blankly off through the flickering candlelight.

Elizabeth began talking, but her speech was incoherent. Her voice kept changing pitch, and it was as if she were two people, first one and then the other.

As she talked she began to grow angry. She demanded that the objects of her anger respond to her, and when they didn't her rage only increased.

"Answer me," she cried, and the voice was not her own. "I want to know why you did it! Why did you leave me here? It's dark here, and it's cold. It frightens me. Why do you want to frighten me? Why can't I come out of here and be with everyone else?"

There was a silence, as she waited for an answer. But there was no answer.

"You're all alike," she hissed. "All of you. None of you have ever changed. You love *her*." She kicked at the body of the cat, and it fell at the base of the cavern wall. "You always pay more attention to her. Why can't you pay attention to me, too?"

And then she seemed to change again, and she stared down at the unconscious Jeff. "You're where you want to be now, aren't you? I wouldn't help you that day, would I? So you put me down here, by myself. But I knew you'd come back. And you'll stay with me this time. This time you'll stay. You and *all of them*."

Elizabeth snatched the knife from the ledge where it had long lain hidden and whirled to face the children. *"You'll all stay with me now!"* she screamed.

She fell upon the body of Kathy Burton, hacking at it with the knife, chopping wildly, tearing at the flesh of the corpse. When it lay dismembered, she turned to Jimmy Tyler.

He screamed as the knife plunged into his stomach, then fell gurgling to the floor of the cavern as she drew it out again and stabbed at his throat. He wriggled beneath her, his body responding reflexively as the knife cut at him. Elizabeth lay on top of him, the knife flashing in the yellow light of the candles as she continued to slash at him. In her fury she did not hear the low moans that came from Jeff Stevens as he slowly regained consciousness.

He was trying to remember what had happened. He'd been in the dark, and somebody had pushed him. He'd been falling. In the cave. He was in the cave. But it wasn't dark any more. Instead, there was a yellowish glow, as if candles were burning. And sounds. Strange, gurgling noises. He opened his eyes and tried to move his head.

He saw Elizabeth. His stomach heaved as he realized what she was doing. She was stabbing at something, but there was so much blood he couldn't see what it was. He heaved himself to his hands and knees and looked again. It was a little boy. Elizabeth was stabbing a little boy.

"No!" he cried out. He tried to get to his feet, but he was too dizzy. He saw Elizabeth turn, and heard her speak.

"You!" she cried. "You made me do this, Daddy. You did it to me, and now I'll do it to you. You'll stay here with me, Daddy. You won't leave me alone again."

He knew then that she was insane, and he tried to protect himself, but there was nothing he could do. His mind, still numb from his fall, seemed incapable of deciding which muscles to move, and his arms and legs wouldn't respond properly. Through hazy eyes he saw the knife flash out at him, but he felt nothing. He only saw the blood gush from his arm. Again he tried to move away, or raise his arm in defense, but he felt paralyzed. Terror welled up in him, and the knife was flashing at him. Again and again. Soon he saw nothing. He wondered why he felt no pain. It should hurt, he thought; dying should hurt. But it did not hurt, and Jeff Stevens drifted slowly into death. As the fog began to close over his mind, Jeff began to pray.

Elizabeth continued to slash at him long after he died, and when she was done his body was no longer recognizable. It lay in pieces, scattered across the floor of the cavern, mixed with the dismembered corpses of Jimmy Tyler and Kathy Burton. And then her rage was spent, and Elizabeth sat in the midst of the gore and stared curiously around her.

"Why did you do that?" she said softly. "I don't understand why you had to do it. They didn't do anything to you. They were your friends. And besides, it all happened so long ago. So very long ago." She crawled across the floor of the cavern, and knelt over the skeleton.

"You shouldn't have done it, Beth," she said, her voice a little stronger. "You should have left them alone. They weren't who you thought they were. He wasn't your father. Your father died a long time ago. And the others. They weren't my parents, and that cat wasn't Sarah. It was only a cat, Beth. A poor, helpless cat. Why did you make me do it? I don't hate them, Beth. I don't. It's you who hate them. It's you who hate all of them. Why can't you leave them alone? They didn't do anything to you. None of them did. *None of them.*" And she was angry again, but now she was angry at Beth, poor Beth, who had died so long ago.

Elizabeth grabbed one of the arm bones and raised it over her head.

"Die!" she screamed. *"Why won't you die and leave us alone?"* She brought the bone down, crushing the skull. "Die," she whispered once more. "Please die, and leave me alone."

And then it was over. Elizabeth stood up and walked to the rope ladder. She didn't blow out the candles; they would die of their own accord. Nor did she pull the ladder up from the shaft. There was no need to now; she would not be coming back, nor would anyone use the ladder to escape. Elizabeth crept through the tunnel and emerged from the hole in the embankment. She began climbing upward, away from the cave.

In the darkness, Sarah stared down into the flickering yellow light below. Then, slowly, she began making her way down the ladder.

Sarah worked slowly in the pit, trying to fit the pieces back together. When she was finished, she found the canteen of water she had dropped down the shaft so long ago. She put the mouth of the bottle to the lips of each of the dead children, and tried to make them drink.

Then she sat down, and looked around her.

She sat for a long time, waiting.

24

It was four thirty when Dr. Charles Belter wound up the meeting with Jack and Rose Conger. He was not convinced that anything had been accomplished, nor was he convinced that anything needed to be accomplished. He had spent the better part of the afternoon not in attempting to second-guess the direction that Sarah's illness might be taking, but in reassuring her worried parents. That was half the battle, he had discovered, in dealing with a case like Sarah's. The parents read too many books, and of the wrong sort. They were convinced that their children were turning into some sort of monsters, and no matter what happened, they projected the worst. His job, he had found, was not so much to treat the child as to calm the parents.

And he had succeeded. As they drove home through the rain they felt better about everything. Dr. Belter had told them not to worry. They had faith in the doctor; they wouldn't worry. The rain came down harder, and they could feel the temperature dropping.

"Early winter this year," Jack commented as he turned off the Conger's Point Road. "This could turn into snow any time."

"I always like the first snow out here," Rose said. "Sometimes I think the house was designed for winter. The snow seems to soften it somehow." She looked through the rain to the old house, looming up ahead, and felt a strange sense of foreboding. It's the weather, she thought. Rain always makes the place so gloomy.

The phone started ringing as they opened the front door.

"Got it," Jack called, and picked up the receiver with one hand as he unbuttoned his dripping coat with the other. "Hello?"

"Jack? Barbara Stevens. We just got home from playing golf—"

"In this weather?" Jack said, disbelieving.

Barbara chuckled. "Some of us will play in anything. But I'll tell you something, just between us. That old shack that serves as a clubhouse needs a new roof."

"It needs a new everything, but there aren't enough members to do it. Besides, I doubt that anybody but you would be out there on a day like today."

"It was pretty wet," Barbara admitted. "Anyway, 1 was just wondering if Jeff is over there. He was supposed to be home all afternoon, but he isn't here. And since he doesn't really know anyone yet except you, I thought he might be playing with your kids."

"We just got in ourselves," Jack said. "Hang on, and I'll find out if he's here." He set the receiver on the table and turned to Rose, who was watching him curiously.

"Barbara Stevens," he said. "She's wondering if Jeff is here."

Rose felt a sinking sensation in her stomach. She was remembering a similar telephone call, a call that had come from Kathy Burton's mother only days ago. How many days? She couldn't remember. Her feeling of foreboding increased.

"What's wrong?" Jack asked his wife, seeing her face lose its color.

"Nothing," Rose said. "I was just thinking—" She broke off. "Nothing," she said again. "I'll call Elizabeth."

She stepped to the foot of the stairs and called upward, her voice echoing through the house. In a moment they heard a door open and close, and footsteps approaching the head of the stairs. Then Rose saw her daughter.

"Hi," Elizabeth said. "I didn't hear you come in. I was reading."

"Didn't you hear the phone ring?" Rose asked curiously.

"Yes, but when it stopped after the second ring I figured Mrs. Goodrich had gotten it. Is it for me?"

"No," Rose said. "It's Mrs. Stevens. Is Jeff here?"

"Jeff?" Elizabeth asked. "He left hours ago."

The feeling of foreboding flooded over Rose.

"Then he was here?"

Elizabeth nodded. "Oh, yes. He came over right after you left. He said he wanted to hunt for the cave."

"The cave?" Rose frowned.

"You know. The legend. He said it doesn't exist, and he wanted to go look for it. He wanted me to go with him, but I wouldn't. I told him it was too dangerous. Besides, it was raining."

Jack, who had been listening to the conversation between Rose and Elizabeth, picked the telephone up again.

"Barbara?" he said. "Apparently he was here, but that was early this afternoon. Elizabeth doesn't know where he was going, but apparently he said something about wanting to hunt for the cave."

"The cave?" Barbara asked. "You mean the one on the embankment on the Point?"

"I guess so," Jack replied. "If there really is one. It's mostly just an old family legend. No one's ever found it."

"The embankment's dangerous, isn't it?" Barbara said, worry sharpening her voice.

Jack decided to be truthful. "Yes, it is. That's one of the reasons we've kept the legend going. It's been a useful tool for keeping children away from a dangerous place."

"I know. Rose told me about it when we moved in. We told Jeff to stay away from there."

"Then I'm sure he did," Jack said reassuringly. "He probably just decided to go for a hike and lost track of time."

"I don't know," Barbara said, the anxiety in her voice rising. "He doesn't know the area, and he's usually pretty responsible about things."

"But he's a teenager," Jack reminded her. "They can be counted on not to be counted on."

"I suppose so," Barbara said doubtfully. "Well, I won't start worrying for another hour. If he isn't home by six, I don't know what we'll do."

"I'm sorry I couldn't help you more. If he turns up here, we'll call you." They said good-bye, and Jack hung up the phone. He turned to Rose, and the worry he had not allowed to show in his voice was etched on his face.

"It's like the others, isn't it?" he said.

Rose nodded mutely. It was too much like the others. And then she remembered Sarah. Sarah had not been standing behind her sister at the head of the stairs. She glanced upward and saw Elizabeth still standing where she had been, waiting to be told what Mrs. Stevens had said.

"Where's Sarah?" Rose said, finding her voice.

"Sarah?" Elizabeth repeated the name. "In her room, I guess. Or the playroom." She fell silent and appeared to be listening. "Just a second," she said. "I'll look."

They heard her footsteps in the hall as she made her way first to Sarah's room, then to the playroom. When they heard her approaching the head of the stairs again, and did not hear the soft murmur of her voice speaking to her sister, they knew that she had not found Sarah. Elizabeth reappeared at the head of the stairs and started down.

"She's not up here," she was saying. "She's probably with Mrs. Goodrich."

As they began searching downstairs, Rose knew they would not find Sarah. Instead of joining in the search, she went into her little office and sank into the chair at her desk. For some reason she found some security there, some security she was suddenly sure she was going to need.

"Well," Jack said, trying to keep his voice steady. "She isn't down here, either. Mrs. Goodrich thought she was upstairs."

"She's got to be here," Rose said desperately. "Look upstairs again. She might be in our room, or the guest room. And the attic. Look in the attic."

She did not volunteer to join in the search, for she was sure it was useless. Sarah was not in the house. Rose sat in her desk chair and listened as Elizabeth and Jack made their way systematically through the house. There was a silence as they searched the third-floor attic; then she heard them on the second floor, and finally coming down the stairs. They came into the small office, and Jack shook his head. "Nothing," he said. "She's not here."

"I didn't think she would be," Rose said. "Not when she wasn't in her room." They looked at one another, unsure of what to do next.

"The barn," Elizabeth said suddenly. "Maybe she went out to the barn." Without waiting for an answer from her parents, she left the room, and they heard the front door open. And then they heard Elizabeth scream.

It was not the same sort of scream they were used to from Sarah, the frustrated scream of a child who finds herself unable to communicate by any other means. Elizabeth's was a scream of horror. It froze Jack and Rose momentarily; then they were on their feet, racing for the front door. They found Elizabeth on the front porch, staring wildly out at the field. They followed the direction of her eyes, and Rose felt a scream emerging from her own lips. She was able to suppress it only by clamping her hand over her mouth.

From the woods, a small form had emerged, and was
now making its way across the field toward the house.
It was Sarah, and even from here they could see that
she was soaking wet and covered with mud. And there
was something else. Something that streaked her face
and arms, and stained her clothing with a redness that
they knew was not mud.

It was blood. Sarah was covered with blood.

"Jesus God," Jack muttered, his mind almost unable
to accept what his eyes were seeing. And then he remembered that Elizabeth, too, was watching the strange
apparition that was coming slowly across the field. He
took his daughter's arm and pulled her into the house.

Elizabeth seemed dazed, and she did not resist as
Jack led her upstairs and into her room.

"Stay here," he said. "Don't come downstairs until I
come up to get you." He looked at her closely, and saw
that her face was pale and she was shaking. "Are you
all right?"

She nodded, and her mouth moved. "What's wrong
with her, Daddy?" she said in a small voice. "Is she
hurt?"

"I don't know," Jack said. "But it will be all right.
Just stay here, and it will be all right." Elizabeth, suddenly seeming much younger, peered up into his face,
and he gathered her into his arms. She began sobbing
quietly.

"It's going to be all right, honey," Jack whispered.
"I'll take care of her." He rocked her gently, and she
calmed down. He laid her on the bed. "Try not to think
about it," he said. "I have to go down and help her now,
but I'll be back in a little while. Try not to think about
it," he repeated, and knew that there was no way she
would be able to blot what she had seen out of her
mind.

Rose was still standing on the front porch, her hand
still clamped over her mouth, and tears were streaming down her cheeks. Sarah was still in the field, getting

closer to the house, moving slowly, the object she carried dragging in the mud behind her. It was getting colder, and there was snow mixed with the rain now.

Small sounds started to come out of Rose as she tried to come to terms with what she was seeing. The object in Sarah's hand was clearly visible now, and as the realization of what it was came to Jack he had to fight down the rising nausea in his stomach.

It was a child's arm, and it had been severed at the shoulder. It seemed to be badly lacerated, and the blood was slowly oozing from it, dripping from the ragged stump that bumped through the mud behind Sarah.

Sarah seemed unaware of the rain and snow, or of the cold. She moved forward steadily, her vacant eyes fixed on her parents as they stood on the porch waiting for her. Jack wanted to go to her, to pick her up and carry her home, but he was unable to. Helplessly he stood next to his wife as their daughter came toward them.

And then she was home. She stood at the bottom of the steps to the porch and stared blankly up at them. Then she lifted the severed arm and held it out, presenting it to them as if it were a gift.

The hysteria she had been holding back swept over Rose. Her mouth opened jerkily, and the scream that had been struggling in her throat burst forth to resound across the field. The trees in the woods almost seemed to tremble with the screams that tore out of the tormented woman's being. Her eyes began playing tricks on her, and all she could see was the arm, the bloody arm, suspended against a background that was fast going black. It seemed to grow before her eyes, and then all she could see was the stump, the ragged flesh surrounding the bone. Her screams rose to a hysterical pitch.

Elizabeth's first scream had awakened Mrs. Goodrich, and she had sat peering dazedly at her television set, unsure whether or not it had been the source of the sound that had awakened her. When she began hearing Rose's screams she realized that it had not been the television. She got to her feet and headed stiffly for the front of the house.

The anguished cries grew as she approached the front door, but it wasn't until she was on the porch that she realized the cause. Her eyes widened at the sight of the bloodied, mud-covered child. She fought down the nausea and glanced at Rose, quickly realizing that it was the mother, not the daughter, who needed immediate attention.

"Take care of Miz Rose," she commanded Jack. She moved forward and, swallowing hard, disengaged Sarah's fingers from the wrist of the dismembered arm. Taking Sarah by one hand and holding the grisly arm in the other, she led Sarah into the house. She took her quickly to the kitchen, and stood her in front of the sink. Then she wrapped the arm in a towel and set it aside. She began working on Sarah, stripping her clothes from her and wiping her off. Then she wrapped the child in an old blanket from her own room and went to the phone. She dialed the number for the police station and asked for Ray Norton.

"Ray," she said. "This is Mrs. Goodrich out at the Congers'. You'd better get out here fast. Something bad's happened. And bring a doctor with you. That one from White Oaks, if you can get hold of him. He knows us."

The police chief started to ask some questions, but the old housekeeper cut him off.

"When you get here," she said. "I've got other things to do." She hung up the telephone and returned to Sarah. The child sat meekly waiting, and offered no resistance as Mrs. Goodrich led her upstairs to the bathroom.

Mrs. Goodrich's command had brought Jack to his senses. He grabbed Rose and shook her.

"It's all right," he said. "Mrs. Goodrich is taking care of her." When Rose continued screaming, he shook her harder and yelled at her. *"It's all right!"* he shouted, and her screams suddenly stopped. She stared at him, her mouth working, her eyes wide.

"Come on," he said. He led her into the house and forced her to come with him to the back study. He poured two large tumblers of brandy and handed one of them to Rose. "Drink this," he commanded. "You need it."

Wordlessly she accepted the glass and drained half of it. Then, shakily, she sank to the sofa.

"What shall we do?" she breathed. "Oh, God, Jack, what shall we do?"

"Call Dr. Belter," Jack said quietly. "I'll call Dr. Belter. And Ray Norton." But neither of them made a move toward the telephone. They simply sat there, staring at each other, trying to assimilate what they had seen. They were still there, sitting in the study, when Ray Norton arrived.

He had been getting ready to go home when the call came. He had known immediately that something was wrong. Very wrong. In all the years he had known her, he had never known Mrs. Goodrich to use the telephone. So he called the White Oaks School and told Dr. Belter to meet him at the Congers'. Then he had gotten into his car and raced out the Conger's Point Road, using the siren for the first time since he had had it installed.

The front door stood open, and he didn't bother to ring the bell. He went in and closed the door behind him. He could hear water running somewhere upstairs, but there were no other sounds. He started for the stairs, then changed his mind and went down the hall to the back study. He opened the door and saw Jack and Rose Conger sitting quietly by the fireplace, their faces pale. Neither of them moved when he came into the room.

"Mrs. Goodrich called me," he said softly. "She said something happened out here."

"Yes," Jack said dully. "Only we don't know what." He fell silent, and Ray Norton moved closer.

"Are you all right?" he said. "What happened?"

"You'd better call Dr. Belter at the White Oaks School," Jack said. "I was going to do it myself, but . . ." His voice trailed off again.

"It's done," Norton said. "Mrs. Goodrich told me to call him. He's on his way." He paused, unsure whether he should wait for the doctor before pressing Jack and Rose for information. Whatever it was, it seemed to be over now. He got a feeling of shock from the house, but not of emergency. It was as if something terrible had passed over them, leaving them stunned. He decided to wait for the doctor. He noted the empty glasses in the hands of both the Congers, and, though he supposed that he shouldn't, he refilled them.

"You look like you need this," he said gently. He sat down, and together they waited for Dr. Belter. The sound of running water upstairs suddenly stopped, and the house was silent. Then Rose began to cry, very softly.

It was almost thirty minutes before they heard the doorbell ring, and Ray Norton stood up to answer it. Then they heard the heavy clumping of Mrs. Goodrich's feet coming down the stairs, and the murmur of voices. A moment later the housekeeper opened the study door and let the psychiatrist in. Without waiting to be asked, Mrs. Goodrich came into the room and closed the door behind her.

"I put her to bed," she said. "She's asleep. And I looked in on Miss Elizabeth. She's scared, but she's all right."

Dr. Belter looked curiously at Jack and Rose Conger.

"What happened?" he said, and when there was no

answer, he turned to the housekeeper. "What happened?" he asked again.

"Well," Mrs. Goodrich said shortly. "It isn't pretty, and I don't know for sure what it's all about. I was in my room, watching television, and all of a sudden I heard the most awful commotion. It was Miz Rose, and she was screaming. 'Course, I didn't know who was screaming till I got to the front porch, and after I got there I didn't pay much attention. It was Miss Sarah. She was standing there, in the rain, all covered with mud and blood. And she had something in her hand."

"What?" the doctor asked when the old woman fell silent. Mrs. Goodrich shot a glance toward Rose. "What was she carrying?" the doctor pressed.

"It—it was an arm," Mrs. Goodrich said. "It's in the kitchen. I left it there when I took Miss Sarah up to the bathroom."

"Oh, Jesus," Ray Norton breathed. He looked helplessly at the doctor, wondering what to do. Dr. Belter realized he would have to take charge for the moment.

"You'd better come with me," he told the police chief. "I don't see what good it will do right now, but we'd better have a look at it."

The two men went to the kitchen and unwrapped the bloodstained towel. Ray Norton felt his stomach rebelling at the grisly sight.

"A child," Dr. Belter said. "It's the right arm of a child."

Norton nodded dumbly. "How old?"

Dr. Belter shrugged. "Hard to say, but it looks like a small child. No more than eight or nine."

"The same age as Jimmy Tyler," Ray Norton said softly. "And the blood hasn't coagulated yet."

"It couldn't have happened very long ago," the doctor said. "It must have been this afternoon."

They rewrapped the arm and returned to the study. Ray Norton looked at the Congers uncomfortably.

"I know this is going to be hard," he said, as gently as he could, "but I'm going to have to ask you some questions."

"I know," Jack said dully. "Can Dr. Belter take Rose upstairs? I think she ought to lie down. I saw everything she saw."

"Of course," Norton replied, signaling the doctor to take Rose from the room. He waited till they were gone, then sat down opposite Jack.

"What happened, Jack? Take your time. I know it must have been awful, but I have to know what happened."

"I don't know. We got home from White Oaks, and Sarah wasn't in the house. We searched, and then Elizabeth said she might be in the barn. She was going out to look, and when she got to the porch she screamed. Rose and I went out to see what was wrong, and . . . we saw her." He winced a little, seeing the gruesome scene once more. "She was covered with blood, and she was dragging that—that thing. God, Ray, it was awful."

"She was coming out of the woods?"

"Yes."

"Well. I know this isn't going to be pleasant for you, but I'm going to have to put together a search party. If Sarah found that thing in the woods, we've got to find the rest of the—" He broke off, not wanting to say what was in his mind.

"My God," Jack whispered suddenly, "I forgot."

Norton jerked his head up.

"It's Jeff Stevens," Jack continued softly, staring helplessly at the policeman. "He's missing too."

Norton stared back at Jack in disbelief. "Jeff Stevens?" He repeated the name as if he'd never heard it before. "The kid in the old Barnes house?"

Jack nodded dumbly.

"Shit," Norton muttered under his breath. Then: "Are you sure?"

"It's all the same," Jack said hopelessly. "He was in

this area, he didn't show up at home. Just like the others."

Norton stood up. "I'll call his parents. I wonder if his father will want to be part of the search party."

"I suppose," Jack said. "We have to find out what's happening, don't we?" He paused a moment, then went on. "I'll come along too, Ray. The least I can do is help look."

Norton shook his head. "Not you," he said. "You've been through enough."

He went to the telephone and began making a series of calls. By the time he was finished, Carl and Barbara Stevens were on their way over and a search party had been organized. He looked out the window toward the woods. It had begun snowing, and it seemed to be falling harder each minute.

As he watched, the woods slowly disappeared into the snowstorm.

They searched the woods, first in the fading light of dusk, then using lights, but they found nothing. If there was a trail, the snow covered it, and as the night wore on the storm grew. After four hours they gave it up. The search party returned to the house on Conger's Point, but soon they began drifting back to town. There was nothing to be accomplished on the Point. In town, where there were no Congers to overhear, the people of Port Arbello could talk.

In the house on Conger's Point, only Ray Norton and Dr. Belter remained. They sat in the study with Jack Conger, and the three of them talked. There was no talk of whether something should be done with Sarah; only of what should be done. Jack Conger was tired. He was tired and he felt terribly alone. He sat with the doctor and the police chief only because it was his daughter they were discussing, his family. But he was beyond caring what they decided to do. He would do whatever had to be done. He poured himself another drink and seated himself by the fire. He envied Rose, who lay sedated and asleep upstairs.

Dr. Belter was just finishing a long explanation of the details of Sarah's illness. When he was done, Ray Norton lit his pipe, something he rarely did, and leaned back.

"Well, I just don't know what to do," he said at last. "I'm going to have to tell people something, you know."

Dr. Belter smiled tightly. "Tell them what you want. If you ask me, which I suppose you're about to do, I don't have any answers. I wish that search party had found something. But they didn't, and we can't change that."

Norton nodded his agreement. "Let me ask you a question. Is it possible, *at all possible,* for Sarah to have killed the children?"

"I don't know," Dr. Belter said hesitantly. He didn't like to deal in possibilities. He had seen so much that he was inclined to think that practically anything was possible. He saw that his answer was going to be unacceptable to the chief of police, so he weighed his words carefully.

"Let me put it this way. I have to say that, yes, it is possible for Sarah to have killed all three of the missing children. I say that not because I think she did, but because at the moment we don't have any alternatives to choose from. If I were you I'd keep searching. If this snow lasts through the winter, I'd continue looking in the spring. Somewhere out there is the rest of that body, and maybe two more bodies besides. And I certainly don't think that you can charge Sarah with anything on the basis of one arm. I admit, it's ugly. I admit, at the moment we don't have much else to think. But you should also be aware that if you try to claim that Sarah is responsible for the dismembering of one chlid and the disappearance of two others, nothing is going to happen. Any psychiatrist you find will tell you the same thing I will. Sarah is not responsible for what she does. She is almost hopelessly schizophrenic. I say almost because with her kind of disorder there is always a chance that she'll come out of it. But even if she does, there's no guarantee that she'll be able to tell you what happened. She probably won't remember. Frankly, if I were you I'd keep the case open."

"And what about Sarah?" Ray Norton said uneasily. "What if she is responsible?"

"I don't think there's too much question about Sarah's future. I'm sure that after the last couple of days the Congers will agree that it's time she was institutionalized. It'll be the best thing for her, and the best for them. They can't go on living as they have been." He looked to Jack, and Jack nodded his agreement.

"When?" Jack said.

Dr. Belter thought it over. "Tonight, I think. I don't see any reason why your wife should have to go through it. It isn't easy to see your child leave your house for the last time. And it will be better for Sarah, too. I can take her to White Oaks for tonight, and we can talk tomorrow about the best place for her."

Jack nodded mutely. He wondered why he didn't feel anything, but he didn't.

"I'm sorry," Ray Norton said. They had moved into the hall, and Ray was standing uncomfortably by the front door, wanting to get away. "If there's anything I can do . . ." His voice trailed off as Jack shook his head.

"Thanks, Ray," he said. "I don't know. I guess I'm feeling numb."

Jack started up the stairs to pack a suitcase for Sarah, and Ray Norton put his hand on the front door.

"Wait a moment, please," Dr. Belter said softly to the police chief.

Norton's hand dropped from the doorknob, but he didn't meet the psychiatrist's eyes. For the last hour he had heard a lot of things he hadn't wanted to hear, and he was embarrassed. He was acutely aware that there was such a thing as knowing too much about your friends, and he had a distinct feeling he was about to hear even more. He was right. Dr. Belter led him back to the study and quickly filled him in on every detail of the Conger cases, both Sarah's and Jack's.

When the doctor was finished Ray Norton stared at him, unable to conceal the animosity he was feeling toward the man.

"Just exactly why are you telling me all this?" he asked. "It seems to me that what you're doing is unethical at best and probably illegal at worst."

Dr. Belter stared at the fire in front of him. He was very much aware that what Norton was saying was true. What he was doing was both unethical and illegal, but he had thought it over carefully before deciding to go ahead. And now it was too late—he had already begun.

"You're right, of course," he said uncomfortably. "And believe me, if I thought there was any other way of going at this thing I wouldn't be doing what I'm doing right now."

"I don't see what you hope to accomplish," Norton said.

"You mean you don't want to see." Belter's reproach was mild. "What I'm suggesting," he said, his voice hardening, "since you want me to spell it out, is that I think there's a distinct possibility that Jack Conger might be involved in all this mess."

"I don't see how," Norton observed. "You yourself admit that he was in your office when at least one and possibly two of the disappearances took place."

"That's not quite true. We don't actually know when the disappearances took place. All we know, really, is when and where the children were last seen. And, as it happens, they were all seen on or near the Conger prop-

erty. As for when they actually met with . . . whatever
it is they met with, we don't know, do we?"

Norton reluctantly agreed. "Just what are you pro-
posing? That I charge Jack Conger with killing three
children? Granted, I suppose we could use your files to
establish a record of previous assault, but where does
that get us? Without any bodies, and with you yourself
acting as a witness for an alibi, there isn't a chance in
the world of making it stick."

"And, of course," the doctor added, "you don't think
he had anything to do with it."

"No," Norton said flatly. "I don't."

Dr. Belter leaned back in his chair and folded his
hands across his stomach. "Then what do you propose
to do?"

"Nothing," Norton said. "Come spring, I'll have
those woods searched again, and I'll have a good search
made for that cave. Other than that, I propose to see
what happens next. If any more children disappear, I'll
reassess the situation. But if you want my opinion, I
think it's over with."

"You really think Sarah did it all?" the psychiatrist
asked in disbelief.

Norton nodded. "I'm no shrink, but for my money she
did it. And I'll stick to that opinion till I have something more solid to go on. The word is already all over
town that Sarah Conger went berserk—those aren't my
words, but they're the ones that will be used—and she's
going to be put away. And in a town like Port Arbello
a story like that counts for a lot. The town will calm
down, and when the word gets out that Sarah's been
taken wherever you take her it'll calm down even more.
I don't propose to stir it all up again, and I don't propose to have the whole town talking about something
that happened to Jack Conger a year ago. I assume I
can count on you not to tell anyone else what you've
told me?"

"That goes without saying," Belter said stiffly. "But

do me a favor, will you? Talk to Jack Conger. Don't grill him, just talk to him. You don't even have to do it officially."

"Why?" Norton demanded.

Belter smiled thinly. "Just to prod him. You might be absolutely right—he may have nothing to do with all this. But then again, he might. In any case, my professional opinion is that he's pretty near the end of his rope emotionally. If you let him know that you're aware of that, it might make him nervous. Nervous enough to make himself get some help before something happens that he is mixed up in."

"I'll think about it," Norton said noncommittally. "If there's nothing else, I have a lot of work to do." He stood up, and the two men shook hands formally and coldly. When the police chief had left the house Dr. Belter thought for a while about the two folders in his office and the look on the policeman's face as he'd left. Norton, he knew, would not be coming for the files. And he wouldn't press the matter himself. Tomorrow he would seal Jack Conger's folder and put it away in the dead files, the special cabinet he kept for the records of patients he didn't think he'd be seeing again.

Suddenly weary, he turned and went upstairs to help Jack, who was just finishing with the packing. He looked as though he'd been crying.

"I'll give her a shot," Dr. Belter said, "and she won't even wake up. You can be at school tomorrow morning if you like. It might make things easier. For you and your wife, if not for her. Frankly, I doubt she'll even be aware of what's happening. I'm sorry, but I imagine all this will make things worse for her." Then he smiled, seeing the expression on Jack's face. "Don't forget," he went on, "we don't really know what goes on in the mind of a child like Sarah. Often I suspect that a child's schizophrenia is much harder on the family than it is on the child. A person's mind generally takes him where he wants to go. Sarah will be all right. Maybe not by your standards, or by mine, but she's living where she wants to live. All we can do, really, is wish her well."

"But what's going to happen to her?" Jack asked dazedly. He picked up his child and began carrying her downstairs. He knew it would be the last time.

Dr. Belter waited until they had reached the front door before he answered Jack's question.

"It's hard to say," he murmured at last. "With Sarah, only time will tell what's going to happen. All I can advise you to do is go on with your life. There's literally nothing you can do for Sarah." At the look of pain in Jack's eyes, he relented. "I didn't say forget about her. By all means go on loving her. But it's time to stop living your lives around her. You and your wife and Elizabeth are still a family, you know."

Jack wondered how much of a family they would ever be again.

"If I can be any help to you, please let me know," Belter went on. "It isn't the end of the world, you know. It's just been a very bad year. For you, and everyone else in Port Arbello. But it's over now." He held out his arms to receive the sleeping child.

Jack looked once more into the face of his daughter, and kissed her gently.

"I love you," he whispered. "I always have. I'm so sorry, my baby. So very sorry."

Then he placed his child in the doctor's arms, and Sarah Conger was taken away from the house on Conger's Point. As he watched the car taking his daughter from her home, Jack Conger wondered if it would, indeed, be all over now. He hoped so.

He stood alone in the driving snow and watched the taillights disappear. He raised one hand in a final salute.

"Sarah," he whispered. And then again: "Sarah . . ."

25

A week passed, then two. Port Arbello began to return to normal, though it was a slightly different normal. Most of the children returned to walking to school, but some of them kept on riding. "What happened once could happen again," some of the parents were saying.

Three days after Sarah walked out of the woods, Carl and Barbara Stevens put their house on the market. Rose Conger was surprised when she got the listing for it, and turned it down. She explained that she was taking some time off to recuperate, but that was only part of the truth. The rest of it was that she couldn't face seeing Barbara Stevens again.

Marilyn Burton continued to operate her dress shop, and people noticed that she was beginning to talk to herself. For a while many of the women in Port Arbello made an effort to drop in on her as often as possible, but it didn't seem to do any good. After a while they stopped dropping in, and if Marilyn Burton's habit became worse, no one knew about it.

Martin Forager did his best to keep the talk alive, but as the days dragged on and nothing else happened, people began to tell him to let it be; they'd just as soon forget. He couldn't, of course, and few nights passed without Marty Forager suddenly standing up in the tavern and drunkenly demanding that someone find out what really did happen to his daughter. After a while people stopped paying attention.

Jimmy Tyler's parents acted as if nothing had happened. They kept his room just as it had been on the day he disappeared, and always set a place for him at the table. Mrs. Tyler told everyone that she expected Jimmy home any day now, and that the waiting was hard. But she also insisted that she was holding up well under it and it would all be over soon, when Jimmy came home. The people of Port Arbello clucked sympathetically, but shook their heads when Mrs. Tyler wasn't around. They saw another Port Arbello legend in the making.

For Jack and Rose Conger, the weeks after Sarah left their home were difficult. Rose stayed in the house almost all the time; after the second week she telephoned the Port Arbello Realty Company to tell them she would not be back. They were not surprised; rather, they were relieved. They had been trying to figure out the most diplomatic way of telling her that her services would no longer be necessary, that Conger was no longer a name to be proud of in Port Arbello.

Jack Conger couldn't stay at home. He had a paper to run, and he had to try to act as if nothing were wrong. It was impossible, of course, and he imagined that people were looking at him strangely even when they weren't. He found that he was spending most of his time barricaded in his office, talking to no one but Sylvia Bannister.

Sylvia had come into his office on his first day back at the Port Arbello *Courier* and had closed the door firmly behind her.

"Are you going to be all right?" she had asked him without preamble.

"That depends on what you call all right," he had said. "I intend to go on living, and go on working, if that's what you mean."

"I suppose that's what I meant," Sylvia had said. Then she had left his office as abruptly as she had entered it.

The Congers told Elizabeth that her sister had finally had to be put in an institution, and she had accepted it without further explanation. She had not asked any questions about the day Sarah had come out of the woods, and while they thought it was a little odd, they accepted it gratefully. Neither Jack nor Rose wished to discuss that day, and they counted themselves lucky that Elizabeth, too, seemed to want to forget it.

In early November, about a month after Sarah was sent to the Ocean Crest Institute, Jack and Rose Conger were sitting in the small study at the back of the house. Jack was reading; Rose was trying to read. Without knocking, Elizabeth came into the room and sat down on the sofa beside her mother. When Rose looked up to see what she wanted, Elizabeth was staring at the portrait of the young girl that hung above the mantel. Rose glanced up at the picture.

"Sometimes it's hard to remember that she isn't you," Rose mused. Elizabeth looked at her mother sharply.

"Well, she isn't," Elizabeth said petulantly. "I don't think she looks anything like me at all."

Jack set his book aside and smiled at his daughter. "You wouldn't have said that two years ago, or three. Of course, you're older than she was when that picture was painted, but when you were that age you looked exactly like her."

"I'm not like her," Elizabeth said flatly.

"Well, no one said you are, dear," Rose said. "All your father or anyone else ever said was that you looked like her."

"I don't want to look like her," Elizabeth said, her face growing slightly red with anger. "She's an awful person, and I don't want anything to do with her. I wish you'd take the picture down."

"Take it down?" Rose said, puzzled. "Why on earth should we take it down?" She examined it once more, trying to see what her daughter could dislike in it. She could see nothing.

"Because I want you to," Elizabeth said. "I think it should go back in the attic, where you found it."

"I don't see any reason to put it away," Jack said. "I should think you'd be proud of it. Not every girl has a portrait like that of herself."

"It isn't me," Elizabeth insisted, her anger swelling. Her parents glanced at each other nervously.

"Well," Jack said, hesitating, "if it means that much to you—"

"It does," Elizabeth declared. "I never want to see that picture again. I hate it." She paused and glared at the picture, at the little girl who looked so much like Elizabeth smiling down at her. *"I hate you!"* Elizabeth suddenly shouted at the picture. Then she ran from the study, and a moment later her parents heard her pounding up the stairs to her room. They looked at each other again, and there was worry in their eyes.

"What do you suppose brought that on?" Jack said.

Rose thought about it a moment, and when she spoke it was in a manner of thinking out loud.

"She seems to be changing lately. Have you noticed it? She isn't like she used to be. She's starting to get a little sloppy. Just little things. And she's started arguing with me. It used to be that if I asked her to do something she either did it immediately or it was already done. Lately she's started arguing with me, or simply not doing what I ask her to do. And she flat out refused to do something for Mrs. Goodrich the other day. You should have heard Mrs. Goodrich!"

Jack chuckled. "I have heard Mrs. Goodrich. Thirty years ago I flatly refused to do something she told me to do. I heard her then, and it was the first and last time I ever refused to do anything she asked me to do."

"I suspect it'll be the last time for Elizabeth, too." Rose smiled. Then her smile faded, and her voice grew serious again.

"But, really, Jack, haven't you noticed it too? Or is it just my imagination?" Rose bit at her lower lip anxiously. "I'm afraid my imagination works overtime these days."

Jack thought it over and realized that Rose was right. Elizabeth had been changing, but it wasn't anything serious, as far as he could see. Elizabeth, in his opinion, was simply beginning to act like any other thirteen-year-old girl.

"I wouldn't worry about it if I were you. After all, she's been through just as much as we have, and her life's changed just as much as ours. We can't expect her to be the same as she always was. You're not and I'm not—why should she be?"

"I don't know, really," Rose said thoughtfully. "I'm not sure I'm even worried. In a way, it's kind of a relief. She was so perfect, she sometimes made me feel incompetent. I could never handle Sarah the way she could."

Jack seemed to stiffen, and Rose realized that it was the first time either of them had mentioned Sarah in a month. They hadn't been to visit her yet; it was almost as if they were trying to pretend that she hadn't existed. But she had.

The next day they drove to Ocean Crest, forty miles south of Port Arbello. It was close enough to make visiting Sarah easy, but far enough away so that Port Arbello would be able to feel safe. Sarah would be there for a very long time.

It was a difficult visit. The child sat in front of them, her enormous brown eyes fixed on a spot somewhere in space, somewhere Rose and Jack could not go.

She did not resist when each of them embraced her, nor did she respond.

"She's always like that," the nurse explained. "So far she hasn't responded to anything. She eats, but the food has to be put in her mouth." When Rose seemed to be on the verge of tears, the nurse hastened to explain.

"It isn't anything to worry about," she said. "Sarah's had a bad trauma, and she's reacting to it. She's temporarily withdrawn, just as normal people do. Except that she was already so withdrawn that now she's practically shut down. But she'll come out of it. I'm sure she will."

They made the drive home in silence. When they were in the house Rose said, "Fix me a drink, will you? I feel like I need one. I'm going up to say hello to Elizabeth."

"Kiss her once for me," Jack said. He headed for the study as Rose disappeared upstairs.

A couple of minutes later, when Rose went into the study, she found her husband standing in the middle of the room, staring at the empty place on the wall above the fireplace.

"It's gone," he said. "She put it back in the attic."

Rose stared at the blank space herself, then went to the study door.

"Elizabeth!" she called.

"What?" The muffled shout came through indistinctly from upstairs. Rose's eyes narrowed, and she went to the foot of the stairs.

"Come down here," she said sharply.

"In a minute," she heard from upstairs.

"Now!" Rose commanded. She stalked back to the study. A very long minute later Elizabeth walked into the room.

"You used to knock before you entered a room," Rose pointed out to her.

"Oh, Mother," Elizabeth protested.

"Don't whine," Jack said sharply. "It doesn't sound attractive. Did you take that picture down?"

"What picture?" Elizabeth said evasively.

"You know perfectly well what picture," Rose snapped. "The one above the fireplace."

"Oh, that," Elizabeth said offhandedly. "I told you I hated it."

"Where did you put it?"

"Back in the attic," Elizabeth said. "That's where it belongs." Then she marched out of the study.

"Well," Jack said, "I guess that's that."

"I don't know," Rose said. "We certainly don't have to leave the picture there. It seems to me that if we want to hang *our* picture in *our* study in *our* house, *our* daughter is no one to tell us we can't."

"But if it means so much to her—" Jack began.

But Rose cut him off. "It's not that. It's just that she's starting to act like an only child."

"In a way," Jack said softly, "she is, isn't she?"

The picture of the unknown child stayed in the attic.

BOOK II

The Present

26

Ray Norton drove slowly along the Conger's Point Road, partly because he was keeping only one eye on the road and partly because he was getting older, and driving more slowly was a part of getting older. He would be retiring next year, and he was ready. Port Arbello was changing, and Ray Norton was changing, and he no longer felt that he was the best chief of police the town could have. He'd kept this feeling a secret, but he knew it was an open secret. As the years had worn on he had turned more and more of the work of his department over to his deputy chief. Port Arbello had ten policemen now, and even they weren't enough.

Not like the old days, Norton thought as he stopped the slowly cruising car entirely. Everything's changing.

He was parked by the Congers' field, and he was watching the work that was going on in the woods on the far side of the field. An apartment complex was being built there, and though Ray Norton didn't approve of it, even he had to admit that, for what they were doing, they were doing a good job. The complex would fit well on the Point, long and low, snug to the ground against the north winds of winter.

As he watched the building progress it occurred to him that what he really resented was not the building itself, but the fact that the building would spell an end to what had become, for him, an annual tradition.

Each spring for the past fifteen years Ray Norton had spent several of his days off searching the woods

for some trace of the three children who had disappeared
that autumn the snow had come early. The first spring
he had been joined by a search party, and they had
combed the woods for days, then moved on to the embankment, searching for some trace of the missing children or the entrance to the cave that was supposed to be
hidden there. They had found nothing. Whatever might
have been there had vanished with the snow. They had
continued the search for the cave until one of the searchers lost his footing among the rocks and nearly lost his
life when he tumbled to the stony beach below. After
that people stopped showing up for the search. From
then on Ray Norton had searched alone.

He had never found anything, but the search had become a habit with him, and each spring he would return
to the woods, make a careful search, and then move
on to the embankment. And each spring he would find
nothing. Well, the search was over now. The woods were
being torn up, and the foundations of the apartment
buildings were being anchored to the embankment.

Ray Norton left his car and began trudging toward
the woods. You never know, he was thinking. They
might turn up something I missed.

From the old house at the end of Conger's Point,
Elizabeth Conger watched the white-haired police chief
making his way slowly across the field. Each spring she
had watched him, and each spring she had asked him
what he hoped to find.

"Don't know," he would say. "But I can't just let it
go. Something's out there, if something's anywhere. And
I'll find it, if it's there."

She had often wondered exactly what it was he hoped
to find, and what he would do if and when he found it.
It would have to be this year, or it wouldn't be at all.

She glanced at a clock and saw that she still had
three hours before it would be time to leave for Ocean
Crest.

• • •

SUFFER THE CHILDREN 345

Sylvia Bannister was driving north, and it had not
been her intention to make any stops until she reached
Maine. But when she saw the sign for Port Arbello she
turned off. As she drove toward the town she wondered
why.

She had left Port Arbello a year after Sarah's com-
mitment, and had not been back in the fourteen years
since. Now, as she drove into town, she decided that it
was time to take one more look at her past.

She intended only to drive around the square, but
she found herself stopping at the offices of the Port
Arbello *Courier*. Before she went in she glanced across
at the grim old Armory, still unchanged from the old
days. So, she thought, Rose never followed through on
her project to convert it to a shopping arcade. Just as
well. She pushed open the door to the *Courier* and knew
at once that Jack Conger was no longer there.

Everything was changed, and most of the old staff
was gone. But she spotted one familiar face, a face that
looked at her curiously.

"Miss Bannister?" the person said, and Sylvia realized
that the young man had been a copy boy when she left.
Now he was an editor. Things *did* change.

"I was looking for Mr. Conger," she said doubtfully.
"But I get the feeling he isn't here any more."

The young man stared at her. "You mean you didn't
hear?" he asked. "He died. Nine or ten years ago."

"I see," Sylvia said. "What about Mrs. Conger? Does
she still live out on the Point?"

The young editor shook his head. "Only Elizabeth.
Mrs. Conger died the same time that Mr. Conger did."

He didn't explain, and Sylvia left the office. She almost decided to leave Port Arbello and continue north-
ward, but she changed her mind. She wasn't sure why,
but she wanted to see Elizabeth Conger. She turned
her car around and headed out the Conger's Point
Road.

The house hadn't changed, and Sylvia parked her car

in front of the porch. She glanced out at the woods as
she mounted the steps, and a chill ran through her body
as she wondered what had really happened out there.
She noticed the construction as she rang the bell.

A tall and strikingly beautiful young woman answered
the door and looked at her curiously. From the blond
hair Sylvia Bannister knew at once who it was.

"Elizabeth?" she said.

The young woman nodded. "May I help you?" She
thought she knew the woman from somewhere, but she
wasn't sure. And so many strangers knocked on her
door, asking her questions about the past. Questions she
couldn't answer.

"I'm not sure if you'll remember me," Sylvia said.
"I'm Sylvia Bannister."

"Of course," Elizabeth said, opening the door wide.
"My father's secretary. Please, come in."

Sylvia glanced around the house as Elizabeth led her
through to the back study. Nothing, it appeared, had
changed.

"I don't know why," Elizabeth was saying, "but we
all seem to wind up living in here. I hardly ever use
the living room any more, and Mother's old office is
completely closed off."

"I heard about your parents," Sylvia said gently. "I
just wanted to stop by and tell you how sorry I am."

"Don't be," Elizabeth said. "It may sound harsh, but
I'm sure they're happier now."

"Do you mind if I ask you what happened?" Sylvia
asked.

"Not at all. It's been almost ten years since they died,
and I don't mind talking about it any more. And maybe
you could answer some questions for me. If you don't
mind."

"Not at all," Sylvia said. "I'll tell you whatever I
can."

The two women sat down, and Elizabeth told Sylvia
what had happened to Jack and Rose Conger.

"It happened about five years after they had to send Sarah to Ocean Crest," she said. "Just after my eighteenth birthday, to be exact. Of course, we'll never know exactly what happened, but Dad took Mother out sailing one day. And they didn't come back. Everyone assumed there had been some kind of an accident, but a week after it happened the manager of the marina, I can't remember his name, found all the life preservers from the *Sea Otter* stuffed into one of the lockers. Since Dad was always careful about things like that, they decided that it wasn't an accident after all. Apparently Dad just took Mother out, and sank the boat with both of them on it." She paused a minute and seemed to think. "I've started to put it all together, I guess. At the time, of course, it didn't make any sense to me at all. But over the years I've started to find out more and more about what must have been happening to him. I think I can understand it now. I think it just got to be too much for Dad. Apparently the town never stopped talking about what happened that fall, and somehow they got the idea that Dad was involved in it. Anyway, you know how Port Arbello is. They have long memories, and stories get worse every time they're told. Toward the end Mother wouldn't leave the house at all, except if Dad took her on a trip out of town, and Dad ... well, I guess he just got tired of having people staring at him all the time."

"Why didn't they just leave town?" Sylvia asked.

"Why don't I?" Elizabeth asked. "I guess for us Congers this place is home. It isn't easy giving up everything that's familiar to you. Dad could never do it, and I can't either. Besides, there's Sarah to think about too, you know."

"Sarah?" Sylvia's eyes flickered with interest. "How is she?"

"Much better," Elizabeth said. "As a matter of fact, she's coming home today, for the first time."

"Will she be able to stay?"

"Not this time. But eventually, we hope. Not that Ocean Crest is a bad place to be. Actually, she's very happy there."

"Yes," Sylvia said, "I imagine she is."

"But we still, or I should say she still, has to remember what happened that day she came out of the woods with that—that thing in her hands. It's the only thing she still can't remember. She remembers what happened between her and Dad—" Elizabeth suddenly stopped talking, and stared at Sylvia in embarrassment.

"It's all right," Sylvia said. "As a matter of fact, I can probably tell you more about that incident than Sarah can, even if she remembers it."

"Could you?" Elizabeth asked. "I don't know why, but I've always felt that it was the major cause of what happened to Dad and Mom."

"It undoubtedly was." Sylvia sighed. "Jack talked a lot about it to me. We were very close, you know."

Elizabeth nodded. "There's been some gossip. I was never very sure how much truth there was to it, but I knew Mom and Dad weren't getting along. Especially after Sarah got sick."

"That was the root of the trouble," Sylvia said. "Jack was never the same after that terrible day in the woods." She fell silent for a minute, then continued.

"We had an affair," she said stiffly, her face coloring. "It didn't last long, only a year. I finally broke it off. I don't know why, really. I suppose partly because I felt sorry for Rose and partly because I was afraid of what would happen when it came to an end. Often, it seems, it's easier to handle endings if you bring them on yourself. So I ended the affair, and left Port Arbello. And do you know," she went on, "when I left I had the feeling that for Jack, life had ended. I suppose that sounds conceited, but I don't mean it to be. It didn't have anything to do with me. He just seemed tired out. Really, when I think about it I'm surprised he held on as long as he did."

Elizabeth nodded. "I think he did it for me. I don't think it was any coincidence that he killed himself right after my eighteenth birthday. He waited until I was old enough, and then he just sort of—went away . . ."

"It must have been terrible for you," Sylvia said.

"It was, at first. And it still isn't easy. I've had to sell off some of the land just to support myself and Sarah. I decided to get rid of the woods. It seemed like they'd been in the family long enough. I guess I hoped that if I got rid of them, and that awful embankment, it would get rid of the legend and the gossip as well."

"I'm sure it will," Sylvia said. Then she glanced at her watch. "Gracious. If I'm going to get to where I'm going, I've got to get started. Thank you for telling me what happened to Jack. Have I been any help to you at all?"

"Of course," Elizabeth said. "I'm glad to know my father had some happiness in his life." Then she too glanced at the time. "I'm sorry this has to be such a short visit," she went on. "Come back and see me again?"

Sylvia assured her that she would, but both women knew that they wouldn't meet again. Elizabeth waved to Sylvia as she drove down the drive, then glanced once more at her watch. She still had an hour before it would be time to leave for Ocean Crest. She went to look in on Mrs. Goodrich.

Though the old housekeeper had never admitted to her true age, Elizabeth was sure she was well into her eighties. She still lived in the little room next to the kitchen, and did her best to keep up the pretense that she was looking after Miss Elizabeth instead of the other way around—brewing fresh coffee for her each morning, and managing to put together something that passed for lunch, though Elizabeth had grown accustomed to waiting for the old woman to fall into her afternoon nap and then going to the kitchen to fix something to tide herself over until dinner.

Elizabeth was worried about Mrs. Goodrich; it wouldn't be much longer until the old woman would need full-time care, and Elizabeth didn't see how she was going to afford it. Unless what the doctors had told her was true, and Sarah really would be allowed to come home. She tapped lightly at Mrs. Goodrich's door.

"Is that you, Miz Rose?" the ancient voice quavered. Elizabeth shook her head a little, in sorrow. More and more lately the old woman had been mistaking Elizabeth for her mother, and Elizabeth supposed that it was a sign of increasing senility.

"It's me," she said gently. "Miss Elizabeth." She opened the door, and the old woman stared at her blankly. Then her mind seemed to clear, and she smiled tentatively.

"Oh, yes," she said uncertainly, "where's your mother?"

"She'll be in later," Elizabeth promised, knowing that later Mrs. Goodrich would have forgotten that she had asked for Rose. The first time this had happened, Elizabeth had tried to explain to the old woman that Rose was dead, and a look of horror had come over Mrs. Goodrich's face.

"Oh, dear," she had clucked. "What'll become of poor Mister Jack now?" Elizabeth had stared at her for a moment before she realized that the old housekeeper must have forgotten what had happened. These days she simply ignored it. She closed the door.

Elizabeth glanced around the kitchen now, and thought she ought to do the dishes and save Mrs. Goodrich the effort. Her arthritic hands could no longer hold on to wet dishes, and she had a hard time seeing what she was doing. But Elizabeth found she didn't mind having the role of servant thrust upon her. Mrs. Goodrich had served her family well for a long time.

The least they could do for her was take care of her in her old age.

And besides, Elizabeth didn't really have much else to do. Without being aware of it, she was becoming more and more like her mother, sticking close to her home, going into Port Arbello only when there was shopping to do or errands to be run. It did not occur to her that, at the age of twenty-eight, she was beginning to behave like a spinster twice her age. Nor did it occur to her that her lifestyle seemed odd to many people.

Elizabeth Conger was, in actuality, fairly content with her lot in life. She had her home, which she loved, and she had her cat, an ancient Persian she'd named Cecil, after the one that had disappeared. Her father had brought the kitten home to her soon after Sarah had gone to Ocean Crest. The cat was decrepit now, and needed a great deal of care. Elizabeth had considered having Cecil put to sleep, but hadn't been able to find it in her heart to do it.

She glanced around the kitchen again and wondered where to start. Then, just as she had made up her mind to do it, she changed her mind and decided to go for a walk instead.

She looked in on Mrs. Goodrich once more and found the old woman sound asleep. As she was putting on her coat at the front door, she felt Cecil rubbing against her ankle.

"You want to come along too?" she asked the cat. "I know you, though. You'll be perfectly happy walking for about ten feet, then you'll want to be carried."

The cat looked up at her and mewed.

"Oh, all right, come on," Elizabeth said, opening the front door. The cat bounded out into the bright spring sunlight.

Elizabeth, seeing Ray Norton's car still parked on the Point Road by the field, decided to go over to the woods and watch the construction. She had avoided the woods for years, until she had had to walk the property

with the real-estate agent she had listed it with. Even
then she had not felt comfortable about the woods or
the embankment. But now, with the construction work
going on and the area bustling with activity, it had lost
its threat, and she found she enjoyed going there.

She found Ray Norton sitting with his back to a
tree, patiently watching the work.

"May I join you?" She smiled.

The old policeman looked up in surprise. "Well, look
who's here," he said. "Since when are young Congers
allowed to play out here?" His eyes were twinkling, and
Elizabeth laughed softly.

"Not that young any more," she said. "And besides,
it's all different since they took over." She made a
gesture that encompassed all the men and machinery
around them.

"Hmph," Norton snorted. "If you ask me, it was
better the way it was."

"I don't know," Elizabeth mused. "I know I shouldn't
say it, but I'm kind of glad it's all happening. For the
first time in my life I feel comfortable out here." She
stared out to sea for a moment, then spoke again.

"Mr. Norton, do you suppose there ever really was
anything out here?"

"For instance?" Norton countered.

"Oh, the cave, I suppose. I know you've been searching for it for years, and you've never found it, but
you think it's here somewhere, don't you?"

"I don't know," the old man said. "For a long time
I didn't believe it was here, then I did believe it. Now
I don't know what I think. I guess when you get to be
my age that's normal. At least I hope it is, because
it's the way I am."

"Will you be coming back?" Elizabeth asked him.
"I mean, when all this building is done and there are
people living here. Will you still come out each spring
to look around?"

Norton shook his head. "I doubt it. For one thing,

I'll be retired by this time next year. And for another, this place just won't be the same. If I don't find what I'm looking for this year, I won't find it."

Elizabeth stood up and patted the old man on the back.

"You'll find it," she reassured him. "Whatever it is, if it's here you'll find it." She glanced at her watch. "I've got to get going," she said. Norton looked at her curiously.

"Sarah's coming home today," she explained. "Just for a visit, to see how it goes. But it'll be the first time in fifteen years." She paused, then winked at Norton. "And I didn't even clean up the kitchen," she added. "I thought it would be homier that way." She turned and started back through the woods, picking her way carefully through the brambles. Twice she caught her foot. She'd be glad when it was all cleared away.

The old policeman watched her until she had disappeared into the trees, then turned his attention back to the workmen.

So she's coming home, he thought. Well, that's nice.

If he was going to find anything after all these years, he was going to find it today. He made himself comfortable and kept on watching. It was all right; he didn't have anything better to do. When he thought about it Ray Norton realized that he hadn't had anything better to do for fifteen years.

Three hours later, as Ray Norton looked on, one of the pile drivers setting the foundations for the apartment complex broke through the roof of the upper cavern. The light of day shined dimly down on the gates of hell.

27

Ocean Crest Institute, which had dropped the word
"Mental" from its name several years ago, sprawled
over twenty-five acres of woods and lawns on a bluff
above the Atlantic. It looked as much like a resort hotel
as its management could make it, and it was able to
keep its costs within reason only through the grace of
an enormous endowment that had accumulated over
the years from the bequests of wealthy families grateful
for the care and discretion that Ocean Crest had shown
their members whose eccentricities had gone beyond
the harmless. No bars marred the view from the windows of Ocean Crest; instead, bulletproof glass had
been installed in the units that housed those patients
deemed to be dangerous. Sarah Conger had lived in one
of those units for four years, never knowing that she
could not have left by one of the windows. She had
never tried. Residents of Ocean Crest rarely tried to
leave; if they ever wandered off, it was usually through
confusion, not a desire to escape.

After the first four years Sarah Conger had been
moved out of the security unit and into a small house
that she shared with three other adolescent girls and a
housemother. An outsider, not knowing that all the girls
were victims of mental disorders, would have thought
them only unusually quiet. There were rarely any out-
bursts of any kind from the girls. Rather, they lived
as close to a normal life as Ocean Crest could make for
them. The director, Dr. Lawrence Felding, was totally

committed to the idea that the mentally ill need "asylum," not treatment. If you want someone to be normal, Dr. Felding maintained, you have to treat him as though he is. People, he had discovered, tend to live up to nonverbal expectations much more readily than to stated orders.

On the other hand, Dr. Felding saw to it that very little at Ocean Crest was left to chance. What he had done was develop a level of planned spontaneity that seemed to work for his patients. Often residents of Ocean Crest were surprised to discover that a friend known for months, or even years, whom they had always assumed to be another resident, was a psychiatrist. The doctors of Ocean Crest happily conducted therapy over card games, picnics, and "chance" meetings in lounges.

It was only when residents were being considered for discharge that formal meetings were held with doctors. And after fifteen years at Ocean Crest, Sarah Conger was starting to have formal meetings with her doctors.

"How does it feel to be going home?" Larry Felding was asking her.

Sarah lit a cigarette nervously and shook the match out before answering. "It doesn't feel like going home at all," she said. "I've spent more than half my life here. This is home."

Larry Felding laughed easily. "Careful. If you say that in the wrong place, people will say you're getting institutionalized."

Sarah grinned at him, and Larry Felding remembered all the years when Sarah Conger had never grinned, had simply sat mutely staring out at the sea, her face expressionless. Her silence had been complete for three years, and it had been another five before she had begun to speak in complete sentences. When she had been at Ocean Crest for ten years she finally smiled, and it was then that Felding had begun to be hopeful that she would eventually recover. For the last year or so it had been rare that Sarah Conger was not grinning. Her good humor faded now only when someone tried to talk to her about the events that had occurred just before she had come to Ocean Crest. Then her grin would fade, and she would become uncomfortable. She could not remember what had happened. Larry Felding was sorry that he was going to have to kill that grin now, but he didn't see any way out of it.

"While you're at home, Sarah," he said, "I want you to try to remember."

"Remember?" Sarah said, the grin predictably fading. "Remember what?" Felding looked at her over the top of his half glasses, and Sarah squirmed. "All right," she said. "I know what you're talking about and I won't pretend I don't. And I know I have to remember all of it." Then her smile sneaked back onto her face. "Of course," she said slyly, "if I don't remember, I can't be discharged, can I?"

"No," Felding replied, examining his fingernails. "But I could always kick you out for malingering, couldn't I?"

"Not you," Sarah said complacently. "You couldn't kick a squirrel out of here." Then she turned serious again. "I think I'm afraid to remember, Larry. I really think that's what it is."

"Bully for you," Felding commented. "After fifteen years you've finally discovered that we don't face what we're afraid to face. Shall I put that on your chart?" Then he leaned forward and the banter left his voice. "Of course you're afraid, Sarah. When you do remember, it's not going to be pleasant. In fact, I'm afraid it's going to be very unpleasant. But you won't remember all of it at once. It'll come back to you in bits and pieces, like the day in the woods with your father. You won't have to face it all at once. But you have to face it. Otherwise we won't ever be able to call you 'well,' whatever that means. So while you're at home I want you to try to remember what happened."

"All right," Sarah said reluctantly. "I'll try. But I'm

not going to promise anything. Is there anything special I should do? Anything that might help to jog my memory?"

Felding shrugged. "Who knows? You might try wandering around in the woods or the field."

"The woods are being torn down," Sarah said. "Elizabeth had to sell them off to keep this place going, remember?" Her infectious grin was back, and Larry Felding decided not to disturb it again. He sighed in mock embarrassment.

"I know," he said. "But I have to pay for my Rolls-Royces some way." He stared out the window at the battered Chevy that was technically his, but which everyone at Ocean Crest used as a sort of public transportation system. He saw another car pulling into the slot next to his.

"Speaking of Elizabeth, here she is. Are you ready?"

"I'll go get my bag," Sarah said, standing up. "I suppose you'll want to have your usual private chat with the family."

"You've been here too long," Felding said sourly. "You're catching on to how this place works." Sarah winked at him, and he smiled back at her. "Tell Elizabeth to come in, will you?"

"Okay. How long shall I take to get my bag? The usual ten minutes?"

"Get out of here!" Felding cried, and Sarah fled, giggling to herself. She met Elizabeth in the hall.

"Hi," she said. "Larry wants to talk to you, but I think I just upset him. Go in and calm him down." Still laughing, she left the building and started across the lawn to the house she had been living in for the last five years.

Elizabeth tapped lightly on the open door and stuck her head inside. Felding's eyes were twinkling when he looked at her.

"Come in," he said, waving. "I just kicked your sister out."

"She said she'd upset you. What happened?" Elizabeth wasn't sure whether she should be concerned. When Felding laughed, she relaxed.

"Sometimes I almost wish for the old days when she didn't say anything at all. She takes a very strange pleasure in needling me. Was she like that when she was a child?"

"From the day she was born. She was sassy, but she was happy. It made it all the harder when she got sick. She was so different all of a sudden." She was silent for a moment, remembering. Then she shook off the memory and met Dr. Felding's eyes. "Sarah said you wanted to talk to me?"

"Yes. I always like to have a little chat with a resident's family before they go home for the first time. To prepare them for anything that might happen."

"And something might happen with Sarah?" Elizabeth asked anxiously.

"I don't know." Dr. Felding was frank. "It all depends, really, on Sarah."

"Sarah? I don't understand."

"I've asked her to do something while she's home," Felding explained. "I've told her that I want her to use the time to try to remember what happened that day she walked out of the woods."

"I see," Elizabeth said noncommittally. "Is there anything you'd like me to do?"

"Only if you want to."

"If it'll help Sarah, I'll do anything," Elizabeth said earnestly. "You know that."

"Well, you don't need to sound so serious. I don't have anything terrible in mind. Tell me, is the house much different from when Sarah left?"

Elizabeth shook her head. "That house hasn't changed much in generations, let alone years." Then her expression clouded over a little. "Except for Sarah's room," she said, half apologetically. "Mother painted it and got rid of all of Sarah's things."

Felding's face fell a little. "What do you mean when you say 'got rid of'?" he asked.

"If it's important," Elizabeth reassured him, "they're all still there. In our family 'get rid of' means put in the attic. I'm sure all of Sarah's things are up there. Is it important?"

"It's hard to say. It could be. What I'd like you to do is go through all of Sarah's old things with her. Make an adventure out of it."

"It would be." Elizabeth smiled. "I haven't been up in that attic in years. In fact, I'm not sure I've been up there since Sarah came here." She thought for a moment. "Once, maybe, but that's all."

"Then it should be fun," Felding said. "Who knows what you'll find up there. And something might jog Sarah's memory."

"I feel sorry for her, in a way. That was a terrible day. I don't remember too much about it myself. Just seeing Sarah across the field, all covered with—" She fell silent, as if forcing the memory from her mind. "Well," she said shortly, "anyway, I feel sorry for her. I suppose she does have to remember it all, but it seems a shame, after all these years, digging it up again."

"I know," Felding said gently. "But it has to be done."

He heard feet in the hall outside and glanced at the clock. Exactly ten minutes. Sarah was back.

"It looks just the same," Sarah said as Elizabeth turned into the long driveway that led to the house. "Only smaller. I remembered it as being much bigger than it is."

"They say that always happens with a house you only remember as a child. The house doesn't get smaller, but you get bigger. The result is the same. You don't feel bigger, so things must have gotten smaller."

She parked the car in the garage, and they began

walking to the house. Without realizing it, Elizabeth had adopted her father's old custom of using only the front door, and she headed in that direction now.

"Just like Father," Sarah commented. When Elizabeth looked at her curiously, Sarah went on. "Don't you remember? He would never use any door except the front door. It was practically a ceremony."

"I'd forgotten, I guess," Elizabeth confessed. "You really remember that?"

"Oh, I remember practically everything now, even during that year before I went to Ocean Crest. Except for the last few weeks. There are some fuzzy patches, and I can't seem to get through the fog. And I'm not sure I want to. I suppose Larry told you."

"Do you call all the doctors at Ocean Crest by their first names? Or is Dr. Felding special?"

Sarah laughed. "He's not special, except in the way all the people at Ocean Crest are special. We call all of them by their first names. Don't forget, I didn't even know Larry was a doctor during the first years. I just thought he was another nut."

An expression of consternation crossed Elizabeth's face. "How can you talk that way?" she said.

"What way?"

"Referring to yourself and everyone else at Ocean Crest as a nut?"

"Sorry," Sarah said. "I forgot. I usually don't say that in front of outsiders. It seems to bother them, like it bothered you. But it doesn't bother us," she said serenely. "We think 'nut' is a much better word than 'paranoid schizophrenic' or 'manic depressive.' It sounds so much more human."

"I'll never get used to that place," Elizabeth said. "But it seems to work, so I guess it's all right."

"Why don't you check in?" Sarah suggested lightly. "Who knows? If you try real hard, maybe you can be crazy too. But it's not easy," she added, her voice taking on a more serious tone. "It takes a lot of energy to be the way I was for so long. Maybe I was just too tired to talk."

"Like Mrs. Goodrich," Elizabeth said, feeling a sudden desire to change the subject. It was a lot easier for Sarah to talk about her illness than it was for her.

"How is she?" Sarah asked.

"As well as can be expected, considering her age," Elizabeth replied. "She might not know who you are, and she might say some strange things. I just wanted to warn you."

"I'm used to people saying strange things," Sarah said, her grin lighting her face. "Lead me to her."

Elizabeth unlocked the door, and they stepped into the entry hall.

"Just the same," Sarah said. "Just like I remember it." She moved from room to room, taking in everything. "You haven't changed anything, have you. Don't you get bored with it?"

"Bored with it?" Elizabeth repeated. "Why should I?"

"I don't know. I should think you'd want a change now and then, that's all."

For some reason Elizabeth suddenly felt slightly uncomfortable. "I suppose I'm my father's daughter," she said, a little stiffly. "He never wanted things to change either."

"I hope you're not completely your father's daughter," Sarah remarked. "If you are, I don't think I want to go to the woods with you."

Elizabeth felt her stomach knot, and looked at her sister with horror. "How can you say such a thing, Sarah?"

Sarah's grin faded, and she looked into Elizabeth's eyes. "I think we'd better have a little talk, Elizabeth," she said. "I can wait to see Mrs. Goodrich. Where's a good place?"

"The back study," Elizabeth said. "I use it more than any other room in the house." She led the way, feeling uneasy about what Sarah might have to say to her. She decided to fix herself a drink.

"Fix me one, too?" Sarah asked her, and when Elizabeth looked at her strangely, Sarah went on, "We drink at Ocean Crest, too."

She sat down and waited until Elizabeth handed her a glass and took a chair opposite her.

"Look, Elizabeth," she said. "I know you thought I said a horrible thing when I made that crack. But you have to understand some things about me. I know what happened out in the woods, and I know it was a horrible thing that Dad did to me. But it's over. I mean, it's really over. I've been through it all—the pain, the anger, the resentment, everything. And yes, I joke about it now. For a long time that incident with Father was the end of my life. But it isn't any more. It's over with, and in the past. It's like it happened to someone else, and if I joke about it I guess it's just one of the tools I use to deal with it. My kidding about it can't hurt Dad; he's dead. And there isn't any reason that it should hurt you, either."

"It just seems so—so—" Elizabeth groped for the right word, and couldn't find it.

"Macabre?" Sarah suggested. "I suppose it is, but believe me, it's better for me to joke about it than sit in silence and brood on it. So let me be myself, all right?" She smiled, and Elizabeth returned the smile uncertainly.

Elizabeth and Sarah returned to the little study after dinner, where they sat sipping brandy and enjoying the fire.

"Do I really look like Mother?" Sarah asked suddenly. Mrs. Goodrich had insisted on calling Sarah "Miz Rose" even after Elizabeth had explained that it was not Rose but Sarah, home for a visit. Mrs. Goodrich had remained unconvinced.

"Quite a bit, really," Elizabeth said. Then an idea

occurred to her. "You know, all of Mom and Dad's old photo albums are up in the attic. Why don't we go up there and find some pictures of Mother when she was your age? Maybe the resemblance is greater than I can see. And we can dig out all the toys we had when we were kids."

"I detect the fine hand of Larry Felding at work," Sarah chuckled. "But I'll give you credit. You did that very well. And I suppose I can't put it off forever. Let's go up. Maybe something will jog my memory."

The two women went up to the door that blocked the stairs to the attic and found it locked.

"I hope we don't have to break it down," Elizabeth said. "I haven't been up here in years, and I don't have any idea where the key is."

Sarah suddenly reached up and ran her fingers along the ledge above the door. A moment later she had put the key in the lock and the door was open.

"How did you know about that?" Elizabeth said curiously. "I certainly didn't know there was a key up there."

"I don't know," Sarah said with a shrug. "I suppose I must have seen someone put it up there years ago, or something. Who cares? Let's see what's up there." She reached for the light switch and started up the stairs.

"Well, for heaven's sake," she said when they were in the attic. "Will you look at that."

"At what?" Elizabeth said. It just looked like an attic to her, and she didn't see anything odd about it.

"That corner," Sarah said, pointing. "It's so clean. Attics are supposed to be dusty."

It was true. In one corner, where an old picture was propped facing the wall, there was no dust anywhere, not even on the floor.

"That is odd, isn't it?" Elizabeth said. "I can't imagine this old place is so tight. There must not be any vents in that spot."

"You don't suppose Mrs. Goodrich comes up here to clean, do you?" Sarah said.

Elizabeth shook her head. "She hasn't been upstairs in years. Anyway, why would she clean just one corner? Well," she went on, shrugging the mystery away, "Let's get to it, shall we?"

They started going through the attic, and found a box marked "Sarah."

"Here it is," Elizabeth said triumphantly. "Prepare to face your past." Sarah touched the box reluctantly, as if it might be hot. Then she seemed to get a grip on herself.

"No time like the present," she muttered, and opened the box. Inside was a jumble of clothing, children's books, and toys. She lifted each item out, and they all seemed familiar to her. She recognized some of the clothes as having been favorites, and held others up in disgust.

"Ugh," she said. "Remember this?" It was a brown scarf, and Sarah was holding it by two fingers. "I used to hate wearing this, it was so itchy. Why do you suppose Mother didn't just throw it away?"

"It wasn't Mother," Elizabeth said. "It was Dad who insisted on keeping everything. I think the whole history of the Congers is probably up here somewhere."

Sarah snorted. "With the history we have, you'd think they'd have wanted to bury it, not store it," she said. "Isn't there supposed to be some sort of curse on us or something?"

Elizabeth looked at her sister curiously. "I didn't know you knew about that," she said slowly.

"Oh, sure," Sarah said. "Didn't you know? It's all written up in my records, first at White Oaks, then at Ocean Crest. What nonsense. Secret caves and everything."

"Ray Norton's still looking," Elizabeth said.

"Ray Norton?" Sarah said, without any particular interest. "Who's he?"

"The chief of police. Every year he comes out here, searching around in the woods and the embankment."

"Well," Sarah said, "I wish he'd find something. Then maybe I could remember those last few weeks and get on with it." She reached into the bottom of the box. "What's this?"

She held up a doll, one arm of which was broken off at the shoulder. It was an odd doll, old-fashioned, and dressed in a blue dress with ruffles down the front and around the hem. On its head, framing the faded porcelain face, was a tiny bonnet.

"I don't remember this," Sarah said. "Where do you suppose it came from?"

Elizabeth examined it carefully, and an odd feeling came over her. Then she realized that it was the right arm that was missing. Fifteen years ago it had been a child's right arm that Sarah had dragged across the field from the woods.

"I don't know," Elizabeth said, quickly putting the doll down. "I've never seen it before either."

She heard the doorbell sound two floors below, and felt a strange sense of relief at being called out of the attic. She didn't know why, but the doll had affected her more than she thought it should have.

"Who could that be?" she said. Then, when Sarah started to rise, she spoke again. "I'll get it," she said. "Why don't you see if you can find the doll's other arm? It looks terrible without it."

Elizabeth left the attic and hurried down the stairs. She paused before she opened the door. "Who is it?" she called.

"Ray Norton," a voice came back to her.

Elizabeth opened the door and let the police chief in. As soon as she saw his face she knew something was wrong. The blood had drained out of it, and there was a strange look in his eyes.

"What is it?" she said. "Has something happened?"

"Is Sarah with you?" Norton asked.

"She's upstairs," Elizabeth replied. "We've been poking around the attic. What's happened?"

"I'm afraid I have some bad news for you," Norton said. "Can we go into the study?"

"Of course," Elizabeth said. "Shall I call Sarah?"

"No," Norton said. "I'd like to talk to you alone."

"All right," Elizabeth said. "Go ahead. I just want to run up and tell Sarah I'll be a while. Will it take long?"

"No." The old policeman shook his head and started down the hall.

A minute later Elizabeth joined him in the study and closed the door behind her.

"You've found something, haven't you?" she said. "In the woods."

"We found something," Norton agreed. "But it wasn't in the woods. The construction workers broke through the roof of the cave today."

"The cave?" Elizabeth said blankly. "You mean the cave in the legend? But I thought—we all thought it didn't exist."

"I know," Norton said gently. "But it turns out it does exist."

"Was—was there anything in it?"

Norton nodded mutely; then, after a pause during which he seemed to be trying to decide how much to tell her, he spoke.

"I know Sarah was supposed to be here for a couple of days, but you'd better take her back to the hospital in the morning," he said.

"Tomorrow morning?" Elizabeth said. "Why? What did you find?"

"A mess," Norton said. "There were four skeletons in the cave, and the remains of a dead cat as well. We've already identified three of the skeletons. All three of the kids that disappeared fifteen years ago. And Jimmy Tyler's skeleton was missing a right arm."

"You said four skeletons," Elizabeth said softly. "Who is the fourth?"

"We don't know," Norton said. "It appears to be much older than the other three. All we know so far is that it was another child, probably a girl."

"I see," Elizabeth said.

"Anyway," Norton said uncomfortably, "for now we're keeping it quiet. But by tomorrow afternoon the word will be out, and this place will be crawling with people. Reporters, photographers, thrill-seekers. The whole works. And I don't think you'd want Sarah subjected to all that."

"No," Elizabeth said shortly. She paused and her eyes met those of the police chief.

"Mr. Norton," she said. "What's going to happen?"

"I don't know," Norton replied. "I'll know better tomorrow, when I've had a chance to talk to the coroner and the district attorney." He stood up nervously, wanting to leave. "You'll excuse me if I don't stay," he said. "I really shouldn't have come at all, but I knew Sarah was here, and I just wanted to . . ." He trailed off, unsure of what else to say.

"I know," Elizabeth said. "And I appreciate it. Thanks for coming out."

She accompanied him to the front door and watched until she saw the taillights of his car fade away down the driveway. Then she snapped the porch light off and slowly climbed the stairs up to the attic.

As she climbed, she tried to think what she was going to tell Sarah.

28

Sarah slept restlessly that night, and woke several times. It didn't seem fair that she would have to go back to Ocean Crest in the morning, but she supposed that Elizabeth was right and she shouldn't stay in the house with only Mrs. Goodrich. Not that she thought anything would happen, but still, she wasn't used to being on her own, and Ocean Crest had agreed to let her come only because Elizabeth would be with her all the time. And now Elizabeth had to go out of town for the day. She punched at her pillow and tried to go back to sleep.

When she first heard the noises from over her head, Sarah was sure she was imagining them. When they persisted, she began listening. Someone, she was sure, was moving around in the attic. She got out of bed and slipped into her robe, then went to Elizabeth's room. The bed was rumpled but empty. Sarah went to the attic stairs and listened. Movement. Silence, then more movement. She started to go up to see what was going on, then changed her mind. Instead she returned to her room, but left the door slightly ajar. She sat on the edge of her bed and lit a cigarette. The cigarette was almost finished when she heard the sound of footsteps coming down. She went to her bedroom door and peeked out. Elizabeth was coming out of the attic. Sarah watched her close the attic door and return the key to its place on the ledge above it. Then Elizabeth returned to her own room and closed the door. The house was silent, and Sarah returned to her bed.

When she came down the next morning, Elizabeth was waiting for her in the dining room. There was a pot of coffee and a plate of blueberry muffins. Elizabeth smiled.

"This is nice, isn't it?" she said. "I hardly ever use the dining room any more. I seem to rattle around in it by myself. But this takes me back. Coffee?"

Sarah nodded and sat down. She stirred at her coffee. "What were you up to last night?" she asked suddenly.

Elizabeth looked at her in surprise. "Last night? Nothing. I just went to bed. Why?"

Sarah decided not to confront her sister with what she had seen the night before. Apparently Elizabeth didn't want to admit to having been in the attic.

"I don't know," Sarah said, shrugging her shoulders a little. "I just thought I heard something in the attic. I thought maybe it was you." She watched her sister carefully, looking for something that would tell her Elizabeth was holding back information. But Elizabeth looked genuinely puzzled.

"In the attic? I didn't hear anything. But then, I sleep like a log. What time was it?"

"I don't know. Late. One or two, I suppose. I couldn't sleep, so I was smoking a cigarette. I could have sworn I heard someone moving around up there." She grinned at Elizabeth. "I thought maybe it was you, still looking for the missing arm."

"Well, it wasn't me," Elizabeth said. "Unless I've started sleepwalking. Did you take a look?"

"No. I decided not to. Attics in the middle of the night aren't my cup of tea." She buttered a muffin and ate it. "I wish I didn't have to go back this morning," she said.

A cloud seemed to cross Elizabeth's face. "I'm sorry too," she said abruptly. "But it just can't be helped. There's some legal thing that's come up, and I have to attend to it today. Apparently they can't continue with the construction till it's taken care of."

Elizabeth had decided to come as close to the truth as possible without telling Sarah of the discovery of the cave the previous day. "I suppose we ought to get started pretty soon," she said.

They finished breakfast in silence.

Dr. Lawrence Felding watched the two women park the car next to his and slipped the file on his desk into the top drawer. He put on an expression of surprise as Sarah and Elizabeth entered his office.

"What are you doing here?" he said. "Have I lost a day?"

Disappointment was apparent in Sarah's dark eyes, but she tried to keep her voice light.

"I got kicked out," she said. "Actually, something came up and Elizabeth has to be out of town for the day. So here I am."

Felding put on his best puzzled expression. "Why don't you go get rid of your suitcase, and I'll have a chat with your sister," he said.

"The usual ten minutes?" Sarah asked.

"Give me twenty, so I can get all the details." Felding grinned. The grin disappeared as Sarah left his office.

"Sit down," he said to Elizabeth. "I had a call this morning from the police chief in Port Arbello. Horton?"

"Norton," Elizabeth corrected him. "Ray Norton. He came out to see me last night. I guess you weren't surprised when we drove up, then."

"No," Felding said. "I'm afraid I have some bad news for you."

"Bad news?" Elizabeth repeated.

"Norton discussed the whole mess with the district attorney up there. He wants to prosecute."

"Prosecute?" Elizabeth enunciated the word as if she'd never heard it before.

"The D.A. seems to think he can build a case against

Sarah. It seems they've been storing that arm all these years, and it fits one of the bodies they found."

"Jimmy Tyler's," Elizabeth said softly. "I was afraid of that. When Mr. Norton told me about it last night I assumed that must be whose arm she brought out of the woods that day. But it never occurred to me that they'd still have it." She looked up, her eyes appealing to Felding for some reassurance. "But I still don't see—I mean, everybody knows that Sarah was—was—" She faltered, not wanting to say the word.

"Insane?" Felding finished for her. "Of course they do. And, of course, that will be the plea if they try her, and there isn't a chance in the world that she won't be found innocent on grounds of insanity. But they say they have to go through the motions, in order to close the case."

"But what good will it do?" Elizabeth flared. "It won't bring those children back to life, and it won't help Sarah. My God, it'll be awful for her!"

"I know," Larry Felding said uncomfortably. "But I don't see any way to avoid it. If she hadn't made so much progress over the years there wouldn't be any trial. She'd be judged unfit to stand. But, unfortunately, she isn't. Right now she's of pretty sound mind."

"Except she still can't remember what happened that day," Elizabeth pointed out. "How can they try her for something she can't even remember?"

"Well, there isn't much we can do about it. What we have to do now is tell her."

"Tell her?" Elizabeth breathed. It hadn't occurred to her that Sarah would have to be told, but of course she would. Elizabeth tried to get used to the idea. "When?" she asked.

"I think now," Felding said. "It's going to be all over the papers by this afternoon, and she's going to know then anyway. I thought it might help if you were here when I told her." He smiled and added, "You know, it might just jolt her into remembering what happened. It might turn out that she didn't have anything to do with it."

Elizabeth chewed her lip. "That's true, isn't it? God, wouldn't that be wonderful?"

A few minutes later Sarah came back to Dr. Felding's office.

"I'm glad you waited," she said to Elizabeth. "I was afraid you might leave without saying good-bye." Then she noticed the strained looks on both Elizabeth's and Dr. Felding's faces, and she sank into a chair.

"Something's wrong, isn't it?" she said, her eyes flashing from one to the other. "You didn't have to go out of town today, did you, Elizabeth?" Sarah looked at her sister accusingly. "Well, what is it?" she cried. "Please, tell me what's happened."

Larry Felding told her what had happened. What had been found in the cave, and what was going to happen in the days to come. As she listened, the blood drained from Sarah's face.

She couldn't believe what she was hearing.

The cave was real.

Four bodies. One of them with an arm missing.

A dead cat.

A knife.

The blood. The blood and the mud.

She began remembering, and she felt her mind beginning to go numb.

Images flashed before her: Stumbling across the field in the middle of the night. Following someone. Who was she following?

Creeping through the woods, trying to keep up with the fleeting shadow ahead of her.

Rocks. Slippery rocks. Her ankle was twisting. She couldn't catch up. She tried, but then the shadow disappeared.

Darkness, and a closed-in place. And then a beam of light shining in the darkness. And rope, there was rope. What was the rope for?

And sounds. Children's voices. Cursing, yelling.

A shaft. She seemed to be looking into a shaft, and there was light. Light was flickering off something. But what?

A knife. She saw a knife flashing in the yellow light.

And then a face looked up at her. A face. Whose face?

She remembered.

Pain flashed through Sarah's head, and she raised her hands to her temples. She looked wildly around the room. The face was there, there in the room with her. Her sister.

"Elizabeth—" she cried. "Elizabeth . . ." And then another name came to her, a name she had heard in the darkness. "Elizabeth," she cried again, her voice rising in a shriek. Then *"Eliza . . . beth. Beth! Beth!"*

And then something snapped in Sarah's mind, and her hands fell limply to her lap. The color slowly returned to her face, but there was no expression. Her eyes—the eyes that had become so expressive, dancing merrily in the impish face—had gone vacant.

"Sarah?"

Elizabeth said the word softly, tentatively. She reached out to her sister, but there was no response. Sarah sat quietly, and the vacant eyes peered almost sightlessly from the expressionless face. "Sarah?" Elizabeth said again.

Dr. Felding roused himself. It had happened so fast. He should have been ready with a hypodermic needle and a sedative. But it shouldn't have happened so fast. It should have been gradual, should have come back to her slowly, in pieces. But it had all crashed in on her, and she hadn't been ready for it. She hadn't been able to handle it. Sarah Conger's mind had closed down again. He wasn't sure why, but he knew that for Sarah it was over. The past had locked her in its grip again. He looked helplessly at Elizabeth.

"I'm sorry," he said. "My God, I'm sorry."

"What happened?" Elizabeth faltered. "What's happened to her? She's all right, isn't she?" There was a note of desperation in her voice, and Felding pressed a button under his desk that would signal a nurse to come in with a sedative.

"She's all right," he said soothingly. "She remembered, that's all. It all came back to her."

"But," Elizabeth stammered, "but look at her . . . she's—she looks like she used to . . ." Elizabeth began softly crying as she realized what had happened. Her sister was gone again, and this time she might never be back.

It wasn't until late that afternoon that they let Elizabeth go home, and even then Dr. Felding insisted on driving her. They were followed by someone else from Ocean Crest, who would bring the doctor back.

"I don't think we could have stopped it," Felding was saying. "It was too fast. She just caved in. I don't know what to tell you."

Elizabeth felt numb. She kept hearing Sarah's voice calling her name. "Elizabeth . . . Elizabeth . . ." And then that other name. Beth. Beth. Something stirred deep inside of her.

"She loved you very much," she heard Felding saying now. "That's why she was calling you at the end. She wanted you to help her." He reached over and patted Elizabeth's hand, and wasn't surprised when she withdrew it. They were in the Conger driveway now.

"Do you want me to come in with you?" Felding asked gently.

Elizabeth shook her head. "No," she said, "but thank you. I'll be all right. Really I will."

Reluctantly Felding let her get out of the car alone, and watched her until she disappeared into the house. Then he parked the car, and got into his own as it pulled up behind Elizabeth's. He glanced at the house once more, then drove away. One day, he thought, the past will let go and Sarah will be free.

Elizabeth sat in front of the fireplace, staring at the blank space above the mantel. The name kept running through her mind.

Beth.

Beth.

Sarah hadn't been calling for help. She had been accusing. But whom had she been accusing? Elizabeth struggled with her mind, feeling there was something she should remember. Had there been somebody in the attic last night? Had Sarah really heard something? She decided to go up and look around.

In the attic she found herself drawn to one of the far corners, a corner she hadn't been in for years. The corner where the old portrait lay.

Elizabeth picked up the portrait and leaned it against one of the rafters of the sloping roof. She looked at it and couldn't remember why it was that she had wanted it taken out of the study. The child was so pretty, all dressed in blue, with ruffles down the front and around the hem. And a little bonnet perched on the head, only partly covering the blond hair that cascaded over her shoulders. Elizabeth decided to take it back downstairs and rehang it in the study. Then she glanced at the spot where it had lain, and she saw the doll—the doll with the missing arm. It was propped up on what looked like an old book, and the book seemed to be familiar. She decided to take all three things down to the study.

She carefully hung the portrait over the mantel, adjusted it to be sure it was straight, then stood back to admire it. It was right, she knew. It belonged there.

She propped the doll on one of the chairs, the strange old-fashioned doll. Then she noticed that the doll was dressed the same way as the girl in the picture. It must have been her doll, Elizabeth thought. Beth's doll.

Elizabeth seated herself in the wing-back chair. Beth's

doll, she repeated to herself. Why had she thought that? Was that the name of the girl in the portrait, the girl who looked so much like herself?

She picked up the old book and opened it. Somewhere, on the edges of her memory, she thought she had seen it before. A long time ago.

It was a diary, handwritten on lined, yellowed paper, and the writing was that of a child. The words were carefully formed in a clear, old-fashioned hand that bore the odd look of a young person practicing penmanship. Much of it was faded and illegible, but Elizabeth could make out pieces of it.

He keeps looking at me.

He was watching me today. He watches me when I play in the field.

My father tried to hurt me today.

I wish he'd go away. I wish my father would go away. Mother wants him to go away too.

He tried to hurt me again today. Why does Daddy want to hurt me?

There was more, but Elizabeth couldn't make it out. She turned the pages of the old diary slowly, then closed it. She reopened it at the front and reread the inscription on the first page. It was written in a strong hand, a masculine hand, and it had not faded. The initials under it were the same as her father's: *J.C.* The diary must have been given to the little girl by her father.

She set the diary aside and stared up at the portrait. It was your diary, she thought. It was yours, wasn't it?

Cecil, her ancient cat, came into the room then, and nuzzled against her leg. She took him into her lap. She stroked the old cat for a long time and continued to stare up at the portrait.

Late in the evening, Elizabeth stood up. She glanced at the broken doll one more time; then, carrying Cecil, she walked to the kitchen. She opened the knife drawer and took out the largest of the knives. Without bother-

ing to shut the drawer again, she went back to the study
and stared mutely at the portrait.

"All right," she said at last. "All right."

Cradling the cat against her bosom with one hand and
holding the knife with the other, Elizabeth Conger
walked slowly out of the house.

She started across the field, toward the forest and
the embankment beyond. As she walked through the
night, the odd inscription in the diary ran through her
mind over and over:

Suffer the Children, it had read, *to Come Unto Me.*
Elizabeth Conger was answering the summons.